Footprints

A World War II and an end-of-empire story of love, loyalty and betrayal.

After a bewilderingly rapid defeat and surrender, two young Indian soldiers survive appalling conditions in German PoW camps. With no leaders they can trust and in a country they know little about, Yaqub and Barkat eventually resolve to escape in Alsace, join the allied army in France, and fight once more. Footsore and half-drowned, they stumble across a snowy mountain landscape. Uncertain who they can trust, they encounter unexpected help. And fighting their way towards them are other *outsiders*, soldiers from distant lands, whose stories briefly merge.

Nearly seventy years later, Saira and Will leave England for their honeymoon in Alsace and try to trace what happened to her grandfather during his escape.

Why did Yaqub find it so hard to talk about his war experiences? What does Grandmother Amina need them to discover? Does anyone even remember the Indian PoWs after all this time? And what is the significance of a tiny stuffed elephant?

HELEN BLACKMORE

Footprints

ISBN 978-1482373455

Footprints

Prologue

It wasn't his life that flashed before him as his frozen limbs ceased to paddle and the water swamped, black, over his head. It was just one staccato image which appeared, vanished and reasserted itself. A girl's face smiling lovingly, welcoming him – was it to his home? Singing alluringly, stroking his wet hair. Vaguely he sensed splashing and tugging nearby, but it didn't matter any more. Then shouting, more distant, a military voice, commanding, German. He didn't care, he wasn't going to jump to orders any more. He realised that the face was not real. The journey was over. The high hopes of their escape, the walking and walking, half starved. He had been so sure he would see her again. But now there would be no ordinary life, no children, no grandchildren. That was not to be his fate. Just a tangle of weed and stinking mud as he sank.

1

Wedding overture

Up on the hill, above the slate rooftops, the sails of the Foxhill windmill glinted as they turned in the early morning sunshine. Birds (Will would know what kind) were chirping in an absurdly cheerful way. Fat pigeons waddled outside the newsagent's below, scavenging scraps of crisps, mushy peas, chips, samosas and ketchup. They were disgusting.

Saira held back the curtain, reluctant to go downstairs. It was easier to focus on the street trivia than to think ahead. A surge of dread. No, no, it's what she wanted. But just supposing her parents had been right all along. Her mother's voice floated up the stairwell. 'We're taking the decorations up to the hall. We should be able to get the key now. You enjoy your bath and wait for Rabia! We'll take food later.'

Saira hurried downstairs and gave her mother a big hug, careful not to crush the armful of ribbons, flowers, tinsel and gauze. It was odd to see her father sitting in his armchair at this hour. On a normal day he'd have been at work by now. He couldn't resist a repeat grumble. He seemed to find it reassuring to return to the well-worn theme. 'It still seems a strange place to choose for a wedding, when there are so many nice hotels.'

'Dad, the old school has changed since the dark ages when

you went there.' Saira was conscious that she too was repeating herself. But what else could she say? 'They've transformed it inside. You wait, you'll love it. And the photos will look great with the old mill behind.'

Her dad sniffed. He didn't want to be cheered. He didn't normally think much about what the relatives would say. But this whole marriage was fraught with family disapproval. Especially his older brother's. He was sure he'd be put to shame in the dingy old school hall with its wall bars and vaulting horse and old crates of milk bottles. The whole thing was a disaster. How had he raised such a hot-headed, obstinate daughter? 'I'm going to get a newspaper!'

The atmosphere lightened when Rabia arrived clutching her beauty box. Rabia was the giggliest of her giggly cousins. But she was a genius with hair. She'd done loads of wedding coiffures, for all kinds of people. The girls retreated to the bathroom with a pile of towels her mother had left out. Saira was amazed how soothing it all was. She even started to laugh herself as Rabia teased her about their 'shopping' trips in the early days of her – well you couldn't call it a romance then, it was all very casual and innocent – when Saira had been meant to be with them, but had disappeared for a pre-arranged coffee with Will. And why was it so soothing to have someone else massage and froth your head and hair, trickle endless rinses and perfumed conditioners and then brush in slow, careful, sensuous strokes? But the curling tongs weren't so relaxing. There was always the worry that it might look too tightly curled, too artificial, like one of those crinolined ladies on Grandmother's traditional English biscuit tin.

Downstairs everything seemed chaotic. More cousins were hovering, already dressed in their finery. Her dad had retreated to the garden with his paper. Her mother was still up at the old school. Various aunts bustled in with tureens, shouted a few instructions, called her mother on their mobiles, then in an effusion of good wishes and kisses headed off to the hall with the food. Saira's young brothers were getting very restless and Saira called down the garden to her dad to take charge of them. Only her grandmother seemed calm, and made her sit down next to her, while she stroked her hand and talked about nothing in particular. Saira laid her head gratefully on Amina's bony shoulder, remembering all the times she had been her refuge from the storms at home. But it was disconcerting how small and brittle she felt these days.

When she went back to her room to change and looked out of the window again, she could see her dad and brothers on the lawn – playing cricket, of all things, among more indignant pigeons. She was glad her mother was up at the hall with the food, otherwise she'd be fussing, insisting on more jewellery. She smiled indulgently as Rabia slipped the cool, satiny dress over her head, making sure her hair remained undisturbed, murmuring, 'Oh Saira, I know you said it would be dead simple, but the beadwork is exquisite, and you look stunning!'

Something about the smell of cut grass, the excited shrieks of his younger sons and the feel of the ball, which he absent-mindedly polished on his best suit, brought a rush of memories to her dad, in which he was 'Sid' again, – Sid, the outwardly confident teenager, taking on England on behalf of Pakistan and for the honour of Minerva Street. He had to remind himself to hit gently, towards their outstretched hands. This was, after all, only a small back garden, not the vast demolition site at the bottom of Minerva Street. And the philosophy these days was to encourage and praise children – to pander to them rather than expose them to rough lessons in self-sufficiency.

And what a silly yellow plastic bat, more suitable for beach cricket. When he thought of the solid, wooden bat he had saved so hard for. All those early morning starts in semi-darkness on his paper round. His dad hadn't understood about pocket money, but had shared his pride in the new bat, slipping out in the evenings after he got back from work to cheer on the Minerva Street Pakis. What would he have thought of his granddaughter's marriage? Would he have approved or disapproved? He'd always been so proud of her achievements. More than mine, he thought ruefully. And Dad had liked Will enough as a lad, coming round to play with Asif.

But things were different then. It was all multiculturalism then. How quickly things had changed again. He felt the stress of complying yet again with new values and expectations – well, they were really the old ones, returning, reinforced. All his life he'd tried to fit in. But still it wasn't good enough. The wedding ceremony would be an absolute nightmare. All the disapproval from the hard-liners.

'Run! Run!' his sons were shouting, as he stood still in a haze of memories and resentments. He lumbered down the grass, allowing himself to be run out, knowing how angry his wife would be if he got hot and sweaty. And he'd better make sure the boys didn't skid and get dirty, or there would be trouble. 'Go and ask your grandmother if it's time to set out,' he ordered, 'and bring me my watch from the bathroom, – if you can get into it, with all this fuss and paraphernalia everywhere!' The boys laughed at this strange new word and scampered off.

He headed towards the kitchen for a glass of water.

'So far, so good!' Will whispered to Saira, wondering, as he heard himself, where such a quaint sounding phrase had sprung from. A proverb, perhaps? He'd never seen Saira look so beautiful. She'd been very secretive about what she'd wear for the wedding. Just murmured that it would be simple, modest, traditional and that one of her aunties, who'd been a skilled machinist, would make it. She looked like a princess.

'Even your dad's cheered up.' It was odd that one of the few things he remembered from his family's arrival before the ceremony, was Sid's surprise at the changes to the old building. He'd been going on about the vanished brown tiles, cream paint and gurgling radiators and how he could hardly recognise this elegant turquoise and lemon function room with its mirrors and chandeliers.

Saira smiled, looking directly at him for the first time. His dark hair was flopping adorably across his face, which looked paler than usual and more pointy. 'Love you, Will.'

Will looked across the crowded room. Everything was becoming clearer in his mind now. The earlier part of the morning and the ceremony seemed to have gone smoothly. Just as well they'd prepared. Now for all the relatives. He and Saira had made a pact to greet everyone individually and make sure they moved out of their family groupings and mixed. Perhaps he'd better start with his nanna. He didn't want her coming out with any of her unfortunate remarks. Her trouble was, she never realised.

As his gaze hovered (it was remarkable how much noise the guests were making now), he noticed that everyone near him had laden plates. The two mums had thought there would be problems with the food. But everyone seemed to be gamely sampling a bit of everything, and relishing it. He wasn't sure he could eat anything yet, though. He smiled back at Saira, his confidence returning. 'Had we better start circulating?'

Saira was looking a bit dazed, as if in disbelief that it had all finally happened after all the arguments. Was she also feeling desolate at the prospect of leaving her family? After all, she'd hardly ever been away from home without them before. And now it was final. She looked towards her mother, who was engrossed in serving food, then smiled weakly at Will. 'Go on then. I'll do my bit.'

Will set out in search of the troublesome old lady. Where on earth was she? He was amazed at how many turquoise hats there were. Had his relatives all bought a job lot for the wedding? He was relieved to see that they seemed to be mingling of their own accord. He'd rather expected to see all his side (well, the older ones, their own friends would be fine, of course) congregating round the more familiar food and not venturing to talk to Saira's family. But both families were beginning to introduce themselves. He overheard fragments of conversation as he moved between the groups.

'... very proud of Saira. She works with computers. It's a very good job ...'

'... he was at school with her brother Asif, you know ...'

'... how it will turn out. But her parents insisted on a long separation before they were even allowed to be engaged ...'

'... honeymoon in Alsace, we understand. It sounds a bit different ...'

He smiled to himself. At least he and Saira had given them plenty to talk about!

Ah! There Nan was! He caught a glimpse of the large turquoise hat with its cheeky feathers protruding behind a couple of Saira's tall cousins. She appeared to be conversing volubly with Saira's grandmother, who hardly spoke any English, but who was nodding as if she understood every word of his nanna's chatter. He hoped Nan wasn't trying to witness to her. She kept telling him she'd been praying daily for poor dear Saira's salvation, ever since they got engaged.

But before he reached the two old ladies, he got waylaid by his best man flapping about the champagne. 'No, like I said, don't hand it round, just keep it low-key, for those who want to serve themselves! There's plenty of sherbet doing the rounds.'

He pressed on. Whatever his nanna was on about, he thought he'd better rescue Saira's grandmother from the barrage of words. He was very fond of Grandmother Amina. She had been quietly supportive of Saira through all their terrible months of enforced separation and parental disapproval. And she had one of those beautiful warm smiles, which always made him feel the world was a better place. 'Stunning hat, Nan!' he observed, bending to kiss her. He hesitated over being so familiar with … should he call her Grandmother now? … but his nanna's companion smiled and offered her cheek, murmuring something.

'You're honoured, mate! I've never seen her do that before! And she's wishing you every happiness. She says she wishes my grandfather was here to see you both wed.'

Turning, Will realised that Asif was standing behind him. Great. He must be providing a running translation service to the old ladies. He might have guessed. There was always one of Saira's family hovering round their elderly relative, making sure she could cope. 'Never seen you in robes before! You look impressive!' Will ribbed him. 'Where's the wife and baby? Can I leave you in charge of these two? You know how Nan never stops talking!'

Asif pulled a rueful face, 'Yeah, I remember!'

'And thanks for everything. You know. Sorting me out. And the imam said some really good stuff, even if he couldn't actually marry us. It made a difference, him knowing me.'

'You should try some of this chicken, pet,' interrupted his nanna, pointing at her plate. 'It's ever so spicy and fruity and really nice. What did you call it, Asif love?' As Asif turned to answer, Will realised that he could stop worrying about his nanna. He looked back at Saira. She was now chatting with her girl cousins and introducing them to some of her work mates. As he moved off to re-join her, he could hear his nanna's shrill voice starting to ask, 'Now this honeymoon of theirs, in Alsace, isn't it? Something to do with her grandfather and the war …?'

Saira's grandmother smiled benignly at the extraordinary little figure in front of her, with the dyed hair and feather head-dress. She had quickly realised that it was Will's grandmother – on his mother's side, she thought. She was glad that dear Asif was there to interpret the rapid flow of words.

'Yes. Alsace,' she replied, pronouncing the word carefully. 'My late husband never talked to us about what happened to him during the war, Mrs. …' She hesitated, realising she wasn't sure of her name.

'Oh, call me Betty, everyone does,' Will's grandmother interrupted Asif's translation. 'And my Bill was the same. Strange, isn't it? You'd have thought they'd have wanted to share their experiences.' She thought the plain, grey-haired lady looked sharply at her. 'But he clammed up. Couldn't get a word out of him till just before he died!'

Grandmother nodded and continued, '… but there was just one time. It was when dear Saira was doing a history project at school. They had to interview people who had taken part in the war.'

That struck a chord with Asif, who'd done the same project the year before. So he made the grandmothers laugh by explaining how his group was allocated some old Polish chap with an accent they couldn't understand, who'd been all over the place, in the Pacific and things, in places they'd never heard of. He thought their report must have been a real mess, and it certainly didn't get a great mark, like Saira's had. He remembered that another group had talked to a woman who'd worked in the munitions factory that had been bombed – that was more exciting. And other groups did a Jewish refugee and a man who'd fought in Malta. 'But it never occurred to me to ask Grandfather, like Saira did,' he concluded. 'Then again, he might not have opened up to me. Saira was always his favourite, wasn't she? He never helped any of the rest of us to buy a car!'

His grandmother laughed and reminded him that his sister had worked much harder than he had at school. As for the car, she was a girl and she needed to get safely to and from college.

Asif refrained from translating this bit. Instead he said to Will's nanna, 'Anyway, he didn't tell Saira any of the bad bits about the fighting or prison camps. She was only a kid then. He told her all about how he and his friend escaped from the Germans in Alsace. The exciting stuff. The best bit was when they'd only just escaped and hid in this underground fort place, and the Germans came and stood right by them!'

Betty gasped, 'Oh my goodness gracious! That sounds just like one of them war films. You know, that one with the horse they used to jump over!'

Amina looked a bit puzzled, but continued to explain that Will had also always been fascinated by the escape story. So when they were planning their honeymoon, and they didn't want to do what other couples did, flying hundreds of miles away just to lie in the sun on some beach for a week, it had been Will who suggested going to Alsace. He thought they could track down the place her grandfather escaped from and the fort where he had hidden which he'd said was part of the Maginot Line defences. And then they could try and retrace the rest of his walk to freedom. 'He said it's very pretty there, with lots of old houses and historic castles.'

'They grow grapes there, too, I've heard,' Betty added. 'Make lots of wine. They'll be able to do a bit of wine-tasting!'

Asif pulled a face, but politely said nothing. He looked down at his grandmother, but she had a strange far-away look in her eyes. She must be day dreaming about his grandfather, he thought.

But his grandmother had no intention of telling them what she was thinking about. Jealousy was not a pleasant thing, even after all these years. 'Why don't you try the lamb?' she said hastily. 'As you like the chicken, I think you will like the lamb too.' And she instructed Asif to take Will's grandmother over to the table and see that she was well served.

It took a while for Will to do the rounds. As he moved from one group to another, he heard Sid (odd how he could use the old nickname, now all the explosions had died down) saying confidently to a large group of men, 'No, no, we are quite reconciled to it now. We must move with the times.'

Old hypocrite. Everyone knew how he had exploded at the very idea of Will and Saira even meeting together, and had imposed that year's separation on them! Then Will noticed his own father, smiling politely amid Saira's uncles. Sid was saving face. 'Wonderful food!' Will commented as Sid expansively beckoned him over to join the group. 'My Nan is even going for seconds! We were expecting her to be a bit picky, but she's quite converted.'

There was a brief silence, in which Will realised his choice of words was careless, then Sid laughed, 'It's hard to imagine, these days, how hard it was to get all the right ingredients over here when I was a boy. Now, when you think of all the Asian supermarkets …'

Then as Will moved off, he ran into his Islamic 'guide' – he'd declined the title of teacher – and was introduced to his wife. Will was really touched to hear their good wishes, and on the spur of the moment drew them towards his mother, who was pausing from serving, fascinator (thankfully not turquoise) slightly askew, and looking a bit harassed. She'd often asked him about the instruction he was receiving, so he knew she'd be interested (and it would distract her from grumbling again about his failure to get his hair cut for the occasion).

Once they were chatting, he turned to Saira's mother, Parveen, and the aunts who were helping her, and told her (choosing his words more carefully than he had with Sid) how beautifully all the arrangements were working out, and especially the food. Next he made sure he spoke to the distant aunts and uncles on his side that he only seemed to see at weddings and funerals, then went outside to check that all the children were happily playing under his sister's supervision. 'Can we throw the confetti and things yet?' they asked hopefully.

Amina hovered, plucking up courage, as Will chased after the children shouting, 'Definitely no confetti! Just bubbles!' and pretending to be horribly fierce. He'll make a good father to Saira's children, she thought, and may I live to see them. She walked up to him, and he looked surprised. 'Is Saira OK?' he asked anxiously. She nodded, marshalling her words.

'I want to ask you something. Something special.'

It was an extraordinary day. And this was the last thing Will had expected. He listened quietly, trying to mask his shock as she explained. He reached out to touch Amina's hand, wanting to reassure her. 'We'll do our best. But after so many years – I'm not sure we'll find anything – I'd hate to disappoint you.'

'Saira?' she asked. And he promised not to discuss it with his new wife until it felt the right moment. She smiled trustingly at him. 'You try?' she murmured and slipped back to the crowded room. How many years had she carried this round with her? Thoughtfully, Will strolled in to find Saira.

'It's taken me ages to get round everyone and back to you!'

'Ah, the trick is just to stand still!' she laughed. 'Everyone just comes to you then.' He realised that the cousins had moved on, but one of her colleagues was still with her. Oh no, hadn't she thought to tell Jacinth to dress a bit more demurely? But somehow Jacinth and demure didn't go together. She was leaning forwards, so her cleavage was even more visible, saying, 'Just ignore Will! You've got him safely under your thumb now.'

Sid interrupted the banter to announce that Saira's cousin Waseem was ready to take the photos, and he wanted to start off with just Will and Saira against the background of the old windmill.

As he posed them, Saira couldn't help smiling at how relaxed and proud her dad was now looking, compared with his gloom earlier that morning. Obviously none of the relatives had made any adverse comments. In fact, looking round, everyone was happily engaged, chatting amicably and still nibbling sweet delicacies.

'And one of Uncle and Auntie in front of his old school with his children and their husbands and wives,' Waseem commanded.

The photographs seemed to take forever. Will hated the fact that he and Saira couldn't relax, having to be in every group. His smile seemed increasingly artificial, though Saira still looked fresh and radiant. In fact she too was feeling exhausted by the time the car arrived to take them away from the festivities. She felt her irritation must show as Waseem insisted on still more photos of them getting into the car. 'Absolutely essential! You wait, you'll love them!'

At last there were kisses all round from her mother and sisters and a special hug from her grandmother. She wondered vaguely through her tiredness why Will was saying 'We'll try' to the frail old lady. Did he think their marriage would be that difficult?

Amina nodded. She didn't understand why knowing more had become so important to her. She hadn't brooded about it during his lifetime. They had been too busy just dealing with each day as it came. But now, in the loneliness, she was aware of the silences, and all the things that everyone had shielded her from. She didn't want to be protected any more. Was it jealousy? Or was it just something that came with age, this desire for simple truth, to see your life as it has really been?

Her thoughts were interrupted as that flamboyant girl – what had Saira called her strange friend from work? – shouted out above the family farewells, 'Throw your bouquet!'

Laughing, Saira tossed the flowers in Jacinth's general direction. Amina was amused to see how disappointed the girl looked when a cousin next to her caught it. But she seemed irrepressible. As the car was pulling away and all the guests were shouting and waving, she could hear Jacinth's voice rising above them, 'Remember all your work mates as you wallow in Temptation!'

What did the girl mean? It seemed to have shocked Saira's father, though Parveen was smiling. Amina sighed. So many things she didn't understand.

2

Desert

Will stood up, stretched. These airport seats were not comfortable after a few hours. He went to pick up an abandoned newspaper.

'Surely most people don't read newspapers on the first day of their honeymoon!' Saira teased.

Will's retort that most people, hopefully, don't have such a long, unexplained delay at the start of their honeymoon was a bit obvious. 'And at least I'm not checking my phone all the time. Though I will if this lasts much longer.'

He looked at his watch. None of the flights listed on the airport's departures board had taken off during the last couple of hours, and no reasons were being given. Everyone was restless around them, and there were speculations about terrorist threats. 'If it's a terrorist threat it could take days,' Saira said gloomily. 'Asif got caught up in one several years ago. And it definitely didn't help having a Muslim name. I wish I'd got my passport changed in advance!'

'I could get us some coffee if we have to wait much longer,' a half-hearted offer before Will got engrossed in the news. He hadn't had time to check out the current Libyan situation during the last couple of days with all the wedding preoccupations. But over the months he'd eagerly followed the accounts of the desert fighting, trying to fit modern place names and desert conditions over the eccentrically spelt details that Saira had written down all those years ago when her grandfather briefly talked about his war and its inauspicious start in Libya back in 1941. He looked at the pictures of burnt-out tanks littering the desert, and wondered if seventy-year old corroded parts of tanks, petrol cans and cartridge cases also lay buried in the layers of sand below these latest casualties. 'Still fighting to liberate Sirte,' he observed.

He'd known little, apart from Yaqub's story, about Libya (and not much more about Tunisia or modern Egypt) when the 'Arab spring' revolutions had hit the headlines earlier that year. As he'd looked at the maps and traced the advance of the modern rebel fighters across the Libyan coastal desert he'd wondered whether Saira's grandfather had been any clearer about where exactly he was seventy-one years earlier. And had there been for him the added question of why exactly he was involved in a war so far from home?

Yaqub sat with hundreds, probably thousands, of others in the desert. They had sat there for three days without food or water apart from the meagre contents of their personal water bottles. In silence they sat on the sand not daring to speak, with the Germans patrolling aggressively between them. Just waiting. He wondered what the Germans were going to do with them.

Other men from his unit sat near him. He kept his eyes on his friend Barkat. He wished he had his bravado. Barkat was an extrovert and showed initiative, – that's probably why he'd recently been promoted to naik, – though there was nothing even he could do now. Occasionally, when the dust from

German vehicles swirled up and enveloped them, they would loose sight of their guards, but Yaqub was too scared to shuffle closer to Barkat. He wished they were allowed to speak to each other. The silence was terrifying.

As he sat there, there was nothing he could do but reflect. Images from his great adventure hazed and dissolved in his mind. He saw, with a heavy heart, his family clustering round him back in his village, fifteen months ago They had been so proud, when he had gone to enlist at the wartime recruiting office of the British Indian Army. The Bengal Sappers and Miners were looking for tall, strong country boys who were used to hard work in the fields. Like himself. He was just seventeen. And so proud. For, despite having only the most basic primary schooling, his acceptance meant that he would bring much-needed income back to his family. But now, would he ever see his home and family again?

An unknown man near him began to groan and beg for water and the picture faded. Yaqub felt guilty. How could he tell this man that the lack of water was partly his fault?

A German boot kicked the moaning man into silence. Yaqub, his gaze submissively lowered, pictured his dusty, desolate companions as they had been back in India, where they'd done their training in Roorkee. How boisterous and exuberant they'd all been when they'd first arrived there fifteen months ago, all hundreds of miles from their homes. And how naïve. They'd been so carefree, too. He'd met Barkat there. Barkat, who also came from Kashmir, though from further north, nearer the great mountains; the boys in his family had traditionally joined the army, so he'd been more knowing than Yaqub. Nevertheless they were just two country lads. But how smart they had looked in their army uniforms! They'd saved up and gone into town to have a photograph taken to send home. He smiled wryly. They looked nothing like their photos now.

They had trained for a whole year and thought they knew it all. Especially after they had been transferred to the Third Indian Motor Brigade. They were raring to go and fight the far-off war for their King Emperor. They had been so excited when the order had finally come one night to assemble with their uniform and luggage. For all of them the journey, by special train to the huge port city of Bombay, had been the longest of their lives.

He could see them on board ship, their uniforms still immaculate, watching the endless waves plunging and rolling them forward. Rolling them 3,000 miles towards Egypt in Africa. They were kept busy with lectures, weapons training and with marching round the decks. Between bouts of miserable sea-sickness (for he, like most of the others, had previously experienced nothing more turbulent than the lake near his village and the mighty river Jhelum), they would talk about their destination, Africa. Two boys, who had been educated by Irish priests, remembered that much of Africa was coloured pink on their maps, like England, the mother country, and recounted tales of jungles with strangely named animals like zebras, chimpanzees and hippopotamuses. Their officers laughed and told them that they would be in desert and wouldn't find any striped zebra, heavy hippopotamuses or huge chimpanzees, just tiny scorpions. And even then, they would probably find the common body lice far more troublesome than the scorpions. They would disembark at Suez and then they would re-train for desert conditions before joining up with an experienced division like the 4th Indian Division that had already fought bravely in Libya and helped to liberate cities. Of course they had all wanted to set off for the fighting at once and join up with the war-hardened troops. They felt they had done enough training and were already well prepared.

But Yaqub had definitely not felt prepared for the chaos and confusion of war. Their training in India and on board ship had been very orderly. At the new training camp outside Cairo it remained disciplined. They were supplied with plenty of spades and pick-axes, enabling them initially to dig deep trenches for their tents, so that they would withstand the terrible desert winds. Their cooks had a hard job trying to keep the swirling, stinging sand out of their cooking pots. For Yaqub, well used to working in the fields back home, the endless digging of military trenches was no hardship, though he was more interested in learning about mines and desert minefields. But sometimes exercises they were expecting did not take place if transport did not arrive. Some of the equipment and weapons seemed to have gone astray, for they were permanently under-equipped. But at least during this period their officers were in contact with what was happening around them.

The real chaos and confusion had begun when their exercises at the training camp came to an end after only twenty days. They had known for a few days that something was about to happen. Barkat seemed to have contacts everywhere, – in the cook house, in supplies, even among the tailors, – and he'd heard from one of the signals operators that a lot of troops were being moved from Cairo to Greece. Barkat rather liked the idea of going to Greece, where Alexander and his brave soldiers were born. So he was quite disappointed when their orders finally came through. They were to proceed towards Libya. Why Libya? Yaqub remembered the long, un-comfortable journey along the coast of Egypt. The trucks they were allocated were battered and worn and broke down frequently. They all had to stop and wait each time one needed repairing. It was worse when the winds were strong and the powdery sand got in the gear boxes and oil sumps. And often the batteries could not be charged. There was a pause for more desert training at Mersa Metruh. Then off again. Did anyone know what they were meant to be doing? It seemed as if they just kept moving forwards in fits and starts in their erratic trucks towards Libya, not knowing if there were other troops near them or whether they were on a lone mission. But at least they could now erect an overnight camp very rapidly between the patches of camel grass and the cooks were good at producing meals wherever they were, Yaqub thought. And they were all cautious with their water rations.

As they got nearer to the Libyan border, they camped outside Sidi Barrani. There their officers took the opportunity to remind them of the bravery of the 4th Indian Division, who'd fought there against the Italian army three months earlier, before being sent south. Yaqub looked forward to meeting up with these veterans and hearing in person about their battles, but his hopes were dashed as they were told that the 4th had not yet returned from the south.

From there onwards, they were aware of earlier battles, as they drove between ruined buildings and had to proceed cautiously in case the roads were still mined. As they crossed the border into Libya, Yaqub was glad that the Italians had already been defeated and forced to retreat. But he wondered why his regiment had suddenly been sent there. Were the Italians trying to come back? Or perhaps the rumours about the Germans were true? They passed Tobruk, but the name meant nothing to anyone. It was just more ruined buildings, one of them like a big fort with barbed wire. One morning they had heard a plane above them. One of the officers said it could be a German spotter plane, spying on troop movements. But nobody knew anything definite.

When orders finally did come through, they were told that they would be moving inland the following day. Their orders were to turn south-west before the Jebel Akhtar mountains. Yaqub could see these green mountains looming ahead of them, and thought how pleasant they looked after the desert. He was sad that the orders were to skirt the green mountains till they reached an important desert crossroads at Mechili, where an old fort stood.

That night they had such a feast. Their cooks had negotiated the purchase of a number of goats from among the ruins they'd passed through. He remembered how, as the temperatures dropped rapidly, he had wrapped his blanket round him as he sat, sniffing the goat-and-spice scented air. It was odd how, though they didn't often talk about their lives back home before the war, something about the familiar scent had stirred memories of home and families. 'When we return home, after fighting bravely, I shall marry my cousin,' Barkat had declared. 'She is as fair as the brightest star up there in the clouds.' Yaqub remembered how they'd all laughed affectionately at their naik's wild exaggeration, and the unmarried lads had joined in with exaggerated descriptions of the girls they were expecting to go home and marry, though he had stayed silent. He hadn't wanted to sully Amina by talking about her, – her gentle laugh, her rapid hands as she sewed, her beautiful, downcast eyes. His bride-to-be. His last thought before he had fallen asleep had been that when they reached this Mechili place he really should write home again. It would feel a long time since his last letter.

But now there would be no letter. Yaqub shuffled in the

sand, trying to find a new position, without the German soldiers thinking he was moving. Glancing quickly around, he wondered whether Barkat had somehow moved a little closer to him. He did not look as far away now. It occurred to him that when they first arrived from the coast they must have driven right over this spot where they were now herded, silent and hopeless. The very name Mechili would be forever accursed.

At first Mechili had seemed a tranquil place, after the wrecked tanks and wooden crosses, witnesses to previous fighting, which they had passed on the way. The whole area was dominated by the old fort. Apparently it had been built by Turkish people. Yaqub was amazed how many strangers had occupied this desert before them, all fighting, destroying, occupying and rebuilding. But the conquerors in turn had been defeated and their buildings had decayed. The fort was not much more than a few mud and stone houses on a mound beside some water cisterns. And now it was his own Indian Motor Brigade that was setting up their camp around the old fort.

His unit probably explored more of the area than other troops, as they were ordered to set up the water supplies. They had to organise everything so that the dusty men, the cooks, the washermen and the vehicles – not to mention any other soldiers and vehicles coming through – should have sufficient. They went out on well reconnaissance, always on their guard, finding the ancient underground cisterns and ensuring that they were clear of drifted sand, to allow them to be topped up by natural rainwater. He enjoyed this task. At the end of the first day he fell asleep, exhausted, only half aware of a dull sound ahead of them, like distant firing.

But that first night it was something much closer that

disturbed his sleep around dawn. The sounds were very familiar, but the tall men in dark robes standing nearby, watering their animals, were not. He was initially alarmed: his unit had been put in charge of the water supplies, and here were these strangers giving the army's precious water supply to their sheep and goats. They seemed to have no fear of the Indian soldiers; it was as if they knew the sleeping men were defenders, not enemies and they indicated that the water had always belonged to the nomads of the desert. The soldiers were fascinated as they could understand some of the shepherds' Arabic words despite their strange accents. They picked up, using gestures as well as shared words, that German warriors had arrived from the sea to the west many days ago, and that they were now on the move. They were moving fast towards this very place. They had vehicles, which had eight wheels and strong armour and did not break down. The shepherds had also seen, ahead of the Germans, many other soldiers in different uniforms, scrambling over the rocky terrain, as if in retreat. They should start to arrive here once the sun was high in the sky. The shepherds had known they had to take their flocks to different grazing grounds, further inland from the ones they usually used at this time of year.

As he listened, Yaqub felt ashamed that he had put his army loyalty before the simple needs of the animals and their herdsmen. He thought of his village back home. He wondered how the family crops were. How would they harvest them with so many men at war, far away from their family land? He asked these men if they had crops, or if they were always on the move, for he was always curious to learn new things about these lands far from home. It was Barkat who interrupted, pointing out with some urgency, that if the Germans were approaching, they should inform one of their officers, not stand around gossiping about crops. He wanted the herdsmen to go with them and explain what they had seen. But the strangers were ready to move on. The soldiers should pass on the information to their superiors. All the flocks now were watered. So the herdsmen and sappers exchanged blessings and farewells, and the animals and men moved off into the desert. Yaqub observed that they did not take any of the tracks, which were now well marked by army truck wheels. They must have thought they were too dangerous. They were soon hidden from view by rocky outcrops.

When Barkat, with Yaqub to back him up, went to report their conversation, they got the impression that their officers had known for some time that the Germans had landed on the coast ahead of them, but had been told that the Germans were expected to wait there for reinforcements. Their officers reassured them that any patrols would be at least 250 miles away. Yaqub thought it was strange that they seemed disinclined to listen, as local herdsmen, who knew the seasons, the terrain, the water and the grazing, would also know the distances and the dangers much better than foreign armies with their outspread maps and sporadic radio communications.

'We would have been informed if the Germans were on the move,' one of the havildars said patronisingly, 'I expect you misunderstood.'

It soon became clear, however, that the herdsmen's sightings were only too accurate. A few hours later, patrols spotted movements in the hills, and everyone was put on high alert. In the distance field guns could be heard. Barkat learned that the wireless personnel were not picking up any signals. He passed on the order that, until instructions were received, they were to fire on anything that moved. Yaqub was confused, because, according to the herdsman, there were allied troops retreating towards them, ahead of the Germans. But their officers were taking no chances. So for seven hours they fired, ignoring cries and shouts.

Finally, some counter-instructions must have been received, as orders filtered down to cease firing. Yaqub stared in horror as a succession of soldiers on foot, as well as men who still had operable vehicles, started to cross the sandy waste they'd been firing across. They were hot, bedraggled and dirty, but someone said that their uniforms were British and Commonwealth. They'd been attacking their own side. Yaqub could hardly believe it. What had happened to their communications? Why was it all so chaotic? He didn't understand. This war was not how he'd imagined.

The newcomers' vehicles were in a dreadful state. They had come over rocky terrain, and their tyres were ripped, their springs ruined, and their engines damaged by grinding in low gears all the time. Their water and spare fuel were all used. Yaqub and Barkat's group were kept very busy, but at the same time they managed, despite the language barrier, to satisfy their curiosity about the new arrivals. One small, cheerful man who helped with distributing water to his fellow newcomers said that he and his mates were from London. He pointed out some tall, tanned men in strange hats and said they were Australians. They had also suffered from poor communications and they had received either conflicting instructions or none at all. But they'd been able to bring with them twenty-four anti-tank guns. 'We'll be able to defend this place properly now,' he concluded.

Inevitably the snatched conversations turned to food. The new arrivals still had plenty of European-style food. Yaqub was relieved for them as he knew that their own cooks had mainly Indian rations, which he couldn't imagine these Englishmen (or Australians) eating. But, noticing how badly their desert boots as well as their vehicles had suffered on rocks and ravines, Barkat directed many of them to their own camp cobbler, so they were able to be of some assistance to these experienced troops.

The whole day continued to be confused, with troops arriving and some troops leaving, once they'd taken on water and petrol and their vehicles had been given hasty temporary repairs. It reminded Yaqub of the busy railway station in Bombay, with people rushing in all directions. He fell asleep that night wondering whether some of them would still be here when the enemy arrived, or whether the Third Indian Motor Brigade would be facing them alone.

When he woke the next morning everyone was saying that the Germans were close. One of the patrols had captured men in German uniforms and brought them back to the camp. Were they advance enemy patrols? Everyone assumed the main army would not be far behind. Barkat rubbed his hands, and told his men with some relish that it looked like they might soon have their first battle.

Then at 9 am the shelling began. The hardened troops who'd joined them and remained there seemed unmoved by it, saying it was only light, but to Yaqub and his companions, new to real warfare, it was terrifying. Even Barkat went rather quiet. As the day wore on, the shelling seemed to be coming not just from the western route, but also from the mountain crest to the north. In the late afternoon Barkat discovered from one of his contacts (how did he manage it, Yaqub wondered, for he'd been completely unaware of the event) that a German staff officer with a white flag had demanded their surrender. Barkat was incensed. Why should the enemy think they would surrender, he shouted? They were soldiers of the King!

Later that evening an English General was rumoured to be approaching. Yaqub broke off from his tasks and watched with interest as their own Major went to meet him. They heard that he'd taken command, and felt more confident.

But the next day things got worse. It was still very confusing. Even the Australian anti-tank guns didn't seem able to dislodge the German guns. Everyone was hoping there would be support from the air, but no planes appeared, though they kept looking up at the skies. At mid-day the Germans demanded, for the second time, that they should surrender. Yaqub was proud that the English General refused. After more attacks, in which Yaqub saw some prisoners being taken, a third surrender demand was made. This time Barkat actually saw the white flag. After they refused, the artillery barrage began, and seemed to be coming from all around them. The men were all instructed to stay in position. As the cooks prepared to distribute the evening food, Barkat pointed out grimly to Yaqub that they were now surrounded on three sides. Around them were wounded men who needed to be taken to the makeshift area where the medics were at work. It was horrible to hear them groaning. And there were dead who needed burying. The firing was getting closer all the time. Then Barkat pointed to the south. In the distance, near the salt pans, they could make out tanks. About sixty of them, Yaqub estimated. He felt trapped and helpless. He didn't want to end his life here, in this foreign desert, far from home.

He was not surprised when later that night, orders were received, from the General himself, it was said, who had summoned their Commander, that all troops defending Mechili should withdraw. Barkat growled that it made sense, although the only way left to them was back, eastwards. Yaqub recognised in the orders the names of places through which his brigade had come such a short time ago. They were all to head for El Adem, outside Tobruk, apart from his unit, which was detailed to stay behind and render unfit all the drinking water that other units could not take with them. They should leave nothing that would help the Germans.

So Yaqub and his tight-knit group spent all night carrying huge petrol cans and dumping quantities of petrol in all the wells. Their task was periodically disturbed by enemy field guns firing in the darkness. Yaqub's heart was heavy as he thought of all the sheep and goats who'd drunk there earlier. The water would be too polluted by the petrol for them ever to return, he thought. As dawn approached, they completed their task and prepared to join the retreat eastwards.

But the first light revealed an unnerving sight ahead. Units of their brigade were still there. Later they learned that only the lead trucks had broken through and the rest had turned back. There were also many of the vehicles belonging to other troops. There was no longer an escape route. What should they do?

They could still hear firing, both intense artillery and light machine gun fire, both round the waiting column and up on the high ground to the north west. As they looked that way, some armoured command vehicles broke out and headed towards the column, but they were soon forced to a halt by a hail of gunfire. Then Yaqub saw German officers for the first time. They encircled the vehicles. A man got out. 'It looks like that English general,' Barkat whispered. The man was holding a white handkerchief. Other senior officers got out of the vehicles. Yaqub watched in horror as they were led away by the Germans. The man was still clutching the white handkerchief.

'He's surrendered!'

As the word went round, all the remaining units threw down their weapons and also surrendered. Yaqub and Barkat did the same. Yaqub was relieved that their ordeal was over, but stunned by how quickly it had happened. This was so different from how he had imagined war.

Yaqub and Barkat were herded with the other sepoys to an open space away from the remaining vehicles. The Germans seemed very efficient. They instantly separated out all the officers and led them away from their men. They couldn't see their Major among them. Perhaps he had reached safety. But it was terrible to watch the others being taken away. Now there was no-one to explain what was happening, or negotiate with the Germans or reassure their men. Would the Germans just shoot the remaining men?

An order was shouted and repeated. They should sit. So they sat down on the sand as ordered. They remained seated all day, hardly daring to move. But some men who had their kit bags, later managed to doze against them, without moving too much. Yaqub marvelled that they could sleep in such a terrifying situation. And all the time, more unknown soldiers were being rounded up and brought to sit with them. Time, like the desert, stretched and stretched, without explanations, ahead of them.

After a night sitting out there, the second day dawned to a chorus of coughing and spitting as men tried to clear their throats of the desert dust. And then came the humiliations of hundreds of men needing to relieve themselves under the eyes of the guards. And still no water or food was brought to them. The sun seemed hotter than usual and there was no shade. Yaqub dared to take no more than an occasional small sip from his water bottle as he had no idea how long it would have to last. More prisoners continued to join them. There must now be thousands of them herded like goats on the bare sand. This had been their first battle of the war, Yaqub reflected, and it would be their last. How could they have surrendered after such a short time? He did not know what would happen to them. Perhaps they would be left to die there.

As the third day dawned, Yaqub's parched lips could hardly open to murmur his morning prayers. Their situation seemed hopeless. The man next to Yaqub continued to whimper that he would die without water, till Yaqub risked whispering harshly to him, 'Be quiet. There is no water. We have poisoned it all with petrol. We did our job thoroughly. There is nothing left for any of us. We are all as near to death as you are. Only the mercy of Allah can preserve us.'

On the fourth morning Yaqub watched with relief as the cramped bodies in front of him were organised, at gunpoint, into a standing, broad column which at various commands started to shamble forwards. He was shocked by how little they now resembled a proud army. He was still, thanks to the enemy's sense of order, with the men of his unit. As their turn came, Barkat urged his men to remember they were soldiers of the British Indian Army. They should stand as tall as they could and march proudly and show the Germans their worth. But they found it hard to march, packed shoulder to shoulder, close enough to drag along any companions who collapsed from dehydration. It felt more like shuffling and hauling than parading. They were ordered to leave the dead. They could only hope that the last men would be allowed to bury them.

The huge procession moved slowly towards the sea. Above them a plane criss-crossed watchfully. Yaqub thought that to the pilot they must look no more than a trail of ants. They were not told where they were going or what would happen to them.

Amina woke early. She often did, though 5 o'clock, which she could see on the old-fashioned big round alarm clock face, was a bit earlier than usual. She lay awake, thinking of the wedding the day before. She was so grateful it had all gone smoothly. With her family you could never be sure. How she wished Yaqub could have been there to see it. At times she'd felt that he been standing there next to her, then turning, had found it was only Asif, being unusually solicitous. Married life seemed to be settling him too.

But Saira had always been the grandchild she felt closest to. And that year when her son, in his fury at what he considered Saira's deception and Will's unsuitability, had ordained a complete separation from Will, had brought them even closer. It had reminded her so vividly of her own wartime separation from Yaqub and all the months and months of not knowing where he was or even whether he was safe.

There had been that first letter written when they'd just landed somewhere in the African desert, which they'd only learned much later was in Egypt. His parents had taken it to the elderly letter-writer to be read out to them all. Particular details stuck in her mind still, how big their ship had been, with mighty engines below and so many men down in the dark heart making the steam, and many more up on the decks hosing down and polishing. He'd said it was like a lighted village, floating on the sea, until they had to cover the round window holes with black to become invisible. She'd found it hard to imagine that so vast a ship could roll so much when the waves got big. She remembered he'd concluded by asking how the crops were doing and telling his brothers to work hard to help their parents. There had, of course, been no personal message for her. After all they had not been married then. Some days she dreamed of what it would have been like if they had married before he left, as some of the village girls had done. Would she be happier? When she looked at her cousins she wasn't sure. Perhaps it was even harder for them, alone in their new families. No, her parents were right to say they should await his return. And it would be such a joyful wedding when the war was finally over.

But then there had been such a long silence. No further letters from him. Finally, one morning, Amina had seen Yaqub's little brother, Yousaf, approaching their house. There must be news at last. But this time he came slowly. It was a very official letter, he said, stumbling over the word official, – with printing and a badge at the top. Father thought Yaqub must be dead. Why else would it be an official letter?

Amina thought she had prepared her heart, during the long weeks of silence. But she hadn't. It plunged to her feet, leaving her empty of spirit and unable to walk. Her mother and sister had taken her arms, and forced her to move forward. This time there was no gossip, no sense of occasion. The letter-writer scanned the typed words on the page, and said, 'There was a big battle in the desert. Yaqub was taken prisoner by the Germans.'

There was a babble of sound. 'What will happen to him? How long will he be a prisoner?' The old man scratched his head. 'They will keep him until the war ends.'

There was a stir in the departure lounge and people started to push closer to the departure boards. Will put down the newspaper, reflecting that it couldn't be long now before the rebel Libyan fighters found their hated president hiding out in the desert or in the cellars of collapsing Sirte. He wondered if he'd be taken prisoner, like his soldiers, or shot on the spot in revenge for all those years of misery he'd inflicted.

Saira grabbed his arm. 'The flights at the top of the board being called to the departure gates. I don't know what the delays were all about. But it should be our Baden-Baden flight soon!' She reached for her phone. 'They might have heard at home about delays and be worried. I'll let them know it's going to be OK.'

3

A small bar of soap

Saira and Will lay back in the headily scented water, surrendering to the relaxing sound of trickling water, wallowing in this most unusual of their wedding gifts.

Extending a languid hand to stroke Saira's breasts, Will at last felt free from all restraints and conventions. This small chamber in a palace of self-indulgence was a world apart from all the anger, fear, separation and loneliness that had scarred the last years.

Like yesterday, the family house felt so empty. It hadn't changed. It was just that there was nothing to look forward to, now the wedding was over. Like yesterday, it felt such a long time since Amina had woken. And today no one was at home. She'd watched as everyone left for work or school, just as they used to. The fridge was full of food, so there were no small tasks of chopping or cooking to occupy her restless hands, let alone her mind. In the end Amina took the breakfast crockery out of the dishwasher and stood at the sink, frothing up the water with the sponge on a stick, just to keep herself busy.

This whole honeymoon thing had unsettled her far more

than she'd let on to anyone. She knew that Alsace had been Will's idea, an acknowledgement of the time he'd first really noticed Asif's sister. How bright and confident she must have been, determined to catch the attention of the muttering back-row boys, as she stood up to present her account of her grandfather's war. No wonder Will had been hooked all those years back. She blushed to remember how eagerly she had listened from the kitchen as Yaqub reluctantly marshalled his thoughts for his granddaughter. Surely something he said would explain a little of the void. But it hadn't.

She started with the glasses and cutlery, sponging each over and over again as if to bring a new sparkle to the everyday. After the official letter informing them that Yaqub was a prisoner, there had been initial rejoicing that he had not been killed in battle, but then, as the silence grew longer so did their fears about what the Germans might do to enemy prisoners they'd consider inferior natives. And all they could do was wait.

And now Saira and Will had flown to Germany, as if it held no fear for them. At least they would only spend today there. It was the nearest convenient airport for Alsace, they said. She wished she could send a message to them. She'd asked her son (her old fingers could not manage the tricky little keys and letters), but he'd just laughed and said that you didn't interrupt young people on a honeymoon. If only she knew they were all right.

She moved on to the plates, and it struck her that perhaps she was just being selfish. Was she really worried about them? After all, Germany was a different place now. Was she just anxious to know if Will had remembered? It had taken so much courage to speak to him. Why had she felt too ashamed to speak to her granddaughter? Was she afraid it would tarnish

Saira's memories of Yaqub? Will would have to explain carefully. Oh dear, she'd been such a pathetic coward. Angrily she started to scour a pan that was perfectly clean already.

Unexpectedly, Saira found that she too was enjoying the sensation of the water caressing her limbs. Initially the high dome of the Doric Spa's reception area had been intimidating. She could imagine the pallid Victorian invalids in their bath chairs being wheeled beneath it to their hydrotherapy sessions. And how were those armless classical statues a good advertisement for the treatments on offer? But she'd giggled as Will, riveted by the corpulent naked bodies strolling round the pool beyond, had hissed 'they all look as if they've been eating the full German breakfast for years on end!' She'd refrained from pointing out that he'd just eaten plenty of the hotel's breakfast spread, but then pulled a face. There was no way she was going to parade around like that.

But she'd been reassured by the private room they were shown to in the modern suite. The shadows from the tall bamboos outside flickered across the walls, the music was soothing and the water looked warm and inviting. She could see why Jacinth had chosen it.

As soon as her colleagues in IT support had heard that Saira's honeymoon trip was starting from Baden-Baden, Jacinth had insisted that she and Will should spend their first morning luxuriating in the spa waters. 'You guys will be exhausted after the wedding and the flight. And besides you can't just stay overnight in Spa-city and then buzz off. You have to do a bit of pampering and healthy living!' Jacinth's boyfriend was a dedicated football fan, so of course they'd gone to Baden-Baden during a previous World Cup, and whilst he'd trekked off to all the England matches, she'd spent a fortune on various thermal baths, facials, ayurveda massages, rasul baths, cream baths, herbal wraps, hot stone massages and saunas. 'You'll just love it!' she'd promised.

'But I don't do naked,' Saira had protested. 'Not in front of other people. You know that!' But her colleague was not to be diverted from her brilliant idea. In between dispensing invaluable computer assistance down the phone line, she'd scoured the internet for 'suitable' spa experiences. Towards the end of the afternoon she'd shouted, 'Temptation! That's it!' She called Saira over. 'Look, you could hardly object to this one. It sounds a great package. You get a Japanese room all to yourselves – look it's all cedar wood and natural stone. You get warm running spa water, celestial and meditative music, a bamboo garden, and a fragrant oil massage for body and spirit. Wow! That's new since I went. You just so must try it!' Jacinth with an idea was unstoppable. She must have done an instant whip-round, for a couple of days later she'd coolly booked a 'Temptation' session for their first morning. Saira had been so embarrassed and rather annoyed that Will and his mates just thought it was a real laugh.

But now Will wasn't laughing in that kind of laddish way that she didn't really like – he had more of a dreamy, sensuous smile. She had been rather frightened of him that first night together. Perhaps they'd made a mistake staying at an anonymous airport hotel, with the roar of planes taking off and landing all night They'd thought it would be easiest for what should have been an early morning flight. But the room had been so drab and soulless. It had smelt of stale cigarette smoke tinged with a sweet and sickly air freshener and had just looked so beige. She knew Will had had girls before he met her and would have had sex with them, so would know what he was doing. But his hungry expression had frightened her, and though she knew he'd tried to be gentle it had hurt. She'd done her best to hide it, but he'd known. It had been an unkind first night – definitely not the bed of roses of romantic tales.

Seeing her wince, Will guessed she was reflecting on their first night. It had been pretty grim. And afterwards she'd turned away from him. Surely this was not how marriage would be? Thank goodness for last night's reprieve. The hotel his parents had booked for them in Baden-Baden had been so cool and elegant. Saira had loved their room as soon as she saw it – the silvery grey and cream linen, grey walls, black-tiled bathroom and tall vase of sultry cream roses. Even the folds of the cream curtains had glittered with silver swirls. After dinner and a stroll under the stars, they had stood at the window looking down at the lit streets, and then quietly Saira had slipped out of her clothes, stretched out voluptuously on the grey sheets like a purring cat and held out her arms to him.

As the music shifted mood and a new perfume seemed to be added to the swirling waters, a mischievous smile played round Saira's lips. 'I guess the sound of cascading water is becoming our theme tune. Remember the fountains in the Market Square? The day they were frothing with washing-up liquid?'

'I still think I popped more bubbles than you!' said Will, idly casting his mind back to that chance meeting. He'd been back in Foxhill from uni, working at a pub in town, and had just come off a shift, and she'd been waiting in the market square for her cousins. He'd never taken much notice of her at school (he just knew her as Asif's sister, who went around with a crowd of Asian girls – though she had done that amazing war project). But he'd recognised her and for some crazy reason he'd challenged her to a bubble-bursting contest. They'd acted like a couple of small kids. And then they'd had that first coffee together.

Water plashed and dripped as Will lifted his foot and ran his toes down Saira's slim leg. 'I can hardly believe we've made it to here! I was just lying back enjoying it all, thinking of the bubbles, and then your Dad's furious face flashed across my mind. Trust him to ruin it!'

His mind went back to those early meetings after the bubble contest that he'd let her think she'd won. It had been very casual, just sitting over a coffee and catching up with what had happened to friends from school. It had been surprisingly interesting as they moved in such different circles now, so they knew quite different stories. And somehow he had found himself looking forward to his innocent Saturday afternoons with Saira. He suspected that she never mentioned them at home or even told the cousins she was meant to be with. Then, when term started and he went back to Manchester, he felt as if something bright and sparkling had gone out of his life. 'I don't think I'll ever forget your Dad's face when I was hauled into your front parlour!'

Saira laughed; she could now, though it had been dreadful at the time. It was her mother who'd noticed the letters. Saira had been surprised when Will started writing – so old-fashioned. But it made her realise how much she had missed the laughs she'd had with Will. She missed his face as he listened attentively. She missed his gentleness, his sarcasm, his doubts, his... well, everything. His letters were hesitant at first. Then they got more fluent. To her amazement it sounded as if he was actually getting quite involved in his course. He described how he'd 'discovered' the library (where had he been all this time?). There was a hint about a previous girl-friend that he seemed to have split up with (she read that bit several times, just to make sure that was what he was saying between the lines). And then her mother had started to take an interest. 'Same hand-writing!' she observed. 'Who do you know in Manchester?'

Saira expected a big row when she told her mother about meeting Will. 'Asif's friend?' Of course she remembered him coming round years ago. 'Quite a polite young boy,' was her only guarded comment. But her mother was subtle. Up till now both her parents had been quite liberal. They'd always said that their daughters need not have arranged marriages, but would always be consulted and allowed to make their own choices 'with our advice, of course!' But now it seemed as if that freedom was a fiction. It was almost as if her parents were saying, 'So you want a boyfriend? We'll show you suitable boyfriends!' For, all of a sudden, they were entertaining innumerable friends and relatives, all of whom had a sullen young single son in tow.

At first Will just thought it was funny when Saira wrote describing all these family get-togethers. But for some reason he felt threatened when Aqeel was produced with his family. He remembered him from school ('That bespectacled nerd?' he wrote, 'I just can't see you two together'). That was when Will came home for the weekend. To Saira's surprise, he said he wanted to come round to her house. She could hardly believe the consternation this produced. Her mother took no notice when she said, 'Look you don't need to clean and cook madly like this! You don't need to impress him. He's very casual!'

'Impress!' her hitherto kindly, gentle mother shouted. 'Of course I don't want to impress him. He's a nothing! A nobody! But even a nobody should be shown proper hospitality.' All the family was there. Asif had been summoned, leaving his new wife at home. Saira sat with her sisters and mother and grandmother in the back room. To her huge embarrassment she could hear Asif hissing to his old friend, 'Look, just lay off my sister, right?' as he opened the front door and took Will into the formal front room.

'We never called it the parlour!' Saira remarked irrelevantly. 'That's so Victorian!'

'Your dad really lost his cool that day.' Up till then Will had retained fond memories of Sid (who for some odd reason had kept his schoolboy nickname, even among his children's friends) joking around with them outside the school gates, and when they called round to play with Asif. He hardly recognised this enraged man, shouting that he always knew that at heart Will was just like all British boys that he saw every night, drinking themselves stupid and having casual sex with girls. His daughter was never going to become like those tarts out on the town in their droves in their skimpy tops and skirts, drinking and behaving in an abandoned fashion. There was no way Will was going to bring shame on his daughter. Even now it was a scary memory.

Saira never heard the details of what her father said to Will. Her mother kept her occupied making the tea and preparing the cups and plates, but it was her older married sister who was sent in with the food. She could hear her father's raised voice briefly as the door opened and closed. But that was all. Finally Saira was sent for. She had never seen her amiable father look so stern. He told her that Will had promised not to try to see, phone, or text her again until they had both finished their courses, and were qualified and working.

As if in tune with their memories, the background music changed from bamboo piping to a high, haunting voice which sounded as if it was singing of love and loss. And for a few moments they reflected on how they'd both coped with the long separation. It had been hardest for Saira, still at home. After Will had left, Saira raged and wept. She couldn't believe that he had coolly accepted her father's dictum and just walked away. He couldn't care, after all. She'd been just a passing whim. And he'd given up as soon as the going got tough. She felt humiliated when she overheard her father telling her mother that he was convinced the boy would forget their daughter after a while. And even more humiliated when they acknowledged how hurt she must be feeling, but how she was bound to come round to their way of thinking. 'She's a sensible girl. She'll see what's right for her.' But two days later came the first letter, starting, 'Dear Saira, I never promised your father that I'd stop writing.' And after that it was that sense of what was right for her that she'd wrestled with during the next dreary months. Her parents were relieved because outwardly it seemed as if she was even more attentive to her prayers and Koran studies. But all the time she was sifting, weighing prayerfully, considering her allegiances, her obligations, her path forward.

It had been easier for Will. He'd not wanted to meet anyone else, so had cut down on his social life and really concentrated on his studies. He'd been amazed to discover how interesting pollution in all its forms could be when you really read up all the possible solutions and he'd had a couple of placements during the holidays, which had kept him away from Foxhill and any temptation to try to catch sight of her in town with her cousins. Then, after finals, he had concentrated on finding a job and trying to appear a man of prospects to her abruptly Victorian parents.

Saira took deep breaths of the scented air. 'What do you think finally changed their minds?'

They'd discussed this endlessly before, but had never come

up with an answer. Saira knew that her parents had always loved her and wanted the best for her, but she couldn't account for their eventual climb-down. She was unaware of how her steadfast loyalty to them and to her faith shone through her equally determined wish to go on seeing Will. Perhaps too, they were pleased with the way Will had respected the ban, and had worked hard (not to mention his 2:1 degree).

'We brought you up to know right from wrong and to act with honour and integrity,' her father had finally said at the end of their unhappy year of enforced separation. 'And now we are trusting you to live that out, young as you are. It is a burden that we place on you.'

A few months after the ban had been lifted and they were meeting again, Will had decided that he needed to know a bit more about Islam if he was to understand Saira better. 'Not that I'm thinking of converting, mind!' he'd warned Asif, who'd merely said, 'We're not into conversion, man, not like your lot!' Will suppressed a grin. History had never been Asif's strong point, he thought. Nevertheless, after consultation with the imam, Asif had put him in touch with someone, 'just to guide your reading, mate, and discuss anything you can't get your head round'. Will didn't know whether to laugh or be offended, but in fact he'd developed a real respect for his scholarly guide. He was a physics lecturer, and his impersonal, unobtrusive style suited Will. Will did wonder if his 'tutor' had put in a good word for him with Saira's family. But that wouldn't be enough, he knew.

Will could have made a joke, his automatic response to big questions, but he was unexpectedly serious. 'I guess it was you, Saira. You convinced them you were dedicated. That you'd stay faithful to Islam. Not compromise or be corrupted by my wicked ways.'

'Who would like the first massage?' asked a rather sexy voice. Saira could hardly believe that during the moments they'd been drifting sensuously in the water, a whole hour of 'real' time had passed. She felt disinclined to stir. 'OK, I'll go first,' said Will, thinking she might be hesitant about exactly what kind of massage the unknown white-clad woman might be proposing.

As she watched him step out of the Japanese bath and into the proffered thick white towelling robe, Saira's thoughts turned to the days ahead. It seemed an amazing luxury to have ten days all to themselves, without any of their families fretting, pressurising or cajoling. It was their time. It was ironic, really, that they hadn't escaped completely from family ties, but had chosen to look for traces of her grandfather's wartime experiences.

That single photo Saira had seen of her grandfather in his army uniform before he set out from India had shown such a handsome young man, tall and lean next to his sturdier companion. He was much younger than she and Will when he was taken prisoner by the Germans. She thought how bewildering his experiences must have been. She wondered how he could have survived three years of imprisonment. She wondered if he'd had to face pressure because of his religion and race. She'd seen horrific films about the treatment of Jews in concentration camps. Would the Germans have treated the 'inferior', 'native' races in an even more bestial manner?

Yaqub lost count of the time his surrendered brigade spent being herded northwards, first to the coast, later onto boats and then onto a series of trains. They must have looked like a crowd of dirty beggars when they finally descended with their kit bags from that last train, for the people lining the neat German streets gazed at them in disgust as they were marched towards a barbed wire enclosure which seemed to stretch for miles.

They soon learnt that this place was called Annaberg. The prisoners had not known what to expect of a permanent prison camp, but got the impression that this place had been created just for them – the Indian soldiers of low rank. They had been separated out from the other Mechili prisoners for some reason. It had its own guards, brutal men, who disdainfully supervised their cleansing and delousing on that first day and then continued to treat them like dirt.

There were thousands of them, crowded in there, leaderless and demoralised. They rapidly learnt to respond to and call out the individual prison number that was now their only identity. Some days they were forced to stand for hours. From the start, their rations were so meagre that they gradually became very weak. Yaqub would tell himself firmly that it must have been worse than that back home during times of famine. But they could see (especially later, when they worked outside the camp's barbed wire) that Germany was prosperous and the people well-fed. Yet the PoWs had to subsist on a cup of hot water or sometimes acorn coffee in the morning, and later in the day some bean soup or some of the cabbage the guards called 'sauerkraut' or some potatoes. Occasionally there was a little strange meat in the soup, but whatever it was they had all reached the stage where they were glad of the added sustenance, and there were no protests. The Germans had disdained all along to pay any heed to all the important caste and religious restrictions. There was bread too, a heavy, black bread, made from a rough grain and wood pulp, bearing no resemblance to Indian bread. Once a week they were given eight loaves of this bread to share between twenty-four men.

After months of this, some men were too weak to stand upright for long at parade, and others could not walk the distance from their barracks to the latrines without falling over. It was pitiable to watch men who had been strong young soldiers, shrivelling up and falling down like old, old men. A few just gave up the struggle and lay in their own excrement. Men began to suffer from tuberculosis. One man from Yaqub's block was taken away to the hospital block and never returned. Men suffered and died. They had each become a mere prison number, treated as if they were devoid of reason or feeling. And in fact normal feelings were vanishing. Yaqub thought less and less about his family and about returning to them, as hope receded. Like the others, he just followed the guards' orders and concentrated on surviving one more day. It was then that Subhas Chandra Bose appeared in their camp.

They had been in the Annaberg camp for over six months before the first food parcels were sent by the Red Cross. The prisoners didn't know that they should have received them earlier, but that the Red Cross had not been allowed to inspect their camp before. It would have lessened the impact of that man Subhas Chandra Bose if these additional rations had arrived sooner.

There was a lot of discussion in Yaqub's hut about how long they should make the food last, and whether any more would arrive. Some men had had tears in their eyes when they opened them and found a selection of familiar foodstuff, such as atta flour, dhal, rice, ghee margarine, Nestles milk, sugar, cheese, and fish. That first night they were very cautious and used only small quantities, but there was an air of festivity. 'Do you remember our last big feast, in the desert, before the battle?' Barkat asked, as for the first time in months his comrades relaxed and joked. 'I haven't dared think of that goat before. It was so good, so spicy, so filling.'

And then a second parcel arrived the following week. The men could hardly believe it. Yaqub was particularly touched by the bar of soap in his parcel. The next morning, he resolved to take full advantage at ablution time. As he stood in line, he could not remember how long it was since he had felt truly clean before morning prayer. He sniffed the soap with pleasure and stroked his calloused finger along its smooth surface. This piece of soap had no dirt-engrained cracks or gritty texture. It was large enough to hold in his hand and slide around. It was not just a slim flat pebble of soap, used and worn down by many bodies before his. It was perfect.

Then he hesitated momentarily. It was possible that this generous soap and food allowance was a trap. Other men, even men he'd previously respected, had brought shame on themselves and the Brigade by betraying their loyalty to King-Emperor and Army for food or for fine clothes. Maybe soap and clean water were the latest allure. You could no longer trust anything to be what it appeared.

But then he laughed at himself. Even if it was an enticement, it didn't matter. He could make the most of it, enjoy a full ablution, create a lather that would slide the grime from every pore of his body, leaving him cleansed and wholesome. But since he already had the soap in his grasp, there was no way he could be persuaded by it to treachery. He would simply wash, pray and make sure he relished the early morning sunshine outside as he marched in line, head held high, through the shabby streets to the factory. Moreover he would hope for the day's blessings to continue with a cup of that strange watery coffee before the day's labour began.

It was his turn. He began to wash his face and slowly rippled his soapy fingers though his matted hair. It was a while since his head had been shaved during delousing. He liked the feel of it growing back, now it was no longer stubbly and prickly. As he massaged his neck and shoulders he thought of how vulnerable they had all been to temptation in those long months as prisoners.

If you are evil, how do you subvert thousands of defeated troops? You remove their leaders, you starve them till they are almost too weak to move, tell them the British are brutal imperialists who are losing the war and then you promise them fine food and smart new uniforms and a chance to overthrow the British and establish a free India.

Yaqub scrubbed his chest vigorously, wishing he could reach his back. He recalled the day the Germans told them that there was a leader from their country who wanted to talk to them. It's true he was an Indian, but, unlike them, Subhas Chandra Bose was a highly educated man and from far-distant Bengal. He seemed to be a friend of the Germans, for the guards and even the commandant appeared to defer to him, so he moved freely among the prisoners, giving speeches and talking to individuals. He had a strange way of speaking to them. They were all sure that he had never been a soldier or faced battle. But he talked in military terms. He talked of loyalty, but he said the only loyalty that mattered was that to their own country, India. He had no praise for their past training and discipline. For he said that the British were being defeated ignominiously everywhere, just as they had been at Mechili. He insisted that only German discipline and training would win India back from the British. He wanted five hundred men to volunteer to be trained by the Germans then be parachuted into India to undermine the British there.

Yaqub and Barkat had been both puzzled and horrified

when some men accepted his words straight away and raised their hands to volunteer. They were puzzled, because, like many of the others, they were not familiar with political arguments. They were offended when Bose had said he knew that they had only joined the British Indian Army for money, because their families were poor and exploited. They were shocked when he said that their oath of loyalty to the British was meaningless.

'A man who can un-say an oath he has given on the Koran has no honour or truth,' said Yaqub firmly. 'My father and my father's father have served in the British army,' agreed Barkat. 'How could I dishonour my whole family by even listening to such seditious words?'

But they recognised that the words of Subhas Chandra Bose were powerful ones, which would sway others. He told them all that now, while Britain was weak, they should think of their own country, and should rise up to help defeat the British and free India for ever from their oppressive and unjust rule. He told the weak and defeated prisoners that they could be free again. They would no longer fight for the British in a war that had nothing to do with them. They would be brave again and fight with heroism against the oppressors of their own country, for their own families and their own plots of land. They should no longer be overawed by the British, for the British were losing this war. Just look how they had crumbled at Mechili! The British were now like a dead snake that people continued to fear. If the prisoners would only shake off this fear, victory and freedom would be theirs.

Yaqub's musing was interrupted by a shout from the queue behind him, telling him get a move on, but he ignored it. He was not usually selfish, but today was special, and he blotted out the noise. And for the moment there was no guard nearby to bludgeon him into speeding. He noticed he was scrubbing his legs with rhythmic vigour as he remembered the rallying speeches that Bose had made. That man had a mesmerising way of speaking that quickly persuaded some of the Indian prisoners to join him. Some joined because they were ambitious and were seduced by promises of promotion, rank and proper pay and benefits. A few were sly and cunning and keen only to save their own skins rather than free India. Many were just weak and desperate. They were hardly idealists.

But Barkat had summed up their distrust of Bose, 'That man has never experienced poverty and injustice. Why does he speak like that? He is a man who has received all the benefits of British education and jobs. He sounds more like a politician who wants power for himself than like the oppressed under-dog he speaks about.'

'If only they had not taken our officers away,' some of the men in their barrack hut lamented after one of his speeches. 'We would know what to think if they were with us.' But Yaqub felt that for the first time, they all had to think for themselves and make their own assessment of the persuasive words. 'But all our Indian Officers have already joined his new Legion,' pointed out the waverers. 'We only have his word for that,' Barkat told them severely. 'He may be lying or at least exaggerating to trick us.'

Yaqub washed his feet, relishing the softness of the now rather scummy lather between his toes and against his hardened soles. More than ever he was convinced that they had to think for themselves and stay true to their sworn loyalty, whatever the hardships. An image came back to him, that had haunted him since their surrender at Mechili. There all the fresh, young, defeated Indian troops had followed orders, as they were accustomed to do, and had sat mindlessly in the desert, not daring to move. But there had been one man, a stranger, not from their brigade, a tall white man, who had initially crouched near Barkat in an attitude of submission. But after several hours of sometimes dozing and sometimes watching carefully, this man had simply stood up, taking advantage of dust swirling up from passing vehicles, and walked confidently to one side, indicating that he was going to urinate. He had not been stopped. He had just walked away, with an easy confidence, and then disappeared into the desert. No shots had been fired at him. He had just taken his chance courageously. Yaqub wondered if he was safe and back fighting somewhere.

Slipping the soap into his uniform pocket, Yaqub finally allowed another man to take his place at the ablutions. He wished it was easier to get dry. He didn't like his clothes to become damp. He dressed thoughtfully. Yes, each man now had to take responsibility for his own survival. Just like that man in the desert had done.

That winter in Annaberg was particularly tough for the prisoners who were set to shovelling the snow from the roads. It was hard, freezing work on the meagre rations. By now, the banks of snow at the sides of the road had grown higher and more compacted, the winds had become more bitter, and their uniforms provided scant warmth or protection. It was no wonder that some of them, who had so far resisted the fine words of Bose, were easily 'converted' by the Germans' promise of ample food and warm new uniforms. These men vanished from their midst, and were sent to a special camp for 'proper' German army training. Barkat always said that many of those men had chosen that way to survival, without believing it would really harm anybody else.

Yaqub was thankful that his Arbeitskommando was

allocated to a factory and it was mainly indoor work, apart from sweeping the yard and loading and unloading. Yet even here there were unexpected temptations. A month or two after the first soap and food parcels arrived, they were allowed a mid-morning break, which was unheard of. They weren't at first sure what they should do. Some of the men went outside to smoke cigarettes they had saved from their parcels. Usually the factory workers ignored them. But this day, a group of women workers, still in their overalls, went out and joined them. Yaqub had stayed inside, but he could hear laughter, and when they were back in their barrack hut that evening the men joked lewdly about how forward the women had been and how one of them had taken a particular fancy to Ali Muhammad.

The morning breaks continued for a week. Yaqub noticed that several of his compatriots were becoming very bold with the German women, and that they were managing to slip away together. But, after what turned out to be the last break, Ali Muhammad and the others did not return. Yaqub never knew whether they had been caught in compromising acts and threatened, or whether the women had simply made the gullible prisoners offers or promises that had swayed them. For at the end of that week the Germans told the remaining prisoners that Ali Muhammad and the others had signed up to be trained for the new Indian Legion. The guards pointed out that they too would have women, food and fine uniforms if they joined. Barkat, who was in a different work-party, had also noticed that the Germans were using their own women to trap and blackmail men into joining. They agreed that it was incomprehensible that the German women could act like that. Their own village women would never behave so degradingly. Women like that were to be found only in the towns, the bazaars. And for white women! From everything they heard it was absolutely impossible for the aloof British memsahibs to behave in such a way as these German fraus.

There were no more breaks at Yaqub's factory, and the women workers no longer talked to them. Yaqub was glad of that and started to count his blessings. The weekly food parcels, soap, a cup of hot coffee that morning and the approach of warmer weather … he must have come to a standstill, for the factory foreman suddenly swiped him round the legs with a broom handle, shouting the by now familiar refrain, 'Schnell! Schnell!', before shoving the broom into his hands and ordering him to get sweeping.

Yaqub immediately set to work with an outward show of docility. But inside he felt strong. He knew that the naïve army recruit who had once unquestioningly followed orders had come a long way. He had learned to judge events and fine words for himself and to make his own decisions. And, even after all these months of degradation, his decision was to stay loyal to his army oath whatever the hardships and however long their captivity.

Amina felt no better. How were the dear children after a night and a morning in Germany? She did hope they'd soon be in France. She got out the vacuum cleaner. The house was perfectly clean and her son and daughter-in-law had forbidden her to help with heavy tasks nowadays. Nevertheless she turned it on. Its roar submerged the worst of her thoughts and soothed her.

It would be idyllic to lie on his stomach for days on end,

thought Will, having fingers anointing and pummelling him with fragrant oils. It was a weird thought that somewhere near here Saira's grandfather had come to his final prisoner of war camp, after the privations and hardship of Annaberg Camp. But Will found it surprisingly difficult to imagine privations and hardships whilst those firm but sensuous fingers were working on him. He gave up trying to reconcile the contrasts and succumbed to the perfumed manipulation.

Finally the fingers lifted their pressure and he lay glowing and contented until the voice interrupted, asking if he would like to relax in the bamboo garden, with a glass of chilled fruit juice.

'It is now the turn of Madam for her Temptation massage.'

4

Borderlands

Still tingling from their massage, Saira and Will went to the poolside café for the final part of their spa package – not a mere lunch, but 'a spiritually revitalising repast'. They were both laughing at the thought of more food so soon after their monster hotel breakfast, but enjoyed selecting their salads and choosing from the array of exotic fruits. Will just wished he could take Saira to bed now. He'd never seen her look so sensuous and indolent.

'What plans?' he asked idly. He felt, suddenly, as if he was in some kind of timeless zone, which bore no relation to the outside, real world.

'Well, we could stay here for ever. Jacinth would approve!' Saira allowed her eyes to rest momentarily on the rotund basking bodies. 'On the other hand, perhaps not! Tourism or quest?'

Will sensed that she was as keen as he was to start looking for traces of her grandfather. He also knew how little they had to go on. They had been so busy planning the wedding and all its complications, that there had been little time for additional research. Her grandfather had just said that his last prison camp was in Alsace, near the Maginot Line. Will had discussed it with his friend Luke, who was working for the year in

Strasbourg, and they'd decided the prisoners might by that stage have been divided up into smaller work-camps, on the other side of the Rhine from the main PoW camp in Baden-Baden. Luke had been unable to get over for the wedding, because of a broadcast he was involved in, but had promised to meet up with them that evening in Strasbourg and to help them plan a route in Alsace, saying that some of the background research he'd done for a previous programme might be useful to them.

'Maybe the quest should wait till we hear Luke's ideas'

'Right, it's tourism then. We could do a quick drive through the Black Forest or wander round Strasbourg.' Then before Will could answer, she added, 'How about spending the afternoon in Strasbourg, getting a feel for the place?'

'And the shops, you mean!'

After nearly three years incarcerated in Annaberg, the men in Yaqub's hut sensed an uneasiness among the Germans, and began to compare notes. Their prisoner numbers had dwindled from the original ten thousand, due to deaths and to all those who'd 'volunteered' for the Indian Legion and been sent off to training camps in other parts of Germany. But there were still thousands of them left. Over those years most of them had picked up some basic German words and phrases, mainly commands. They tried to listen out for familiar words when they were working, so as to get an idea of how the war was progressing. But they couldn't make much sense of what they overheard, though the German guards would taunt them by telling them of constant German victories.

But recently, they agreed, the German factory workers and guards sounded concerned about Russia. Whose side were the

Russians on? None of the prisoners had been too sure at first. Barkat thought they'd once been told, long ago in training, about a pact between Germany and Russia. So what were they now doing that so worried the Germans? It sounded as if it was something that threatened Annaberg. Why would they do that if they were allies? Perhaps they were against Germany after all. If they came, would the Russians free the prisoners or would they kill them? Everything seemed very confusing.

Then one morning their work in the factories came to an abrupt end. There was no call to line up for work. They were all confined to barracks without an explanation. Everyone was speculating about this unexpected break in routine. In the afternoon they were ordered to line up outside with their blanket, personal things and any remaining rations.

Yaqub and Barkat stood in line, clutching their scant possessions. Everywhere stood Germans with wads of typed papers from which they were calling out prisoners' numbers. Their numbers did not get called for a long time, so they stood for several hours, wondering what was happening and whether the Russians were approaching. All the time other men were being led away through the camp gates.

It was dusk before they were finally called. They were led off under guard in a file of about fifty. The streets were very quiet, but they saw occasional faces watching from behind the curtains. At the railway station wooden goods trucks were waiting for them.

'I've got strangely used to being here,' whispered Yaqub, 'I'd almost rather stay here!'

'What will happen to our Red Cross parcels?' wondered one of their group.

'Perhaps the new place will be better,' said Barkat optimistically before they were silenced.

Their group was ordered into one truck, and they could see more groups arriving and being marshalled into the other trucks. The doors were slammed and bolted behind them. After a long wait, they heard a whistle and felt the jolt as a steam engine was connected, then, after a fierce hiss of steam, the chain of goods trucks lurched forwards into the unknown.

There were some benches so they took it in turns to sit on them. Those without seats sat on the floor. The men nearest the outside tried peering through the gaps in the wooden slats, but they could make out little outside. There were occasional halts, but the German place names meant nothing to them.

'Just imagine if this train was taking us all back home!' said one the prisoners. 'What I wouldn't give to see my family and home again.' Everyone wished that he hadn't voiced this thought. As the months and then years had slowly passed, their hopes of seeing their families again had diminished. Yaqub could hardly remember the face of the girl he had once been going to marry. It was stupid to stir up old dreams.

Outside the airy pleasure dome the afternoon was grey and drab as they collected their hired car from the hotel car-park. Will got thoroughly bored with the flat landscape as they drove along the Rhine plain, never seeing the river. As they took the Strasbourg turning, he gazed at the grey range of mountains straight ahead of them, the wartime border with France.

Saira had a quick look at the guide book (ostensibly a gift from her small brothers, along with a map) and read aloud the section on the Vosges fauna. 'Deer, roe, wild boars, badgers, foxes, marten, stoats, chamois, lynx, great grouse. But sadly the bears are extinct now. The boys would have liked it if we got half-eaten by bears!' It sounded as if there were parts of the range where you could no longer walk freely, as the peaty bog was being damaged by the tramp of walkers' boots. 'Every boot leaves a permanent trace!'

As they approached the bridge over the Rhine, Saira and Will had their first married argument. Saira suddenly suggested that it would be good to stop and look at the great river that formed the present-day boundary between France and Germany. She felt there should be a sense of occasion in crossing from one country to another. 'Besides, it would be fun to watch those huge barges going up and down the river!' But Will was getting increasingly ratty. He was still getting used to the gears and hand-brake being on the wrong side (not to mention the traffic), and the road signs were driving him mad – were those ones just lorry routes? Then they changed abruptly in appearance and in language. German became French, and he found it hard to adapt. And at the same time they were actually crossing the Rhine sandwiched between juggernauts. 'Too late!'

Once, he supposed, they would have paused at the border control and customs (as they'd done on family holidays as kids), but nowadays the heavy traffic flowed unchecked past the deserted border control he could see out of the corner of his eye. They seemed to be hurtling towards unknown place names within Strasbourg, with no opportunity to pull over.

'Concentrate on the fucking map,' he yelled at Saira. 'Tell me which way to go!'

At the end of their long rail journey from Annaberg Camp, Yaqub and the rest of the train-load spent short periods in different camps. There must have been about a thousand of them moving between camps. At a big camp near a place called

Baden-Baden, they were split into smaller workforces and moved again. There were rumours that they might be heading towards defeated France. It was a matter of indifference to them. They were still prisoners of the Germans.

Of all the camps, the one near Strasbourg was the most depressing. They had become accustomed to wooden huts surrounded by barbed wire and guard towers. At least the huts were in the open air, however windswept. But when, after a long march from the railway, they arrived at the latest prison-camp gates, they were confronted by a vast stone building sunk into a grassy hillside, with a wide water-less moat between it and them. As they marched through the gates and descended into the moat, the damp walls, churned-up mud and patrolling dogs depressed their spirits still further. It was like a mighty fortress from some long-ago war.

They were marched through the huge doorway and as metal doors clanged shut behind them Yaqub felt like a condemned prisoner who might never come out alive from beneath the hill. He let himself be pushed down stairs to the basement, level with the floor of the moat, where they were counted into large cell-like dormitories. Yaqub's, like the others, was bare apart from three tiers of deep shelves. They were expected to sleep crammed cheek by jowl on these.

Later they were escorted along a dank corridor to the latrines and washroom. He soon discovered that there was never enough water for so many prisoners. He became accustomed to sharing the same water, which got dirtier and dirtier as more men queued up to use it. The latrines were also completely inadequate for the number of men, and he was disgusted to see the maggots crawling beneath the wooden seats. Each day when a lorry arrived to pump out the excrement, a dreadful smell assailed them, whether they were in their dormitories or the corridor or even exercising outside in the sunken moat.

All exercise was out in the moat, surrounded by snarling dogs straining at their leashes. He could see nothing of the world above and beyond the rim of the moat, and felt forgotten by time. Twice a day the sentries brought jugs of the eternal potato and cabbage soup. Unfortunately the Red Cross parcels had not caught up with their whereabouts and the soup hardly gave them enough nourishment to keep going. Then, when the parcels eventually arrived, they were a great disappointment, as they were the standard ones with corned beef and pork luncheon meat, and no rice or other Indian ingredients. There were other prisoners in other parts of the fort who were delighted to be offered some of the tins of meat, and most gave something in return. Yaqub and his comrades also traded some of the tins for cigarettes with some men who weren't German guards, but who did jobs around the fort. Barkat thought they were civilians. Two of them spoke some English as well as German (and French they said). The mention of French confused Yaqub, so one day when the guards were occupied, he and Barkat tried to find out from one of the civilians where they were. 'Here Germany? Here France?'

The answer was more complicated than they expected. That night they told the rest of prisoners in their dungeon dormitory that, as far as they understood the man, this Strasbourg place was in Alsace, and Alsace was a frontier area, sometimes part of France and sometimes part of Germany. It had been French before the war. But the Germans had annexed it, whatever annexed meant. Anyway, now that it was like part of Germany, the men had to fight in the German army and the French language was banned. They were even forbidden to wear French hats called berets. The man had told them that if they wanted to escape, they still had to cross the plains and then the mountains of Alsace to reach occupied France to the west and then England.

'Escape?' None of Yaqub and Barkat's fellow prisoners had really thought of that before, as they had no idea of where they should head for in Germany. But now that this French/German civilian had put the idea into their heads, they started to discuss the possibility. Apparently some of the prisoners who had been there before them had escaped at the point when they were being moved on to the next camp. Yaqub thought back to the desert at Mechili, and the unknown English prisoner who had coolly strolled off into the desert. 'Perhaps we have all been too passive up till now? Perhaps now we know that we are near France …'

'But,' Barkat reminded him, 'the man also said that if we are moved to a smaller work-camp here in Alsace, it would be easier for us to escape from there, as there are likely to be fewer guards than in the bigger transit camps.' Their dormitory got quite excited by the idea, and discussed it late into the night.

Barkat and Yaqub had saved the most interesting piece of information till last. They got the impression that the man had been a bit uncertain at first about revealing it. But remembering their generosity over the tinned meat, he'd decided to trust them. Apparently, both in France and in this part of Germany which had once been French, there was a secret organisation of people who were resisting the Germans and who would help escaped prisoners to cross the border into France. They were known as the Resistance. They would not be on their own if they escaped.

It was a great relief when, between Saira's map reading and

Will's interpretation of road signs, they eventually found a large underground car park in the centre of Strasbourg. They left the car there, and headed on foot into the old town. After the busy roads, it was really relaxing to stroll by the canals and along the narrow streets. Saira loved the old timbered houses whose upper stories jutted out above their heads. And the glass-topped tourist boats on the canals looked fun.

They checked into the small hotel where Luke had reserved a room for them. The hotel was an old-fashioned one right in the centre, and Saira loved the view from their attic room, over the steeply sloping rooftops to the cathedral tower. As they still had a couple of hours to spare before Luke finished work, they headed for the cathedral square. It was thronging with tourists, 'living statues', roasted chestnut sellers and surreptitious beggars. From the cathedral steps soared the ethereal voice of a male soprano. 'Creepy!' Saira observed uncomfortably. The quaint, timbered gift shops were overflowing with postcards, pottery and furry miniature storks. 'Tacky or what?' sneered Will. But Saira was gazing in amazement at the tier upon tier of sculpted stone figures round the cathedral doorway and over all the surfaces.

They followed a surge of tourists behind a woman with a raised scarlet umbrella through the cathedral doors and into the vast interior. The milling crowds and babble of languages made it seem more like an airport terminal to Will. He felt more at ease when they finished their internal inspection and climbed up and up the tower, though he lost count of the number of stairs. From the viewing platform, they could see the whole of Strasbourg spread out below and the open countryside beyond, stretching out towards the Vosges mountains.

'Your grandfather's mountains!'

Then, at Saira's insistence, they took a boat trip along the canals in one of the glass-topped boats. It was very peaceful. The head-phone commentaries murmured on about the old buildings they were passing. As they went through a narrow lock, and as the lock gates closed on them, fellow tourists stared down curiously at them from the quay above. The boat paused below the modern European Parliament buildings, which looked vast from the water, then turned slowly back.

'It's an international city,' enthused Luke when they joined him on the cathedral steps after the boat trip. (Saira was a bit disconcerted by the kisses on both cheeks – he hadn't been like that in England). 'It's really buzzing when all the members of the European Parliament are in session here. You can hear a bizarre mix of languages in the bars and restaurants. Talking of which, me and the lads have got something a bit special planned for you tonight.'

Back at his flat he introduced them to the four French guys he shared with, made some mugs of tea, then he gave Saira a folder of notes, print-outs and leaflets. The bad news was, he announced, that he hadn't been able to discover the location of any Indian PoW camps. None of the older people he'd spoken to during his programme research and interviews, 'and many of them were only children during the war, of course,' remembered ever having seen Indian prisoners. And the camps had probably been destroyed after the war.

Saira felt a real sense of let-down. She'd thought Luke had discovered something more definite through his local contacts. She tried to explain to him about the warning boot-print sign in the guidebook, and the momentary surge of encouragement it had given her earlier. 'This sense that whatever you do, however small, leaves a permanent footprint behind. You know, they always make it sound negative, like a carbon footprint or like you're destroying the environment, but it could be a positive idea too. But now you're saying that all those Indian prisoners left nothing behind to show that they were here.'

'Not quite nothing,' one of Luke's friends, Bastien, tried to cheer her up, desperately thinking of traces. 'If you start in the right place, you can still see memorials, street names and forts from the war, and people living near these places will remember things.'

'And you haven't waited for the good news,' Luke pointed out. 'Three bits, in fact. First, I'm pretty confident I've identified the Maginot Line fort where your grandfather hid. Second, I've come across a definite indication that there were some Indian soldiers at Schoenenbourg, which is near a town you said he mentioned. You should start there tomorrow. Third, you're going to meet someone tonight to get you in the mood. He's too young to remember the war, but his father's war-time experiences will interest you. I was lucky enough to interview his father for our wartime memories programme. Nothing to do with the Indian Army, but it will give you some colourful background. Parallel lives and all that.'

'Hungry now?' he continued, 'Our treat. We're taking you out to dinner!'

Saira started to explain that eating out could be complicated. But Luke looked smug. 'No worries! We've got it all sorted!' With that, he led them all in a straggling procession down small side streets towards one of the canals. They stopped outside a narrow shop front painted dark blue, with a hanging wrought-iron sign showing a camel and a palm tree. Habib's Tunisian Restaurant.

'It was always a great place for students, but it's gone a bit more upmarket since Habib took over from his father. Food's great. A suitably North African start to your journey in your grandfather's footsteps. Seemed appropriate. Shame it's not Libyan, as you said that's where he fought, – but you can't have everything, and it's the next country on the map, and its soldiers fought for France! Not to mention it's halal, Saira. Didn't I tell you no worries!'

The door had one of those old-fashioned jangling bells as they went in, and Habib himself came forward to welcome them. The inside was sparkling with the patterned light from perforated metal lampshades reflecting off tiles and mirrors. Richly-coloured cushions were spread around the low tables by the entrance. Even the floor was bright with tiles and rugs.

There was something very intimate about the atmosphere. Habib flourished the colourful menus, asking Luke and his friends (obviously regulars) if they liked the new menu design, and then concentrated on Saira and Will, determined that they should experience the best dishes. 'Tunisians have the most delicate dishes and are the best cooks in North Africa,' he boasted. His English was excellent (he modestly claimed that all restaurateurs spoke every tourist language). 'And here we recreate for you the perfumes and savours of a starry night in a desert encampment,' he recited as if from a script.

Luke laughed at the hyperbole. 'This man has never left France! He's no more camped in a desert oasis than you or I have!' Habib grinned, pointing out that he had actually been on holiday there and that his father had lived in the desert, especially earlier in the war. It was his father who had started the restaurant, to recreate the authentic food of his childhood. 'Later I come and tell Saira about him. But first, enjoy my food!'

There was something about Habib's style and courtesy that did indeed make them feel like honoured guests at a banquet.

'I don't think I've ever eaten so much!' said Saira, leaning back, as Habib bought them another pot of mint tea. The last of his other customers had been served, and he could finally sit down with them and chat.

He told Saira how much he wished that his father could have met her grandfather, but that he had died two months ago from a heart attack. 'It is so good that you record him, Luke. He was so happy when his memories are heard on the radio. It was very special to him.'

'It was fascinating. He was a great character, Habib. Tell Saira about him.'

Habib told her that his father had started the restaurant after the war. He explained that during the war, his father had fought in North Africa, Italy and across France, finally being wounded in a desperate battle to liberate a tiny village north of Strasbourg. At the end of the war, he'd come back to that village to marry the French girl he'd met and fallen in love with whilst wounded.

Saira was fascinated. Although her grandfather had only been in a single battle, and then had spent most of the rest of the war imprisoned, she was fascinated by the story of another colonial soldier fighting for his mother country. 'And I always like a romantic ending!'

'I knew you'd find it interesting!' crowed Luke triumphantly. Will suddenly remembered Amina, and realised he hadn't had a chance to tell Saira. Later, he thought, as Luke and Habib started to compare dates. They worked out that Saira's grandfather had been in captivity for nearly two years before the tide began to turn and Habib's father was fighting in North Africa and then Italy. Habib said he'd been in really famous battles like Monte Cassino in Italy, but that later many of his regiment were wiped out in battles in France that were hardly remembered nowadays, like the one in December 1944 on the snow-capped Hohneck, one of the highest summits of the Vosges.

Luke snapped his fingers. 'December! It would only have been a month or so before that when your grandfather and his friend were trying to cross the mountain border in the opposite direction.'

Forty Tunisians were killed on the Hohneck, Habib continued, and one hundred and twenty-one captured, but the survivors, including his father, had fought on eastwards and northwards across Alsace, till, in March 1945, they reached his mother's small village on the German border.

Unable to be silent for long during this story he already knew, Luke interrupted to point out that what was really odd, like their paths really should have crossed, was that her village was fairly close to the Maginot Line fort, where he was pretty sure Saira's grandfather's hid. Habib nodded and added proudly that there was even a street in his mother's village named after his father's Tunisian regiment.

Will seemed very impressed by the military exploits of Habib's father, and Saira wondered whether she'd be trivialising everything by asking hesitantly, 'Your father … how did he meet your mother? Was it … was it easy for them to mix with the French girls? Was it permissible for white girls to mix with the coloured troops? My grandfather always said that the Indian other ranks were not expected to talk with the English memsahibs back home.' She hoped that she hadn't been too direct.

But Habib answered her seriously, saying that you had to imagine how it must have been in France at that time. There must have been such euphoria at finally being liberated – it would have been a time of rejoicing and recklessness. And also for the women – their men had been away for so long, conscripted into the German army, fighting far away, many of them sent to the Russian front, with no news as to whether they were alive or dead. The Germans would have stripped their villages of food, animals, fuel and valuables. Their lives over the war years would have been lives of harsh drudgery. They would have welcomed the liberating troops with open arms and hearts. He also pointed out that during the occupation some French girls were known to have slept with Germans to gain a few rations or other favours. 'And of course Tunisians are many times more handsome than the Germans – and our soldiers were many times braver!'

Habib got up and fetched a photograph from inside the house. 'My mother and father on their wedding day. He married her as soon as he was allowed to return after the end of the war.' Saira laughed. 'Yes, he is very handsome!' How trustingly his mother was looking up into her new husband's eyes. It forced Will to reflect; anything was possible; but what could Grandmother A. possibly hope they'd discover after so many years?

It was getting late by now. The candles in the pierced tin lamps were burning low and flickering. All the other customers had long since left. 'We should go now,' Saira said regretfully. As Habib brought their jackets and they stood in a group by the door, ready to leave, Saira asked, knowing Luke would already have asked, but still wanting to be sure, had he never heard people talking of seeing Indian prisoners of war in Strasbourg or round the villages?

Habib made a gesture of regretful denial. 'No, I never knew there were Indian prisoners around here. I did not know even that Indians were fighting for the English in the war. Then Luke tell me about your grandfather. I wish he and my father have the possibility before they died to meet and talk together about the war and their lives afterwards. But I wish you good chance to find out more!'

Three days after Yaqub's conversation with the civilian, the order was given to assemble in the moat with all their possessions. With some relief, the Indian prisoners lined up in the moat while it was still dark. Anywhere would be better than this dismal semi-underground prison.

After being counted and having their possessions searched, they were led up the ramp towards the gates. Yaqub took a deep breath. It was wonderful to come up from the depths of the moat into the fresh early morning air. The fort was on the edge of a village, facing out across farm land. They walked along tracks between fields, feeling almost like free men, despite the shepherding German guards. Yaqub was puzzled at how the previous prisoners had escaped. Surely they would have been so easily spotted and shot down in the flat countryside? Perhaps they only travelled at night.

After a while they came to another village. It was very shabby but still pretty. There were large timbered houses with big courtyards. Hens were scratching in the courtyards and women were standing at water troughs, scrubbing clothes. There were huge slatted wooden barns which smelt musty. They passed an ornate fountain in a square, but they were not allowed to stop to drink. It made Yaqub feel very sad. Although the houses were quite different from those in his far-off home village, the sight of the women at work in the fields and courtyards brought back all kinds of memories.

But the women kept their eyes fixed on their work, and nobody, not even the small children, seemed to take any notice of the straggling column of underfed men. Perhaps too many prisoners had already passed that way. It was too common a sight. And it was not their concern. It was only later that Yaqub learnt that the women could have been shot for talking to the prisoners or even offering them a drink of water.

'That was a wonderful extra wedding present!' said Saira, hugging Luke outside the restaurant, and bidding farewell to his friends. She slipped her hand into Will's as the two of them strolled back along the canal towards their hotel. The rippling reflections in the water added to her sense of trying to grasp new ways of looking for the past.

'Habib's father ...' She trailed off uncertainly.

'He sounded quite some guy, fighting his way across the icy mountains, liberating villages!' prompted Will.

Saira tried to explain that hearing about his very different war experiences had nevertheless made her grandfather's story more vivid, – had given a sense of all these strangers criss-crossing the landscape, not knowing how they fitted into the bigger picture. 'But it somehow made me believe that, even though no one so far seems to have seen the Indian prisoners, we really will find out what happened to Grandfather. Luke and Habib have between them made me believe that the quest is on!'

Will wrapped his arms around her and kissed her. 'Of course it is! And we will!'

They didn't feel inclined to study Luke's folder of information when they got back to their hotel room. Saira was floating in a haze of well-being, with that day's memories of the perfumed massage, the view from the cathedral tower, the boat trip on the canal, Habib's food and his affirming tale of his father's parallel war, all swirling round her mind. Will undressed her and led her to bed. Perhaps his own sense of identity had been reinforced by the conviviality of the evening with his old mate Luke, for at last he felt free of her fiercely protective family and community. And for the moment even the quest for Grandfather Yaqub seemed a far-away wisp of an idea. He could finally be himself and express his desire for her and explore her body to his heart's content.

5

Chalk traces

The graveyard was a surprise to them both.

In the morning Saira still felt a glow, the closeness of cherished intimacy, which she felt must be so obvious to the handful of people in the bar where they lingered over their coffee and croissants ('A bit of a change from yesterday's monster breakfast!') and looked Luke's folder. 'Bless him! He's printed off a list of suggestions for today.' Against item one, Schoenenbourg churchyard, Luke had scrawled, 'A convincing starter clue about nearby Indian PoWs?' Saira felt a rush of hope that they were on the verge of momentous insights into her grandfather's experiences nearly 70 years ago.

The church stood at the top of the hill in the village of Schoenenbourg, overlooking a patchwork of fields. Saira parked the car under the shade of an old tree. This time she had been driving while Will did the map reading, guiding them out of Strasbourg in a northerly direction up the motorway. This seemed to work better. Privately she thought she had adapted more rapidly to driving on the right than he had. And he was happy as he was convinced that he was the better map reader. 'You can see how vulnerable this bit of France was,' he said thoughtfully, 'so close to the German border to the north as well as the east.'

From the church they strolled down the lane to the small cemetery. It was so still and peaceful. Saira realised that when she'd read in Luke's note that two Indian soldiers were buried here, she'd still imagined endless rows of identical gleaming white war graves, like the ones she'd seen on web-sites. But here on the edge of the village, the cemetery was a more informal arrangement of family tombs from all epochs. Dour black marble slabs, smiling angels, wrought iron crosses, colourful flowers (some real, some plastic), enamelled photographs, and engraved tributes from family and friends jostled within the walled space. An old man was changing the water in a vase on what looked, from the photo on it and dates, like his wife's grave. She felt it was a friendly, well loved village graveyard. And the view was stunning.

It was easy to spot the two plain white headstones against the far wall. For they were at a different angle and slightly apart from the others. They were unadorned. For their dead there were no flowers, photographs or family tributes. But the headstones were spotless. The inscriptions recorded the names of a sepoy and a rifleman from the Indian Army who died in November 1943. Luke's note suggested a road accident.

Saira tried to picture what these two young men had been doing. They must have been prisoners, as at that date there was no fighting in the area. The liberating armies didn't arrive for another year. 'Do you think they stole a car or lorry to try and escape then careered out of control?'

'Or 'road accident' could be a grim euphemism. They could just have been shot dead by guards while trying to escape.'

'Maybe they weren't even trying to escape. They could just have been walking along one of the country roads to work on a farm or in the forest when a passing vehicle skidded into the file of prisoners and killed these two.'

She felt sad that they had died so far from home, but content that their bodies lay in a loved and sacred place. She murmured a prayer. She wished that she and Will had some flowers for these two strangers who, unlike her grandfather, had not survived their captivity.

As they turned from the graves to head back to the car, the old man looked up from his wife's grave and fixed his gaze, curiously, on Saira. When he spoke, his accent was difficult to understand, not like school French. But he pointed to her hand then touched her skin, seeming to draw attention to its colour. 'I think he's asking if you're a relative of one of the dead soldiers.' Saira shook her head. The man looked disappointed. So Will seized the opportunity to ask the man if he knew anything about how the men had died and where they had been imprisoned. The man indicated over his shoulder with his thumb. Did he mean nearby? Then he said portentously, 'Pfaffenschlick' which made Saira want to giggle.

She explained haltingly that her grandfather had been in the Indian Army and had been imprisoned somewhere in the area. So she was interested to learn more about any Indian soldiers. The old man finally smiled, satisfied that he'd been right about a connection. He got out his pipe, and rammed in some tobacco, as if preparing to tell a long tale.

'No one knew at the time how they died,' he said equally slowly and more comprehensibly. 'The Germans kept quiet about these things.' Then he put the pipe in his mouth and began to light it, uttering a few tantalising words between each puff.

Assembling his scattered words, they gathered that his father had told him, but that was after the war, for as children they were scared of the Germans, and looked away when they marched past with prisoners, well his father had said that at one time there had been Hindu prisoners in the army camp by the Maginot Line. Mind you, that's only what his father said. He hadn't taken much notice at the time. Saira's heart turned over as he mentioned a prisoners' camp close to the Maginot Line. She gripped Will's arm.

The old man had got his pipe going now, and suddenly launched into a longer, faster barrage of words. They tried to focus on the main words, though Saira was distracted by the idea that his pipe might go out as he waved it over his shoulder. But it seemed that the old army camp, back there, had later been abandoned by the army, and was now derelict. Well, the huts still were falling apart, but recently a young couple had bought the big stone administrative building. And while they were restoring it, do you know what they found? Well, his sister's son's daughter had been doing some work up there. The owners were Parisians, he thought. And these Parisians had found some strange writing. On the walls and ceiling beams, it seemed. His great-niece said they must be magic charms. Then some friends of these Parisians had told them that they were in the Hindu language. Well, that just goes to show that his old Dad had been right about there being Hindus there in the war, doesn't it!

He stubbed his pipe emphatically in Will's chest, then, realising that it had gone out, began the tedious process of re-lighting it, merely shaking his head as Will asked him if he could show him on the map where the old camp was. But then, re-lit pipe in one hand, he traced on the ground with his walking-stick his own instructions, concluding, 'follow the sign to the Maginot fort'.

Will took some photos of the graves, then they strolled back, hand in hand, to the car, with the old man shuffling behind them. Quickly scanning Luke's notes, Will pointed out that

Luke thought that a different Maginot Line fort and camp only a few miles further on were where Grandfather Yaqub had been. 'But I think we should investigate this place too. It sounds a possibility. And Luke could be wrong!'

'If only I'd asked Grandfather what his prison camp was called!' Saira lamented for the umpteenth time, as the old man waved them on their way. 'But it wasn't important back then.'

From the moment they arrived at their new camp, Yaqub and Barkat felt much happier. It was hard to pinpoint why. For they were still prisoners and their guards were still German. But the huge file of prisoners who had set out from Annaberg had been whittled down into smaller groups throughout the journey. And after they left the inhospitable Strasbourg fort and took the train north, groups of prisoners were disgorged at different stations. Some of them ended up in camps nearby, and they would meet up on occasional work-parties. So it was partly the size of their camp. It seemed very small after their previous camps – just a handful of long wooden huts really – and so more intimate. Even the guards seemed much more relaxed. Perhaps they had concluded that they had a docile work-force since none of their prisoners had ever tried in the past to escape into the unknown countryside. Perhaps they too felt far from home, on this side of the wide Rhine river, where most people now spoke French. But that small camp definitely felt more relaxed.

It was on the edge of the forest, at the foot of a mountain. Through the barbed wire of the camp they could see military lorries passing, and could hear the constant bumping of railway trucks. All their work was now logging in the forest, and several times they were led through the forest past a point where they could see the trucks disappearing into or emerging out of a huge concrete entrance in the mountainside. The entrance was heavily guarded, and they guessed there was some kind of secret, underground factory in there. They were intrigued, but glad that they were not put to work inside the formidable mountain.

Yaqub loved the resinous smell of the freshly cut wood, and the feeling of near-freedom which the outdoor life in the forest gave them. On fine days, when they ate their lunch under the trees, they could almost pretend for a few moments that they were free men enjoying a carefree picnic in the forest. And even when their break was over, and they were ordered back to work, their guards were not nearly as strident or brutal as the Annaberg guards had been.

Some of them were no older than Yaqub and Barkat. One of them would compensate for his youth by a bullying or disdainful manner, and another always asked sarcastically if they needed some elephants to help them move the logs faster. He never tired of this little joke. But most of them were civil and one would even show them photos of his wife and two children back home. He would grow surprisingly sentimental as prisoners clustered round to look at his photos, saying he was missing the youngest's first steps and maybe her first words.

But it was Benoit who made the biggest difference. Yaqub had always been curious about how things worked, and why. So it was inevitable, when they returned one evening from the forest, that he would stop to watch the stranger (in overalls, not German uniform) on a ladder who was adjusting overhead cables with assured fingers. He'd always been surprised that their small camp in the middle of the forest was supplied with electricity, and without thinking, he blurted out a few words.

'Where from electric?' He was embarrassed that he had so few words in German (most of them commands that the guards would rasp out). Barkat knew more. But then Barkat wouldn't have asked about the electricity. To his surprise the man smiled, and pointed towards the mountain gateway and then downhill. And that was the beginning of a cautious friendship.

Benoit didn't work there every day. Over the weeks, Yaqub pieced together various facts – he was a civilian; he lived in the nearest town with his family; he was French, and, like everyone, he now had to work for the Germans; before the war he had been involved in the building of the huge fort under the hill for the French; and now he did all the electrical maintenance in the fort, here, and down in the army camp, where the guards stayed. Had they not heard of the Maginot Line in India? It was very famous.

Seeing Yaqub's blank look, Benoit got out pencil and the notepad he always carried with him, looked over his shoulder to check that no guards were watching and began drawing. Yaqub was amused to see that Barkat was now interested and listening too. First he drew a squarish outline, and said that was France. Then he added waves on the left and bottom for the sea, then wrote DEUTSCHLAND in big letters on the right. Along parts of the top and down the right he drew a thick line with turrets: a line of forts like a big wall, he explained, to defend France from Germany. Then he marked an X in the top right corner to show where their camp was.

It was useful that Barkat was hooked. He had more army English than Yaqub did, and discovered that he and Benoit could communicate better in English than German. So he asked the obvious. Why hadn't the chain of forts kept the Germans out of France then? Benoit drew arrows attacking from the right, then crossed them out, shaking his head. He explained that the German army had not attacked from the east, where expected and where the line was therefore strongest, but (more arrows) through gaps in the north. When Paris was conquered and France had surrendered, the undefeated Maginot Line forts were also ordered to surrender without a fight.

At this point one of the guards appeared, but on other days he told them more about the building of the defences; about the French troops who'd occupied the nearby barracks during peace time; about all the food and weapons the French soldiers had assembled in the underground fort and how they could have held out there for months and months behind the massive impregnable concrete walls, against siege or attack by tanks, shells or bombers. Yaqub began to appreciate his new friend's sadness at seeing the fort surrender, despite its strength.

Barkat was less sentimental, and wanted to know why Benoit still worked there. Yaqub nodded knowingly as Benoit said that after the French surrender, the Germans still needed men like him, with specialised knowledge, to maintain the water supply and electricity, especially when they decided to make use of the huge bomb-proof underground chambers of the fort to manufacture and store aircraft parts. So, as the electricity (like the water) at their camp, as well as at the soldiers' barracks, came from the underground fort, he worked on all three. And of course the presence of so many Germans meant the need for plenty of wood for construction as well as firewood. So that was why, with most of the local men recruited into the German army, they needed the PoWs to do their menial logging work. Barkat was interested to hear that, as he'd often wondered why the Germans needed so much wood.

And these fascinating conversations with Benoit weren't their only friendly contacts with the people outside their latest camp. Occasionally, if they were working further away from the camp, they would pass old men and young boys who were too old or too young to have been forcibly conscripted into the German army. One day a woman who was cycling with her children, dismounted, and tossed some cherries from her basket to the passing file of prisoners. The guards said nothing as the prisoners picked them up, so her children scooped up more cherries in their hands and ran up to the men, distributing them. Somehow they felt like real soldiers again, and their eyes lit up and they pushed back their shoulders and marched on proudly. After that, if they had received food parcels, they would store little things in their pockets which they could give to these kindly passers-by. They loved watching the children's eyes light up when they gave them pieces of chocolate. And the guards here seemed much more tolerant of contact.

Once Yaqub had a warm over-shirt pressed into his hands by the kind-faced woman they'd now seen several times. He looked at her in disbelief, and then looked guiltily towards the guards. He knew that such a gift could never have been either offered or accepted at Annaberg and the other camps. He was afraid that the woman would be struck to the ground for her temerity. But one of the guards seemed to know her quite well, and came over and chatted pleasantly to her, and said nothing about the shirt. Yaqub was overwhelmed. He was so glad he knew the proper German word of thanks, but wished he could say something French and more elaborate. But he smiled and laughed his gratitude for this unexpected warmth, until one of the other guards decided that perhaps he ought to hurry their prisoners along.

Earlier, the sight of the white and pink blossom on the fruit trees had stirred up Yaqub's memories of home which he had for so long tried to suppress. And seeing the fields in need of ploughing and planting had made him restless as he thought of sowing time back home and wondered how everyone was coping with many of their young men away at war. Then one day, after the overwhelming gift of the shirt, his group passed a girl sitting under the shade of a tree, outside her house. Her head was bent over some white material, and she was sewing. The breeze tugged at her hair and, as she brushed it away from her eyes, her gesture reminded him painfully of how Amina would do just that. He wished he hadn't noticed. It made him aware of how long ago he had given up hope of ever seeing her again. When he spoke to Barkat about this fresh stirring of hope, he realised that his friend was feeling the same restlessness along with the changing surroundings and season, and they recalled the words of the civilian in the Strasbourg camp. But as they discussed possibilities in more detail they could not see how they could successfully evade their guards, still less get safely though this land full of Germans to the sea and freedom.

Barkat insisted that they needed to know much more about the area first. So in the evenings, as their comrades shared their day's experiences, they set about building up a picture of their surroundings. By now, a few privileged prisoners had moved from logging to working in the villages in gardens and others were doing seasonal work in the fields. Those who helped with weeding and pruning in the vineyards were amazed that the fruits, when ripe, would be wasted as undrinkable alcohol which both the French and Germans seemed to prize. They concluded that the families for whom prisoners worked in the village were pro-German and had contacts with the camp, seeming to both socialise with the Germans and do key jobs on behalf of them. The prisoners were beginning to understand a bit more about the division of loyalties in Alsace between people who wanted to remain part of France and those who were happy that Alsace had been re-taken by Germany and were profiting. Yaqub and Barkat were also realising that they might need to learn some French as well as German words and also know who they could trust, before they could think realistically about escaping.

‘It's very small!’

They had driven past the enclosure before they realised that these must be the former army huts the old man had told them about. ‘I'm sure Grandfather said that about a thousand of them had been transferred from Annaberg to Alsace. This is far too small.’ Nevertheless Saira reversed. As they stared at the ramshackle barracks, they both agreed that however much the Germans had crammed the prisoners together, they wouldn't have managed to fit a thousand in here. But then Will reminded her that they had probably been allocated to several smaller camps. Perhaps different camps for different work?

‘We'll never know if we don't ask.’

So, despite their initial doubts, they walked up to the main stone building, which looked large and official. A surprisingly young woman (she looks no older than me, thought Saira) answered the door and gave them a very welcoming smile. ‘You have heard about our salt?’ she asked in good English. That was disconcerting. But it turned out, by one of those weird co-incidences, that this remote spot in France was one of the best places to buy Himalayan crystal salt and Himalayan salt crystal lamps. Saira couldn't help laughing.

But when Saira explained about her grandfather, the young woman couldn't have been more obliging. She steered them round the children's bikes in the hallway and took them straight up several flights of stairs into the attic rooms. Saira blinked, almost disbelievingly, in the dim light as the woman pointed out the words chalked on different walls and over a doorway, words in Hindi script. 'Maybe this section was used as a prayer room for the Hindu prisoners.'

'Nothing in Urdu?' Saira asked hopefully. 'My grandfather's written language. The old man in the cemetery only talked about Hindus.'

The woman gave an almost apologetic little smile as she said that it seemed that often all Indians were referred to as 'hindous' in France during the war. 'But I wish you could have seen downstairs. We found very different looking words written on the beams down there when we were renovating. Friends told us they were Urdu or Arabic. So you would have known what they said. But we were hurrying to convert that floor into a workshop, and didn't think too much about it, and they got obliterated in the process. We were so busy working all hours to set up the business in this derelict shell, we had no time to look into the past. It was only later, when we were more settled and looking at the possibilities of the attic rooms, that we realised there were these words too. Later, as we heard that these former French barracks were probably used by the Germans for their Indian prisoners, we began to wonder if the Indian prisoners had been allowed to use these large rooms for religious observances.'

Although the Urdu (or Arabic) words had been destroyed, Saira felt excited again. She wondered what the prisoners had written. Perhaps they were comforting words from the Koran. And up here, there was something about the musty air in the attic, that seduced her into imagining the faint, one-dimensional shapes of Indian soldiers flitting through the dark rooms, superimposed one on top of another, gaunt yet smiling. She sighed, wishing that the ghosts would somehow come into clearer focus in the photographs Will was taking.

Will too was moved by the experience, even without rustles from ghostly figures. He could see how it had affected Saira and he wanted her to have a tangible reminder of this unexpected touching point with the past. When he had finished taking photos, he asked if they could see what they were making there. When they were shown the manufacturing area and the shop, they chose a pretty, pink, heart-shaped candle-holder made from the salt crystal.

Back in the car, Saira unwrapped and gently stroked the polished, curving outline of her candle holder. She felt how lucky they'd been to meet the old man and learn about this camp. 'I suppose the two dead soldiers must have been from here.' She wondered if her grandfather knew the men here. It was so close to where Luke thought his camp had been. Why did it give her such a thrill to feel close to his wartime experiences when they must have been so painful and unendurable that he could never talk about them?

Will was examining his map. 'We must be almost at the Schoenenbourg fort as well.' He checked Luke's pamphlets. 'Right. This fort is open to the public and Luke says that although he doesn't think it's the one where your grandfather hid, it would be worth looking round, to get a feel of a Maginot Line fort. However, it's nearly twelve, and it doesn't open until two.'

'I can't believe the French still manage to take two-hour lunch breaks!' exclaimed Saira, thinking of her snatched tea and sandwiches at her desk by her phone. 'So, why don't we drive on a few miles to the place that Luke suggests as more likely to have been Grandfather's camp?'

Will was beginning to feel that coffee and croissants formed a very skimpy breakfast, so he agreed that could drive on to the more distant camp and look at the outside, with the proviso that they then found some lunch. 'After all, Luke was definite that we can't go inside either the camp or the fort at Hochwald.'

'And then, if you still want to, we can come back here and spend the rest of the afternoon looking round this fort!' Saira continued happily. Their quest was really taking a very satisfactory direction.

Sid sat in the taxi rank, getting impatient. It had been a bad morning. Hardly any movement in the waiting queue of shiny green taxis. There would normally be more heavily-laden shoppers than this. He wondered whether to give up and go home for lunch with his mother. He was worried about her. She had been very restless since Saira left with Will.

It was all Will's fault. If he hadn't suggested Alsace, it wouldn't have stirred up old memories. It was all a bit of a puzzle, though, as, when they were kids, his dad had never said much about his time there, or about his escape. So why had the honeymoon journey unsettled his mother? The only thing he remembered, which seemed to have something to do with the war, was that his dad had always been big on loyalty and had drilled that into his sons. A bit odd, really as the Brits had hardly welcomed them with open arms. So, even back then, they'd known they had to protect their mother and learn English fast so they could translate for her and run errands to the strange shops and there was an unspoken rule that they had to pretend everything was all right at school.

And look at him now. He still hadn't lost the habit of trying to shield his mother from hurtful things. He turned the key in the ignition and pulled out of the line. He'd give her a pleasant surprise.

'Look out for a sign for the air base,' Will read out from Luke's notes as they drove along a narrow country lane.

'Air base?'

'It might have been your grandfather's camp.' Spotting the sign, Saira pulled into the large car park opposite the gates of the base. She stayed sitting at the wheel for a few moments. She felt hesitant about getting out. This looked quite different from the decaying barracks at Schoenenbourg. For a start the high enclosure looked shiny and modern, although she couldn't see any aeroplanes or runways.

More of last night's conversation started to come back to Saira. She got out of the car and crossed the road to the gates. All she could see were a lot of freshly painted, pink, white and cream buildings surrounded by neatly clipped grass and roads. 'I didn't think an old prison camp would look all pastel-coloured and innocuous like this. I thought it would look more like the Schoenenbourg one only bigger.' She half-closed her eyes. She tried to imagine the neat buildings with barbed wire round and prisoners shuffling aimlessly in striped uniforms like you saw in films. (Or was that concentration camps? Did PoWs get to wear their army uniforms still? But then they must have been captured in tropical, desert kit). She couldn't picture them. Or perhaps they wouldn't be idle. Perhaps they'd be staggering round, emaciated and half-starved, under heavy tree trunks or piles of the logs they'd cut in the forest. But she saw nothing. 'No way. I just can't imagine him here. I can imagine immaculately uniformed Germans here, but not the prisoners.'

Will sighed. He knew Luke had explained last night. Didn't she remember anything? But perhaps she was too excited after the chalked words over at Schoenenbourg. He summarised patiently: 'Well, this might not in fact have been where the prisoners were. It would definitely have been the French barracks first, then the Germans could have kept these quarters for their own use and had other rough, makeshift huts erected for the prisoners somewhere nearby. Anything temporary like that would have been destroyed after the war. Now both these buildings and the old fort are used as a French radar base, a tracking station.'

Ah, radar base. That's why there weren't any planes visible. And that was why, Saira recalled, Luke had said they couldn't visit the old Hochwald fort. It must be pretty sensitive. She vaguely remembered that he'd said they did special visits by arrangement, and he'd checked, but that this week wasn't convenient. She now muttered under her breath something about how with a Muslim name it might never be convenient, and Will looked at her in surprise. Nobly shelving thoughts of lunch, he suggested that they could drive up towards the forested hill to see if they could see any traces of the exterior entrances to the old underground fort.

Part way along the first road they tried, they were stopped by a huge sign saying 'Terrain militaire. Accès formellement interdit'. Forbidden! And they couldn't see anything from here. Perhaps it wasn't altogether surprising, Saira thought. Radar must all be a bit hush-hush. She turned the car round.

The second road led steeply up the hill through the forest to a crossroads at the top. Will made an excited sound, 'Did you see the sign? Col de Pfaffenschlick!' As he tried to pronounce the word, Saira recognised the word the old man had said. It was certainly steep enough for a nasty road accident.

They decided to take the turning to the right to see if they could see the radar dome that Will remembered Luke mentioning. As they drove slowly along, there were clearings in the forest in which they could see strange, small, rusting domes set into concrete. 'They may be dome-shaped, but they definitely don't look like modern radar!' Saira wanted to get out and look more closely, but Will pointed out that the notices along the roadside all said it was military territory with restricted access. 'We'd better not get ourselves shot!' he joked. 'We really can't go any nearer! So it's definitely food time. I'm starving. No more messing about. How about that place we passed, you know, with the eagle sign. We can also ask them,' he added persuasively, 'whether anyone has heard about the Indian soldiers here during the war!'

One warm summer morning, when he came to the camp after a few days' absence, Benoit could barely contain his excitement. Yaqub and Barkat had begun to realise how fiercely pro-French he was, despite working for the Germans so conscientiously. He was too late to speak to Yaqub or Barkat before they left for work, but he found a pretext to stay on until they returned in the evening, so that he could whisper the good news that the Allies had landed in Normandy. All the prisoners were very excited and hoped this would mean that they would soon be freed and sent home. But things seemed to move very slowly after that, and there was no hint of release.

It was so frustrating that nothing seemed to change, but finally, in August Benoit passed on the news that more Americans together with the Free French Army had also landed near Marseilles in the south of France and this time they were making unimaginably fast progress northwards. 'Soon they will liberate us too,' he rejoiced. That evening Barkat said reflectively, 'We shouldn't just be sitting here waiting for them to fight their way towards us and liberate us. We should be helping those soldiers to liberate the area. Surely it is our duty to escape and join them!'

All that week, whenever they were out of earshot of the Germans, Yaqub and Barkat spoke of little other than this Allied advance. The idea of once more being part of a fighting force rather than passive prisoners stirred their imaginations. Besides, they felt their war had ended ignominiously early, in their very first encounter with the German army. But they were careful not to say much in front of their companions. They had been surprised at how negative their friends had become about escaping. Ever since hearing that the Allies were approaching, many of the prisoners seemed content to sit out the rest of the war in relative safety. They knew that their families were receiving their army pay while they were imprisoned, so they reasoned that it would be better to stay put for the time being rather than risking their lives. And also there was one fellow-prisoner that Yaqub and Barkat had never trusted. So they waited till they were on their own with Benoit then asked him if he could help them to escape and join the approaching army. Benoit was amused by their fierce faces but he was clearly scared by the enormity of what they were suggesting. All he would say was that he'd have to think about it.

When Benoit next spoke to them, he said that he'd reflected long and hard about their idea and that it would in fact probably be fairly easy to help them escape from the camp. He knew several underground hiding places in the nearby Maginot Line fort. Places that the Germans wouldn't know about. They could stay hidden there until the liberating army arrived. The other prisoners would probably be moved back to Germany itself, to a safer camp, as the Allies got closer, whereas they would then be free to emerge and join the Americans.

But Yaqub and Barkat wanted to be on the move as soon as they escaped. They begged Benoit to give them maps, so they could make their way across Alsace towards the French border and the approaching armies. Benoit was dubious. He said the roads were now heavily patrolled and there were constant troop movements. Any two young men would be instantly questioned as they should be fighting in the German army. And then it would be obvious that they were Indians. They could never remain inconspicuous whilst endeavouring to find their way round all the inhabited areas and the patrols. He was sure they would be recaptured or shot straight away – and either would endanger him and his family too. He was very afraid of vicious reprisals. If suspected of helping them to escape, he and his whole family would be deported to the concentration camps.

A few days later, Benoit's fearful mood had changed. He was full of optimism, for he brought the news that Paris had been liberated. Soon the rest of France would be freed. All those who supported France had been celebrating discretely, though the pro-Germans had been dismayed. But he said that although it was such good news, it also meant that it would be even more dangerous in the areas like this which were under direct German rule. In fact, he feared that the Germans might be extra vindictive as they retreated and defended, both in the east of France and here in Alsace. For they would be determined to hold on to Alsace and fight back from there.

Despite that, he was now more hopeful that if he helped them to escape, he might eventually find someone who could guide them on their proposed journey. But it would still not be easy, so they'd have to hide for a short time, as he'd originally suggested, in the Maginot Line. When Barkat said that they had heard about people called the Resistance, and how they helped men to escape to occupied France, Benoit shook his head. Yes, there were these brave people in the Resistance. But he had no contact with them. Perhaps people were cautious around him, because they knew he worked for the Germans and was careful not to criticise them.

Yaqub and Barkat found it hard to hide their mounting excitement from their fellow-prisoners. But fortunately many of the Muslim prisoners were preoccupied with discussing how and when exactly they would manage to celebrate the approaching Eid-al-Fitr. Under cover of the preparations, Benoit was able to show them plans which he'd drawn for getting into the Maginot Line fort. He had decided that they should enter the fort well away from the big munitions entrance through the trees. He made them memorise the directions which he then tore up.

The restaurant was busy, and rather old-fashioned with its red-and-white checked table cloths, huge carved sideboard and black beamed ceiling. Will was content to eat his way through the menu of the day. The main course was an enormous mound of boiled white cabbage garnished with chunks of smoked pork and sausages. Looking at his plateful, Saira was relieved that they had agreed to make her a salad, omelette and potatoes instead. But they both agreed that the apple tart dessert was delicious.

With most of her customers served, Madame, like Habib the night before, was happy to chat with her new customers, though she didn't sit down with them. Unfortunately she didn't know anything about the wartime history of the airbase, as her family had only bought the inn in the late fifties. So she shouted out to the remaining customers to see if any of them had heard talk of Indian prisoners during the war, but everyone shook their heads. Most of them worked at the radar base, but had come recently, and hadn't heard about any Indians being imprisoned there in the past. They thought the Germans had used it themselves. And they certainly hadn't heard of any Indians hiding in the mountain in the Maginot Line fort.

'If there had been any strangers hiding underground,' a local man added, 'the malgré-nous would have seen them!' He tipped sachets of sugar into his black coffee and, stirring slowly, explained that men like his father and uncles were compulsorily conscripted into the German army and sent to the Russian front. If they survived, and if they managed to escape, they made their way back to their village and hid underground in the fort where the villagers took food to them every night. ('Like some of the men Luke was involved in interviewing,' whispered Saira). They would have known if there had been Indian escaped prisoners hiding there too.

Although the response was negative concerning any Indian PoWs, Saira was heartened by the friendliness. After all, they already knew that there had been Indian prisoners at the other camp at Schoenenbourg. On the spur of the moment, before they left to tour the fort there, she asked if l'Aigle had a room for the night.

Yaqub could hardly believe what he could feel in his hand. Benoit had just surreptitiously pressed something large and metallic into it. A key! As Barkat joined them, he explained that it was a duplicate of the one he used to open the security doors in the course of his work on the Maginot Line. He had continued to test them on the layout of the underground passages, till they had a clear mental map and understood which passages to avoid because they led to the areas used by the Germans. Now he thought it would be a good time to try and escape, with the grape harvest about to start. Work parties would be needed for the picking, so some of the guards would be re-allocated from the forest to the fields. They should try to stay on logging duty and secrete some of their food in the forest. He didn't know how long they'd have to hide in the Maginot Line as he hadn't yet found anyone to guide them, so they'd need a supply of food. The key should be safe enough with them tonight, but he urged them to find a hiding place for it (and food) the very next day in the forest.

As Benoit had predicted, a few days later the Germans re-organised the working parties. They seemed to be very anxious, all of a sudden, not only to get the grapes harvested rapidly, but also to shift the timber from the forest. The roads around them seemed full of army lorries transporting animals, timber, foodstuffs and wine. Benoit said it was all bound for Germany, before any Allied attack. He thought that during this period of intense preoccupation for the Germans they might find a chance to melt into the forest while they were working, and head for the fort. He would come and find them in the agreed hiding place, as soon as he could.

Yaqub felt happy that the time had at last come. They had managed to save and hide enough food, along with the key. And now the weather was beginning to change. The nights were getting colder and the autumn rains and snow would start soon, making forest work less pleasant. Barkat chided him for such selfish thoughts. Surely what was important was that they would soon be back in the fighting!

As Yaqub and Barkat looked around them, they wondered if, after their escape, they would ever set eyes on the men with whom they'd been cooped up for the last three and a half years.

Together they'd suffered and surmounted the deprivation, starvation and temptations of Annaberg. They'd helped each other when the labour was too hard. They'd looked after each other when they were ill. They'd shared the scant news in letters from home. They knew the nightmares of each man who'd shared their hut or dormitory. They felt sad that couldn't share their plan or make their farewells.

But the next day, without any explanation, all the fatigue parties outside the camp were cancelled. Yaqub and Barkat were horrified. Did the Germans suspect something? Had they missed their chance to escape? The others were pleased to have a day's rest and couldn't understand their friends' dejection. When the work groups were organised the next day, still with no explanation, and they were taken to the usual part of the forest. Yaqub was so relieved. But the disruption had alarmed them, and they resolved to escape that very day, before it was too late.

After a morning's hard work in the forest, one of the guards returned to the camp taking four prisoners to bring lunch back to their group. The guard who remained was the young one, the one who sometimes showed them his family photographs; one of the prisoners had recently carved a rattle for his new baby. Yaqub and Barkat continued to work diligently, as they always did, so he had no reason to be suspicious. Then, while he was bending over inspecting some blunt tools, they gradually edged further and further away from the group, watching the young guard all the time. It all seemed too easy. Then, as the guard straightened up, they quickly rolled into a hollow created when a rotten tree had crashed to the ground, wrenching up a ball of earth in its roots. No one seemed to notice their absence as the food arrived. During the afternoon's work they crawled further away and hid again until the sun got lower in the sky.

They heard their names being called as the wood-cutting party was rounded up. They expected one of the guards to come looking for them, but of course they were short-staffed and still had to guard the other prisoners. Eventually the guards stopped shouting for them, and led the file of prisoners away. Silence.

After about an hour, and fearing that it would get dark before they reached the right section of the fort, they decided to make a move. They went cautiously back to where they had hidden the key and food. They knew that the tins would have lasted, and to their relief, the dry food had not been eaten by any of the forest animals or insects. Pocketing the key and food, they scrambled up the hill, through the trees. Once over the ridge they paused. Ahead of them lay open country. The forest had all been cleared, and below them lay fields and orchards. Further along the ridge they could see a big wall of concrete. They realised they would be easily visible against the hillside as they searched for the metal door that Benoit had described. But it was no time to hesitate. Taking a deep breath, they bent double and moved rapidly towards the concrete expanse. It had been easier than they had expected.

6

Maginot Line

A concrete wall reared up in front of them, its gateway gaping like a mouth in the hillside. Saira stopped in her tracks. She hadn't been as enthusiastic as Will about visiting the Schoenenbourg fort as this wasn't the actual fort where her grandfather hid; she'd been more interested in finding the camp from which he escaped. But as Will pointed to the two metal cloches above the gates and she imagined automatic rifles pointing at them, she felt suddenly transported back to her grandfather's war.

She brushed away Luke's leaflet and notes that Will was trying to show her. She just wanted to absorb the atmosphere as they walked towards it. 'Just tell me the highlights!' So Will rapidly told her that it was smaller than the Hochwald fort, that this would have been the rail entrance for munitions and goods, and that the troops would originally have used a smaller entrance, which was later dynamited by the Germans as they retreated in 1945. 'Luke doesn't think your grandfather would have entered his fort by either of the main entrances, but by a gate his electrician friend used, somewhere less obvious, probably one of the forward combat blocks, as the Germans were still using the main rear part of that fort.'

There was a ticket office just inside the gate, where they

were warmly welcomed, and a lady explained that all the parts that they could visit had been meticulously and lovingly restored to how the fort would have been when the French occupied it at the start of the war. 'We want you to be able to experience how it was then.'

Will explained about Saira's grandfather, and how they'd been to look for the Hochwald fort first. The lady smiled again and told them that they'd probably get a far better idea of what it had been like in her grandfather's day from looking round their Schoenenbourg fort. 'Over at the radar base everything has been modernised, from the main entrance to the control areas. You're better off here, where we've tried to preserve things!'

Saira nodded happily. She was surprised to learn that they could explore the fort on their own, following the arrows and information panels, though the lady warned them that there would be stairs and several kilometres of walking. Saira soon realised, after they'd descended a level, why the woman had first checked that they were happy to walk. For the image that was to haunt her afterwards was of that long, long, curving tunnel, its rail tracks glinting, as it disappeared into the distance towards the far-off combat blocks.

As they cautiously approached this more remote section of the fort, they could see in the last of the daylight that the massive concrete walls were pitted from gunfire. That must have happened in the days before the mighty fort surrendered, Yaqub thought. There were chunks of concrete and rock lying round the base of the walls. Benoit had told them that this was a part of the fort in which he only worked occasionally on maintenance as the Germans had never used it.

Benoit had so often talked to them about the underground fort. He was very proud of how modern it was, especially his electrical equipment. 'More modern than anything you can see in civilian life,' he would enthuse. And he had told them that it was so vast that underground rails had once transported supplies and ammunition through the main tunnels from the rear storage and living areas (which the Germans had now turned into a factory) to the network of forward fighting areas with their observation and machine-gun posts. Even so, when they found the entrance he used, they were overwhelmed by the size of the tunnel in which they found themselves.

But they did not linger. Although Benoit had said that the Germans were only using the rear section, near their camp, they were careful to create no sound which might echo. This was difficult as this area was no longer lit, and they had to feel their way down the corridor, counting off on their fingers the side tunnels and the massive metal doors (which had to be unlocked and locked behind them) until they reached a junction where Benoit had told them to turn. At the end of this tunnel, which seemed to be a dead-end, they felt the doorway to the chamber in which Benoit had instructed them to hide.

First Saira and Will stared at the engines and trucks and the rails stretching away down the corridor. 'Luke said you can take a ride in some of the other forts, but not here,' Will recalled. 'Shame about that.' Then they branched off to explore the 'safe' areas situated close to the ammunition entrance and furthest from the fighting blocks. The dormitories, kitchens, generators and hospital as well as a lot of stores were here.

Will was most interested in how everything worked, and there were enthusiasts on hand in the power-generating plant to explain the details of how the electrical current came in from outside, was transformed and distributed to power everything from the trains and the turret engines right down to the cooks' potato peeler. He assumed that this would be the main area in which the man who had helped to hide Grandfather Yaqub and his friend would have worked.

Saira was more interested in the details of everyday living conditions and lingered much longer in the kitchen, with its storerooms, cold room, washing-up area, huge stainless steel cooking pots, isothermal containers for conveying food by rail to the outlying combat posts, tiled butchering area, not to mention the wine cellar (how typically French she thought). The electric coffee percolator and potato peeler which stood on the floor were so huge that they came almost up to her chin! She tried to imagine what cooking underground for six hundred troops would be like. Apparently they kept enough stores to last for three months. She wondered how much was left by the time the fort surrendered. There was a big hatch for serving food, but nowhere, apart from the corridors and dormitories, for the troops to sit and eat.

Of course, all that was irrelevant to their quest. Her grandfather would never have seen this rear section of 'his' fort. And she wanted to be able to picture the kind of area in which he would have hidden. Will had initially toyed with the idea of it being among the central electrical installations which Benoit maintained, but they now realised that this would have been located in the area the Germans were using. From what she could understand, his hiding place was most likely to have been far away from German activity, which left the combat blocks almost a mile away down the long corridor. How she wished she had asked her grandfather more questions. But then as a teenager, working on her project, she had never imagined that she would one day visit one of the forts in the area where he'd escaped and hidden.

Another feature he had mentioned was a storeroom, and they saw any number of those. For, as well as the food stores, there were stores for shells, stores for electrical components, stores for medical equipment, even a store for coffins, – you name it and there seemed to be a store for it. Saira was quite prepared to believe that the fort could have held out against the enemy for ever.

After looking round the dormitories and the infirmary, they went back to the main tunnel, and started to walk along it. After a while, despite her growing sense of anticipation, Saira agreed to turn off to look at the command centre, which, the label explained, was situated half-way between the rear barracks and the forward action posts. They examined all the panels and photos to see how the information from the look-out posts would have been rapidly processed and precise orders transmitted to the firing positions. Saira was amazed by all the telephones, each linked to a specific observation or firing post, and Will tried to work out the chain of command. Then once more Saira became impatient. It was all fascinating, but was very obviously not the kind of area where her grandfather would have hidden in 'his' fort. They turned back into the main tunnel and continued along its length towards an artillery block.

By now their eyes were well accustomed to the darkness. They could tell that it was the combat block which Benoit had told them about, as small patches of the night sky could be seen where there were openings that must have been for observation and firing. In the dimness they could make out bunk beds, which they guessed must have been for gunners or observers resting between their duty-shifts. They were pleased that they were still there, as Benoit had mentioned that civilians had been ordered to strip the fort of arms and equipment, including the steel beds, so they could be sent back to Germany. Later they found an alcove with a single bed. Perhaps for an officer. There were still some army blankets on the bunks. In fact it looked as if it had been vacated in a hurry. They could make out scattered tin plates, a few mugs, and an old magazine. There were no signs of food though. Either the surrendering French troops had taken every last mouthful with them, or rats had long since consumed any scraps.

After they had offered their evening prayers, they laid their food on the table and divided it into seven portions. They were sure that Benoit would somehow find them a guide so that they could leave their underground hiding place within the week. Though small and no longer fresh, their first meal as free men tasted special. When they'd finished, Yaqub leaned back, stretching his hands up and clasping them behind his head. 'I would never have thought, during those miserable years at Annaberg, that we would ever dare to take our lives in our hands and escape! Allah has indeed been good to us.'

Barkat tried one of the bunks, relishing the well-stuffed mattress. 'Free men at last! And those foolish fellows are still slaving away for the Germans! I wonder what happened when they found out we had escaped!'

That night they slept soundly. The excitement and stress of escaping had left them too exhausted to lie awake worrying about what felt a remote chance of being discovered. And it was wonderfully peaceful without the snores, grunts, insomniac pacing and nightmare ravings of the other inmates. When they woke in the morning they agreed that these were the most comfortable quarters they'd been in since they'd set sail from Bombay.

There was a surprising amount of light coming into their room. Perhaps the gun apertures been damaged before the fort surrendered, but they were pleased not to be in darkness, and to be able to mark the passage of day and night. They could now see that there was a separate section with a wash basin and also a European-style toilet. There was even soap and a cut-throat razor lying on the sink. Yaqub wasn't sure he'd fancy using it though, but he was glad that there was still water from the tap. They also noticed that there was a poster tacked to the walls, which showed a woman in a tight, revealing dress, dancing with a French soldier, with other couples in the background. They were surprised that the men had been allowed to put up such a picture. Later as Barkat was folding his bedding, with as much care as if he expected a kit inspection, he found a pile of postcards under his mattress. When he saw the subject matter he couldn't resist showing them to Yaqub, who gasped and looked away, guiltily. 'They wouldn't do that!' he protested.

After a while, Barkat tired of the postcards and replaced them beneath the mattress. He began to drum his fingers on the table. 'I never expected it to feel so strange to be resting, at leisure, with no work to do!' They laughed, and agreed that it would do them good to relax for a few days, as it sounded as if it would be a long walk to reach the Americans. 'We might be able to see the mountains we've got to cross. There should be a good view from up there,' suggested Yaqub.

They scrambled up and looked cautiously out from the observation slits, and were delighted with the magnificent views they got across the countryside. They could indeed see mountains. 'But we're being stupid,' laughed Barkat. 'Of course it must be Germany and German mountains in the distance ahead of us. They'd hardly be firing at France from here! That won't be the way we've got to go.' Closer to them they could see smoke drifting from distant chimneys beyond the ranks of coiled barbed wire. Then, to their surprise, they noticed, much closer to their look-out and isolated by the barbed wire and metal anti-tank obstructions, some stunted trees with apples and pears still on the low branches. The trees had somehow escaped the onslaught and explosions but must have become inaccessible to the villagers.

'It would be a shame to waste them, and Benoit never said that we weren't to leave the fort at night!' said Yaqub tentatively.

Entering the artillery block near the end of the tunnel Saira had the most peculiar sensation of immediacy. On one side there was the most enormous piece of machinery, like a turret, disappearing up into the roof, which immediately attracted Will's attention. She looked across the chamber to where there was a small rest room for the crew on duty or in reserve and an even smaller wash-room. She immediately felt that this was the kind of area in which her grandfather could have hidden.

But, when Will called her over and pointed out how the enormous counter-weight was used to raise and lower the gun turret, she wasn't so sure. She knew that her grandfather would have been absolutely fascinated by the way it raised the gun apertures above the ground level so that, as Will explained, the two guns could be swivelled towards the identified enemy targets then loaded and fired by the four gunners perched uncomfortably in the cramped area at the top. But she was sure he'd have mentioned such a marvel to her if he'd seen it

– even if he thought that, as a girl, she wouldn't find it as interesting.

'I can't quite see Grandfather and his friend manipulating that monstrous rising and falling turret just in order to look out at the apples and pears he harped on about!' She turned to the attendant, who spoke good English and was interested to hear her grandfather's story. He was a mine of information and suggested that maybe the two men could have hidden in one of the infantry blocks and looked out of the fixed cloches and if they were quite slim, they would even have been able to crawl out of the damaged gun embrasures at night to explore.

'They'd have been thin all right! They were positively malnourished in the prison-camps', Will interrupted.

Unfortunately, according to the attendant, none of the infantry blocks at the Schoenenbourg fort were currently open to the public, although, when they had finished looking below ground, they could wander round above ground and look at the outside of the cloches over the infantry blocks. Equally unfortunately, he continued, they knew very little about the period between 1940 and 1945 when all the forts were in German hands, and he had never heard any rumours of escaped Indian prisoners hiding inside this or any of the other forts. He did, however, know that there had been Indian prisoners at the adjacent old barracks, having been told about the Indian writing on the walls.

He was really pleased to hear that they'd actually seen the words, – at least, those that were left. Saira asked if he'd heard about the two Muslim soldiers buried in the village churchyard, adding that the old man had talked only of Hindus. The attendant laughed and confirmed what the woman at the barracks had told them, that in those days all the Indians were referred to in French as 'hindous'. Probably no-one knew much about the different religions. And yes, it was true that the driver had lost control of a lorry, which had come careering down from the Col de Pfaffenschlick, killing those two prisoners in the process.

Saira couldn't help giggling again at the funny name (and got an odd look from the attendant), but she felt encouraged by this very specific addition to their growing information. She really regretted that they couldn't visit an infantry block, as she respected the attendant's intuition. Instead, she went and sat on one of the four bottom bunks, and tried to imagine it without the brightness of the electric lights. Would they have been able to tell night from day or how fast the time was passing? She began to sense why they might have been keen to get out at night. She was surprised at what a strong sense of affinity she felt with this underground maze and how easily she could imagine her grandfather here.

Her imaginings were brought to an abrupt end when the phone rang (was it one of the original ones?) and the attendant picked it up. He nodded as he listened, then replied, 'Only two English.'

Putting the phone down, he told them regretfully, that it was only fifteen minutes to closing time, and that it would probably taken them that long to get back to the main entrance. Apparently they were the last visitors that day. When they checked their watches they were amazed at how long they'd spent underground, though Saira realised how cold she'd become.

'Can I just take another quick look round,' she begged, unwilling to leave so abruptly. She touched the walls, breathed in the musty air, and took photos of more intimate details like the bunks and sink and table before they set off on the long march back along the tunnel and up the stairs towards daylight.

It was only their second night there, but it felt wonderful to be squeezing out, like naughty schoolboys, through one of the damaged gun apertures. They assumed it was the Germans who had removed the weaponry. They were as cautious as ever as they headed for the fruit trees, for there was always the possibility that the ground had been mined or that there was unexploded ammunition lying around, or that the Germans would be on some night patrol. They picked as many apples and pears as they could carry, and then, heedless of the cold night air with its hint of frost, they lay on their backs on a rock in a sheltered position where they would not be visible silhouetted against the sky. They munched their spoil and gazed up at the starry skies. The stars were just so bright and clear and occasionally they spotted a shooting star falling earthwards.

'It takes me back to when I was a boy, tending sheep,' sighed Barkat. 'But our orchards were not these straggly, pock-marked affairs. I think we must have the most beautiful orchards in the whole world, with apricot and almond and tall walnuts trees. And in the valley there are the mulberry trees.'

Yaqub pictured them in his mind. 'You will see then again,' he predicted. It was good to regain this conviction, so long lost.

They began to shiver, lying out there on the rock, but neither of them wanted to relinquish the sense of freedom and tranquillity in the middle of this mad war. Eventually, though, they brushed themselves down and made their way back into their hiding place. 'Tomorrow night,' they promised each other.

Saira grabbed a cardigan from the car, before they climbed up the grassy slope above the fort. There were little paths where everyone before them had explored. She was amazed when they came across a thicket which still had rusting barbed wire coiled round and round itself. 'Can this really be wartime stuff?'

She was surprised at how much was visible above ground. This fort could never have been totally hidden or secret. Will remarked that the Germans seemed to have flown over and photographed the line as it was being constructed, so it certainly wasn't secret. And then the Germans had avoided it when they invaded. He pointed ahead of them to some metal domes protruding from concrete bases. 'Now we know what those rusty domes were that we saw on the unpronounceable radar hill. Cloches. One of these might even be over the infantry block the helpful man mentioned.'

'It all looks like some military teletubby territory!'

Adopting the most frightful phoney French accent, that he'd read in his dad's old comics, Will stood on one of the nearer, shallower metal protuberances, declaiming 'And 'ere we 'ave ze tourelle. 'E go up and 'e go down wiz ze machinery we 'ave been seeing below. And pouf! Ze enemy 'e die.' Then he leapt ahead. 'And over zere, mesdames, messieurs, we 'ave ze cloche fixed. 'E do not go up and down. But – bang! 'e shoot! You die!'

'Idiot! We've never met anyone who speaks like that!' As she walked past Will, who was still perched on the last cloche, she saw that below the mound was a concrete wall with recessed slits. When Will caught up with her she was looking thoughtful. 'I'm just trying to imagine that those birch trees over there are apple and pear trees!'

As the days passed, Yaqub and Barkat spent longer and longer out on the hillside at night, and more of the daytime sleeping. They began to wonder when Benoit would come and fetch them. Surely he must have found a guide for them by now? In fact they were dozing in the mid-afternoon when he finally arrived to check up on how they were. He was laughing at their laziness as he woke them.

He continued to laugh as he recounted the 'news' of their escape. When he was last at the camp, the other prisoners had rushed up to tell him that their friends Yaqub and Barkat were missing. They told him that no-one had noticed their absence at lunch-time in the forest or indeed until it was time to return at nightfall to the camp. The guards had counted, then called the names of their missing companions. Fortunately they had decided that Yaqub and Barkat must have become separated and would have made their own way back to the camp, for they would have nowhere else to go. So they had marched their remaining prisoners back to base. Benoit described how he had pretended to look very surprised by this news and had said firmly that Yaqub and Barkat had been very foolish and would certainly be caught and killed. However, since then he hadn't seen the young guard who had let them wander off in the forest. It was rumoured that he had been disciplined and sent back to Germany.

Then, with a flourish, Benoit produced half a loaf, some goats' cheese and some coarse wine. 'We celebrate!' He apologised for the scanty provisions, but, as they knew, civilian food was rationed and the Germans creamed off the best. He insisted that they should have a glass (well, tin mug in fact) of wine with him and it seemed ungrateful, after all his kindness, to refuse. So they lifted their mugs and drank together. They didn't quite follow Benoit's rousing but convoluted words about the three fundamental French values – Liberté, Egalité and Fraternité, with the emphasis just at this moment most definitely on Liberté, but they understood that he was talking both about their freedom and the freedom of France.

'And you're not the only free men hiding down here,' he added. He hadn't dared tell them while they were in the camp, but there were also young men who'd escaped from the army and were hiding in a different section of the fort, nearer their village, where the women could bring them food at night. 'Liberté France! Liberté Alsace! Liberté Benoit! Liberté Barkat, Yaqub! Liberté prisonniers!' Barkat proclaimed, rather overdoing his new French word.

The wine was more potent than Yaqub and Barkat had realised. No wonder it was forbidden. That night the apples and pears in the orchard above their heads remained unpicked, as they slept more profoundly than they had for years.

Madame back at l'Aigle was really interested to hear about the tingling feeling Saira had experienced both in the artillery tower at the fort, and also afterwards as they had climbed around the humps and bumps above the fort. Saira was still disappointed that they hadn't seen any pear trees or apple trees among the cloches.

'But,' said Madame encouragingly, 'everyone says this area was really famous for its cherry trees before the war. And in those days most of the small farmers would have little plots of orchard and fields up on the hillside. So I can easily imagine your grandfather and his friend in our fort looking out at apple and pears trees.'

Up in their room, Saira lit the candle in the heart-shaped pinkish crystal holder which Will had given her. She turned off the overhead light, and sat watching the warm pink glow flicker and spread. 'I'm not sure I can sense all the negative ions flooding the room, as the blurb says! But this feels like a symbol of the many positives from today!'

Will reflected, 'I think I can see why you didn't get any feeling of the past at the airbase, although Luke's pretty sure it's the most likely camp for your grandfather. But at least we can be sure that he and his fellow prisoners were in the area, perhaps in a separate special camp.'

'Graves and Hindi inscriptions are pretty conclusive,' Saira agreed, 'even if you want to mock my strange sense of reaching out to touch the past inside the artillery block and up above the infantry block.'

'Would I mock?'

That night Saira felt closer to Will than she had ever done before. Was it just the fragments of long-buried history that they had shared that day? When he stroked her outstretched body, she felt as if the flickering pink glow was intensifying in brightness as she floated weightless and giddily desirous. And then, against her tightly-closed eyelids all the colours of the rainbow were flashing into unbearable brilliance. As Will entered her, she shivered and the colours seemed to siphon to a distant point of unattainable green brightness to which she and Will were hurtling through a long, long tunnel.

At first their days of freedom in the Maginot Line had passed reasonably quickly. But now, locked in a small underground store-room with no openings to the world above and no hint of light, Yaqub and Barkat were fretting at what felt like a return to captivity. For, after the initial days (about seventeen, they thought) of comfort in their airy 'bedroom', Benoit still hadn't found a guide for them but had suddenly become fearful for their safety. He'd overheard that some top-brass German military would be inspecting the whole underground system in order to draw up plans to use the fort for defence in the 'unlikely' event of their troops being forced by the advancing Allies to retreat further than they had already. So he had insisted on moving his friends from their comfortable quarters to this cell-like empty store room under a staircase, to which he had a separate key. As the metal door clanged behind them it felt as if their hard-won freedom had been stripped away. How ironic that they had escaped from the PoW camp only to be locked away again. They fell to bickering.

'It's a stupid hiding place. Why did you agree to it?'

'Me? I wanted just to set off walking towards the setting sun and France. It was you who agreed to hide here first!'

'I never wanted to hide like an animal in a burrow! I was the one who wanted to find the Americans as soon as possible. We'll never get to help the liberating troops if we just cower underground!'

'He's never going to find someone to guide us. We should just set out on our own.'

'That's even more stupid!'

'We might come across those secret Resistance people.'

'We can hardly go around asking for them.'

But their angry whispers ceased when the lights in that section were suddenly switched on. After the darkness, they seemed harsh, almost blinding. They crouched in the corner with their backs against the corridor wall, not daring to move. After an hour or two of brightness, they heard footsteps and German voices further up the tunnel. The approaching footsteps paused right outside their storeroom door. They heard a rustle of papers and more discussion, as if plans or lists were being consulted. But, to their immense relief, no one tried to open the door and look into the corners, and the party moved on. A few hours later, the lights were switched off again. The inspection must have been completed.

But after the shock of so nearly being discovered by the Germans, they were unable to relax again. They must have spent two or three days in the darkness in the corner of the store-room, dozing fitfully, arguing, and eking out their stale bread and the last of the pears they'd gathered. How they missed their midnight sorties to the abandoned orchard above ground, the scent of the night air, and the sound of the wind in the dried grass.

They began to feel that they might never see the outside world again. And they were worried because Benoit had not returned. Had he been caught? Had the Germans realised he'd helped them? Was he ill? Had he been transferred?

As they also thought longingly of their comfortable previous quarters, Barkat remembered the postcards he'd showed Yaqub. 'I don't think I want to die here without ever knowing a woman.'

Yaqub wasn't sure how to respond to Barkat. He didn't want to show his inexperience. He'd been very shocked when he'd first heard other recruits talking lewdly. He didn't know whether they were boastful inventions or the truth and hadn't dared ask more. He'd thought Barkat was equally inexperienced, but then Barkat had shown him the postcards with a curious relish. So he asked, in what he hoped sounded a neutral tone, 'Do you remember the women we saw in the doorways in Cairo? We could have had them any time. Lots of the men did. Were you ever tempted?'

Barkat gave an odd laugh. 'They looked so beautiful and so languid. And Ali said that they would do anything you wanted.' He admitted that he had been tempted at first and had even gone up to one once, thinking that he was far from home, and no one would know if he satisfied his curiosity and desire. 'But then I saw her neck. Under all that paint and bright colour on her face, she was an old woman. And then I remembered all the terrible things we were told about that wasting, disfiguring disease that would never leave us or our children or our children's children, and I ran away.'

'And Ali was sure that some of them were really boys. How could he be so sure? Do you think he was just pretending to know so much?'

Barkat consoled him with the thought that those who talk most do least.

And Yaqub reflected, 'No, I don't want a dirty, backstreet experience, or even the strange acts in the postcards. I want to love a woman and feel all those things the poets speak of. I want her to be the mother of my children, the grower and harvester of my crops, the carrier of water that will forever refresh me, the companion of my life ...' He tailed off, as Amina's beautiful face floated through the claustrophobic walls. It had been a long time since he'd been able to visualise her like this.

'I never realised that you were so poetical!'

'But,' Yaqub confessed more candidly, dismissing the pure image of Amina, 'I also want to know what it is like to sleep with her. The poets only hint at that. They don't explain the detail!' he stopped, fearful that he'd betrayed too much ignorance.

Barkat began to talk about the girl to whom he had been promised, concluding, 'It has nothing to do with her, this desperation. I am getting to be an old man. And I need to know more.'

As they were falling asleep later, they both knew that the other would also be dreaming of a beautiful unknown woman in their arms.

Yaqub was woken from his dreams (he couldn't tell whether it was night or day) by a distant sound of cautious knocking, which got closer. Then he heard his name called. He woke Barkat, but they remained silent. It could be a trap. 'Yaqub! Barkat!' It sounded like Benoit. They risked a single bang on their door.

And suddenly there was Benoit unlocking their door and hugging them. He was smiling with relief. He was saying how stupid he was. How stupid to have forgotten which of the many store-rooms he had locked them in!

He pushed some bread and some cheese into their hands and a glass bottle of water. They ate and drank gratefully. And then Benoit announced, 'It is getting too dangerous to keep you here, and I have at last found someone to guide you across the mountains. Come!'

7

Scenic route

Saira stirred her coffee. The fourth morning of their honey-moon and everything felt flat. Will was still showering and she hadn't waited for him. Yesterday they'd found what they had hoped. Will had wanted to see the Maginot Line and she had wanted to understand more of her grandfather's wartime experiences. And they had. They'd done both and she'd felt so happy. But now she felt almost ashamed of their night-time ardour. Freud's legacy to callow students, debasing symbols: tunnels and sex. Pathetic. It exploited her grandfather's sufferings. She was pathetic. And what now? Luke's notes were useless. 'No idea which route your grandfather would have followed across the mountains.'

She prodded the book her brothers had given them to one side. That couldn't help. She unfolded the map, jolting her cup as she did and peevishly wiped the spreading stain. That long ridge of mountains, north to south, roads crossing it east to west. Footpaths zig-zagging. She skipped to the end of his note: 'Have you brought boots?' as Will slouched in. Madame appeared immediately, as if she'd been lurking, with a coffee and a solitary croissant. He glanced at the outspread map. 'No plans,' she said, flatly. 'I've no idea what to do today.'

Will leaned forward, then hesitated. 'There's something I need to tell you.'

As they silently followed Benoit down the tunnels, Yaqub was assailed by unexpected doubts. Up till then he'd been excited at the thought of taking their fate into their own hands after the years of blindly following orders. Years in which someone else had always been in charge, marching them here and there, ordaining tasks, shouting and disciplining. But now there was no master-plan. Just their own will to escape from everything known and reach the unknown. Would they find the Americans out to the west? Would the Americans welcome them? Would they get killed in subsequent battles? What would their parents think if their fellow prisoners returned safely and they did not? Benoit had mentioned a guide. But Yaqub sensed that ultimately they would now be responsible only to each other for their mutual survival. It was a frightening but also exhilarating thought.

It was good to feel the fresh air on their faces as they emerged once more into the outside world. But the weather had changed whilst they'd been locked away in the store-room. The nights had been cold and clear during their night sorties, but tonight there were no stars, the rain lashed their faces, and it was slippery underfoot as they scrambled through the anti-tank trenches.

It was soon obvious that Benoit was not a countryman. He had no instinct for moving silently or merging into shadows. He seemed desperate to hand them over as quickly as possible, as he blundered across the bare hillside. They were thankful when he stopped at a disused hut on the edge of the forest where they waited, glad of the shelter from the driving rain.

But the man who sidled into the hut soon afterwards did not inspire them with confidence. He was an old man. He would not look at them. He mumbled and muttered. His accent was strange to them with its choking, throaty sounds. They could not recognise any words he was saying, but he sounded as if he was grumbling and hopeless.

'You will call him Wilhelm,' said Benoit. He looked very anxious, Yaqub thought, as if he wasn't too sure about this old man either. He explained that 'Wilhelm' didn't want them to know his real name; that he spoke only the local Alsace dialect, so they might find it hard to understand him; and that he had worked in the forest all his life, so knew it well. He could guide them better than anyone. At that point, the old man interrupted rudely and Benoit nodded and tried to find simple words, 'he says that for two days, troops move up to the border; there are soldiers and convoys on all roads and tracks, also the accustomed patrols. He says it will be difficult to find a place to cross the border.' More gestures and words. It seemed that Wilhelm thought that the safest direction would be southwards, hugging the forested mountains, before swinging westwards towards the border. 'But things change all the time, as the Allies approach. You have to trust him.'

Benoit was clearly anxious to be gone, whether or not his two Indian friends had understood all his words. 'My family,' he murmured. 'I must return to them.' He held out his arms to first Yaqub and then Barkat and hugged them both and kissed their cheeks. They found it hard to know how to thank him enough for all the risks he had taken for them. Even more, they wanted to tell him how much his friendship had meant to them. All Yaqub could give him was a twist of paper containing some curry powder from a tin in the last food parcel before their escape. 'Frau,' he whispered. He hoped his wife would know how to cook some spicy meat with onions and vegetables to remind Benoit of his Indian friends. Barkat added, in their usual mixture of languages, words to the effect that they would never forget his tremendous kindness and thanking him on behalf of their parents as well as themselves, for helping them to escape.

Wilhelm was muttering and beckoning impatiently. As they began to follow him, Barkat whispered to Benoit one of his newly acquired French phrases, 'Vive la France!' Benoit raised his hand briefly in farewell as they headed off through the trees. They looked so vulnerable. He hoped he would never see them again. How he wished they had agreed to stay in their hiding place. But Barkat, in particular, was an obstinate young man. He admired their optimism. But it was a dangerous time.

He sighed as he turned to start his long trudge back to the town. Then, deliberately, he dropped Yaqub's farewell gift down a hole by a tree. He would not risk the pungent smell of the spices tainting his clothes or home and betraying him to the Germans or their spies.

It might have been his strange smell (was it the sour stink of wine on his breath as he mumbled?) or his uncouthness (he would not look at them or speak directly to them) or his lack of concern as to whether were following him as he slid in and out of the shadows, but from the moment that Benoit disappeared from their sight, Yaqub and Barkat felt uncomfortable with Wilhelm. They had to trust him as their guide, but there was something about his shifty look that made them feel he could as easily betray them to someone offering higher payment. For Barkat thought straight away that Benoit must have bribed him to lead them.

But he knew the forest and was sure-footed even in the dark. Yaqub noticed that they never followed any paths. Wilhelm deliberately steered them away from the tracks which followed the contours of the mountain. So it seemed that they were always climbing, then descending, then listening attentively before crossing a path or track or stream. Then again the ascent, the descent and the listening. All the time, Wilhelm was cocking his head, listening for sounds from the ridge above them. His one concession to communication was to point up into the damp mist which hugged the ridge and make a gesture of someone shooting down at them, presumably from some fortified place.

At one point they saw a tiny stone building. Yaqub expected their guide to swerve away from it, as he seemed to be avoiding all signs of habitation. To their surprise he approached it and knelt before the grille in the doorway and crossed himself. Imperiously he indicated that Yaqub and Barkat should do the same. Barkat whispered that he thought it was probably a shrine to a forest saint who would protect them, so they too knelt and bowed their heads. Wilhelm nodded, as if that was the best that could be expected of heathens.

As they moved on through the dark forest, they occasionally heard rumbling sounds, and realised that they were approaching roads with night convoys. Each time Wilhelm waited for a long time, listening and peering into the darkness, before they slunk across the wet, shiny road.

Yaqub had thought that they were really fit after their long summer working out in the forest and hauling logs. But the steady tramping was producing a different kind of tiredness. Perhaps it was because they had no idea of where they were going, or whether they were really making progress. The forest all looked the same to him, and with all the ups and downs, it did not feel as if they were making any progress upwards and towards a mountain pass. He had expected their walk to freedom to seem exciting, despite all the dangers, but all he was feeling was a tired numbness of brain and body. He started to whisper to Barkat, who agreed that they must have softened up while they were hiding and doing nothing. But then Wilhelm looked angrily at them, as if he despised them. He held his finger in front of his lips for silence. Despite his age, he didn't seem to be tiring. He forced them on.

Eventually, after many hours it began to get light and the old man slowed down. They realised that he was scanning the forest for a secure place to rest during the day. They hadn't passed a single house or hut during the night. Wilhelm wasn't risking any human contact. But on the edge of a small clearing he approached a stack of long tree trunks. He prowled around, looking to see if there were recent wheel-tracks nearby. Clearly satisfied that no vehicles had approached since the trees had been felled and stacked, he indicated a tarpaulin-covered shelter the woodcutters had left and ushered them in. He mimed and muttered that they should stay quiet and take the opportunity to sleep. Yaqub and Barkat were quite relieved when the old man lay down apart from them in the furthest corner and closed his eyes. Despite the lack of water to cleanse themselves, they knelt to perform their dawn prayers, including thanksgiving for their continuing safety. Then, exhausted, they too fell asleep almost immediately, scarcely conscious of the dampness of the ground.

When they woke, it was still light outside. Wilhelm was munching some black bread. He didn't offer to share it with them. He gestured that he was going ahead of them to look round, possibly make some enquiries. They understood that he could move freely, whereas they had to stay hidden in daylight. No movement. Stay.

After a couple of hours they began to wonder whether he

was really coming back, and then there he was right by them. You had to admire his skill and silence in the woods. He seemed very uneasy, though without the words to make them understand. He tugged his ear uncertainly, then joggled Barkat's elbow, pointing to the ridge above them. Thanks to the fact that some of the trees had been felled, they could see a section of the ridge clearly outlined against the sky and the jagged shapes of two ruined castles. Perhaps he had wanted to go that way. Wilhelm held up both hands several times, fingers upright. They guessed he meant ten, twenty, eighty, a hundred Germans up there in the ruins. Heavily armed too, judging from his gestures of shooting. He shook his head. Clearly they weren't going to risk that route. He pointed south-west again. Then from a very grubby bit of cloth he unwrapped some bread. This time he gave them a piece each. They ate it with relish then Wilhelm urged to follow him from the clearing into the darkening shadows of the forest.

'You know how interested you were in the story of Habib's father and mother and their romance?' Will started tentatively. 'Do you think there is the faintest possibility that something similar happened to your grandfather? No, don't look so shocked. It's taken me a while to take it in.'

'But he never would …'

'It's something your grandmother said. At the wedding. Furtively.' Saira smiled at the word 'furtive'. Will could come out with unexpected words. She tried to imagine her grandmother looking furtive at their wedding.

'Seriously furtive! It seems she always suspected something. She didn't say why. Just that she had never discussed it with him. How things were then, I suppose.'

'Still are, in traditional families. But why now?'

But Will didn't know that either. 'There wasn't much time to talk. All she said was that she thought it must have happened at the end, at the Russian's house. And could we try to find out more. She looked so imploring.'

Will watched Saira, as she tried to comprehend the unexpected request, and wondered if he dared ask for an additional croissant. One flaky bit of nothingness wasn't really enough to keep a guy going. Madame looked surprised, but brought an extra. Saira reflected. Her grandmother had never struck her as fanciful. There must be some basis for her suspicions. Had they stirred up the long-buried thoughts with their talk of Alsace and a honeymoon there? Had there been a glint in her eye when they'd first mentioned the possibility to her? And why had she spoken to Will and not her? Perhaps she hadn't wanted to destroy Saira's image of her grandfather, so nearly didn't say anything to either of them. Had she hesitated until it was almost to late? 'So imploring,' Will repeated. Perhaps her grandmother had seen the soft side of Will, the kindness beneath his laconic humour. Or perhaps she knew he wouldn't ask too many questions, especially with so many people around.

And then he dipped his croissant first in the coffee and then the jam. 'Oh, that's gross!' It reminded her of the downside: the occasional moodiness or bad-temper, a certain sarcasm and liking to have his own way. Though his single-mindedness over the Maginot Line yesterday had paid off. She'd never expected to feel so close to her grandfather. It was hard to know how they could follow that. Perhaps, she should take this ludicrous suggestion seriously. Perhaps, now they'd seen where his escape began, it would be good to try and find the place where it had ended.

'Oddly enough, it was the only place name that I remember him mentioning in his account of his escape, the place where the Russian lived. So it's possible it had happy memories for him. Forge-les-Eaux, he called it. I always pictured a big, strong, Russian blacksmith! But he never mentioned a woman.' She searched the index of villages on the back of the map, turned it back over and found the spot, on the other side of the mountains. 'It looks a tiny place, so it might just be possible to see if anyone remembers a Russian there, It must have been a bit unusual in those days.' She sat back. It might be a really bad idea to go stirring up the past. Would it really make her grandmother happy? 'Were you thinking of today?'

Will looked horrified. He'd always imagined following the escape route in order. Except that they didn't actually know the escape route. The old man had told Saira about the hardships, the detours and the people, but no names. Perhaps he and his friend never knew them. 'What does our self-appointed tour guide suggest for today? Have you got Luke's notes?'

Saira wiped her hands on her serviette before reaching out for the folder. Sometimes, he thought, she could be obsessively neat, a bit too like her mother. Were these things hereditary? 'The first bit's not much help. He writes: sorry, absolutely no idea what route your grandfather and his friend would have taken across the Vosges. Any border crossing would have been pretty hairy! But you're in luck as this Friday there's an organised walk that's well worth going on. From time to time some old men lead this ramble along the forest paths their fathers took in the war when helping young Alsace lads to escape over the border to occupied France. It's called the Sentier des Passeurs (= path of the smugglers – sounds like drugs or old rum and lace, but actually these were people-smugglers!). You should do it! P.S. Have you got walking boots???'

Will rather fancied that. A border crossing! He could imagine a thick mist, dense trees, German patrols, a youthful guide with a wooden staff and perhaps even a dog. That would be so much more atmospheric than driving tamely past a signpost on the old national boundary that probably now said 'Welcome to Lorraine'.

Practical as ever, Saira went back to the map, struggling to find the starting point of the walk. It turned out to be much further south than she'd assumed her grandfather would have crossed. She hesitated. Will pulled the map towards him, seeking ammunition for his orderly progress concept, then pointed out in his most reasonable voice that if you drew a line from where they were now to Forge-les-Eaux and the house of the Russian, it would pass quite near the start of the walk. 'We could treat the line as a hypothetical route, drive along those wiggly little mountain roads for a couple of days, spend the Friday walking an authentic war route across the border, then drive on the next day towards a bit of detective work around the hypothetical girl at the end of the journey.' He poked the map again. 'Look, there would be lots of ruined castles in the mountains and waterfalls if we started in that direction today.' He looked at her hopefully. She'd definitely twitched at the mention of castles.

'You win!' she said in resignation. 'Actually, I quite like the sound of doing a bit of normal tourism today. We never had fancy foreign holidays like you did as a kid. We just went to family in Pakistan!'

Will was about to protest about the 'fancy', then realising that quiet reason had prevailed, and she looked much more cheerful than when he came in, drained his coffee cup in silence.

For the next two nights they kept to the forest, avoiding the crags above and the plains and villages below. Once they were terrified by a crashing sound in the undergrowth above them. Had they finally been spotted by German soldiers? Old Wilhelm looked at them pityingly and screwed up his eyes to a small piggy shape and made tusk shapes with two fingers by his jaws. But he made them stay quite still until the thudding of the invisible boar receded. And again they paused for long, listening periods before they crossed any of the tracks and especially a wider road.

But, once they were safely over that road, there was a new worry. Wilhelm was now on less familiar territory. This was not the way he'd originally intended to take. He no longer knew every fold and crevice of the forest floor. There were times when they had to turn back, defeated by the brambles which had invaded the forest since the foresters went to war. There were places where the streams had overflowed and created stagnant impassable stretches of boggy ground, which had then frozen at the edges. Progress was much slower. And they could see that Wilhelm was uneasy.

On the third day Wilhelm spent much longer away from them. It was still raining heavily and both Yaqub and Barkat were disheartened. He had indicated that he was going into the big town whose grey shape they could see through the mist and rain on the plains below. They didn't know why he wanted to go into the town. Up till now they had been avoiding all signs of habitation. They wondered if he was hoping to find another guide to take over. Someone who knew this stretch of terrain better than he did.

When he eventually returned, he handed them some bread and strong-smelling cheese. It was unusual for him not to have some too. He also looked rather guilty as he gave it to them. Perhaps he had already eaten in the town. Though it felt more as if he was placating them. Why? Before the grey daylight faded, he led them from their hiding place to a bushy promontory looking across the valley. And then they understood.

The town lay below, to their left. Running from it, criss-crossing each other and then disappearing towards a pass in the higher mountains on their right they could see four threads. There was a busy road, with camouflaged lorries moving up towards the border and files of labourers being marched under guard in the other direction, towards the town. There was a river glinting silver even through the rain. There was a broad railway line with coils of smoke rising from engines pulling chains of goods trucks. And finally there was a canal, which looked as busy with loaded barges as the road was with trucks. Wilhelm indicated that they would have to cross all these. And then he pointed to himself and the direction from which they had come. They realised with a shock that Wilhelm was giving up on them. He was going home and leaving them here. He was too old and scared to face the seemingly insurmountable obstacles ahead.

'I don't think I've ever seen so much forest before!'

Saira was still stunned by the contrasts of the late afternoon light. Driving through the hills, you suddenly plunged into shadow and coolness, and then, rounding the contour, you were back in a world where the sunlight played on each leaf and blade of grass. Abruptly, having seen a small wooden sign 'cascade', she pulled into the verge on a bend.

Will got a fright as she walked towards the edge of the grassy verge, and pulled her roughly back. 'Idiot! Look at the drop!' The ground fell away below them, as if the bending road was just a shelf against a rocky precipice. They looked down onto a dense mass of treetops, all different shades and textures, like an unending quilted duvet. 'But it looks as if you'd just bounce up again from those cushions of green and gold!'

They'd spent the day scrambling up to castles perched on rocky pinnacles, and reading histories of long ago rivalries and wars. All those feuds and betrayals. All those fortifications. And now all in ruins. Saira had pictured the vast halls with their vanished lords and ladies in their long velvet robes and ornate head-dresses, minstrels, falconers, huntsmen and servants. Will, with his mind still on their quest, had wondered if the Germans had used the strongholds during the last war in their defence of Alsace. In between each castle and its legends, they plunged once more into the forest, hardly meeting any other cars on the narrow, winding roads, apart from in the town to which they'd driven down; after crossing the river and railway there, they had driven up into the forested hills again. Will was now beginning to feel that he had seen enough castles for one day, so the sign to a waterfall was a welcome diversion.

Irregular, worn steps, led down the from the signpost into the green mass below. The tufts of grass were still lush on either side, and the forest felt ancient as they climbed down into it. This was not a uniform single-species forest with bare brown ground between the neat rows. This was something more mysterious. Vast oaks and venerable beeches spread a canopy of colour, but still let in the sunlight. A footpath led through the trees, seeming to be drawn towards the sound of water. They paused in a clearing, and Saira's imagination continued to work on the information they'd absorbed during the day. 'It's so peaceful and timeless. Remember that hermit we read about? The one who lived alone in the forest and talked to all the animals and birds? He'd have lived in a forest glade just like this, close to the water, in harmony with nature.'

Will was picturing a totally different scene. He was wondering how it must have felt to be a fugitive, a bewildered, escaped prisoner, dependent on a stranger, terrified of capture, tramping exhausted through a hostile forest. He thought any forest would have seemed pretty bleak in the winter of '44. He suddenly remembered another leaflet in Luke's folder. 'Apparently there were loads of little forest railway tracks, for logging, in the old days. You can still ride along a section of preserved track in one of the old steam trains.' Privately, he thought it might have been more fun to have spent that afternoon riding on an old logging train, rather than seeing quite so many castles, even if he had suggested them. 'I wonder if your grandfather – couldn't they have hidden away among all those logs?'

'The Germans probably searched all the trains pretty thoroughly.' Saira was ruffled that he'd interrupted her romantic picture. 'And, anyway, he never mentioned a train.'

They walked further into the depths of the forest, entranced by the apparent stillness, then noticing the scuffling of small birds in the undergrowth, the cawing of larger birds and creaking of branches overhead, and always the cascading of the waterfall ahead. Eventually they found themselves at the foot of a steep rock. The shadow was more profound. Above them were the jagged outlines of ruined castle walls. It was beginning to feel sinister. 'Let's press on to the waterfall,' Will said hastily, 'we've done enough castles for today'.

The waterfall was spectacular. They just had to scramble

down its rocky sides to the bottom, to get the full effect of its power as it hurtled down to the dark pools below. They sat on boulders, dangling their feet in the darting, curling eddies. Then suddenly they were cold. They looked at their wet, peaty feet in dismay. Saira pulled some scrunched tissues from her bag. 'Best I can offer!'

Their partly-dried feet felt clammy as they put on their boots and walked back up the hill to the car. A slight mist was creeping round the trees, filtering the remains of the daylight. 'I've got an even better offer.' Will reached for the rucksack he'd left on the back seat. 'Chocolate!'

Wilhelm shrugged, seeming to express no regrets or concern for their future, then turned his back on them and was soon absorbed into the silent forest. This was the first time they had been truly alone. Even in the long periods in the Maginot Line, they had known that Benoit was out there, making plans for them. They had been in the company of herded men for so long, that it was hard to know what to do in this unknown terrain. Barkat was the first to pull himself together and take charge. 'I am not going back. If this is the only way to reach the Americans, we'll wait till it gets darker, then we'll cross the road and all the rest below.'

'Can you swim?' asked Yaqub doubtfully. 'I know we did all those exercises with pontoons and rafts and things, but I was never very good, as you know – you were quite rude at the time. And it wasn't in the dark, in fast flowing water.' But even as he said it, he knew it was the only thing they could do, by night and not knowing what awaited them beyond the quadruple barrier of the road, river, railway, and canal. 'If we ever get across that lot, we need to avoid going anywhere near that town. It will be dangerous.'

In fact it was a long time before they reached the river. Crouching low, they zig-zagged downhill in the gloom from tree to tree. But the road seemed to have non-stop traffic and patrols. So they flung themselves into the ditch by its side and stayed there for a long time, listening to the rumbling wheels above them, most of them heading from the town on their left towards where William had indicated the border was. When eventually the rumble and clattering fell silent and they raised their heads and saw that the road was temporarily clear, it felt unnatural – as if a trap had been laid for them to walk straight into. Nevertheless, with beating hearts, they took this chance and bolted across, tumbling breathlessly into the ditch on the other side. This one was unpleasantly wet, so, checking the road was still quiet behind them, they quickly scrambled out.

It was further to the river than it had looked from above, and they felt exposed on the open ground away from the forest, but the river itself was quieter and there appeared to be no one around. Barkat led the way into the water, knowing Yaqub's fear. He pointed at the boulders, suggesting that they should move from one to another. Much of the time they could wade, boots slung round their necks, but in places there were unexpected dips where the water had churned round the rocks, and then they got soaked as they fought against the rapid flow of the water. In addition to his struggle to keep his footing, Yaqub expected at any moment to hear an unseen sentry shout or to feel a peppering of gunshot. He felt very cold as they reached the other side and his boots had got wet. He was shivering as he put them on and found it hard to lace them with his trembling hands.

He got even colder as they waited by the railway track. Barkat was afraid that it might be overlooked by some signal

136

box or plate-layer's hut and insisted on investigating further along the line, while Yaqub lay still, head down, against the clinker embankment. His wet clothes felt as if they were stiffening and freezing onto his bony body. His mind too felt numb. When Barkat was finally satisfied, Yaqub managed to haul himself upright and stumbled behind Barkat across the line, no longer caring whether there was an approaching engine or guards.

'Only the canal now,' Barkat whispered encouragingly, seeing that his friend was in a bad way, his face anguished with cold. He propelled Yaqub towards the black canal. The tow-path seemed deserted and the barge nearest them showed no signs of being guarded. Barkat looked for ropes and, using those and the side of the boat, eased himself down into the water with only a slight splash.

Yaqub, however, was clumsy with the cold, hardly feeling the rough rope against his hands, letting go too soon and landing awkwardly in the water. He splashed noisily to stay afloat as Barkat swam ahead of him. Afterwards he couldn't say if his legs had become entangled with rope or weeds or whether it was the cold that made his limbs feel bereft of muscle and like soft, impotent ribbons; he was aware only of being dragged down inch by inch into the velvet water.

It was a surprisingly peaceful feeling as he ceased to try to move his legs and succumbed to the enveloping chill. He had heard tales of strange tailed women, who sang as they lured sailors to their death. But the face he sensed illuminating the depths was a loving, familiar, but long-neglected face, smiling welcomingly, holding out her arms to him. He would just sink into them.

But now there was a lot of noise, muffled by the water but nudging insistently at his brain, and his shoulders hurt as something was wrenching them, trying to lift him from his clammy bed, hauling, cursing, insistent. As his head was forced above the water and his lungs filled, he spluttered, shouted and thrashed out.

As if in answer, a German shouted command was heard from further along the towpath they had left and a light flashed on, searching the water. Before Yaqub could make another sound, Barkat hit him hard, almost loosing his grip, then began to drag his friend's inert body towards the shelter of a tethered barge. Yaqub's last thought was that he would never see Amina and his family again.

Barkat's arms ached as he held onto Yaqub. He might have been the sturdier of the two, but Yaqub was tall, and, despite being undernourished, his wet body was unbearably heavy. He wasn't sure how long he could hold on to it. If only he could prop or hook it on the side of the barge. But the light was still searching the water. He could only wait and endure and hope neither of them froze to death. He was determined they should not be re-captured after coming so far. If he could just keep Yaqub alive a bit longer.

He never knew how he held their two bedraggled bodies flattened against barge. Barkat feared his mind was beginning to wander. He no longer felt focussed on the danger. He was afraid he might be loosing his grip on Yaqub. And if they did get out, how were they ever to get warm again? He focussed his mind on warmth. He imagined all his favourite hot foods. Even the wretched prison soup would be welcome if it was piping hot. He pretended he could feel the warmth of the food spreading through his body, bringing it back into action. Hot, something hot, they must find something hot.

Above them on the tow path, he heard a squishing sound, – perhaps bicycle wheels in the mud. Barkat forced Yaqub's body, against his own, further into the angle between the barge and the dank, glistening canal wall. The bicycle stopped. Barkat looked up fearfully. A head in a black hat appeared over the top, and two eyes looked straight down at them.

8

Resistance

The geraniums were the clincher. Saira still felt shivery after their walk, despite the car heater. In the fast-rising evening chill the scarlet flowers flamed out against the light from the diamond-paned inn windows. 'You wanted to do quaint,' observed Will. 'Can't get much quainter than this.' A stream ran down one side of the village street, overlooked by ancient-looking timbered houses. Saira agreed that it was a fairy tale village inn.

The woman at the desk was initially welcoming, as she ushered them up the polished wooden staircase and showed them three large bedrooms with comfortable armchairs and massive wooden wardrobes. As Saira chose the double-bedded room looking out over the street, Madame gave them a curious look. Will went into his usual rigmarole about just married, honeymoon, retracing the footsteps of Saira's grandfather. Out of habit, he asked if anyone had ever mentioned escaping prisoners of war passing through in the last war – especially Indian ones. 'Never!' said Madame abruptly, and stalked out.

Down in the dining room they found the immaculately starched tablecloths and phalanxes of cutlery and wine glasses rather intimidating. The elderly waiter spoke English deliberately and almost offensively as he guided Will through the menu, ignoring Saira. She was hardened to such reactions, but, although the food was good, the discrete hostility cast a gloom over their meal. 'Quaint' outside had somehow turned to 'cold' inside.

Over dinner they again mulled over their findings so far. Saira was still excited by the previous day's visit to the underground fort, military graves and the inscriptions in the old barracks. But they were both surprised that there were no stories here about foreign prisoners. The Indians must have seemed pretty exotic. Surely stories about escaping ones would have circulated? But perhaps they had now strayed too far off the trail? Even so, they were both puzzled by the way Madame had clammed up.

The dark figure on the tow-path above their heads whispered in English, 'I am Philippe.' He pointed back along the canal in the direction he had come. 'Backwards that way, I did see a chain. Very old and green with weed. But it is possible you can climb it.'

Philippe. That was the word that Wilhelm had kept repeating before he'd vanished back into the forest. They hadn't known what he'd meant. But now Barkat felt a huge surge of relief as he realised that Wilhelm had made some kind of plan for them. Unless it was a trap. But Barkat knew that they had to get out before they froze to death. He had to risk it.

He began to tow Yaqub along the canal wall in search of the chain. The movement seemed to rouse Yaqub. Barkat was aware of him coming round and beginning to move, and hissed fierce instructions to remain silent, they were safe. He rather doubted his reassuring last words, but what else could he say? They were two half-drowned creatures in an unknown place.

Afterwards he remembered little of their numb struggle up the chain as he pushed Yaqub towards to Philippe's outstretched hand and the safety of the tow-path. Yaqub seemed dazed, not understanding how he came to be there or why there was a strange face. But then Barkat was uncomprehending too. They just stumbled silently behind the shadowy figure with its bicycle, as it skirted round the dark houses on the edge of the town. The wind whipped through their sodden clothes, and they were oddly relieved when the figure reached a quiet road and turned along it, towards the houses. They could only trust that they were not being taken straight to the German authorities. At least no one seemed to be out on the streets, for the two dripping figures would have instantly attracted suspicion. Their rescuer led them rapidly to a house on the corner of a square, in the shadow of a tall building that Yaqub hazily registered as a church.

Once they were indoors, Yaqub could see that the tall man they had followed was much older than he'd thought, for he'd walked like a young man. But he had a mass of white hair, a wrinkled forehead, and observant eyes. A plainly dressed woman emerged, flung her arms round Philippe, then smiled a welcome at them. She pushed them into the kitchen where a stove blazed and poured huge kettles of water into a tin tub. She brought them soap, some worn towels and a pile of clothing. 'You will wash and become warm,' urged Philippe, 'then we shall eat.'

The soup which she brought them afterwards was thick and delicious. So different from prison soup. As she ladled it out, she explained that she would not give them much. She guessed their stomachs were not used to rich food, and they must eat slowly. Because she spoke slowly and used her hands expressively, Yaqub understood what she was trying to say, for he knew from the Annaberg treachery how ill people could make themselves when large quantities of food were unexpectedly presented. Afterwards she gave them some semolina. It was a long time since they had tasted milk. It was flavoured with something they did not recognise. 'Zehr gut,' Barkat said slowly, and the couple clapped delightedly.

They sat in a contented daze, hardly able to believe they had been brought to somewhere so warm and safe, until Philippe said, 'Wilhelm told to me you want to cross the mountains to the Americans.' They could pick out the main words, and nodded vigorously, although it hadn't been a question. Philippe's wife had been looking at them appraisingly, and said something rapid to her husband, who seemed to agree, and translated, 'We do not think it possible to make you look like our local men. You look so different So it will be too dangerous to use the trains.' This was too much for Barkat's limited English, though both he and Yaqub recognised the word 'train'. However, with a little German, a little English and a lot of gestures and smiles, they finally understood. And they immediately agreed. They knew how long it had taken them to dare to cross the railway line.

'But I will do my best to get you on foot to the border and arrange another guide. But the day after tomorrow is Sunday, so we must wait.'

Yaqub and Barkat were mystified, but finally he made them understand that he was the pastor of the church and would have Sunday services to lead. He also explained that they would have to remain well hidden as plenty of people, including Germans, would come to the house during the day. For the church and house were close to the barracks. As a pastor, he was equally available to Alsatians and Germans.

'But on Mondays and Tuesdays they know I am often

144

visiting the old and the sick in distant farmhouses, so it will not surprise them that I am not here.'

Barkat nodded. He understood both 'Monday' and 'Tuesday'. He tried to explain how happy they were just to be there with the pastor and his wife. He wanted to say how much it meant to sit in a house, like guests, and to share a meal. He was almost crying at the normality. It had been so long. It was nearly four years, such long, long years, since they'd marched onto their ship in Bombay.

As Philippe nodded gently, the two men started to tell him where they were from and what life in their villages was like. Yaqub too began to weep. Philippe's wife held his hand and wiped his tears just as his mother would do. All Yaqub's years of bravery melted away as he sobbed. He could not imagine now how he had crossed that road, that river, that railway, and that ... But how had they crossed the canal? He could not now remember anything about the canal apart from cold, black water. Barkat had to tell him, minimising the part he had played in his rescue, concluding contentedly, 'and now we are warm again and safe here.'

'You are completely fatigued,' said Philippe, after he'd listened intently to their broken tale. 'I think you are both very brave. And you owe much to your friend,' he smiled at Barkat. He led them upstairs to a bedroom with a huge wardrobe. To their great surprise he stepped into the wardrobe, among some hanging clothes, and removed a wooden panel at the back. He ushered them through into a tiny room, almost filled with a large mattress and quilts. 'You will be safely hidden here, but do not make a noise. Sleep now. God bless you both.'

'May I join you?' As they sat by the fire in the bar having

an after-dinner coffee, one of their fellow-diners approached them. He introduced himself as a Paris-based business man, but born in Alsace. He said he couldn't help overhearing them during dinner. 'You sounded puzzled about the reticence of local people. But there are things you should understand about Alsace during and after the war.'

This sounded ominous. But in fact he was charming and spoke excellent English with a passionate intensity. As he sipped his cognac, he observed that the war had been difficult for everyone in France, but it had been far worse in annexed Alsace and Moselle. Loyalties were far more complex here than in the rest of France.

'For example, when the last war started, some old people, like my mother's parents, still spoke only our Alsatian dialect and German. That is how they had grown up, and in 1918 when we became French again, they never learned to speak the new language. So as a child my mother spoke French at school and dialect at home.'

He said that there were plenty of people who in 1940 welcomed the return of German orderliness and efficiency. 'Probably my grandfather did, although it was not something that was spoken about after the war.' He explained how the war was a very frightening time in which no one could trust their neighbours. People could never be sure who was working for the Germans and who was against them. There were denunciations. There were deportations. Unlike the rest of France, the men of Alsace had fought in the German Army in the First World War and were forced to do so again from 1942 onwards. 'My father was one of them. He did not dare to try and avoid this compulsory military service or even to escape from the Russian front where he was sent, for he knew that my grandparents would be sent to concentration camps in

Poland. He had seen that happen to others before he left.'

Saira shook her head in disbelief. Although they'd been told earlier about the 'malgré-nous' escapees hiding in the Maginot Line, she hadn't realised the drastic reprisals their parents could have suffered. 'But what about the Resistance?'

Their new friend explained how much harder it would have been to work with the Resistance in Alsace. His mother, who remained in her village, never heard whispers of anyone there daring to do so. It was only after the war that they learned that there had been some very brave people on their side of the border as well as in France. 'But it was all very hidden. The punishment was death. And there were plenty of people who would betray you. You must also remember that at that time there were parents here who were proud that their sons were in the SS.'

'In the SS!' Will exclaimed.

'Oh yes. There were SS men from Alsace, including two of my father's class-mates. So everyone had to be very careful what they said. After the war, more became known. There were the trials and the revenge. My father said only the skeleton of one of those former class-mates was returned to the devastated parents.' He ordered another cognac as he concluded, 'So many dreadful things happened during and after the war that it was better not to enquire about afterwards. And many people have remained silent, even if they did nothing shameful. It is my generation that thinks our children should learn more about those years of fear.'

As the gloomy waiter brought his cognac, he had another thought. 'Did you know that the only extermination camp on what is now French soil was here in Alsace, quite close to this village? Many French political prisoners and those caught resisting the Germans, spent time there. Many died – from

147

malnutrition, hard labour and the freezing cold. And others were shot or executed. Everyone knew about the death camp. Such terrible events.'

Saira and Will were shocked. They had not heard of a concentration camp in France.

Their companion sounded bitter as he told them that despite everything they had suffered in Alsace, after Alsace was given back to the French at the end of the war, the French government did not really trust the people of Alsace. 'The French reacted as if we had all collaborated, despite the fact that the loss of life was seven times greater here in Alsace than all the other areas of France. In order to obtain certain jobs, people from Alsace had to prove that they and their parents were French by birth, which was very difficult, given our chequered history. My oldest brother, for example, he was born German, but the rest of us, born after the war, were automatically French. And a cousin of mine, born during the war to parents who were born during the previous German administration, found it hard to become a doctor. Also, as my father was to discover, it could also be very difficult to get a French passport, especially for those who'd been forced into the German army, as the French still considered them German.'

He paused reflectively, then said, 'It must be hard for you, coming from England, to understand what it is like to be constantly shuffled and torn between two countries.'

Saira hastened to assure him that she understood only too well. 'My grandfather – the one whose footsteps I am trying to trace – was from Azad Kashmir.' She was not surprised when he looked puzzled – the partition of India was probably not something the French studied. It was her turn to give a potted history lesson about how India had been one country under the British, and so her grandfather had fought in the Indian

Army, which had Muslims and Sikhs as well as Hindus. But after 1947, when India and Pakistan became separate, independent countries, both countries claimed and fought over Kashmir. 'It is the most beautiful area. Visitors used to love the mountains and lakes. My grandfather's part now belongs to Pakistan and the other part to India. But many of the people of Kashmir just want to be Kashmiri'. She knew she was over-simplifying the complex social and political situation massively, but she wanted him to know that she understood what he was trying to say.

The man's face lit up. 'Like the people of Alsace. So perhaps you will also understand how, after the horrors and treachery of the war, it was better not to look back at what had happened. People picked up the pieces as best they could and endeavoured to fit in with French rules and requirements. And to this day many people prefer not to talk about the things that happened in the war, that their parents witnessed, or that they saw as children. That's why some people are unwilling to talk to you. It is not personal.'

Saira and Will had warmed to him as he had earnestly filled them in on history. They were amused too, because, although his English was so good, he also used his hands and expressive face like a comedy Frenchman. And now he was looking apologetic and saying that he hoped they didn't mind him just coming up to them and lecturing them like that. 'But then it's not often I overhear someone talking of a soldier from the old India who passed this way in the war, and wanting to know more.'

Saira hastened to reassure him that she had found his explanation really interesting and helpful. She realised that they could have read up more about the wartime history of Alsace beforehand, but said that it meant far more to her to hear about the experiences of ordinary people.

'So will you go to the concentration camp?'

He smiled at their startled faces and explained that the camp existed still, although desecrators (probably neo-Nazis) had tried to burn down the original buildings. 'It is called Le Struthof. Everyone here knew about it in the war. It is quite close to here, beyond the village of Natzwiller. Resistance workers who were caught were sent there. As non-combatants they were not protected by the Geneva Convention, unlike your grandfather and the thousands of prisoners of war. They just vanished, as if into the night or the fog, with no reports to their families and no subsequent outside contact. Medical experiments were also done on 'undesirables'. A visit there may help you to understand those terrible times.'

Saira started to explain that they were only interested in places where her grandfather might have been, but Will broke in, 'Well, we hadn't planned to. But perhaps we should.'

Yaqub and Barkat must have slept for a good twelve hours, aware only of the imperious ring of the doorbell breaking through their dreams. It was a very busy household. For the safety of all of them, Philippe's wife brought their meals up to their little hidden room. It was strange to have a woman sitting with them as they ate. She brought up their clothes which she had dried, and sat and mended the tears and patched the holes. Meanwhile they were glad of the spare clothes she had found for them the night before. And all the time she talked in her quiet voice. Most of it they couldn't understand. But it felt as if the words were immaterial and as if she was telling stories to two very dear sons. Yaqub tried to tell her that he wished he could stay there, and to thank her for her kindness, which still brought tears to his eyes. Barkat, however, was stern about the need to move on. Their hostess just smiled and went on sewing.

On the Sunday they were alone for most of the day. They could hear the organ and the singing from the big church. It felt very calm. Again Yaqub thought how good it would be to stay there for ever with the warm comfortable bedding, the warm tasty food and the warm friendliness of Philippe and his wife. But he knew they would be on the move again once the evening service was finished.

It was a zone of silence. Remote, up a winding road. Le Struthof. Saira and Will walked wordlessly, next morning, through the concentration camp gates, and saw the tiers of huts, precipitous on the hillside.

There was a lot to assimilate, both in the huts that had been reconstructed after the hate-fire and in the sombre, black walled museum. Will felt quite angry with a group of foreign students chattering away despite the injunction to silence, and seeming not to absorb the impact of what was in front of them. But perhaps it was their only way of coping with a death camp. He himself found it hard not to feel false sentiments, what you 'ought' to feel when confronted with evidence of experimentation, gassing and cremation.

Saira was much more affected than she had expected. She had set out on this journey, thinking about her grandfather's escape, – about reckless heroism and adventure. She had not wanted to think about the realities of his earlier imprisonment. But now this windswept hillside and its high, double, barbed-wire enclosure, its 'ravine of death', its black huts, its watchtowers, its gallows and its crematorium block, were making her face up to all the horrors of imprisonment that her grandfather hadn't talked about. No wonder he had remained silent.

As they looked at the photographs and read the history, she kept telling herself that at least Grandfather hadn't been forced to build a long road up to his own camp, or quarry granite for Hitler's monuments, or sleep in the shadow of the smoking crematorium chimney, or dread the human experiments and the gas chambers down the road. 'It couldn't have been quite as terrible for him,' she kept murmuring. 'His wasn't a death camp.' Though when they stood below the gallows, and read about the deportees being forced to watch their fellow-prisoners being hanged, she whispered to Will, 'It must have made a difference to them, the Geneva Convention, surely? They wouldn't have dared to treat our soldiers like this?'

Will privately wondered whether sadistic camp guards (who would actually want to be a camp guard?) would have worried too much about such distinctions, but he kept his mouth shut.

Throughout the morning the clouds had been gathering and closing in on the exposed hilltop site. Saira shivered as she retreated to the car to say her noon prayers. They seemed particularly significant today in the face of so much evil in the world.

Will got quietly into the back seat. He never found it difficult to keep their agreement to respect each other's beliefs (however minimal his own had become). However, today, he felt unable to continue on his assumption that human nature and endeavour were all that was provable. As he meditated on the betrayals and atrocities they had read about, especially the medical experiments, he found his despair over human nature turning into a litany familiar from his younger days, as he punctuated each fresh image with a silent 'Lord have mercy'.

He felt some comfort doing this. There was no sudden revelation from the heavens. But he began to have a sense that instead of turning away from a God who seemed to permit cruelty and injustice, it might be possible to align oneself – himself, even – more closely with a God who abhorred mankind's every act of cruelty and injustice. He smiled at Saira as she finished, and he moved into the front seat, next to her. 'You're a very good influence on me!'

'But of course! What did you expect?' Then, noticing that the low clouds were producing some very dramatic effects, Saira got abruptly out of the car to take some even more atmospheric photos. Will called out of the window 'Who didn't even want to come here? And now you want to record it all!'

'I don't think I ever tried to imagine what day-to-day survival in a prison camp would have been like for Grandfather and all his comrades. I know this is different, but those jolly black and white films about plucky British officers planning brave escapes didn't capture the bleakness and isolation that hits you here.'

As she got back in the car, she said, 'You know those photos we saw in the first hut, the ones showing this as a popular skiing area before the war? Imagine if you were one of those who'd once skimmed and swooped like a bird down those slopes, and then a few years later found yourself shivering, crouching and fearful for your life among hundreds of prisoners in one of those wooden barracks behind the barbed wire.'

It was pretty amazing that her grandfather and his friend had found anyone prepared to help them escape. If any act of resistance on their own soil led to this cruel place, who on earth would willingly put their life on the line for a couple of unknown foreign fugitives?

Late on Sunday evening, Philippe's wife had tears of compassion in her eyes as she urged them to keep the clothes that she'd found for them, especially as Barkat lacked a warm over-shirt like Yaqub's. 'It will be cold in the mountains now that the snow has come, especially if it freezes. You must wear all the clothes to stay warm!' They were especially glad of the hand-knitted long socks she gave them to protect their bruised and bandaged feet. As they came downstairs, there was more thick hot soup on the stove to set them up for the next stage of their journey.

Before they left she and her husband bowed their heads and she murmured what sounded like a prayer for their safety. Then she produced two battered black felt hats for Yaqub and Barkat, which would hide their features from curious passers-by. As she put them on their heads, she kissed them both lightly on each cheek and held Philippe in a tight embrace. Her look was a strange mixture of calm trust and desperate pleading.

Snow was falling as they left, and the street looked different from how it had – was it only two nights before? – when they'd staggered bedraggled and frozen towards Philippe's haven of safety. The snow was helpful in that it muffled their footsteps. But on the other hand they left a trail of footprints behind them. Yaqub pulled his hat further over his face, pleased with its warmth and protection. But, again, they saw no-one out on the street as they walked quietly out of town then slipped into the protective orchards. From there they headed towards the hills and forest. Philippe was striding ahead like a young and vigorous man, but stopped and smiled encouragingly as they caught up. The snow was now falling faster and as they looked back they could see that it was already beginning to cover their tracks.

Once in the forest, they noticed that Philippe didn't have the unerring instincts that Wilhelm had. Nevertheless, they felt safer with him, as if his obvious concern for them would ward off evil. And, unlike Wilhelm, Philippe seemed to have friends and contacts throughout the forest. He deliberately headed for several remote forest houses, knocked openly on the doors in order, it seemed, to exchange information before continuing their journey. No-one seemed surprised to see him on their doorstep in the middle of the night, or to see the shadowy figures of Yaqub and Barkat behind him. Yaqub began to wonder if he regularly helped people to get over the border.

Despite the stops, they made good progress that night. The whitening forest was very beautiful, but the ground would become treacherous once it froze. As the sky began to get lighter, they turned aside to a huge barn, and scrambled up a wooden ladder and tumbled into the mounds of hay, where they slept soundly all day. Philippe must have left them and gone to warn the owners, for they were woken, as the daylight was fading, by a plump woman in a blue overall who brought them plates of hot food.

After eating, they set out once more into the darkness. Although the forest was thick, in places the snow drove fiercely under its canopy and they were grateful for the broad-brimmed hats which Philippe's wife had given them.

As they climbed higher, they could hear the distant sounds of bombardments from the other side of the mountain. 'Americans?' Philippe nodded and whispered that they were approaching the border. Barkat got very excited at the thought that they were finally getting close to the fighting and would be part of the great battle.

But the news when they stopped at the next isolated house, not far from the border, seemed to disturb Philippe. He tried to explain to them that with both the American and French liberating armies pushing the Germans back towards the mountains on the French side, the occupying Germans were becoming desperate and brutal. They were making a big stand to defend the mountains and Alsace and force the allies to retreat. They didn't understand everything, but noticed that for the first time, Philippe seemed hesitant. He pushed them inside the dark, dusty house. The owner resignedly hitched up his trousers and shuffled off to boil up some old chicory coffee for a warming drink. They sat down at the kitchen table to rest and, in the faint candle-light, Philippe began to marshal the objects on the table to help him make a map.

Here lay the border, he said, just ahead of them. And here, just over the border lay these villages. Two months ago, there had been British parachute drops (here he raised both clenched fist, and opened them in mimicry of the parachutes billowing open and dropping to the ground) of weapons, ammunition, radios and men. They landed near these villages. Naturally, when the Germans found no trace of them, they suspected all the villagers of aiding the French resistance by hiding the men and weapons. The Germans knew the weapons would be used against them if the Allies got closer. So many villagers were rounded up in vicious reprisals. There had been hundreds of deportations. No one knew if they were still alive. The old man had just informed Philippe that the search had now been renewed for anyone still hiding out in the forest and for any remaining weapons. The area ahead was swarming with German troops.

Again, Yaqub and Barkat couldn't follow all of this explanation, but understood about the resistance and present danger. The old man brought their coffee, and told Philippe more. In the broad river valley beyond those villages, the Germans were now blowing up bridges and railway lines and forcing the villagers to dig huge anti-tank ditches across the valley. They were also fortifying positions up in the hills. Anything to slow down the American advance. It would not be safe to cross the border in any of the usual places. 'We change our plan,' Philippe said, without trying to summarise. As they drank their bitter coffee, he talked rapidly with the old man. In the end, he seemed resolved.

There was something in the way that all these people unquestioningly accepted Philippe, provided him with the latest information, and helped him plan, that made Yaqub finally realise that these were no casual encounters. These mountain people were like a trusted network of information and help. He pointed at Philippe and the old man.

'Resistance?'

But Philippe just smiled and put his finger to his lips, as if such things were better not discussed.

9

Schnapps

It was an early start on Friday morning. When they drove up to the railway station, Saira's heart sank. She'd been expecting an intimate stroll along winding paths, crossing the border with a guide who would recreate the experience of the passeurs leading a handful of prisoners to safety and freedom. Instead the car-park was thronged with all these professional-looking walkers. There must have been nearly a hundred of them.

She'd been looking forward to shaking off the gloom that had filled her at the concentration camp yesterday, and to sharing the sense of joy that must have been her grandfather's as he escaped from the Nazi tyranny of the camps and crossed into France. She wanted to be able to tell her grandmother what his walk must have been like and to celebrate with Will his triumph over adversity. When they'd looked again at the map last night, she'd understood for the first time quite how far he must have walked. And now this very private moment had become as public as the death camps had become. A tourist trail, in fact.

It was hard even to spot who their guide must be among the huddles of walkers, but someone seemed to be regrouping the sight-seers into cars ready to move on from the railway station to the start of the path. This station, she thought, must have been the last stop before the station where the trains disgorged their convoys of prisoners for the death camp. She shivered and Will looked concerned. 'Just imagining we were bound for Le Struthof, not a day's hike for pleasure,' she explained.

Will obligingly juggled the two images in his mind as a man waved their car forward to join the others. He imagined the defeated huddles of men shuffling forward to their fate. And here was their procession of cars winding up the opposite hillside, through farms and hamlets where people were just setting off for work down in the town. The convoy came to a halt near a forestry house, parking as best they could on the edge of the forest, at the foot of a broad track.

Again, this was not what Saira had imagined. This was no secret way through dense forest. She eyed the other walkers as they pressed closer to the guide, – all those walking poles, leg protectors, map pouches, fleeces with club badges, many-pocketed rucksacks, and even a pedometer. A few dogs were scampering round as their owners chatted loudly about other walks they'd shared. Distances, times, endurance. Was this just like any old walk to them, with a bit of history thrown in? And then their guide began to speak. Some of his words were blown away by the wind, and his French was a bit too rapid for her, but she began to understand parts.

She thought he was only born towards the end of the war, but his father was one of one of the original smugglers. His father hadn't been conscripted to fight, as he had an essential job on the railway, but he also knew the forest well. And when distraught parents asked him to help their sons to cross the border to avoid being conscripted into the occupying German army, he had risked everything to help them. 'His boss was very understanding and asked no questions.' The guide said that his parents hadn't talked much about the war while he was growing up, but as his father got older, in his seventies, he and his friends would reminisce together about the old days, as they sat drinking in the bar. And one day the old men had the idea of walking the rough route together, and later still of turning it into a commemorative walk. They got a real kick out of re-living the old days. And after his father's death, the walks were still very popular with all kinds of people. Groups like this were spreading the word, and school children were learning a lot. It was important to pass these things on to future generations. So, when he, the son, retired recently, he decided to help to lead the walks. He welcomed them all warmly to the smugglers' trail.

Will got the impression that the walking group was from a different area, as their guide, like several of the people they'd met, was keen to explain the complexities of Alsace's history. And as they set off up the broad track the guide talked also about different forestry philosophies under the French and the Germans. Saira lingered at the back of the group, wanting to sense something of the loneliness and dangers of the forest, but the chattering group ahead made that impossible. As if reading her thoughts, the guide paused again, and as she caught up he was explaining that they were following a logging track, the Route des Allemands, built for the Germans in the First World War by Polish and Russian PoWs, whereas the men like his father would have taken different routes each time, according to where the patrols were thought to be. He then pointed out an enclosed stretch of forest where foresters were trying to encourage some kind of rare bird to breed. They hadn't done French bird names at school. 'Might be a kind of grouse,' murmured Will, vaguely.

But Saira wasn't interested in grouse. The guide's mention of PoWs from the previous war encouraged her to nudge her way to the front of the group and to ask hesitantly, as they set off again, whether his father had helped any PoWs in the last war, in particular Indian ones. But his reply was disappointing. 'No, the military networks were quite separate. They were further over. And there weren't any Indians in this area.' And then he turned to answer a question about bird protection policies.

Disappointment yet again. She'd hoped for more, Perhaps they should give up on trying to trace her grandfather's escape route. 'Further over' was just so vague. And anyway, she didn't think her grandfather had fallen in with anything as organised as a military network.

With the new plan made, Philippe led them out of the dingy house, and took a track leading downhill, away from the border. Yaqub turned briefly and waved to the old man watching from his doorway. But Barkat stopped dead in his tracks, furious. He wanted to head straight towards the fighting, not run away from it. He refused to follow.

Yaqub had a hard job calming him, reasoning that he needed to stay free to help in the liberation, and not throw it all away by running into the arms of the Germans and being put straight back into a PoW camp. Also they couldn't endanger Philippe still further. He had continued walking and was looking back impatiently at them. Yaqub sensed that he was worried because he needed to return to his parish duties back in his town before anyone became suspicious. He was relieved when Barkat caved in and walked on downhill with only the occasional muttered 'Not scared!'

They were both relieved when Philippe turned off the downhill track and threaded his way through the trees following the contour of the mountainside for the next two hours. The forest looked much like all the forest they had trudged through, and it was hard to feel as if they were making progress. But at last Yaqub whispered encouragingly, 'You know, we're finally starting to go uphill again.'

Just as it was getting light, they found themselves in front of an isolated house with a lorry parked outside. Was this part of Philippe's plan? Some small children, looking half-dressed, not yet in their warm top layers of clothing, came running out to Philippe, delighted to see him. So he was well-known, even in this far-flung household.

Their father was obviously not expecting Philippe, and seemed agitated as they went indoors, talking together. Yaqub and Barkat squatted down on their haunches in the corridor and played with the children who showed them their wooden toys. It felt wonderful to relax for a few minutes. But then their mother came and rounded up her children, scolding, as if she was frightened for them. Perhaps it was dangerous for the children to have seen the escapees. Perhaps they would not understand the need for silence. Perhaps they would unwittingly betray their father.

As the children were hustled away, Philippe led them into the kitchen and introduced them to Mathieu, though by now Yaqub was beginning to suspect that the men who were helping them were not using their real names. Mathieu was shaking his head. Philippe explained that Mathieu had been ordered to do some work for the Germans that day, which complicated everything. Yaqub could tell that Philippe was pleading with him. The word 'gazogène' kept being mentioned. And Mathieu was shaking his head. Eventually he seemed to give in. Philippe smiled and turned to Yaqub and Barkat.

'It is very dangerous for him and for you. But it is possible.'

As they trudged up the next stretch of forest track, Will began to wonder why a small van was doggedly tailing them. They were getting close to the border, which the Germans had marked out after the Franco-Prussian war with sandstone boundary stones. This would have been the most dangerous part of the journey, with the border heavily patrolled. To have failed at this point would have been terrible. Beyond the boundary the terrain was much more open. Had it been like that in the war? Would the forest have been more or less extensive, Saira wondered. Even if the passeurs succeeded in crossing the border unseen, they must have feared a bullet in their back on this bare rooftop of the mountain.

The tension was broken as the group paused again and gathered round a small monument, by the path, to the passeurs and to the earlier Polish and Russian prisoners. As they stopped, the mystery van stopped too. Will joked that it must be the stretcher party. But to his surprise an elderly man got out of it and opened the battered doors. He produced two trays on which he set out rows of tiny glasses. Then, with a flourish he brought out a bottle of schnapps and filled the glasses.

The walkers passed the drinks round and the elderly man made a short speech, though Will and Saira could not follow all of it. Was he one of the original passeurs, they wondered. He looked about the right age. A woman overheard their English voices and explained that he had been one of the young men who had been incorporated into the German army, and that he would never have dared to try to escape, because by then everyone had heard of the dreadful reprisals against the families of men who deserted. But he wanted to honour the memory of the passeurs, who risked their lives to save other young men from the battle front. Apparently one of the original passeurs had always taken a celebratory drink of schnapps once he was safely across the frontier and in occupied France. 'So he now offers this drink in memory of their bravery!'

As Will raised his delicate glass to their memory, then took a swig of the burning liquid, he felt in touch with the epic escape and border crossing of Grandfather Yaqub and his friend and added his own silent toast to them.

'Very restorative!' he murmured, returning his empty glass to the beaming van driver. The whole group seemed re-energised, and when the guide suggested that they might like to make a detour and climb the hill ahead to see the splendid views, they set off across the grassy ridge at quite a pace. Saira couldn't believe that the wartime escapees would have braved this bare hilltop. The guide was too far ahead for them to hear all his words, but they thought he was saying that the trees up here had been killed off. Something about differences in forestry policies and types of trees between France and Germany. So perhaps it would have looked different during the war. And anyway, those men wouldn't have been panting off on some stupid detour just to see the view!

It was of course a fine view, and as the cameras came out, and the water bottles, and people sat down for a short break, Saira stood a little apart, reflecting once again on her grandmother's surprising request. She couldn't imagine that in such a tense situation as walking night after night to freedom any PoW – let alone her rather strict grandfather – would have time to form a relationship with a girl. No, it just wasn't plausible. But whatever would have given her grandmother that idea?

The guide came over and explained that they would be setting off downhill to the village of Moussey. This was the

French village which had fed, sheltered and made false ID cards for the smuggled escapees. Will got out their map, and worked out the position of their border crossing and the hilltop. From there it took him a while to find Moussey. Saira leaned over him. She was beginning to feel a bit tired. 'Where?' 'It's a bit further than you want to know! But downhill all the way.'

They set off down a smaller path towards the lush forest below. Saira could have hit Will when he cheerfully commented on how much prettier the forest was on this side of the border, and how he thought the narrow footpaths which zig-zagged downhill gave a better feel for the original route than the broad track they'd followed uphill. All she was aware of was that her toes were being rammed against her boots by the steep slope and that there was no sign of the village ahead. She tried to imagine her grandfather and his friend walking for miles night after night through rain, snow and ice. She told herself she was a wimp, and plodded, uncomplaining, downhill, and then was forced to agree that it was much prettier.

It was Will who chattered on (perhaps he was trying to divert her attention from her tiredness). He was wondering aloud what route her grandfather had taken. 'He must have crossed the border much further north. There would be no reason for them to come so far south. Pity though. I'd like to imagine him on this path, having crossed the border where we crossed!'

'Well he'd hardly have come down these footpaths,' she replied grumpily, 'not in that lorry contraption!'

Yaqub, in fact, never saw where he crossed the border. Mathieu's business that day for the Germans meant that he would be officially crossing the border in his lorry. It was always highly risky to try and smuggle people over, but he was less likely to be searched on an authorised journey. What he and Philippe proposed was that he would use some of the scarce petrol the Germans allowed him for their errands in his ordinary petrol tank.

That would leave the tank of the gazogène – the wartime fuel generator – free for them to hide in. As soon as Philippe said 'gazogène' and mimed them climbing in through the top of it, Yaqub understood. Gazogènes had become more common with the shortage of petrol. They had seen small gazogènes on the back of cars and larger ones on lorries. Ever curious, he had been told that these devices enabled a gas to be generated by burning hand-sized pieces of wood or charcoal in a large tank and the gas could then be fed directly to the carburettor of the vehicle as an alternative to petrol. But he would never have imagined that one day he would be stuffed into one of these fuel tanks to be driven across the border. 'Wait till we tell our fellow-prisoners about this!' he enthused.

'What makes you think we will see them again?' Barkat was still feeling negative. But then he brightened up. 'But imagine riding in a lorry under the very noses of the Germans!'

Mathieu's wife returned without the children. She sat the men down at the huge kitchen table, and brought them steaming chicory coffee, bread spread with delicious dark-berried jam and slices of a strong smelling cheese that made Barkat wrinkle his nose before he tucked in. She was clearly worried about her husband trying to smuggle Yaqub and Barkat over the border. It sounded as if she was trying to dissuade him. He sighed, and spread his hands out on the table, helplessly. 'Big danger!' Yaqub remembered what they had heard at the previous house, about the current German reprisals, deportations and shootings. He heard the children laughing in another room, and felt guilty about the risks their father would be running for them.

However, Mathieu was clearly a man of considerable courage, and over breakfast, he started to make his plans. He pointed to Yaqub, recognising that he had understood more of what was involved. As the cylinder would only hold one man, Yaqub should make the first journey. His wife would hide Barkat in an outbuilding. If Mathieu succeeded in crossing the border safely and also had no problems returning that day, then he would risk a second crossing with Barkat. But his wife still looked uneasy. The current situation was making the Germans very tense and suspicious. And unpredictable, he agreed.

Philippe was the first to leave. He faced a long walk back to his parish. Yaqub and Barkat felt sad to part company with this brave, compassionate man, who had brought them so far and made such an effort to communicate and to learn more about their lives. They hugged him and patted him on the back, and kept repeating words of gratitude, till he broke away, wishing them God speed, and set off down the track in a north-easterly direction towards his town. Yaqub was surprised at his lack of caution, till he realised that without them the pastor could, of course, walk openly.

Then Mathieu beckoned Yaqub to follow him to his lorry. He seemed to be holding his children very tightly to him as he kissed them goodbye, as if he feared he might never see them again. Then he opened the metal cover and waited a few minutes before helping Yaqub to squeeze into its blackened cylinder. There was just enough room for Yaqub as he crouched, feet on the residues of part-burnt wood at the bottom of the tank. As the lorry started up and lurched off in the opposite direction from Philippe, along the rutted forest track towards the border, Yaqub couldn't help wondering when and where (or even if) he and Barkat would be reunited.

The snow may have partially cushioned the jolts and bumps, but nevertheless, after a while in his confined doubled-up position and with only very small air vents, Yaqub began to feel very sick. He hoped he would not disgrace himself by vomiting in the cylinder. That would definitely draw attention to his presence. Fortunately the lorry eventually turned onto a proper road and began to grind uphill.

As the road levelled out, Mathieu braked and came to an abrupt halt. Yaqub began to feel better with the lack of movement, though he did not dare to stretch out. For through the metal walls of the cylinder, he heard peremptory German voices. Had they reached the border? Or was this possibly a spot-check? Or was this where the lorry was collecting or delivering? Probably not, as there were no thuds or bangs. But he could hear, he was sure, the rustling of papers. German officials always had lists of everything.

He juddered as the lorry driver jumped down from his cab, slamming the door. Mathieu's voice sounded firm and respectful as he answered questions. He didn't sound nervous. Yaqub sensed that he was standing right the other side of the gazogène cylinder, between himself and the German. But then an order was barked out, and Yaqub heard footsteps, possibly Mathieu's, moving away and receding. Was something wrong?

There was a long silence. But Yaqub sensed that the German had not moved away. And then he froze in shock. Right against his ear came a loud staccato drumming. It reverberated. Repeated. Echoed. It must be the German, getting impatient. He was drumming his fingers against the cylinder. Such a thin sheet of metal separated Yaqub from discovery.

Then a dreadful thought struck him. The cylinder should be hot, possibly too hot to touch. Normally there would be something burning inside to create gas to fuel the engine. The German would realise that. Border guards must be constantly alert for trickery. Yaqub did not dare breathe as he waited for the realisation to dawn, and the shots to be fired. One into the cylinder. One at his brave driver.

Then, to his immense relief, Yaqub heard Mathieu's voice. It sounded urgent. He must have recognised the extreme danger. He heard the shuffling of papers again. Maybe the driver been to get them stamped. Maybe the guard's thoughts were focussed only on the correctness of the papers. Mathieu climbed back into his cab, and the lorry moved off. And still there were no shots.

It was a few minutes before Yaqub dared shuffle into a more comfortable position. It felt as if they were going downhill but he no longer trusted his senses. He was too numbed in mind and body. All he could hope was that it had been the border, that they were now in France, and that they wouldn't get stopped again.

Neither Saira nor Will had expected to end their walk in another graveyard. But when they were finally in sight of Moussey, a large group that had pre-booked a meal went straight into the village, while the rest picnicked on the edge of the forest. The instructions were to rendez-vous at 16.00 hours at the church. Will felt himself stiffening up as they tried to relax over their sandwiches. He also still felt hungry. He wished that the hotel had packed up more sandwiches for them, for it had been quite a trek. He envied the walking group eating a proper meal in the village. Perhaps they could find a bakery. So they set off in good time for the rendez-vous, downhill and through the village. Unfortunately for him they didn't see a bread shop.

But at the top of the church steps, a few well-dressed people were waiting. They were obviously not their fellow-walkers. They greeted Saira and Will warmly, one of the men switching to English as soon as he realised where they were from. 'English! Then you must come and see our graveyard!'

Mystified, they followed the man. Perhaps he was the mayor or a teacher, with a passion for monuments. Then they understood. Against the west wall was a row of about ten graves similar to the two they'd seen at Schoenenbourg. Commonwealth war graves. Some had flowers on and one had a photograph. Saira eagerly scanned the names. No Indian names. 'Were they prisoners?'

'Parachutists. Mainly shot or executed.' Seeing how shocked they looked, the man explained further that they were all parachuted in by the British, then hidden in the woods, along with weapons, petrol, ammunition and even Jeeps, to await the approach of the Americans (who would be far from their supply bases). 'Many people from the village were involved in helping the resistance. My parents lived near the edge of the forest. I was only a small child then. But even so I remember that some of the parachutists would come down to our house after dark and my parents would feed them. My parents said that it felt as if the Americans were taking a long time to get here, as if there was no hurry. And in the meantime the Germans had plenty of time to hunt down the parachutists, the maquis and all the local people suspected of helping them.'

Will looked at the dates on the tombs. Some were killed in August 1944, maybe around the time that Grandfather Yaqub and his friend started planning to escape and join the Americans. Others had not been found and shot until October, which wouldn't have been long before the two Indian prisoners set out on their long trek.

'They were brave men, the British, and we honour them every year. But the Germans were determined to punish the village as well. All the time they were searching the forests. In one raid, as well as munitions they found a bag containing a list of our villagers who had taken part in the parachute landings. Fifty-two were taken to a nearby prison camp, some were executed at le Struthof and some were transferred to Dachau. Later another forty-two villagers were deported, then even more. Very few returned. Look at the plaque inside the Church.'

Although this was not her grandfather's story, Saira felt very moved by these well-tended graves, and also by the fate of the villagers. After yesterday's visit, she could imagine the suffering of those sent up to the cloud-shrouded camp.

As they turned to go back to the church, her eyes fell on a family grave in the opposite row that included a son who had died in captivity. Her thoughts wandered back to him as they joined the rest of the walkers in the church pews and half-listened to a talk about how those smuggled over the border were helped by the village. She stared at the statue of Joan of Arc looking to the sky and inspiring her countrymen onwards and upwards, and thought of the cost of each act of resistance. Will was looking at the nearby commemorative plaque and counting the number of villagers who'd died: five in the army, three civilians killed, and a long list of those who'd been deported and died in the camps: the repeated surnames danced as he counted, so many from the same families, one hundred and forty-four names in all. A terrible price for freedom. He wondered what had happened to the men who had helped Saira's grandfather. Would they have survived that appalling time of reprisals? Would they too have ended up at the

Schirmeck death camp? But, since Grandfather Yaqub had never gone into the specific details of his journey, with his death the names of those who had helped him and of their villages had vanished. Now they had no way of knowing if they were commemorated somewhere or had died with their help to Grandfather Yaqub and others unrecorded.

After their heart-stopping checkpoint, Yaqub was relieved that the lorry was still on a proper road, but then the driver turned onto a rougher surface. Yaqub wondered whether this was part of the Mathieu's work for the Germans. Perhaps their next stop would be even more dangerous. He was beginning to feel ill again. He wished he knew what was happening. The smell was catching his throat. He told himself he would be all right. He had survived so far. Even with a German tapping the metal against his shoulder. It wouldn't be long now. And Philippe had arranged this. He trusted Philippe, he was a good man. He wouldn't lead him into a trap.

But it seemed an eternity before the lorry stopped. As Mathieu opened the lid of the gazogène tank and the fresh cold air gusted in, Yaqub began to recover. He took his rescuer's hand and climbed shakily out. He noticed that Mathieu's hands were also shaking badly and that he looked very scared as he pointed to the cylinder, tapped it with his fingers and then made the gesture of firing at himself. He too had obviously been terrified by their narrow escape.

Yaqub swayed on his feet as the ground seemed to lurch up towards his face. To distract himself, he focussed on a more distant point, a sliced rock-face. He seemed to be in a small quarry in the hillside. It was a secluded spot. There were no signs of any labourers. Perhaps the Germans currently had other things on their mind than supervising the extraction of monumental slabs of rock.

Mathieu pushed him towards a small shack at the edge of the quarry. Inside there was a rough table with a wooden chest up against the wall for seating. He unloaded the pickaxes from the box, stacking them against the wall, and indicated that Yaqub should climb inside. Yaqub wished he could stretch his legs and body a bit more, but did not complain.

'Bad today!' Mathieu said carefully, gesturing over his shoulder to explain that he had to get on with his real task. Then he shrugged helplessly, as if to indicate that he might not be able to return that day. Yaqub knew that if he was the driver, he would be too scared to repeat the trip after their narrow escape. Covering him with an old sack, Mathieu closed the chest, and left the hut. Yaqub felt very vulnerable. He did not know where he was. He wondered if he really was over the border. He didn't know if Barkat would join him or what would happen if he did. He felt exhausted after his long walk the previous night, followed by the bumpy lorry journey.

He must have fallen fast asleep, curled up in the chest. So he didn't know how much later it was when he was roused by the sound of a lorry approaching then stopping. Was it the same lorry? It was possible that the muffled sounds he could hear were those of his friend being helped out of the lorry's hiding place. He desperately hoped so.

It was wonderful to hear the shack door open and Barkat's low voice calling out, 'Yaqub!' He flung open the chest lid and tried to climb out. But his legs had gone to sleep and he stumbled. Barkat rushed over and hugged him fiercely, then massaged his legs and helped him out. He was quite surprised to see that there were two men in the shadows behind Barkat, – Mathieu and a dark, wiry stranger. They were waving their arms triumphantly and kissing each other on the cheeks. Yaqub had never seen English or German men doing that!

And then it struck him forcibly that they had actually crossed the border. After all these nights of walking, they must now be in France. Soon they would be able to join the advancing American army. He looked at Barkat, hardly able to believe that they had made it to safety. 'We've done it!' Then he laughed, telling Barkat how fearsome he looked, covered in black. Barkat retaliated that he didn't look too clean either, and they rubbed at their faces with their dirty sleeves, which made very little difference.

Mathieu was clearly telling the Frenchman about the dangers of their journey, for he was tapping his fingers, and the Frenchman was looking grave. Was he to be their new guide, Yaqub wondered. But Mathieu did not introduce him. He gave a big sigh at the end of his recital and then smiled and pulled a small rather grubby bottle out of his pocket. He raised the bottle, uttered something celebratory and took a long swig before passing it to the thin man, who did the same.

When the bottle was passed to Yaqub, he thought it smelt abominable, so he merely raised the bottle, murmured something vague and passed it hastily to Barkat. But Barkat was a great actor. Looking every inch as if he was one of their officers in the mess, he lifted the bottle and said in impeccable English,

'Cheers!'

10

Scorched earth

'Sheeers!' Mathieu tried to imitate Barkat. Smiling still, he tucked the nearly empty bottle back in his pocket, slapped the three men on the back, and climbed into his lorry. He looked light-hearted now he had safely delivered his loads. For a while they could hear the growl of the low gears as he climbed the hill, then all fell silent. Yaqub thought of his children rushing up to greet him and his wife's relief and felt very grateful to him for the risks he had taken for them.

They soon realised that their new French guide had no words of English and not much German, but he was a great mime artiste. As they waited for it to get dark again, they almost laughed out loud as he demonstrated how he was a keen cyclist. So after that they referred to him, between themselves, as bicycle-man. They stuck to that name even though he went on to indicate that he was a French forestry worker and that he hated seeing all his beloved trees being sent as timber to Germany. They wondered if that was why he was prepared to act against the Germans and help two unknown allied soldiers – a small revenge for his lost trees, perhaps.

At nightfall they left the hut and followed bicycle-man. He moved fast and stealthily and was very fit. The snow was deeper on this side of the mountain, as he led them rapidly downhill from the quarry. They were crossing more open land, probably high pastures, with copses and numerous small streams. They caught occasional glimpses of hamlets, but never followed the streams downhill towards them. During a brief rest, as they squatted in a snowy hollow in the shelter of a bright-berried holly bush, Yaqub noticed that their guide was listening attentively to the exact location of the gunfire. 'Americains!' he said firmly, pointing ahead. 'Americans!' agreed Yaqub fervently.

In recent days they had heard the shelling ahead of them and had seen the sky flushing red. But as they followed bicycle-man's pointing finger, the red arc was getting wider and brighter. After several hours of walking silently through pasture then forest towards the glow, their guide seemed uneasy. He looked around for an open spot from which to check the source of the brightness. Then, as he headed for a rocky promontory, the whole sky seemed to flame.

Listening carefully for patrols, Yaqub and Barkat followed him out from the protective trees towards the viewpoint. Although they were safely across the border they were still very cautious, as Philippe had told them that the German mountain troops could be hard to spot in their white camouflage gear. On top of the rock, they stopped speechless. Ahead of them in the distance, a huge area was being devastated by flames. This was no mere village. This must be the town they were heading for. Philippe had told them that they should find the Americans had reached a town called Saint Dié and that they would be safe when they got there. 'Les Bosches' growled their guide in despair. The Americans had obviously not reached the town in time to prevent the Germans from laying waste to it.

Then bicycle-man pointed silently to the road leading from

the town and running along the plain far below them. There was an unusual amount of night traffic visible from above, even compared with what they had seen on the other side of the border. But this time it was all going in the opposite direction to them. They could see long lines of lorry head-lights reflecting off the snow on either side of the road. Could this be the mighty German army in retreat?

The morning after their 'stroll across the border', as Will persisted in calling it, once he found how delightfully it riled her, Saira hobbled across their hotel room to the shower. She remembered their decision at the end of the walk to drive on to the town of Saint Dié, close to the village she'd pinpointed where her grandfather's Russian had lived. It had taken them nearly an hour driving in the dark and then they'd had to find a hotel. The rest of the evening must have passed in a haze of exhaustion. Will was thinking, regretfully, that last night had been the first night they hadn't made love. How could they have been so tired that they'd fallen asleep as soon as their heads touched their pillows? They were in danger of becoming like an old married couple.

In the shower, Saira tried to be firm with herself. Now that they'd gained some insight into her grandfather's captivity, his underground hide-out, and his journey across the border, maybe they shouldn't just dismiss her grandmother's concerns, but should be bold in asking questions and really trying to find out more. She realised that, whilst she did not want to discover anything disquieting, it would add a little romantic spice to their quest. Somewhere very close to here, Grandfather had reached the end of his journey across the mountains and reached the house of a Russian, where, just maybe, in the midst of war, he had succumbed (though surely innocently) to love. This was a day for taking risks and looking confident, rather than asking half-hearted questions. She packed away her crumpled walking clothes, and pulled out of her case the top that Will chosen for her. He hadn't seen her in it yet, somehow it had seemed too flamboyant for home. She pulled it over her head and smoothed it down over her hips. Perfect with some clean black trousers.

Behind her Will whooped appreciatively. He'd liked it as soon as he saw it – those swirling scarlet anemones splashed onto that black woollen stuff and those wide sleeves like some kind of kimono. A must-have for Saira. And the first time he'd ever bought clothes for a woman – a bit embarrassing, but look how great it looked. Best not say 'exotic' out loud, though it was. 'Maybe a touch over-dressed, but I feel great. I can almost believe my feet don't ache!' And Saira swept down the stairs ahead of him to the Hotel du Centre's small, dark bar which opened onto one of the town's main streets. The bar was quite busy – mainly men behind newspapers, who seemed to have dropped in for a coffee before work. She was unaware of their appreciative glances as she headed for a free table.

The owner came bustling up with their coffee and croissants. He seemed eager to chat. Saira really couldn't remember much about their arrival last night. But it seemed as if they had told him about Grandfather and his escape, for he announced that after their interesting conversation, he'd got out some old photos and post cards from that time. Would they like to see them after breakfast? Will hesitated, thinking Saira would be keen to locate her grandfather's last refuge, but Saira, touched by the hotelier's interest, agreed, thanking him.

After their second coffee, when most of the businessmen had disappeared, the owner, introducing himself as Gérard, came back with a photograph album and a book, and started talking in a mixture of hotel-English and French with a bit of German thrown in. It was a curiously relaxing mix and very easy to follow. He prefaced his presentation by observing that of course her grandfather would hardly have come to Saint Dié at that particular time, November 1944, as that was when the Germans had burned the town to the ground before retreating from the Americans in a – he didn't know the term in English, but Will thought it must translate as 'scorched earth policy'. 'Yes, they burned everything. They even dynamited our cathedral, despite their promises that they would not.'

Saira looked thoughtfully at them both. 'Grandfather said that they'd been heading for a town. This must have been it. The one they saw in flames ahead of them. The reason they had to take a different route. How terrible. What happened to all the people? To your family?'

Gérard opened the album and pointed sadly at a postcard of an elegant, three-storey building, with long windows with shutters and tiny balconies. This, he told them, was how their family hotel had once looked, before the war. And that was his father as a small child. He was four when the war began. There was his grandfather in his army uniform. That formidable looking woman was his grandmother. She'd held the whole family together after her two oldest sons, mere teenagers, were rounded up by the Germans and sent as forced labour to Germany. 'She thought they'd been taken to dig trenches somewhere nearby. They only took enough food for one day. They were gone for many, many months – nearly two years, in fact. That's my uncle some time after he came back. Look how thin he still is.' A mournful young man with a moustache stared back at them. Saira looked at Gérard, horrified, wondering what his uncles had done. 'But it was like that for all families. All the able men and adolescent boys were taken,' he told them. 'Look at our town.' He opened the book, flipping through the pages of black and white illustrations. Will had seen photos of bombed towns and villages before. But what horrified him most was to see the rubble, piled up in neat stacks all along the grid of roads, with no walls left standing, nowhere obvious to start re-constructing.

To his surprise, Gérard started to laugh. It must have been quite comical, he explained. Everyone living on their side of the river was ordered to evacuate shortly before it was destroyed – anywhere – the Germans didn't care where. His grandmother's first thought was to save all the hotel's best bottles of wine from the cellar and she packed them, and whatever food remained, into a small handcart, under the embroidered linen. His father remembered carrying all the heavy cutlery slung over his shoulder in a pillowcase which clanked and jangled all the way. They all had to wear as many layers of warm clothes as they could, so looked really fat, and his younger sister was carrying silver candlesticks in both hands, with firm orders to hide them under her coat if they saw any Bosches. But the Germans must have been too busy looting other evacuated homes, and they crossed the old bridge safely before it too was blown up. Then Gérard looked serious. They were fortunate, as they had family on the other side of the river. Other families had to set off through the snow, not knowing where to go.

Saira was still surprised by how intimately some people were prepared – in just casual encounters – to share their family history. Her own grandfather seemed to have found it so hard. And as she thought of him, her heart lurched. She'd thought they were so close. But how much had he hidden from them all?

'Does that mean, if your town was completely destroyed,

that the same would have happened to the hamlet where my grandfather ended up? To Forge-les-Eaux? It's so close to here. I'd somehow just assumed it would still be as it was back then.' She stopped, feeling Will's eyes on her and realising she'd interrupted Gérard's story rather rudely. But he smiled and reassured her that she would find it much the same as in the old days. Yes, there would have been fierce fighting all around Forge-les-Eaux, but that was a bit earlier, before the Germans began the policy of burning whole towns and villages behind them.

Suddenly, Saira was anxious to get on with the quest, almost as if the hamlet might disappear while they were talking, before she had a chance to see it. But she was careful to take her time over thanking Gérard for his kindness in showing them his photos, and asking him the best way out of town. And Will suggested they should keep their room and return to the Hotel du Centre that night. He had a feeling that her grandfather's story wouldn't be quite over by nightfall.

✻ 🐾 🐾 🐾

Clearly there was no point in proceeding towards the burning town. Their guide indicated that they should turn aside, make their way down to the plain, cross the busy road, and head for a wooded area on the plain, circling round the massive conflagration ahead.

They crawled down from the promontory into the forest's dark embrace and bicycle-man led them zig-zagging down the hillside. They at times followed or crossed old ditches that seemed out of place in the middle of the forest. They took a short rest in one of these. It was dry and provided excellent shelter. Their guide risked lighting a cigarette. Then he mimed shooting and ducking down and, after some puzzlement, they

183

worked out that he meant that these were trenches from the previous great war.

'Did I ever tell you that two of my father's brothers were killed in the trenches on the Western Front in that war?' said Barkat.

'Often!'

But the thought of the great war such a short time before, with all its deaths, was a sobering one. Yaqub fell silent.

After half an hour of stealthy descent, they started to come across more cart tracks. Sometimes they followed them for a short distance, but more often they crossed them. At this lower level there were signs of recent tree felling and logging. The distinctive resin smell brought back vivid memories of their old PoW work camp. Yaqub wondered aloud how their old companions were. Barkat wondered if the piles of smaller logs meant that they were getting near villages. The sounds of the heavy lorries below them were getting closer. Bicycle-man indicated that they must cross the road well before daybreak.

Their pace slowed as they flitted from tree to tree, always alert. Their guide scanned the gaps between the trees of the dark forest carefully, and chose a place where a broad tongue of trees sloped right down to the road. They found themselves on a rocky outcrop which had caused the road to bend round it. It should be possible to climb down the rock's crevices whilst remaining unobserved in its shadows. Then they had to hope for a break in the traffic.

Close-up it did not look as if the procession of vehicles was an army in retreat. There were few soldiers to be seen other than the drivers. Rather it looked like a giant furniture-moving convoy. The vehicles were stacked high with elegant furniture, timber, metal, paper, textile machinery, bales of fabric, milk churns, vases and paintings. Loot from the burning town.

After half an hour of quietly watching the endless convoy, they heard a clucking sound as one of the lorries beyond the rock came to an abrupt halt. Before the vehicles behind the broken-down lorry could organise themselves to overtake, their guide beckoned them to cross the road. The churned-up slush left no trace of their hasty crossing, but the bare white field on the other side was a clean sheet, which would show every footprint when the headlights started moving again. They just had to hope that the booty-laden Germans had other preoccupations at present. They ran.

They were very relieved to reach a copse of trees before the procession resumed its remorseless progress. They paused to catch their breath. Then they continued, following the lines of field ditches and channels till they reached the railway track. Yaqub and Barkat were surprised to see the metal lines covered with snow, but their guide mimed, with apparent pleasure, that explosions had put the railway out of action somewhere nearer the town.

As they made their way across the fields beyond the railway, the sky slowly began to get lighter. Despite their tiredness, their guide increased the pace, heading for the low wooded hills ahead. It was a pleasure to feel the trees closing protectively around them as they reached the woods. They were able to slow down again, but still walked steadily between the snowy roots, then started climbing gently uphill again. It was lighter now. A grey, freezing dawn. After a while Yaqub stopped and sniffed. Wood smoke. As they edged forward cautiously, they heard the unexpected sound of children's laughter.

Yaqub and Barkat looked at each other in dismay. They were exhausted. They did not fancy another detour. Bicycle-man motioned them to stay hidden. He walked towards the laughter. He was gone for a disconcertingly long time. Yaqub and Barkat crouched behind a tangle of brambles, not daring even to whisper. They were determined they would not be re-captured after such a long walk out of captivity. But when he reappeared he was smiling. He even made mouth and hand gestures – was he meaning food? He beckoned them to follow him.

Surprisingly close to them, through the screen of trees, stood a ruined barn. When they looked closely, they realised that one end of the barn had once been a house, though its roof had fallen in and the upper storey was crumbling. Knocking the snow off their boots, they followed the man as he pushed open a battered wooden door and led them into the barn. Inside was a barrier of old carts and prams, some still loaded with packages. Old men and small boys were sitting huddled on the straw against the comforting warmth of a wall of chomping black and white cows. The men's querulous voices broke off as they looked suspiciously at the two dark-skinned men, but they took their pipes from their mouths and waved them through the broken internal door beyond which the chatter of women could be heard.

A wonderful warmth enveloped them. A dusty old stove was roaring. Huge casseroles were steaming and boiling on top of it. And round it were a group of sturdy, sharp-eyed women with small children on their laps or clutching their skirts. The crowded room looked as if it had not been used for a long time. There were holes in the window panes which had been stuffed with sacking, and thick cobwebs hung from the beams. The few chairs were broken and dusty and there was no cloth on the battered table. But the sound of good humoured laughter hung in the dusty air

One still-laughing woman waved at the stove as if to apologise that nothing was ready yet, but another rummaged in a basket and produced a loaf which she cut into chunks, whilst a third one headed to one of the prams in the barn and brought back a large ham from which she cut generous slices. Some milk was boiled up and poured, together with coffee from a tin pot, into three bowls. Bicycle-man crossed himself and said a quick prayer of thanks over his portion, whilst Yaqub added his now customary prayer of thanks (and one for forgiveness for eating the pig meat, – but it was a long time since their bread and jam at Mathieu's). He was surprised that this ramshackle house had enough food to offer strangers in the midst of war.

The women watched them eat with fascination, as if they somehow expected them to eat differently from them. One of them leaned forward to touch Yaqub's hand. She held it and turned it over, examining the skin colours, and stroked his wrist. It was a gesture of curiosity but trust.

After they had eaten and were warmed through and their boots and clothes were dry, bicycle-man put on his outdoor garments. He indicated that Yaqub and Barkat should stay there. Only he would go out. He should be working now. They assumed he was also telling them that he would send someone to help them on the final stage of their journey.

The children waved him off, then began to edge forward and touch Yaqub, though they seemed more scared of Barkat. Then, overcome with their daring, they would giggle and run back to safety. One of the children sang a few snatches of song, then collapsed in more giggles. So Yaqub sang them a song he used to sing at home with his young brothers. That was a great success, and the clamour when he finished was clearly for more.

After more songs, an older girl was dragged to the front, and the women told her all the questions they wanted her to ask the strangers in her very limited school English. They worked their way laboriously through everyone's names, places of origin (but they had never heard of India) and ages. Some of the women had sons the same age as Yaqub and Barkat, and they mimed that the sons had been taken far away.

Then all the children joined in the mime, producing a noisy tale of Germans in their village. Germans lining up all the able-bodied men and marching them away from the village at gunpoint. Germans stealing mooing animals and squawking animals. Germans taking food. Americans bombarding the surrounding villages. Germans forcing the remaining women, old men and children to evacuate their homes and village and head for the hills.

By then the boys and old men had crowded in and joined in the tale. One of the boys had been ordered by the Germans to drive their cows (Moo! Moo!) to the German HQ (Heil Hitler!) with his grandfather. Boom! Boom! The American shells had started to fall. Boom! Boom! They exploded just so close. He mimed crossing himself and falling to his knees in prayer. They prayed and still Boom! Boom! They were terrified. It was impossible to go forward. They turned round and brought the cows here instead. And now they had milk for everyone. A woman mimed how they had tried to hastily gather up all their winter food, but she had thrown any food they couldn't carry with them out of her window into the street so that the Germans wouldn't enjoy it. And then she and other villagers had pushed their loaded carts and prams through the snow and ice up into the hills to this house. This house? Yaqub thought she was saying that it fell down in the last war, but before that her grandparents had lived here. Now the forest surrounded the ruin. Now it was hidden. Safe. No Bosches.

Yaqub and Barkat slept soundly amongst the villagers and their cows. It was so friendly – almost like being back home.

The next morning and each morning after that it was the children who woke them, stroking their bristly faces, trying on their boots and demanding more songs. And each morning two of the men would return from a dawn reconnoitre with serious faces. It seemed that they had seen from a distance that the surrounding villages were burning. When Barkat tried to ask them about their village, they would shake their heads. It was safe so far. Germans gone. No Americans yet. But they did not know when they could return to it. And Yaqub and Barkat did not know when they would be able to move on.

But despite the uncertainties, the days passed in surprising gaiety. The adults were determined that the children should not feel any of their apprehension. And the children thought it was great fun to be free of school. In fact they set up a pretend school, taking it in turns to be the teacher. They found it hilarious when Yaqub and Barkat joined in, and they made them learn French numbers and even do sums in French. The 'teacher' would smack them severely across the hand every time they gave a wrong answer, as Yaqub would sometimes do just for fun. Then in return, Yaqub taught them to count to ten in 'Indian numbers', and pulled horrible faces at their mispronunciation and threatened to spank them.

It was during 'school' one day that they heard a vehicle bouncing along the snow-filled rutted track towards the ruined house. Everyone froze. A Jeep stopped and a man in American uniform strode towards them, shouting out, 'You're OK folks! Your village is safe. You've been liberated. You can go home now.' The villagers looked uncertainly at each other.

'You're the ones I've come for!' said the American cheerfully to Yaqub and Barkat. They stood up and saluted smartly. This would, after all (they hoped), be their new army. 'I've orders to take you to HQ.'

Then a girl got out of the Jeep and approached the villagers. She had dark, wavy hair held back with a comb, a pale face with big eyes, a long nose and a tiny mouth. Yaqub took in her crimson coat, her thick woollen socks and heavy boots. How delicate she was. He stared, fascinated, as she translated the American's words for the villagers.

The villagers broke into cheers. For them the long war had ended. They hugged each other, tossed the children in the air, someone produced an accordion and everyone went mad for a few moments. With tears of gratitude in their eyes they came to embrace the American and the two Indian soldiers, then broke into excited chatter again. 'They are planning a party already!' said the girl in fluent English. 'They want him to teach them the jitterbug!' It was Yaqub and Barkat's turn to look baffled.

'OK, we'll be on our way,' said the American, ignoring their request and also the celebratory bottle of wine that was being brought out. He headed for his Jeep. The children surrounded Yaqub and Barkat, linking their hands and dancing round, singing one of the songs that Yaqub had taught them. Yaqub wished they could stay and celebrate with them. Barkat was reminding him that the war wasn't over for everyone yet when the American impatiently pressed his horn and shouted, 'Hop in next to me, Eloise! You two, squash in the back! Let's go!'

The children ran down and surrounded the Jeep, begging for a ride in this marvellous American vehicle. The girl chided them gently and kissed some of them goodbye. One of the boys shyly pressed some walnuts into Yaqub's hand. 'He says you're not to forget him!' the girl translated.

Amid cheers and shouts from all the villagers, the Jeep set off. 'They are wishing you good luck,' said the girl. 'You've made quite an impression on them! And,' she giggled, 'they think you are very handsome and brave!'

The driver rested a hand on the girl's leg, rather familiarly, Yaqub thought, and bragged, 'You're wrong there! They were talking about me!' The girl gently pushed his hand away. 'Hands on the wheel, Dwight!' Unabashed, he drove down the hill and a little later along a deserted village street. The girl said that this was where the villagers were from. She seemed surprised that all the houses were unharmed. There was some abandoned food lying in the snow outside one of the houses and some hens squawking in a hen house. 'I guess the Germans just ran out of time,' said the driver laconically.

But, after they'd turned onto a bigger road, the next village was a smoking ruin. Despite the desolation, a French flag was flying defiantly above what must have been the mayor's office. Some people were busy rummaging in the ruins to see if anything could be salvaged. Others were just gazing vacantly at what had once been their homes, as if unable to take it in. But their eyes still lit up as they saw the American Jeep. However Dwight refused to stop. 'Everywhere folk want us to stop so they can thank us, touch us, give us things. But we couldn't save their village. And we can't stop now. Our guys have to keep moving forward, fighting onwards towards Germany.'

On the other side of the village, the Jeep followed a road into the hills. The driver seemed very careful as if he was still uncertain about mines. They could see wrecked vehicles and abandoned equipment poking through the snow in the forest.

When Gérard had shown them the route on the big, framed map in the hotel bar, Will had noticed that there was a monument on the pass they would have to cross. As they drove uphill towards Forge-les-Eaux he suggested stopping to look at it.

In fact they found two monuments. A huge one commemorated the Vosgian Resistance. A smaller one, on a base engraved 'Cross roads of hell 11.44,' commemorated the American 'Cotton Balers' who had fought their way up the hillside to gain this summit. 'One hundred and forty-eight killed and eight hundred and twenty-two wounded,' Will read. 'It must have been ferocious fighting up here in the snow and freezing temperatures.'

'Look at that date. Do you think Grandfather could have passed this way when some of the bodies were still lying in the forest after the battle?' They shivered. Even now there was not a good feeling to this place. Will took some photos then they climbed back in the car.

'We're on a bit of a detour,' announced the Yank as they turned onto a smaller road leading through a devastated area of the forest, where the fighting must have been fierce. 'I'm taking this brave little lady back home to her daddy! She's been running messages and translating for us all over the show, and now it's time for her to go home.'

When they stopped outside an isolated house, a huge bearded man came rushing out and scooped his daughter into his arms. 'Hey Leo!' said the driver, slapping him heartily on the back. 'She's fine and dandy! She's been a grand help to us.'

'I have a man for you,' said Léo, his face suddenly serious. He took Dwight indoors and the two of them emerged carrying a badly wounded GI. Léo was reassuring the man in his curiously accented English, telling him he would be fine now.

'Out!' the American ordered Yaqub and Barkat. 'Stay here.

Our man's in a bad way. I need to get him to hospital pretty darn quick.' He and Léo made the man as comfortable as possible across the back seat.

'Right! I'll be back for you two later,' Dwight shouted over his shoulder as he turned and roared off. 'You'll be okey-dokey with old Leo!'

As they drove down from the Americans' 'cross roads of hell', Saira realised that she'd already formed a picture of the house they were heading for. She knew from what her grandfather had said that it was a remote building in the middle of the forest. In her imagination it had become like Little Red Riding Hood's grandmother's cottage: in thick forest surrounded by wolves and huntsmen.

Once again, Will reminded her that the Russian who'd sheltered her grandfather must have died many years ago, and probably any daughter he might have had. But Saira felt a sense of rising excitement. Somewhere in that forest she was going to see the house in her grandfather's story. The house where her grandmother had convinced herself that Yaqub had fallen in love. And then she might understand what had happened to him there.

The road descended quickly in generous sweeps. The hamlet at the bottom was larger than they'd imagined. There was even a small village shop, which seemed a good place to ask if anyone knew the house where the old Russian had once lived.

A well-built woman with muscular legs bustled across to the counter from the shabby bar area of the shop where she was chatting to a couple of customers. It occurred to Will that they'd learn more if they too sat and chatted, and besides, he was ready for a coffee. Saira was quite happy to absorb a bit of atmosphere, so they ordered and sat at one of the tables. The shop-keeper and the two old men didn't seem surprised by their interest. 'Oh yes. Léo's well remembered. He lived about two kilometres from here, up that valley over there.'

'Of course he died some time ago,' said one of the wrinkled old men lugubriously.

'And his daughter, Marie, died just three years ago,' added his friend. 'She never married, sad really.'

'In the end the house was sold to some Germans. It's ironic really. The old man would have hated that. But who else would want such an isolated house? Especially in winter.' The woman spoke slowly and clearly, so they understood most of her French.

So there had been a daughter. Was there a reason she had never married? Had there once been someone …? But they were too late. The daughter was dead too. Despite Will's cautions, Saira felt shattered. Both Grandfather and his mystery girl. To cover all possibilities, Will asked in his laboured French, 'Was the daughter the last member of his family?'

Then, to Saira's relief, the woman laughed. 'Oh no. His other daughter, his younger one, Eloise, she moved away years ago when she married. She did well for herself, marrying the school teacher over at Saint Loup. I haven't seen her since her sister Marie's funeral.' Seeing their interest she added, 'But you'd easily find her there. It's near Saint Dié. I can check the phone book for her address if you like.'

Both Will and Saira were surprised by how helpful she was. But when she returned with an old envelope with an address pencilled on it, she said, 'We get a lot of people asking about Léo. Especially the Japanese.' She examined Saira, doubtfully. 'Are you Japanese?'

'First time I've been called Japanese,' muttered Saira. And she wondered what on earth the Japanese were doing, visiting this remote spot. The only thing she remembered her grandfather saying about the Japanese was that friends of his who had fought against the Japanese in Burma, had been treated far worse in Japanese prison camps than they had been in German camps. But that was all thousands of miles away, and nothing to do with France.

Feeling that her silence was awkward, Will replied on her behalf, 'No, we're English. But my wife's grandfather came here in the war. He was in the Indian Army.' That obviously meant nothing to the woman. She looked puzzled. 'Well, the Germans won't be able to tell you anything about the old days. But they won't mind you going up there, before you go and look for Eloise. They are quite friendly, though they don't speak any French. Not like Monsieur. You speak well,' she added flatteringly. 'And you're fortunate. The Germans are staying here at the moment. He's come in to buy bread every morning this week.'

As the doorbell sounded, Madame bustled off to serve an old woman who had arrived on an equally old bicycle and was now shuffling painfully towards the bread counter. They sipped their coffees. 'I can hardly believe we'll see the house! And maybe, after we've seen it, we can see this Eloise and find out if either of the sisters had any romantic feelings for my grandfather. Poor Grandmother. Fancy her having worried about it all these years.'

As they left, the shop-keeper shouted, 'Up the valley and turn left up the track by the calvary! Good luck!'

11

The Russian house

'Good luck, soldier!' shouted Léo after the retreating Jeep. 'My house becomes more like a hotel every day!' he confided to Yaqub and Barkat, ushering them indoors. 'Top quality! International clientèle!'

Yaqub and Barkat must have looked bemused. He slapped them on the back. 'Welcome! Welcome!' He waved them to the wooden chairs round the stove, sat down opposite them and pulled out his pipe. 'Now, tell me all about today's guests! Where did our American friend find you?' His daughter came and sat silently down behind her father, taking off her boots and rubbing her ankles.

Yaqub left the explanation to Barkat who knew more English words and was better at putting them together. He was embarrassed that the girl was sitting with them, listening. Now she was unselfconsciously taking off her thick socks and flexing her toes. Yaqub could see where her boots had rubbed her toes red and blistered against her white skin. Surely she hadn't been marching with the American army? And then he felt ashamed of his indelicacy. But should not her father have protected her from their gaze and sent her to be with her mother?

He made himself look away, and examined the room with the intensity of a furniture merchant. There seemed to be a lot of furniture closing in on them. Heavy, carved furniture, glossy with polish and protected with tasselled runners. Oval family photographs stared back at him from the walls, formal and disapproving. Tall gold-and-blue vases adorned the dark alcoves, and on an embroidered mat on the table stood the prettiest bowl of flowers. He focussed on these as Barkat tried to mime how they had crossed the border, crouched in the cylinder. The flowers were rich crimsons, bright blues and vibrant yellows. He hadn't seen such exotic blooms since leaving home. He stood up to touch them, and their sharp edges shocked him into the realisation that they were porcelain. He sat down, feeling foolish, hoping the girl had not noticed his mistake.

'So you have found your way across the mountains from Alsace?' Léo was asking Barkat. 'That is most admirable. Earlier this year we had Indian prisoners wandering through the forest after their prison camp in Epinal had a direct hit. Later the Americans reached us and took charge of them. I was thinking maybe the Americans had missed you up till now.' It was impossible to follow Léo's effusive speech, apart from the mention of Indians and Americans, so Barkat let it wash over him whilst smiling politely.

In the background, Yaqub could hear the murmur of women's voices. After a while, Léo called out, and his wife came in, carrying a pile of blood-stained straw and bits of linen. She was followed by an older girl with a bucket and mop. Léo spoke to them in French, obviously summarising Barkat's tale. His wife dropped an odd little bob curtsey to them, to which they weren't sure how to respond. Her older daughter, introduced as Marie, just stared in an exhausted, resigned way.

'They have been so busy with the wounded,' Léo explained as the women left the room to get on with their work. Again

Yaqub was surprised that the pretty younger daughter did not join her mother and sister. Léo noticed his gaze. 'And as for my brave daughter Eloise, she has her own work.' He leant over and patted his younger daughter's hand. 'The Germans can sometimes be so easily deceived by a charming girl on a bicycle! They are flattered that she chats to them in such excellent German. They don't realise that my clever daughter is also as fluent in English and Russian as she is in French and German. Her father's influence, of course! And they never suspect that she risks her life carrying messages between the Resistance and the Americans and between the Americans and the villages.'

Léo spoke English fluently though his accent was very strange to their ears. Yaqub now strained to make sense of his flow of words. But Barkat was not paying attention to what sounded to him like little more than a proud father boasting. He thought that the American with the strange name would be back any moment to take them to his HQ and that they would need to impress the American Commander. They had to understand the current situation so they could answer properly and efficiently. They didn't even know where the Americans' battle had been. Had it been an important one?

As his friend interrupted Léo's eulogy with his questions, Yaqub felt a bit ashamed. He felt Barkat was being disrespectful of the girl's achievements as he demanded, 'Wounded American here why? Americans fight here now? France free? Barkat help Americans fight Alsace?' A hearty laugh greeted Barkat's abrupt intervention. 'Well, the Americans are not so desperate that they'll take on an old Cossack like me! All the Americans think I'm good for is information on where to find Germans and how many, and drawing useful maps of the forest and its perils.'

'Oh Papa! You know that's not true!' his daughter teased him. 'They also look to you and Maman to bring all their dead soldiers back to life!' Yaqub wished that his English was better, so he could follow her words properly. He could only pick out a few words here and there and felt frustrated. It felt as if it had never before mattered so much. But he could sense the affection between the bearded man and his daughter.

Seeing that Barkat was still impatient for a proper answer, Léo took pity on him and explained slowly, making sure he was understood, that there had been a desperate fight, high up in the hills. He said that the Americans were not as experienced in mountain warfare as the Germans. How could they be? The poor fellows had done all their training on the plains of Texas! So it was hardly surprising that, in the heart of the high forest, an American battalion had been surrounded and cut off by the Germans. For seven days they were up on that hill, unable to move, their food, water and ammunition almost exhausted.

Seven days! Yaqub and Barkat looked at each other, remembering what it had felt like to be surrounded by the Germans. Did they surrender?

'Not the Americans!' said the girl passionately. 'They fought and fought. They were so brave!'

'They brought in more experienced troops to attempt to rescue the 'lost battalion' as they are calling them,' continued her father. 'That's what made the difference. These new troops were hard. They fought hard and they died hard.' He explained that they had to be daring. For the Germans held all the advantage points and had plenty of ammunition. The rescuers were fired on from all directions. It was a case of fighting forward from one tree to another, one rock to another. It was bitter fighting. In the end, those that survived reached the besieged battalion and saved them. 'But on the way, so many wounded, so many killed.'

'Such heroes,' sighed Eloise.

Yaqub followed the gist of Léo's dramatic re-enactment and wished that they had fought like that at Mechili. If they had, maybe she would admire them too. He knew that the Germans had a very low opinion of them for surrendering so easily. But they had only been following orders.

'She didn't see the bodies afterwards,' said her father. 'Because they were fighting in such a remote area, it took a long time to find all the wounded and dead afterwards. She was off with the Americans by then. But we saw the bodies, lined up in tarpaulins, waiting for transport. Already they are saying that they lost more men than they rescued. Such a heavy price.'

Léo sank into silence as he contemplated the waste, then remembered Barkat's original question. 'And why did some of the wounded come here?' Because of the wild remote terrain, he explained, some of the wounded soldiers weren't ever found by the stretcher parties. A few had to make their own way painfully down from the hills. If they found their way back in the direction they'd come from, they would have reached the field hospital, but for others, his isolated house, down this side of the ridge, was the first house they came across. 'That man you saw. He was nearly dead with cold by the time he crawled to our door last week. He must have lain a long time up there in the freezing temperatures before he recovered consciousness.'

Barkat sighed. He wished he could have talked to the brave survivor of such a desperate battle.

'He will be our last soldier,' Léo concluded. 'No-one else will have survived this long out there. Not since the snow came!' With that, he sent Eloise to make some tea for everyone, especially the nursing staff.

When Eloise came in with a wooden tray, Yaqub was surprised to see tall glasses on it, with intricate silver filigree holders with handles. The liquid in the glasses looked red with the light shining through it. The British always had beige tea in white china cups, he thought. Léo misinterpreted his glance and said wryly, 'It is unfortunate that our Russian tea is also wartime tea, mainly tea-dust with no slices of lemon to float in it! But at least, before young Dwight takes you away, you can sit back and experience a little Russian-style hospitality!'

The stone cross looked really old. It stood in a clearing, with some new houses, and they could hear a stream close by. Up a track they could see an older house and it was easy to imagine the forest having once wrapped itself around it. Saira was sure this was the house they were looking for. It had obviously been extensively modernised, with double glazed windows, Velux windows in the roof, a sun lounge, and the shutters painted a bright Mediterranean blue. But they could still see some small rectangular windows under the eaves. Parts of the house looked as if they might once have been barns. Perhaps the small windows had been in a hayloft. In the fenced garden there were scarlet and yellow swings and a slide. On the windows were pretty cut-out white paper shapes. A house with small children.

As they stood looking, a smart woman came to the door. 'Can I help?' she asked in German, then English. Saira smiled gratefully. 'I think my grandfather was cared for here during the war,' she said. 'I'm trying to imagine how it was then.' The woman immediately invited them in, in a surprisingly hospitable way, explaining that she was about to call the children in for lunch, but that it could wait for a few moments. 'You are welcome to look round, but I'm afraid you will find that we have altered everything.'

She showed them a sparkling new kitchen with pale wood units, a large sitting and dining room which she explained was made out of two smaller rooms, the sun lounge they'd added, a spacious bathroom with bright yellow tiles, and the bedrooms, one en-suite, with their vibrantly coloured walls. Everywhere the floors were stripped pine with bright rugs. Saira was disappointed. The woman was right. It was impossible to imagine how the old Russian had lived.

To everyone's surprise, Dwight did not return for them that day, so at nightfall Léo ordered Marie to make up some clean beds for their guests. Meanwhile he went outside, brought in more logs, and closed the shutters. Yaqub noticed that he did not close the shutters at the window by the door, and he watched as Eloise lit a candle and placed it on the window sill. 'To light the way for any wanderers,' explained Eloise, noticing his interest. 'It is our custom.'

That evening, as they sat round the stove, well-fed and basking in the security of this friendly, industrious household, Léo entertained them with stories about his own fighting days, back in the First World War. He was a great story teller, repeating his words to make sure they didn't miss anything. He had such energy and vigour as he described the starry nights, the trenches, the frost-bite and the forays. His wife smiled indulgently, as she sat darning. She had clearly heard it all many times – and probably in many languages too. 'No politics tonight!' she warned, as Barkat asked why he had not returned to Russia at the end of the fighting. Eloise laughed, as she translated. 'My mother has heard quite enough over the years about the Bolsheviks. And she always reminds my father that it was her charms which kept him here!'

Mid-way through one of Léo's tales of heroism and military incompetence, there was a heavy thud against the door, followed by feeble but rhythmic knocking. Léo instantly broke off his narrative and went to the door. The cold night air leapt into the house, and with it a bundled-up man fell across the threshold.

'I was wrong,' said Léo as Yaqub and Barkat helped him to carry the man to a chair. 'Amazingly there are still survivors out there.' His wife and older daughter had already gone for water and cloths. 'Not too close to the stove. He must thaw out slowly, not rush it.'

As the two women tried to persuade the figure to sip some warm water, Léo attempted to unwrap some of the blankets that cocooned him, which were frozen in ridges and troughed with snow. 'German blankets,' he muttered.

'We'll need to keep him down here in the warmth tonight till we know how badly injured he is. Eloise, as you're no help with the sick and wounded, stir yourself and take our two healthy guests upstairs.' As Barkat protested that they could stay and help, Léo shook his head and told them they'd be more help out of the way. There would be plenty they could do in the morning.

Eloise led them up two flights of steep stairs, her skirt swishing. On the top floor, a hayloft ran across the length of the house. The rafters had been boarded over, and straw and blankets had been piled up to form comfortable beds for them. The window openings had been stuffed with newspapers and straw, to keep out the worst of the cold and the chimney stack against the wall was warm to touch. There was a simple marble-topped wash-stand with a china jug and bowl, and below it a chamber pot so they wouldn't have to go outside into the snowy night. On one wall hung a small rectangular wooden picture of a figure on horseback, which glittered in the flickering candle light, all golden and scarlet and white. Perhaps, thought Yaqub, he was some household saint who would protect the wounded man downstairs.

As the woman paused on the first floor landing, Saira noticed a door at the far end. Without meaning to be discourteous or prying, she pushed it open. 'Ah, yes, I am forgetting. You can also go up there.'

Up the ladder-steep stairs behind the door, Saira found herself in the loft, with the sun streaming through the small old slit openings and the newer Velux windows onto the rough board floor. As she stood in the middle of the bare room, Saira began finally to get a sense of the building as it used to be. She visualised bedding on the floor, and her grandfather and his friend stretched out, talking about their epic journey and planning their futures.

The woman smiled apologetically. 'We have intended to make a play-room up here. But we have not yet commenced. I think maybe they have kept the chickens up here – you see some straw still is here!' Saira was relieved that the trendy colours had not yet made their way up here. The walls were still streaked with thin whitewash. She wasn't sure about chickens though, as she could make out a lighter patch of wall where a picture or perhaps a calendar would have hung. Though there were indeed a few wisps of straw.

She stood, as if in a trance, while Will, with the woman's permission, photographed this attic room from all angles, hoping to recapture something of its atmosphere, including shots of Saira, who, most unusually, didn't protest.

'He was here. I know he was,' was all she could say.

The next morning, Léo had lined up some tasks for them. 'It is good for you to be useful before Dwight takes you away! It is a rare opportunity to have some able-bodied young men to help!'

Léo and Barkat busied themselves with mucking out the animals in the barns and replenishing the water supplies, whilst Eloise led Yaqub into a lean-to shed and set him to splitting and chopping the stacked wood into smaller logs for the stove. He felt happy to be able to repay their hospitality in this small, familiar way. He sang to himself as he raised his axe and brought it neatly down, keeping a good rhythm of work. After a while the girl picked up the tune and hummed along with him. He stopped, immediately self-conscious. 'Don't stop,' she urged. 'You've got a fine voice!'

But Yaqub was too embarrassed. 'I'll teach you one of Papa's songs, then.' And she started a jolly, swinging tune, which Yaqub soon found to be ideal to work to. Soon he had a good pile of logs in front of him and the girl helped him to carry them to the big barn next to the kitchen and to stack them neatly along the wall, behind the massive hay cart. Yaqub felt very disturbed and uneasy when her shoulder brushed against his as they stooped and stacked. He was finding it hard to breathe. And yet, when the task was completed, all he wanted to do was to resume chopping and create more logs for stacking.

'Sing again,' he begged the girl. He marvelled at how magical it felt to be chopping logs, in the snowy landscape, to the ethereal sound of this girl's voice. It was no longer the tedious, exhausting task, day-in, day-out, that the Germans had made it.

Then a deep voice joined in, and two tunes began rise and merge with each other, then separate again. Léo brought the recital to an end with his usual hearty laugh. He assured Yaqub that he had chopped twice as fast as any man he knew, and that he deserved a break! 'The women have made our latest wounded soldier comfortable upstairs, and we can sit down in comfort for our soup!'

'Have you seen the soldier?' Barkat asked Yaqub, as the table was being cleared after lunch. The bowls were blotched purple from the rich beetroot soup they'd eaten, and the smell of a strong cheese lingered. Yaqub laughed and said that he had been far too busy chopping wood.

'The women have cleaned him up and he is upstairs now in our attic. When I went up he was either fast asleep or unconscious. But he didn't look American like Dwight, and he's certainly not a German. His skin is darker and his eyes are different. Come up and have a look!'

The man was stirring as they reached the top of the attic stairs. He opened his strange eyes and looked at them and said something. He had the strange, lazy-sounding way of drawling his words that Dwight had. Perhaps he was a different kind of American. But then he closed his eyes again, seeming to sink into insensibility.

Yaqub was keen to continue chopping wood. He had enjoyed his morning's work, but he did not know if he could expect to be accompanied by Eloise again. He hoped it might be possible, though he knew that it was not proper. And yet her father had allowed her to mingle with all those American soldiers. Perhaps war justified many things. And he had to admit that it did not seem to have made her forward or flirtatious.

He left Barkat sitting by the wounded soldier and went out and resumed solitary chopping. 'What are you doing?' laughed Eloise when she finally came out to find him. 'We shall not need so much wood for months! Papa did not intend you to work like a slave! I have been sent to fetch you for tea.' Yaqub smiled shyly, without looking directly at her, then followed her indoors. Had she been wearing that red skirt yesterday?

Will's voice broke in on Saira's silent contemplation of the faded upstairs room. 'We really mustn't keep you from lunch any longer! You said you were ready to call in the children.'

The woman looked relieved. Saira poured out her thanks as they cautiously descended the steep stairs, concluding. 'You can't imagine how exciting this has been for me. I could almost see him here!'

As they walked away, down towards the cross, Saira turned and looked back at the house. She had to admit to herself that it didn't look at all like Little Red Riding Hood's cottage, but what a haven it must have been for her escaping grandfather. She wondered again how long he'd spent there, whether he had fallen in love, and if so, with which of the daughters.

Despite sitting wide-awake and thoughtful for a long time before he lay down to sleep, Yaqub woke early in the morning as he heard the household stirring below him. He went out to the barns and watched silently as Eloise milked the cows. Her fingers were nimble. Her father might claim that she was the intellectual one, but she was also a practical country girl. He

208

was glad about that. Then, realising how surreptitious he was being, almost as if he was spying on her, he hastily put on his coat and went to help Léo shovelling the fresh snow. 'We need to get the milk churns and some eggs down to the main road,' grunted his host. 'We have heard how short of supplies the refugees around Saint Dié are. One of the farmers is collecting as much as he can take for them.'

When they got back, Barkat had finished mucking out, and the fresh manure was steaming on top of the snow-covered dung heap. The sun was coming out, and Eloise and her mother and sister were hanging out the sheets which had been washed the day before.

'Perhaps they will dry today!' Eloise called as he watched.

How graceful she looked, with her arms stretched up in a V as she secured the linen with wooden pegs. Then as Marie hoisted the line high in the air, Eloise secured it with a clothes prop and it billowed with giant white sails. And for some reason that made them all laugh.

After sitting down together to warm up over coffee and bread, Léo fetched his gun, asking Barkat if he wanted to accompany him. The womenfolk resumed their endless round of changing the wounded man's dressings, cleaning the house and preparing the soup. Yaqub felt restless. The only thing he could think of doing was to create more logs. This time he sang Léo and Eloise's tune with his own words as he chopped.

When Eloise came to fetch him, she stopped on the way back to the kitchen by another door at the back of the barn. The door opened into a storeroom whose shelves were densely packed with large glass Kilner jars, all brightly coloured. 'Beetroot, tomatoes, beans, carrots, strawberries, raspberries, pears, damsons,' listed Eloise proudly. 'This year's harvest. They'll last us all through the winter.'

As she reached up for a jar of beans, Yaqub felt a surge of madness. He longed to kiss her upturned face. He backed out hastily, stammering the first thing that came into his head. 'What man?' asked Eloise. 'Oh, the man in the picture in the attic? It's a good story. I'll tell you later. First I must take the beans to Maman! And some potatoes!' She opened another door and he followed her downstairs to a dark, dry cellar with an earth floor and wooden racks round the wall. He helped her scoop out potatoes from the rack into her apron, his hands almost touching hers in the musty dark. He could hardly breathe.

12

Icon

That evening, like the evening before, Eloise lit a candle and placed it in the window, saying, 'I hope there are no more poor, frozen men out there.' As her mother replied, Eloise translated, 'My mother is amazed that our last man has survived so long. From what she can make out, after he was shot, he must have rolled or crawled into a sheltered German dug-out. He must have passed out, and then other bodies fell on top of him, which would have protected him from the worst of the cold. For he wouldn't have lasted so long in a shallow fox-hole.' Barkat turned to Léo and asked where the wounded soldier was from. He still did not think he looked like an American.

'Are you an Englishman? Am I a Frenchman? How simple are these things?' demanded Léo. 'He has fought bravely for the Americans. I hope they appreciate him and his friends.' Barkat looked puzzled. 'He would probably answer you either that his parents are American citizens of Japanese origin, or else Hawaiians of Japanese origin.'

Yaqub's interest was caught, for the German guards had taken great pleasure in telling them that the Japanese had attacked a place with the pretty name of Pearl Harbour, and would soon crush America itself. But the prisoners had long since ceased to believe the news of defeats which the Germans gave them. 'Pearl Harbour?' he murmured.

Léo laughed grimly. 'America, the land of the free! How quickly our fears rise to the surface! Here we were relieved to hear of the Japanese attack on Pearl Harbour. Perhaps it would at last force America to rise up to help Europe. What we did not know was that the Americans, in a reaction of fear and panic, interned every single one of their citizens of Japanese origin, – men, women and children. Some of these brave soldiers fighting here are men from those camps, fighting to prove their loyalty and worth. You two boys know only too well how degrading the prisoner-of-war camps are. And so are the American internment camps. The only way these young Americans could get out of them was by fighting in the army. Others from their regiment are Hawaiians. All of them are very brave.'

That night, up in their attic, Barkat sat next to the wounded soldier for a long time, holding his hand, stroking it gently. Yaqub wondered if he was trying to pass on some hope and courage to the unknown young man. 'How much did you understand? Léo sahib was very passionate, but I did not understand all that he said about this man.' He sat watching the two of them as the candle flickered and burned down.

Barkat was unusually reflective. 'Do you remember at Annaberg, when we listened to the words of Subhas Chandra Bose, and at first he made us proud to be Indian? How he made us question our loyalty to the British who were mere intruders, invaders? This is the other side of the coin. How long does it take before an immigrant is truly accepted? Before this man with Japanese parents and appearance becomes a true American?'

As if he knew they were talking about him, the soldier briefly opened his eyes, and murmured, 'Private Jimmy Onaga' and his number, as if reporting for duty, before he fell back into semi-consciousness.

Barkat tried out the strange name, 'Djimmi … Hello! We friends.'

Above the man's head pranced the magnificent horse, white against a scarlet sky. As Yaqub smiled at Barkat's attempts to pronounce the strange Japanese name, his eyes searched the small picture for meaning. He wondered about its rider, with his long spear pointing down. Perhaps he was not a saint but a Russian or French soldier in some long-ago battle?

As they left the Russian (now German) house, Will noticed that Saira had the same rapt expression she'd had in the Maginot fort. She was obviously back there in the past with her grandfather. He did hope that the pencilled address wouldn't be a let-down after this. Suppose this Eloise, who would be pretty old by now, didn't want to talk to them? Suppose she turned them away? He felt protective. Perhaps they should linger round here a bit longer before confronting her. He suggested following the road a bit further up the hill and having their baguettes somewhere where they could look down on the hamlet and Léo's little house.

It was a spur-of-the-moment suggestion, but afterwards he found it hard to believe that the ensuing encounter was just chance. It was too bizarre. One moment they were just sitting at a conveniently placed picnic-table (the French seemed to like these wooden forest tables and benches at scenic spots), chewing their baguettes and talking about Léo's attic, and the next minute, like some Irish folk-tale, a wizened figure with a back-to-front baseball cap had popped out of the forest, demanded whether they were Americans, and insisted that they followed him, muttering something about 'monument' and 'Hawaiians'.

Will was quite surprised when Saira stood up and seemed prepared to follow this odd stranger. She admitted afterwards that she must have been lulled by the sheer delight of having found Léo's house and the prospect of seeing his younger daughter, almost as if nothing could go wrong and nothing could be chance on this momentous day. She merely shook the crumbs from her lap, and smoothed her new blouse, murmuring 'It must be my flamboyant top. It must look to him like one of those gaudy Hawaiian shirts! Earlier I was Japanese, and now American. I don't know which is worse.'

Fortunately the small man was out of earshot, making his way purposefully along a small forest footpath. He turned and waited for them, and announced slowly and proudly, 'I led the Americans! They would not have found their way through the forest without me.' And then he hurried on again, and Will shrugged uncomprehendingly at Saira.

The next time the man stopped, they had emerged into a clearing with broad tracks, and the man was pointing at a memorial – rather a small one, flanked by two low hedges and two flag poles.

'Of course, I didn't lead them here. But I met some of the men who later died here.' They must have looked puzzled, for he hesitated and asked, 'The lost battalion? You know all about them, of course?'

'We're English,' Will replied, as if that would explain everything, and indeed it seemed to. The man sighed. 'Ah yes, our allies too.' When he fell silent, Will prompted, 'It mentions a Hawaiian regiment'.

Will sensed they were about to get a lecture, as the man

stabbed the ground with his walking pole, adopted a stance and waved his hand once more at the memorial and began to explain how he had just passed his twelfth birthday in October 1944 when the Americans crossed the Moselle and were approaching his home town of Bruyères. He was so proud to be one of the boys detailed to find the advance party and lead them through the forest to a hill above their town. He thought the ensuing battle for Bruyères must have been the Americans' toughest so far, for it took them days to liberate the town, fighting first for the hills and then from house to house. While the town was still celebrating its liberty, the Americans pressed on, but his mother wouldn't let him go with them this time.

His French was clear, with occasional American words. 'She was right too. The slaughter up here in these hills was unimaginable, for the Germans held all the advantage points, and could pick off the approaching Americans. We could hear the constant gunfire, but did not realise how deadly the fighting had become. But eventually it fell silent, and later we heard that all those Americans, including the ones I knew, had been encircled up here in the hills.'

He paused dramatically, then told them how the 442nd had to be recalled from the rest camp to rescue them. 'You know, we were so surprised when we first saw the strange men of the 442nd. We thought all the Americans were so tall, and here were these tiny soldiers, who scuttled along like rabbits. There were many jokes about these Nippo-Americans, as we called them then (we didn't know about Hawaii). But, mon dieu, how brave they were! We were soon full of admiration for these dark-skinned men with their fierce mud-smeared faces. They fought almost to the death. The tanks could hardly move up here and it was quite unsuitable for the heavy artillery. Most of them charged with their bayonets, fighting from tree to tree.'

Will closed his eyes, imagining these small, determined soldiers as their self-appointed guide said sadly that many more men of 442nd were killed than the number of men of the Lost Battalion that were rescued. One of the wounded Nippo-Americans later married the girl – the priest's cousin – who nursed him. And it was he who had this monument built in honour of his fallen comrades.

He paused, puzzled. 'Many relatives of those soldiers now make the journey to this spot. Like a pilgrimage. But why have you come?'

Finally Saira understood why the shopkeeper had at first thought she must be looking for Léo's house, – because of Japanese-American ancestors. 'Well, mine is also a war story,' she replied, 'But a different one, and a long one too.' By now she had looked up all the vocabulary and found it relatively easy to outline her grandfather's imprisonment, escape and arrival at Léo's.

The man nodded. He had heard of Léo. He had also heard of some Indian soldiers in the area. Saira's heart leapt, only to subside as he added 'But they could not be the same men. These men had been imprisoned in Epinal only a few kilometres west of here. When one of the American shells hit their prison camp, many of them escaped and wandered in the forest, and were given food and helped by local people. I don't know what happened to them after that. I think the Americans finally took charge of them.'

Even though it was not her grandfather's story, Saira was excited to hear of more Indian soldiers. Like every detail they'd discovered so far, it gave substance to their own search.

'We affirm a historic truth here – that loyalty to one's country is not modified by racial origins.' Saira was startled as the strange little man adopted a pose and declaimed these lofty words in English. Seeing their surprise, he grinned and explained that they were the words on another memorial which the Hawaiians had erected on the other side of Bruyères. 'I have always found the words on it very moving.'

When they parted, having taken photos of the man standing like a sentinel before 'his' memorial, he said happily, 'Now the English will know all about how I led the Lost Battalion!' 'What a vain little man! Do you think he lurks there deliberately waiting to waylay strangers with his story?' Saira commented as they reached the car and were out of hearing. 'But a bit of luck to hear about those other Indian PoWs.' 'Absolutely,' Will murmured, still wondering why he'd never heard the story of the Lost Battalion before. Now that would have been a really riveting bit of history to have unearthed for his Second World War project back in their schooldays.

❦ ❦

After the girls had washed up the lunch dishes the next day, Marie took up a bowl of soup for the wounded soldier, who was beginning to sit up and speak a few words. Barkat followed her. He seemed to have become very attached to the suffering young man. Eloise beckoned Yaqub to come too. Barkat sat on one side of the makeshift bed, once more holding Jimmy's hand, and Marie sat on the other side, spooning soup and wiping his dribbles with a clean cloth.

Yaqub and Eloise sat on the other bed. Eloise pointed delicately and respectfully at the small picture. 'Yesterday Yaqub asked me who he was. He was a knight (a brave man, like you soldiers) called George. The story says that hundreds of years ago, he travelled for many months on that white horse, over land and sea, until he reached the land if Libya.'

'Libya!' Barkat couldn't resist interrupting to point out that

that was where they were captured. Yaqub hadn't realised that he too was listening, but realised that this detail of Eloise's tale had drawn him immediately into it.

'There he met a hermit (you know, a holy man, a man who lives alone and prays). The hermit told him that it was dangerous to go any further, for the land was being devastated by a terrible dragon.'

Here Eloise had to break off for the word 'dragon' was not one that Yaqub or Barkat had ever heard. She pointed to the bottom of the picture at a dark shape which Yaqub had not noticed before in the shadows. It was a horrible scaly monster. She puffed out her cheeks and blew, her lips rippling, as if blowing fire, until she laughed and had to stop. Even Jimmy was smiling.

Then she resumed her account of how this terrible dragon had demanded the sacrifice (here she mimed slitting her throat) of young maidens, (she laughingly pointed at Marie and herself) and that the only young girl who had not yet been sacrificed was the beautiful daughter of the king. But the hermit told him that the very next day, she too would be sacrificed, unless a knight was found who would kill the dragon.

Barkat noticed that the wounded man was squeezing his hand. He looked at him. The soldier had opened his eyes and was listening, entranced, as he obediently swallowed his soup.

'The king promised to give his daughter in marriage to any knight who would kill the dragon and save her.' Yaqub had followed enough of this to imagine Eloise as the beautiful princess. He wanted to shout, 'I would fight to protect you!' Something must have showed in his expression as Barkat muttered something reproving to him. And even Jimmy looked as if he had winked. But that must just have been the poor man's fever.

Eloise went on to tell, with many gestures and sound effects, how George set out to find the dragon's cave, how he rode past the princess, who was being led to the dragon, and how the dragon came rushing out of his cave with a tremendous roar, like thunder. The two men laughed as she tried to imitate the sound, but the sick man whispered, 'Go on!'

'The dragon was much bigger and more fierce than it looks in that picture. It was as tall as this house and ten times as long. When George struck it with his spear, its scales were so hard that his spear broke into a thousand pieces. The dragon turned on him, preparing to kill him with his poisonous, fiery breath, but, quick as lightning, George drew his sword and pushed it deep into the soft flesh under the dragon's wing, where it has no scales. And so he killed it.'

All three soldiers involuntarily clapped their hands and even Marie smiled. Yaqub immediately wanted to know if he married the princess. 'I expect he did in the story,' she said dismissively. 'But that is just a story. In fact, Saint George is one of the most famous saints in Russia. Really, the dragon represents evil, and Saint George is fighting and defeating all the evil in the world.'

Marie said something, and Eloise translated, 'That is why we moved the icon (that means holy picture) and hung it over the bed of our wounded men. Saint George will protect all those who are fighting now against wicked governments and armies.'

'Good story,' said the wounded man, in his strange drawl. 'I feel safe now,' and he closed his eyes and fell into a peaceful sleep.

That evening, after Marie and her mother had washed Jimmy and put fresh dressings on his wounds, Marie took up some more soup for him. As if drawn by the shared story of the icon, the other three followed her. The injured man always fell into a troubled sleep after the pain of being moved when his dressings were changed. But their footsteps on the steep stairs must have disturbed him. For as the candlelight threw their shadows onto the attic wall, they could see his eyes opening and his lips moving.

'Go for broke!'

Nobody understood what he meant. 'Go for broke,' he repeated. 'That's our motto. That's what we did.' Looking at their puzzled faces he explained, 'It means you give everything you've got. You risk everything you've got, including your life. Like that dragon-killing saint. I sure liked him.'

He looked up at Eloise and smiled. She stroked his hand. 'I'm glad you like our Saint George. And you were very brave too.'

Yaqub felt irrational jealousy. Perhaps Marie did too, as she jabbed the soup spoon against his lips and ordered Eloise to stop flirting and go and get the playing cards.

13

Mists

Could this be her? A skinny old lady bunched on a bench, autumn sunshine playing on her sagging face. A flowered overall. Thick stockings folding around her ankles to collapse on her worn blue slippers. A cat on her lap.

They were later reaching the village of Saint Loup than they had intended. But then they hadn't expected to be diverted by a garrulous old man who had not only met but had actually led the American liberators, however briefly, when he was a boy. Will was worried it might be getting too late to call, unannounced, on Eloise. But Saira pointed out that it was often a good idea to give old people time for a nap after lunch, especially before descending unexpectedly on them. But even calling them 'old people' (for after all her beloved grandmother was old now, and her grandfather had seemed very frail before he died) had not really prepared Saira for this waif-like bundle. Could this possibly be her?

Driving into the small, sleepy village, Will had parked by the church. As they walked up the street from the church, they passed the war memorial. Saira was surprised by how many men in such a small village had perished in the First World War. Then Will pointed to the names of those from the last war who'd died in captivity. 'All civilians!' Perhaps they were men who had been forced to work in Germany. As they read the names of those shot, they wondered what risks Léo and his family had run.

Further up the road, they saw a man sweeping in front of the neat bungalow they were heading for. He looked up and greeted them as they approached, then went back to his task, chatting cheerfully to the motionless old lady on her bench behind him.

Looking up again he observed, 'She still loves her garden'. Then he switched to English, 'Are you American?' Saira shook her head, wondering if this was a step up from being asked if she was Japanese. 'We're English. My grandfather fought in the Indian Army during the last war.' She paused and took a deep breath. So often she'd been disappointed. 'After he escaped from his prison camp and reached France, he was helped by a Russian man ...'

'Ah, Léo!' said the man softly. The woman looked up at that name. 'My dear, these young people are asking about your father!'

'My Papa loves me very much,' murmured the woman, cradling the cat to her. 'My Papa is very strict. I must learn all my lessons well.'

The man sighed. He walked up to the old woman and stroked her wispy hair. 'Léo gave shelter to so many wounded soldiers after the battle. I didn't know the family then. But I know that many soldiers wrote to him afterwards, expressing their gratitude. Three of them even came back many years after the war to thank him – all the way from America. Then they came here to see Eloise too. Of course they remembered her. That was really the first I'd heard much about her wartime work. For a long time after the war, many of the real resistance workers didn't talk much about their contribution.'

He caressed the lobes of her ears, where once, perhaps, she had worn earrings. 'And she remembered them all, in those days, when they came back. Do you remember a handsome Indian soldier as well, my dear?' The old lady looked around her in an unfocussed kind of way, seeming confused by the question.

'Is it breakfast time yet?' she asked.

Saira was devastated. Here, in front of her, after all these years, was the witness to her grandfather's war. The girl Grandfather had never spoken of to his family. One of the two daughters of the Russian man that he had spoken about. Maybe the girl her grandmother had wondered about. And she was completely gaga. How cruel. Everything would now remain shrouded in mystery. She burst into tears.

The old lady looked up at this unexpected sound. 'She's a naughty girl,' she told her purring tabby.

Hugging Saira to him, Will felt he needed to explain to these strangers how tantalising the last week had been and why his wife (he was getting more used to the word each time he spoke it) had pinned so much hope on meeting Léo's daughter after she'd heard she was still alive.

The man looked sad. 'Our minds become treacherous in old age. It is not easy for her. I am so sorry. But it's the end of the day. She's sometimes brighter in the mornings. That's a better time for her.'

He held out his hand to Will then to Saira, who hastily wiped her eyes. He introduced himself as Daniel, saying that he was once the schoolmaster. He pointed to the building with the bell, in the heart of the village. 'They have closed my school and made apartments there now,' he said sadly.

He seemed quite pleased to have people to talk to, but reluctant to invite them in. He said he wished that he and Eloise

223

could be more helpful. It might be better, though, if they returned the next morning. In fact it often did Eloise good to see people and to sit and talk about the past. It was surprising how sometimes, chatting over a cup of coffee, she could become quite like her old self.

Saira nodded immediately. Will smiled, thinking that Daniel sounded rather like a teacher discussing a difficult pupil, – force of habit maybe. 'Come at ten thirty, for coffee. We will be organised by then. I cannot promise that the mists will lift, but we can hope.'

Hand in hand, not turning to look back at the pathetic figure, Saira and Will walked back to the car. Daniel continued his sweeping.

Appearing oblivious to their departure, Eloise fondled her acquiescent cat: Who are they? So many people come and go and tell me things. Did I ever know them? If I just sit here maybe it will become clearer who they are. A boy and a girl. I don't think I have seen them before. Daniel will know. Daniel will tell me. He talks about me as if I can't hear, but I know what he's saying. So they will come back. Tomorrow. When will that be? Is it tomorrow now? Always sweeping! Will he sweep up the past into a neat heap so I can see it all at once? So many people I once knew. They all float and merge before my eyes. Some of them I loved. But no one face will remain still – they are all fluid. Tomorrow they will return. Daniel told them to come back then.

What's wrong with French mattresses, Will wondered that night as he reached out to comfort Saira and rolled heavily against her. Did they always sag in the middle like this? Saira pulled away from him. She had been so happy earlier on. Up in the attic of Léo's house, then meeting the man who knew about other Indian PoWs, and then driving to Saint Loup in the certainty that Grandfather's mystery girl was still alive (she had by now convinced herself that if her grandmother's suspicions were right, it would have been the younger daughter). And now her hope had been tugged away. Not even Will could make that better.

At the same time, Daniel was tucking his wife into bed. 'May the good Saint George protect you and keep away all evil this night,' he murmured, stroking her cheek. It was not something he believed, personally, or any of the saints, but it was something that always seemed to soothe Eloise. He'd gone into the bedroom to find that Eloise had forgotten that she was getting undressed, and was sitting in her petticoat, with one stocking on and one stocking off, just staring at the icon she'd always loved of the warrior on the white charger: One day he will come back and rescue me. One day. Then I will know where I am going.

The next morning was overcast, as Saira and Will drove back to Saint Loup. There was no one outside in the garden this time, so they pulled the metal chain, causing a dull jangle (Will wondered if the heavy-looking bell was a reminder of Daniel's school-mastering days). Daniel greeted them warmly and led them into the sitting room. It was a large room, furnished with glass-fronted bookshelves and comfortable armchairs. It looked like a room which had once been orderly, but had slowly overflowed into disorder. The striped wall-paper was from another era. There was a leather-topped desk under the window, piled high with folders and newspapers.

Eloise was sitting in an armchair, immaculately dressed in

a pale blue skirt and cardigan, her hair brushed and held neatly back with a child's butterfly hair-slide. Saira noticed that she had on surprisingly dainty shoes rather than yesterday's baggy slippers. The cat was nowhere to be seen. When Daniel introduced their English visitors, she waved her hand graciously and said, in excellent English, 'Do take a seat.'

Saira was amazed at the change in her. On the table were some tall glasses in silver holders and a bowl with sliced lemons. Daniel said that he had changed his mind about coffee, and hoped that they liked tea – 'but after all, you are English' – for he had thought the old tea glasses might prompt Eloise's wartime memories. He brought in a pot of tea, while Eloise smiled gently at them. 'These aren't more Americans,' Daniel said, 'they are English people.'

'Do English people like lemon in their tea? I'm never sure.' I think I have seen them before. The girl has lovely eyes. Do I know them? Perhaps they are friends of Papa. No, he is gone now. Or Daniel? I don't think he has English friends. If I just keep smiling, it may become clear.

Saira wondered whether she should begin the conversation or whether it was better for Daniel to broach the subject of her grandfather. Seeing her hesitation, Daniel said, 'This is Saira, my dear. She has come specially to see you.' Oh, they all say that nowadays, it's so tiresome. It doesn't help.

'Her grandfather came to your house in the war, and you all looked after him.' So many came, so many. 'Perhaps Saira will tell you his story, my dear.'

'I should like that.' That's safe enough to say. Oh, why do memories swirl so uncontrollably and never settle into place?

Where best to start? Saira decided to begin right at the beginning, to let Eloise get used to her voice, in the hope that something amid all the detail would remind her of the past.

'My grandfather was born in Kashmir, which was then part of India. During the war he joined the Indian army, to fight for the British,' she began. She told of his capture and escape, but could see no response of recognition in Eloise's eyes. The journey across the mountains obviously meant nothing to her.

Ah, yes, there is something about the girl, but it's not always wise to remember. I will push that away. Not even try to make sense. No one will know the difference. People talk to me as if was a child these days. Not Daniel, though. He still loves me.

Perhaps if she embroidered her tale, Saira thought, remembered the small details that various people, not just her grandfather, had told her. How was it that this frail woman remembered English so well, but not the events? 'It must have been the coldest winter of the war. The snow lay thick on the ground. The mist clung to the trees in the forest. There was a big battle up in the hills, and many wounded men were brought down to your house.'

That's true. They were. And so much blood. Blood on the floor, blood on the sheets, bloody strips of linen they used for the bandages. So much washing. Always wet sheets hanging in the barns – or sometimes outside – to dry. Great white sheets. White snow. We stopped starching. There was no time for niceties. Always ironing, drying and ironing. How I hated that. The blood, the stench, I couldn't clean up those leaking bodies. I just ironed and ironed. Always dirty. Always dirty.

Seeing a change of expression, Saira asked, 'Do you remember the Americans?'

Now they were handsome. So tall, so easy, so friendly. 'Oh yes, the Americans were everywhere. We saw a lot of them.' They could be very familiar, sometimes. They were different from our boys. Very direct. 'There was Teddy. I led him to Saint Dié. And Dwight, he came later to collect the men.' But it was more fun at the beginning. It was such an adventure leading their spies forwards. Did I know their names? Perhaps not, there was too much work to be done then. Too much danger to bother with real names. Yes, there was a before-time and an after-time. 'Sam, Kurt, Lou, Royce ...' But which face goes with those names? What did that very first American look like, the one I found – or did he find me – when I had gone to my favourite spot to hunt for mushrooms? There were still ceps and a few chanterelles, for that was before the snow came, and I had half filled my basket. I didn't want him to see it, for, like all soldiers, he had a hungry look. I tried to hide my basket from him. But he was more interested in making sense of his map. He seemed lost among the trees. I showed him the way. 'My basket was full of mushrooms!' Now she's looking cross. She doesn't want to know about mushrooms. And with her frown all my lovely soldiers are fading away. They all left anyway. 'No, no Americans,' she concluded sadly.

Daniel was more used to these shifts in concentration. He began to talk about the things that he remembered, as a teenager, to give her time to refocus. He talked about the radio that his brother had, and how they would try to pick up British broadcasts. How they buried it in the garden when the Germans approached their village. He talked about going to school in the war. About the terrible bombardments as the Americans got close. About the young men who joined the maquis and were shot after a night drop went wrong. About the deportations which he was lucky to escape, but in which his brother and father were taken. 'It was a terrible time. But Léo was magnificent.'

He thought, perhaps, he could now try to draw Eloise back into the conversation, 'Your mother and father looked after so many soldiers, all those brave Hawaiians, the Nippo-

Americans, we called them!' Will and Saira looked at each other, significantly. 'We saw a monument to them, and heard about the lost battalion they rescued.' Will interrupted. Daniel nodded and turned back to Eloise, prompting, 'Their motto was 'Go for Broke'. The Americans threw them into the worst battles and they proved their bravery a thousand times over!'

'Go for Broke!' repeated Eloise, thoughtfully. 'Such strange words. It had something to do with a game.' A game where you risk everything you'd got. Where have I heard that? Was it on their badges? Or did one of them tell me? 'Saint George knows all about that!' Oh, now I've made the girl frown again. 'I'm sure Saint George heard him say those words.' Heard who? He lay there. At first you could hardly see his face, just his slanting eyes peering out of the Mama's bandages, and he said you risk everything, including your life. 'He was upstairs in our attic. His head was all bandaged. He was the last one.' And my special one was there too, but I don't want to remember that. I shan't tell. I shall talk about something else.

'Will you have a biscuit? We always have biscuits for visitors. We had biscuits all through the war. We had a tin with roses on it and biscuits inside. My mother was a very prudent house-keeper. We always had food that winter of '44, though others ran short, with all the refugees. We had a big store-room full of beans and carrots and …' I wanted him to kiss me there. In that small, musty, intimate space. He was so close. He didn't smell decaying like the others, the wounded ones. He was tall and slim and his face … why does even his face slip away so fast when I try to see it properly again? No, I don't want to see it again. No, not that one. I am glad he went away. 'I don't want him to come back.'

'And do you remember among all your wartime visitors, two Indian soldiers?' asked Saira, thinking the time was ripe now that Eloise was well launched, however randomly, into her wartime memories now. She was excited by the casual mention, among the otherwise incomprehensible things, of the attic they'd seen. 'My grandfather's name was Yaqub.'

'No!' Eloise almost shouted.

Saira thought the old woman looked frightened. How odd she was. The way she remembered some things. A phrase would set her off and then she would lose it. Perhaps, like Daniel, she should just keep throwing out ideas, and see which ones provoked a response. She obviously remembered something about games. 'So what games did you play on the long winter nights? Did you play with the soldiers?'

'Crap!' said the old lady unexpectedly, and Will stifled a laugh. 'One of them had dice in his pocket. He tried to explain, but we didn't understand, and Papa said it was unsuitable. So we taught him belote instead. That was fun. Marie liked that. We played for hours every evening.' *Papa thought we were all cheering up the wounded one. That's why we were allowed to go up and play on his bed. It was fun up there by candle-light. It was never the same after they left. The other one was good, he picked it up quickly. But Yaqub, he used to pretend he didn't understand the rules. He could be so funny. The way he imitated me as he made me explain the rules yet again! Marie took no notice of him. But Papa liked him too. And Papa was so hurt too when neither of them wrote afterwards.*

Suddenly Eloise started to cry. 'I think she may be tired now,' said Daniel, putting his arm round her. 'That's probably enough just for the moment. Why don't we leave her to sleep a little? I can show you her garden, and then we can come back to her, and she will feel refreshed.'

Sleep! Do I ever sleep? It is just one round of jumbled memories with no break, no sleep, no future, no past. Just sitting here, waiting for all memory to cease. For whoever I am to cease. But I am Eloise, and once I had a future. Everything was possible. I could have been betrothed to anyone. I was the popular one. Not like poor plain Marie. She stayed with Maman and Papa. Where is she now? Why doesn't she come and see me? She was the kind one. She was the one who really cared. But I loved the attention, the admiration. Marie said I was heartless. So why am I standing down by the roadside, by the mail box, just waiting in vain for the postman? No, I'm not going to remember him. He was unworthy. Treacherous. His face vanished long ago. Remember instead the mushrooms. Remember instead Sam or Kurt. But who were they? Just names. Just names.

Daniel is showing them the pumpkins now. I can hear his voice outside, excusing me, saying yet again how bright and lively I used to be. Of course I was, everything was at my fingertips then. For a few precious miles, I, like Saint Joan, led a shining army of Americans. Although, of course, they had no silver armour, just drab olive. But they were heroes. And I took them a short part of their journey eastwards. And on the way, as we took a break from creeping from one tree to the next, such strange rations they shared. The tins and bars of concentrated food. So exotic to me. Monotonous fare, they called it. But I felt that I, like them, could conquer the world, do any task, speak with anyone, for I was the one who knew all the languages. I could travel anywhere, even to the remotest Indies. And when Yaqub came, I gave him my heart. I thought he felt the same. I thought he would come riding back after the war on his white charger to claim me and carry me off. I thought he cared. But I told no one. It was our secret. And it was in secret that my heart broke. And now it is too late. So why tell anyone now, after so long.

'I just love them. Look Will, they are simply huge! And those ones, they are such unusual shapes!'

That girl has a gentle voice. It floats in above the rustle of the dead roses that need pruning. I used to love my roses. So many lovely names. And so many bowls of fragrant pot-pourri. But now it hardly matters. Does Daniel tend the garden just to please me? He's a good man. The one who does not leave me. The one who is faithful. I shan't hurt him by telling. These old echoes do no good … I think I can hear lumbering hooves. Are they real or just echoes too?

Will and Saira looked up from the garden in surprise. They could see Eloise hobbling down the front path with unexpected agility. Was she running away in her madness? 'She's heard the cows,' explained Daniel cryptically.

They all went to join her. Sure enough, a herd of cows were being driven up the road. A man was shouting what sounded like extremely rude curses at every beast who strayed. 'He always takes them to the fields in the middle of the day, long after everyone else. Once, someone must have left our gate open, for we found two of his wretched cows chewing and trampling Eloise's lovely flowers. So now she listens out for them!' He reached out his hand to his wife who was swaying like a feather in the wind. 'It's alright my dear, the gate is closed. Your garden is safe.'

Her rush to the gate seemed to have revived Eloise. As she went back into the house, she turned into the kitchen and sat down at the table there, leaving behind the formality of the sitting room. The kitchen was lighter, with cream-coloured wall-paper covered with cheerful red flowers, – poppies, Saira thought. Despite that, they sensed a creeping chaos here too, with sheets of hand-written notes on top of the herb jars, half-full baskets on the floor, and a stack of newspapers overspilling in one corner.

'During the war,' Eloise said, as if there had been no break in their earlier conversation, but clearly prompted by the passing cows, 'we had two fine cows. Really good milkers. Roussette and Gamine. I liked to drink the milk, warm, straight after milking. Milking was the one task that I enjoyed. It was not rushed. It's no good hurrying them.'

Saira tried to picture the cow stalls. Where would they have been before the Germans converted Léo's house?

'It was warm leaning against their bodies. And peaceful.' And one morning he just stood there behind me. He thought I didn't know. Was it the same day or was it later – perhaps later – that he leaned over and tucked my hair behind my ear, and his rough finger tickled against my neck. And then I did turn round, and … but he's gone. He didn't mean it.

'He didn't want to help Papa kill the pig, though,' said the old lady abruptly. 'He kept saying that it wasn't right. But Papa had no one else to help him that war year, with all our men, including the pig-killer, taken away to work in German factories and farms while their own men fought.'

Saira wrinkled her nose. Pig-killing sounded disgusting. And who was Eloise talking about now?

'The pigs had mean eyes, not like the cows. Marie didn't mind them.' She'd give them all the kitchen scraps and watch them snuffling and gobbling. I refused to watch them being killed. And that year out in the snow it was terrible. Even more blood. The blood of the wounded. The blood of the pig. Poor Marie had to hold the bowl to catch the pig's blood. 'How grateful we were that the Germans never came to our house. We were too far from the road, I expect. Other households were occupied. Many lost all their animals that winter. But we were more fortunate. We had plenty of pork and sausages for that terrible winter.'

Was there, any chance, Saira wondered, that this was in fact relevant? The old lady was speaking very coherently. Did she dare press her further? She looked at Daniel for guidance, but he didn't pick up her signal. So she risked asking 'Was it my grandfather who helped to kill the pig?' She couldn't imagine this. Surely he wouldn't have done such a thing. But perhaps a sense of gratitude, of obligation, would have forced him to participate? 'Was it Yaqub?'

'I don't know!' said Eloise angrily. 'His friend helped too. The noise was terrible. I don't know who they were! Is it lunch time? I'm hungry!'

'It's nearly lunch time,' soothed Daniel. 'I'll warm up the soup in a few minutes.'

He obviously thought this sounded inhospitable, as he added, 'I don't know what you two are planning. But there's a pizza restaurant and also a kebab place on the main road, which they say are quite good. But stay just a little longer. We'd like that wouldn't we Eloise? We don't want Saira and Will to go before you've told her all about her grandfather. Do you remember him now?'

Of course I do. How could I forget? 'There were eggs as well, from all our hens.' His fingers were long as he slid them under mine as we felt gently in the straw for new-laid eggs, with the fussy hens pecking angrily around us. 'Other winters, not during the war, but when we were younger, we would all sit round the big table and decorate the egg shells, ready for Easter. Papa was the most skilful.' What made me show him our shoe-boxes of painted eggs, wrapped and put carefully away? He held one in the palm of his hand, his eyes wide with wonder. It was one I'd painted, my best. He blew gently on it, as if he expected it to float away on his breath. I told him to keep it. So he would not forget me! He laughed with pleasure.

He had such a warm laugh. He insisted on going to show it to his friend. But that one wasn't interested. Not artistic. More impatient. Always wanting to be off. He wanted to fight. 'Silly boy!' Perhaps they really were killed in the confusion afterwards, as the officials always said. But I was sure that the paper-shufflers were just fobbing me off. Of course it was possible they were dead, but I didn't think so. I'd have known. I wrote a lot of letters. 'I tore most of them up,' she said helpfully. 'And the rest weren't answered.' Oh dear, I've confused her again. I think I want to tell her, but not Daniel and the boy, not after all these years of aching suppression. But supposing she doesn't understand that?

'Perhaps we really should be going now, if you are getting tired,' said Saira politely, thinking she was losing focus again.

Eloise leaned over the kitchen table and took the girls hand in hers. She held it gently stroking it, and smiling. She touched her wrist wonderingly. Then she looked into Saira's eyes, hungrily, but trustingly. Suddenly she got up and went into what must be the bedroom – Saira caught a glimpse of a blue candlewick bedspread. She came back with a comb and sat down closer to Saira and began to comb Saira's hair, rhythmically, humming under her breath as she did so. So soft, so soft. His was black too, black as the hides of the cows. He asked me to trim it before Dwight took them away. I did him and Marie did the grumpy one. Short back and sides to look smart for the Americans. I rubbed in some of Papa's pomade, so it felt all stiff and shiny, not soft cascades like hers. He was ticklish, though, behind his ears.

Saira found it intimate and curiously soothing. She sat very still as Eloise held up strands of hair and let it run through her fingers. Then she scooped up another handful and held it up behind Saira's ears as if trying out a new hairstyle. Seriously weird, thought Will, though Saira seemed cool about it. Eventually Eloise stopped trying out styles, and combed her hair neatly. 'There, you're ready to go now. You are smart enough to face any interrogation!' she smiled.

The word 'interrogation' caught Will's attention more firmly than any of her rambling animal prattle. He tried one last shot. 'We saw the war memorial as we walked up. It listed civilians who were shot by the Germans. Wasn't it very dangerous, helping the wounded Americans and the escaping prisoners?'

For the first time, she looked at Will directly. 'They were worth it.'

Feeling they were being dismissed, Saira and Will stood up.

She's lovely. I wanted to give him something of mine. But it was too fragile to last. And now I wish I had something to give her.

Will shook hands with Daniel and Eloise, thanking them both for their kindness and hospitality. Impulsively Saira leaned forward and kissed Eloise on both cheeks, and the old lady held her close for a few moments, before pushing her away quite roughly. Daniel also bent to kiss Saira, though in a formal, hardly touching kind of way. 'I wish that she had remembered something to tell you about your grandfather. It must be disappointing. If only you'd come a year or two earlier, when everything was still crystal clear in her mind.'

And the thought that if only she'd asked more while her grandfather was still alive, echoed hollowly in Saira's mind yet again, as they walked down, past the memorial, to their car.

14

Old tunes

The two old people stood on the doorstep, waving them off, like any couple. Then Daniel returned to the kitchen to put the soup on to heat. Eloise made her usual protests about him doing the cooking. He's a bully! He thinks I can't remember how to cook! After all these years! But he didn't want her burning her hands on the hot stove again or dropping a heavy pan of scalding liquid. Sometimes she would forget, mid-way through a familiar routine, what she had started to do. She scowled at him, but he laughed back. It was safer to do that than to get impatient. He hated himself when he got angry with her. Sometimes he could say such cruel things, and he knew it was not her fault. It was better to be restrained, however frustrated he felt inwardly. He only hoped Saira hadn't minded Eloise playing with her hair. He sighed, as he thought how beautiful Eloise had been. Old age was so humiliating.

He's smiling at me now, as he stirs. His soup is never as good as mine, he doesn't add the right herbs.

He'd always thought how lucky he'd been to win her. Everyone knew, however vaguely, that she'd had a glamorous past. After the war, anyone who had any connection with the maquis (and quite a few others who'd in fact done nothing) had a special status, even if they didn't talk about their exploits. He'd known that she'd been in love with someone else and that he was second best. He'd thought it was one of the Americans, most probably Dwight. Dwight, after all, had been around the longest and had most frequent contact with her family, having stayed on at the Epinal base after the others had moved on through Alsace, towards Germany and the horrors of the concentration camps. Then she'd gone off to Paris, and so much time had elapsed before Daniel had met her that she only teased him gently if he asked about her past, chiding him for being jealous and telling him nothing. But something in the odd way she'd made her farewells to the visitors made him wonder, after all these years, about the man she had once loved. Could it in fact have been one of the two young Indians?

Eloise noticed that as he ladled the soup he dripped on the tablecloth. He could be so clumsy. It should be washed straight away. But she felt too tired to bother. The girl had been very demanding with all her questions. Maman always prided herself on her linen. Even in the war, with all those soldiers, the linen would be scrubbed into hospital-like cleanliness. Rub, rub, rub in the cold spring water in the stone trough in the wash-house. Twisting, wringing, feeding the folded heavy linen under the mangle rollers, till it was compressed into a stiff board. Then the impeccable sheets would whip high up into the sky like storks, whiter than the snow below, flying free, tugging the washing line behind them. And the next day, a whole day, spent with the heavy iron, steaming and smoothing every last wrinkle then folding them into submissive piles. His eyes were such a strange shade as he stared at me over the mound of still-damp sheets. I thought they were brown, but in that light there was a hint of grey-green too. So clear. So innocent. I laughed at him and made him help. I made him take the corners, fold, hold the new corners and stand at a distance, holding one end as I ironed other end. He had such grace and delicacy, as his brown fingers traced the white embroidered initials. 'Stand still!' I must have sounded bossy, for he saluted ironically, dropping a corner. With each fold we stepped closer to each other, as if in a formal dance. On the final fold his face was so close to mine. His lips were …

'No closer!'

Daniel looked surprised. 'Eat your soup, my dear. You said you were hungry.' He wished she'd eat more. She was becoming as thin as a bedraggled bird.

A few mouthfuls to please him. It tastes of wool. Nothing tastes nice these days.

It was more efficient some days just to take the spoon and feed her himself. But so undignified. He noticed the cat coming in. He tried to shoo it away from her, but it jumped on her lap and purred triumphantly.

With a start, she remembered herself, and started eating again. We should have fed our guests. Papa insists that Maman feeds everyone who comes to our house. 'Why isn't the girl eating with us?'

The kebabs were excellent. Will looked round at the cramped dining area. He supposed most people must take away or eat outside. There was hardly space inside the tiny kebaberie for the three small tables and the chairs between the plate glass window and the glass-fronted counter. Large mirrors on the side walls reflected the bright blue walls and gave the illusion that the room was larger. Perhaps it was the French culinary influence which made the familiar-sounding kebabs with their colourful, spicily-dressed salad taste so much better than English ones.

'I'm absolutely ravenous,' confessed Saira. 'I had to concentrate so hard to try and follow her. It was exhausting. I don't mean her English, that was amazing. I mean the way her mind kept hopping around. Do you suppose there was any logic?'

'I don't think it meant anything, most of the time,' said Will dismissively. 'Although she remembered the Americans and the food and the animals all right. I kept waiting for her to focus properly and work out who you were.' He picked up his second skewer, and jabbed it for emphasis, as he spoke. 'But then I had a really strange feeling at the end. You know, when I quite deliberately mentioned the Americans and escaping prisoners in the same breath? She seemed to know perfectly well what I meant by escaping prisoners. I'm sure that when she said they were worth it she meant your grandfather and his friend.' He took a bite.

'Yeah, I got the oddest feeling, too, that occasionally she was kind of hiding behind a mask of madness. Well, not that you can call it madness, these days. Would it count as dementia do you think? You're allowed to say that, though it sounds just as bad to me. Confusion sounds kinder.'

'And didn't you think it was odd, seeing her dressed up and doing her gracious hostess thing? I found myself wishing I could see her as the young and beautiful girl she must have been when (or if) your grandfather met her.'

'When,' said Saira firmly. 'We know that he was definitely there that November. And now we know she was there too. She specifically mentioned the winter of '44. So why does she say she can't remember Grandfather and his friend?'

There was something else nagging away at the back of her

mind. Something about that strange leave-taking. It wasn't so much the combing and arranging and combing again, though that was odd enough. She suddenly realised that it was the tune the old woman was humming. She'd thought it sounded familiar.

'Did you recognise the tune she was humming as she combed?'

Will's emphatic 'Never heard it before!' shook her. She'd assumed it was a childhood tune that Will would know too. But suddenly it clicked. Of course! It wasn't some nursery rhyme that English children, let alone French children, would know. It was from a song, a bit distorted, which was why she hadn't recognised it at first, that her grandfather used to sing to her when she was young.

'Lie down for a little while,' Daniel insisted when Eloise had eventually eaten the last mouthful of soup. He knew she'd be exhausted after a morning of trying to focus and that tiredness made her restless and even more vague.

She pouted and began to argue. Maman never lets us lie down in the afternoon. Too much to do. Even when I've walked all night with my brave boys. 'They'd have lost their way without me, you know!' The afternoons are for sewing, Maman insists, while the light is good. No time to waste. That's the one thing she thinks I can do better than Marie. 'My darns are almost invisible, you know!' Daniel nodded, without really listening, tucked the bedspread over her feet and tiptoed out of their bedroom.

Eloise turned onto her side and curled up, warm and relaxed. This last soldier, the Nippo-American, the frozen one. His uniform is in a terrible state. Maman has pounded and

241

scrubbed and Marie has pressed it, and now they can see where the rocks and ice have ripped and pierced it, and they pass it on to me to patch and join. I sit by the window to catch the light, and Yaqub comes in and pulls up a chair next to me and watches as I cut patches out of the hems and stitch them into place. He is silent for a long time, just watching my needle forcing its way through the thick fabric. Then he leans towards me. I hardly dare breathe. He stretches out his hand. Is he going to stroke my sewing hand? Does he want to kiss it? But no, he fingers the fabric. He asks me to cut a small piece for him. So strange. And then he rummages through my scrap bag. He seems to like the thick black from an old dress of grand-maman and asks too for small pieces of white, scarlet, blue and green. He takes a needle from my pincushion – a big one with a blunt end, and some colourful embroidery thread, and steals my scissors, so I'll have to bite the thread off when I've finished. And he laughs and tiptoes away. 'Daniel! Where are my scissors? What has he done with them?'

Saira and Will decided to spend the afternoon back in town in the local museum, getting more of a feel of the town's past, so much of which had been effaced by the war. Saira found the section on local crafts and occupations the most interesting, but then spent time with Will in the basement looking at uniforms and weapons. When they got back to the Hotel du Centre, both of them found it hard to summarise for the friendly owner exactly how much they had discovered from Eloise. It all came out in rather a jumble. But he looked very pleased, and said he thought they'd done really well. It was almost as if he felt responsible for their discoveries.

It also transpired that he'd had another idea. He was a little hesitant at first, saying that it wasn't the kind thing he'd normally suggest to tourists. But then, he conceded, they weren't his usual kind of visitor. There was this man he knew who played the accordion. He used to play in cafés and at weddings, – all the latest tunes. But then his kind of music went out of fashion. However he was now having a bit of a comeback, playing the old tunes. Nowhere glamorous of course, mainly clubs and residences for the elderly. Anyway, he was doing a session at one of the community centres that evening. It would all be very jolly, with everyone singing along and dancing, and, although there wouldn't be many other young people, they'd be welcome to go along, provided they bought a few drinks from the bar there. And he always finished up with old wartime favourites. The hotelier urged them to go and enjoy the atmosphere and chat to the old people about their memories.

Intrigued, that evening, after they'd eaten, they strolled along the river side and over a foot-bridge and headed, as instructed, towards some tall flats till they spotted the community centre. Inside, the session was well under way. Convivial groups of old people were sitting around the tables, with bottles of wine or beer, chatting loudly or singing along. Saira and Will felt a bit self-conscious as everyone seemed to know everyone else. There were some young people, but they were either with their elderly relatives or clustering round the bar. They found a table and Will got some beer and some fruit juice.

As they looked around and talked in a desultory fashion over the noise about what they would do next, now that they'd come to the last point on Grandfather Yaqub's escape route, the accordionist struck up a fresh tune. To their surprise, everyone stood up, and formed a long chain, hands on the hips of the person in front. And, like a long caterpillar, they began an ungainly dance, with legs sticking out first on one side, then on the other. Saira and Will smiled to see the elegantly dressed elderly women and their dapper men looking so foolish, and then they too got swept up to join in. At the end they returned, laughing to their table. Then Will pointed in surprise to the doorway. Daniel was standing there with a brown paper bag in his hand.

They waved, and Daniel came over to sit down with them. Despite his protestations that he couldn't stay but had to get back quickly to Eloise, Will went to get him a beer. Daniel said that the hotelier had told him where to find them. He'd only just missed them. He looked around him, and started to relax and shed his watchful anxiety. He began to tap his foot gently to the familiar tune. 'We used to dance to this. We had big dances in the village on our patronal day,' he said fondly. Then he held out the bag towards Saira. It was old and dusty. 'She insisted that I brought this for you. She wouldn't let me wait until tomorrow, in case you had departed. And she wouldn't tell me what it was.'

Saira took the bag. It was very light and the paper was soft with age. It smelt of mothballs. As she untwisted the tightly screwed corners and felt inside, her hand met more soft paper. She pulled out a ball of greying wood-flecked tissue paper. She fumbled in the creases to find a way in. 'Reminds me of my grandparents and the old tissue paper they used every year to wrap away the hand-painted Christmas decorations,' Will commented. 'It was always the same old pieces.'

Daniel leaned forward intently as Saira pulled aside the wrapping, but wasn't quick enough to catch the toy animal that rolled out and landed, legs in the air, on the wooden floor. Its legs were sturdy, with red discs crudely attached with a sort of green blanket stitch to form feet. As Saira picked it up she could feel the coarse straw of its stuffing under the fabric. 'Look a trunk and tusks!' 'And it's squinting!' Will laughed at the unevenly attached buttons that formed its eyes.

Saira fingered the still bright colours that formed a decorative cloth on the dull, coarse elephant hide. 'Did it belong to your children?' This strange gift – if it was a gift – puzzled her.

'We didn't have children. Perhaps we met too late,' Daniel replied bleakly. 'The strangest thing was that she remembered your name, though we hadn't mentioned it again. When she woke up this afternoon after I made her rest, she dragged a chair into the bedroom, and stood on it. I was so worried that she would fall, but she insisted. All the time she was saying, 'For Saira! For Saira! There's nothing else left now.' And she rummaged at the back of the shelf at the top of the wardrobe till she found this. I've never seen it before.'

Daniel stared, perplexed at the misshapen animal, which Saira had balanced, unsteadily on the table, thinking it combined cheeky and exotic now it stood the right way up. It was clearly a toy, but didn't look as if small fingers had ever played with it or tugged at the bead-like buttons or clumsily attached yellow tusks. And yet the black skin-fabric was quite worn and shiny in places and there was something vaguely familiar about one small patch of colour. Was it the drab shade of old army uniforms?

'One thing is sure, that wasn't sewn by my Eloise! She has always been very neat, artistic – professional even! Did I tell you, that after the war she trained as a maker of ladies' fashion hats? No? I do not really know why. It was not what her father wanted for her.' He explained that Léo had wanted her to become an interpreter or a translator, but for some reason she had rebelled, and decided to do something more frivolous. 'She was always clever with her fingers. So soon after the war ended, she left home and went to Paris, to train with one of the big houses. She must have spent about ten years working there on the latest fashions.'

Saira was only half listening. She looked at Will to see if he was thinking the same as she was. It wasn't something she felt she could say out loud in front of Eloise's kindly, courteous husband. It was a fantastical thought that maybe her grandfather had been the one who had sewn it. A hint of India. A reminder for Eloise of her Indian soldier. A token? A promise? A promise he would return? A hint even of marriage and children? No, she was being fanciful. Something about this squat little elephant had enchanted her and snared her imagination.

Daniel was silent for a few moments then added, 'Of course, I didn't know her then. And this is making me wonder if I ever really knew her. Could I even truthfully say I know her now?' He said it wasn't the confusion, for he was getting used to that now, and could usually work out the invisible links between her statements. It was the sense that there were still secrets, things that she'd never trusted him enough to talk about.

He hesitated again, before continuing, in rather a rush, 'Some people speculated that she had to go away to Paris, that she had to leave home, because … Well things were confused at the end of the war. There were other girls who went away to have babies. Liberation babies. Victory babies. But people saying that of Eloise has always angered me. I think that was just jealous talk. People can be very spiteful. I thought there may have been some special friendship, but that is all. And after the war, she just needed to find herself, in being creative and free-spirited.' He looked down at his hands, and niggled away at one cuticle. 'That's why it's so sad that now she seems to lose that very self that she once prized so much.' Saira smiled sympathetically at him.

'Once my Eloise was so proud. So independent. Now she hardly cares how she looks or what she says.' He felt as if he lived alongside a wilful child, who was unaware of danger, and who had ceased to regard him as a friend and lover. 'Sometimes I think she even forgets who I am. At other times she seems to be constantly criticising me for taking over her old tasks. She must regret her loss of autonomy. But it feels as if I can do nothing right. But today was a good day. She enjoyed your visit. And maybe there is a reason why she wants you to have the little elephant.'

He stood up, shaking his shoulders gently as if to shake off the unpleasant thoughts. And then he inclined his head towards the accordion player, who was striking up a new tune. 'I don't know, my dear, if you dance, but this used to be a favourite tune of ours, and it would give an old man a great deal of pleasure to dance to it one more time.'

Will expected Saira to refuse, and was very surprised when she allowed herself to be led onto the dance floor. She'd insisted on changing into a silver sparkly tunic before they came out, and he felt proud of how graceful she looked, – almost as good as something off a TV dance show. He wondered how she'd cope with whatever bizarrely named dance this was – foxtrot maybe – and was surprised at the ease with which she just seemed to follow Daniel's lead. He felt almost ashamed to see the elegant footwork of many of the old folk around them. None of his generation knew how to dance like that nowadays. He sat and stroked the little elephant, feeling the occasional tip of a rough straw stalk protruding from the seams. A child would have loved this unusual little toy. He wondered if Yaqub and Eloise had actually … no, he didn't think so. To cover his treacherous thoughts, he stood up and applauded as the two dancers returned to his table, and then felt foolish as people turned to look.

Daniel smiled happily. 'Eloise was a great dancer, you know. She always knew the latest steps! She told me once how one of the Americans, Dwight, had taught her to jitterbug. That was 'all the rage' then. I always thought it was him she'd loved …'

To distract him from this delicate question, Will pointed out that he was a great dancer too. And Daniel started to tell them how that had been a song they'd danced to on their honeymoon. Will got the feeling that Daniel didn't often reminisce these days and certainly hadn't confessed to anyone else quite how difficult he was finding it to adapt to the changes in Eloise. Perhaps the rare break from her company plus the beer had loosened his tongue, along with the fact that they were strangers whom he wouldn't have to face again after his revelations. Daniel was describing how they'd spent their honeymoon in Switzerland. 'It was a great adventure! I remember dancing outside our hotel, by the lake, beneath the stars, with the band playing. I was so proud that this beautiful woman had chosen me over all the brilliant young men she must have met in Paris. Just an ordinary schoolmaster!'

Saira noticed him looking at the elephant again as he fell silent. She was startled when he wondered aloud if Eloise had somehow remembered that it was Saira's honeymoon and that's why she wanted to give her a gift, a plaything for any future children. She toyed with the idea of contradicting him, and telling him about the significance of the hummed tune, and that Eloise had realised she was Yaqub's granddaughter. But then she thought that the tune was like a secret code, and that Eloise must have had her own reasons for keeping quiet.

She still didn't think Eloise was as vague as she made out.

Will seemed to be thinking along similar lines as he nodded at Daniel as if in agreement about the reason for the gift and then picked up an earlier theme. 'I expect she always saw far more in you than you realised. And she was right. And now it is your will-power and devotion that keeps Eloise alive to her real self for as much of the time as possible.' Saira was amazed his wisdom and tact – qualities she hadn't previously thought well-developed in Will.

Daniel looked relieved. But then the mention of 'devotion' made him feel guilty as well as grateful. He realised that he'd been gone too long. 'If she wakes up she may wander out of doors looking for me. She may forget that she begged me to bring you the little toy.' He found it hard to express to Saira and Will how much this short break from the minute-by-minute watchfulness over Eloise had meant to him and how it had given him back a sense of normality and his own past. As he stood up to go, he hesitantly asked if perhaps they would write occasionally when they got home. Saira promised with all her heart. 'And tell Eloise how much her gift means to me.'

Soon after Daniel left, they too slipped out, overhearing people reminiscing about the great victory dances as they passed their tables. Saira was reminded of Habib's comments about the euphoria after his mother's village was liberated, the sense that anything was possible. She wondered why Eloise had gone to Paris. She realised she'd like to see Habib again and find out more about how it was when his father returned to find his mother. She thought of the little elephant and wondered whether her grandfather had intended to return to Eloise and why he hadn't.

'What an amazing day! I can't take it all in!' she sighed as they strolled back by the river. The avenue of trees and the street lamps rippled and merged and separated in the water below. She clasped the paper bag in one hand, and Will's firm hand in the other. 'I wonder why she gave it to me, after she'd kept it for so long.' A real sense of sadness overtook her, as she tried to imagine Eloise, as Daniel had described her: a young woman, with all her life ahead of her, much as she must have been when Grandfather met her. She tried again to picture her serious, upright grandfather as a romantic young soldier, overwhelmed by the beauty and courage of this resistance heroine. But perhaps, in the long run, the real romance was Daniel's steadfast caring. She turned her face up to Will's. 'At least you now know what it will be like to look after me when I'm old and grey and confused.'

'It's always worried me, the till death us do part bit. It's an alarming prospect,' Will agreed, smiling. And he drew her to a stop, took her in his arms and kissed her passionately. 'But we'll create some good memories first.'

When Daniel reached home, he was alarmed to see that the lights were all on. Eloise must have woken up. With a sigh of relief, he realised that the front door was still locked. At least she hadn't gone out looking for him. As he closed the door quietly behind him, he could hear his wife humming in the kitchen. She was sitting at the table with her back to him. In front of her was the egg basket and coloured felt tips were splayed around (mainly without their tops, he noticed with irritation). She looked up at him and smiled childishly, and held up one of the eggs she had been decorating. She obviously hadn't prepared it first, but had an expression of great concentration. He held out his hand, curiously, but she wouldn't give it to him. He was surprise how delicately she had traced the colours and patterns. He didn't know she was still capable of such intricate work or such concentration.

'It's very pretty, my dear.'

Eloise began to cry.

15

Black, grey or white?

'C'mon now boys, no time to hang around! I'm finally taking you to HQ.' They had recognised the sound of Dwight's Jeep screeching to a halt, skidding slightly on the compacted snow, even before he leaned out and yelled to them. As they rushed up the stairs to collect their few possessions, Yaqub could still hear his loud voice demanding, 'And how's my favourite girl?'

Barkat laughed at his friend's scowl. 'If you ask me, it's just as well we're on the move, otherwise you'd be persuaded into staying here for ever!' He leant down over the wounded American. 'Soon I fight Germans! Brave like you!' and squeezed his hand. He thought Jimmy was looking much brighter, so was surprised to see his face cloud over. Perhaps he was disappointed that they were leaving. But then Jimmy whispered, 'All that bravery! Will anyone notice? Who was it shot me? My own side!'

Barkat frowned. He couldn't really understand the hoarse, rapid words. But Jimmy continued, 'I was one of the first to get near our boys in the trapped regiment. Close enough for them to see our faces. They took one look and went crazy with their last rounds of ammo. They didn't even look at our uniforms. Just our faces.' His words came tumbling out, now he was reviving and anxious to communicate with outsiders, before he transferred back into the care of the Americans. 'I guess someone told them later. But too late for my buddies. You wait, they'll hush it up.'

While Barkat puzzled over this outburst, Yaqub was lost in his own thoughts. He had picked up Eloise's delicate painted egg shell and was turning it over in his hands, wondering how he could ever carry it safely through all the fighting that lay ahead of them. He took a sock (one of the two pairs that Philippe's wife had given him), wrapped the egg shell in it and tucked it carefully in a pocket. He went over and patted the heavily bandaged hands of their Japanese-American friend, saying hopefully, 'Better soon!' Jimmy sighed. If they hadn't understood, no one else would.

Downstairs, all the family were waiting to see them off. Léo's wife was wiping her reddened, chapped hands, then to their surprise she stood on her toes and gave them each a big kiss on each cheek. Even Marie smiled, and pushed their pack of well-worn playing cards into Barkat's hands. 'She wants you to remember us as you defeat the Germans in the day and play belote at night with the American troops,' Eloise translated. She kissed Barkat lightly, but gave Yaqub a more lingering embrace, whispering, 'You will write to me, won't you?' Yaqub nodded. He felt as tearful as a small child, and could not trust himself to speak. Finally Léo gave them both a bear hug as they struggled to find words of gratitude for the family's big-hearted welcome. 'Come and see us after the war!'

Dwight shepherded them to his Jeep, promising, over his shoulder, 'I'll be back for our Jap.' As the Jeep roared off, Yaqub turned and looked back at the house on the edge of the forest. He realised that he no longer felt any enthusiasm for fighting. Eloise's area was already free. Somehow that was all that mattered now. If only he could stay.

However, Dwight was in a cheerful mood and wanted conversation. He asked them about girls and whether they had sweet-hearts waiting for them back home. Undeterred when Yaqub remained silent, he asked how they were captured and whether they'd seen the German General Rommel. After Barkat had leaned forward and shouted from the back, telling him a bit about Libya, Dwight unashamedly confessed that he'd never heard of any of these places before he joined the army and was sent to Europe. He said he came from a farm. But a much bigger farm than you ever saw in these parts. The fields stretched beyond the horizon. And he would eventually inherit it all, and settle down with his girl, and raise his kids on the family land. 'When it's finally over!' As he chattered on, Yaqub's emotions were see-sawing. He now felt homesick for the few small fields from which his family eked a living. How could he have thought he wanted to stay here? What would his mother have said if he did?

But Barkat felt no such nostalgia, he was just raring to get back with fighting troops. So he changed the subject and started asking Dwight for the latest news of the advance. But as they turned onto the main road, he became perturbed that they were moving away from the fighting. Dwight merely replied 'Heading for HQ! Military orders!' firmly, and Yaqub roused himself and pointed out that they probably needed to get the paper-work sorted out. 'Three copies of everything first, – you know the army,' he said lightly.

However, at Epinal, it seemed more complicated than a few bits of paper in triplicate. They passed through various officials, feeling more passive with every move. They were becoming insignificant pebbles in a huge military game, rather than adventurers who had broken out of prison camp to fight for freedom. At the first desk, their details were written out, and Dwight was handed some kind of receipt. 'For Leo,' he explained before he left them, clapping them on their shoulders and wishing them good luck. At the second desk, the American seemed to find it very difficult to understand them, and passed them on to a third official, who filled in their names and army details on a different form. When they tried to tell their story, just three words were added to the form, at the point when they mentioned the PoW camps at Annaberg and in Alsace. The officer seemed disappointed that they did not know the real names (apart from Léo's) of the people who had helped them. And he seemed quite surprised that they hadn't been in the PoW camp at Epinal. 'All the other Indians were from there,' he said several times. The fourth official read the paperwork, and congratulated them briefly on their escape, and said he would send their details on to the Brits. When Barkat tried to ask why they couldn't just join the Americans, fighting, he was told, stiffly, that they were fighting in different sectors, and that the Brits had wanted all the other Indians returned to them.

They seemed to be moving up the ranks, as they were escorted to a separate office. Here there was an officer with some complicated forms. He said the questions were things the British would want to know. He read out some very long-winded questions starting with words like 'were you ever subjected to or did you ever hear of efforts to subvert …' which they found quite incomprehensible. The officer looked exasperated, but didn't simplify his questions. He tried out some French phrases from a book and then some German ones. Did he think they were spies or something? They shrugged and continued to look blank. In the end the officer just said 'Wait! British Army!' 'I feel like one of the guard dogs when the Germans pointed at them and told them to sit,' whispered

Barkat. 'I still don't see why we can't join in with the Americans before it's too late. They must always need sappers. And they've just lost all those men like Jimmy.'

Barkat's frustration increased with every hour, then every day that they had to spend in Epinal. The pen-pushers, like pen-pushers the world over, seemed self-important and unfriendly. But the liaison men, like Dwight, who would return to the base most evenings, were more welcoming. They would jolly them along and tell them to thank their stars that they were at least being properly fed, American army style!

The highlight of their time there was the evening when some GIs took Yaqub and Barkat out with them. Parts of the town had been quite badly shelled, but there was a real sense of gaiety, even in the middle of winter. The men headed for a bar they knew. It was the first time Yaqub and Barkat had been inside a French café-bar. Lots of old men were sitting drinking and chatting loudly. Some of them cheered the Americans as they entered and insisted on buying them drinks. And Yaqub was surprised at how many girls were there and how friendly they were. He wished he could be there with Eloise, and imagined her face, animated from chatting to so many people. Perhaps he might even have been very daring and held her hand as they listened to the accordion player in the corner. He started to compose a letter to her in his head. But who could he ask to write it out for him in proper English or French?

The Americans took delight in trying to get them to taste the spirit they seemed so fond of. Barkat was feeling so depressed by all the waiting around that he almost succumbed to the you-don't-know-until-you've-tried-it patter. But when he saw the state of one of their companions, who they had to help escort back, he was glad he had resisted.

The next morning one of the GIs, looking no worse after

his night of heavy drinking, stuck his head round the door. 'Hi boys! You're off to Marseilles!'

‡ 🐾
‡ 🐾

'So what now?' Will asked the next morning, sighing at the same time and, spraying croissant crumbs everywhere. 'D'you know, after that amazing ending yesterday, everything feels pretty aimless today.'

Saira agreed, suggesting that the grey weather outside might be partly responsible. She stirred her coffee. 'But the main thing is the sense that we've come to the end of the trail. There's nothing left to discover. Because after being with Léo and Eloise, the Americans just took Grandfather to um – Epinal, wasn't it?'

Struck by the mention of Epinal, Will brightened up, and suggested that they went there to the real end of the journey, before turning round and spending a couple of frivolous days back in Alsace, 'where I seem to remember that you promised me some pretty wine villages.'

Saira had mixed feelings about wine villages and who'd promised what to whom, so agreed it was a good idea to see the place where the Americans interviewed her grandfather and his friend. 'We might find a last piece of the jigsaw.'

The tourist office was their first point of call in Epinal. But the young lady there looked at them incredulously when Saira asked if she knew where the Americans were based at the end of the war. Wherever it had been, it obviously wasn't now a tourist destination. She tried to steer them towards the huge American cemetery nearby even adding, helpfully, that some of the Hawaiian soldiers had been buried there. 'Some of the ones we heard about, I expect,' Will observed. Saira was irritated and persisted with her question, thinking surely someone must know. The girl suddenly looked inspired. One of their tour guides was leading a group round the old town in half an hour. They could ask him.

It was pleasant to wander round the market while they waited, sampling the proffered pieces of cheese and looking at the fruit and vegetables. There were tables and chairs still spread outside the cafés on the old square, as if just waiting for the sun to come out from behind the low cloud. And over the bridge in the newer part of town (had it too been destroyed?) the canal was busy with schoolchildren in canoes, negotiating a marked-out course. Saira enjoyed the buzz of people getting on with their lives.

The tour guide, older and more knowledgeable than the staff member, was, nevertheless, regretful on their return. He really didn't know where the Americans had been based. It was possible that they'd occupied some of the old army barracks and he could tell them where those had been. Why did they want to know? When Saira explained about her grandfather's captivity and escape, the guide was interested. Did they know that there had been Indian prisoners here too? Now that was something he knew a bit about. It was famous because it had been a large camp which had got shelled. No, not by the Germans, by the Americans in their attempts to dislodge the Germans. Some Indian prisoners had escaped, but a lot were killed or injured. Will said they'd heard about some of them roaming the forest. The guide's trump card was that he could tell them where the Indians were buried.

'What do you think? A few more graves at the end of the journey?' Will turned to Saira and she nodded. 'Appropriate, perhaps.'

The cemetery here was, unsurprisingly, much larger than the Schoenenbourg one, and it took them a lot longer to find the military graves from the Second World War. They wandered between graves ranging from monumental to communal paupers', then found the French military graves from the First World War. Finally, right at the back, screened by a hedge, was a secluded strip of later war graves including, at the far end the distinctive British Commonwealth ones. There must have been more than fifty.

'A lot of Sikh headstones,' Will observed, 'but look! A Bengal Sapper and Miner like your grandfather.' It seemed so ignominious for them to have been killed by their own side, however accidentally, after all they must have been through. Saira was just pleased that some rose bushes had been planted in front of the graves. It made them feel more remembered. And somehow, although her grandfather had been more fortunate and had reached Epinal safely, she was glad that they'd ended their search in this quiet place of remembrance.

It was hard to tell if they were being guarded as they left Epinal for Marseilles. It definitely felt as if they were being escorted as they were led to an empty supply lorry. However, Yaqub was pleased that they were not consigned to the back, but offered a seat up front, wedged between the driver and another soldier. The driver didn't say much, but his companion was prepared to chat. He told them his name, but it was a long one, and they couldn't get their tongues round it. He laughed and said it was Polish and told them to just call him Hank. He said he'd been running supplies ever since the August landings.

Yaqub thought back to their days in their last PoW camp, and to Benoit's excitement as he'd told them about the Allied landings. He hadn't thought about Benoit recently. How long ago that all seemed. Practical as ever, Barkat asked the name of the place where Hank had landed, but he didn't recognise it. But when Hank explained that there were several landing places, all to the west of Marseilles, he banged his knee in frustration. 'Marseilles! That's what Benoit said. And that's where we're going. Do you realise that we're being sent backwards all the time, further and further from the fighting? Don't they trust us?'

Yaqub sat miserably in silence. He hadn't expected to feel such a wrench as they travelled further and further from Eloise. He liked these Americans and their informality. He couldn't imagine the British soldiers chatting like this. It made him wonder if he dared to ask Hank ... No, it was unthinkable.

After several hours, when Hank had taken over the driving, he announced that they were going to take a break. He drove into the main square of a small town and pulled up to a halt outside a café. 'Wonderful girl I know here,' he announced with a wink. His companion, who appeared to be called Arnie, remonstrated with him, pointing at the two of them, which confirmed their impression of being under guard. But Hank just shrugged and laughed away all objections.

Yaqub was beginning to like these friendly little cafés. It was dark and warm inside and the mirror behind the bar was all steamed up. The men were wearing berets, drab overalls and huge wooden clogs, which they stamped appreciatively as the Americans entered. Hank made a bee-line for the bar, where a girl with a big ribbon in her hair was wiping glasses, while Arnie, with an air of resignation, sat them down at one of the tables and waited for the owner, in his large grey apron, to come over to serve them. They noticed that Arnie didn't try to speak any French, but just repeated his order loudly, trying to get some fruit juice for them all, after which he relapsed into silence. Sipping his blackcurrant juice, Yaqub guiltily reminded Barkat of prayer time, but this noisy, irreverent place felt quite unsuitable, and they thought Arnie wouldn't let them out of his sight, so they decided to wait till they were back in the truck. 'Besides, we are on a journey,' said Barkat, feeling he'd used that justification rather a lot in recent weeks.

Later, Yaqub was to wish they'd taken more advantage of the easy freedom of the café. He wished he'd gone over to watch the games the men were playing. He wished he'd tried to talk to them about their lives and their land. He felt his glimpses of French life had been so warm-hearted and vibrant despite the war. But at the time he was preoccupied with another matter. So when Hank re-joined them, well pleased with his flirtation with the bar-maid, and boasting of all the French girls he knew along the routes he drove, Yaqub plucked up courage. Falteringly he asked Hank if, as a man who so obviously understood these things, he would be prepared to write a letter in English for him. An important letter. A letter to a girl.

They walked back to the car, through the rows and rows of townspeople, some who had died young and some at a ripe old age, and Saira's thoughts took a new turn. She wondered what it must be like to be as old as her grandmother, with not so many years ahead of her, but with a question which still needed answering before she could feel at peace. 'I can't decide how much to tell her, Will. It feels such a responsibility. Do I tell her that nothing happened, which is half true, or should I be more honest and say that there was a girl to whom he clearly meant something?'

Will hesitated. He had always been puzzled by how much Grandmother Amina's family protected her, always accompanying her, translating, rarely expecting her to speak in public. He suspected that, like his nanna, she was quite a tough old bird, who'd understood, even if she hadn't experienced, more of life than they suspected. 'I always thought that she was the one who stood by you during our year apart. Did you feel she understood how you felt and what it was like to face losing someone? Do you need to protect her? Won't she be able to find her own way of coming to terms with what happened, once she knows?'

Saira was surprised. It was true that she had been very understanding and supportive then. 'But this is different.'

'Is it?'

It was many days before they arrived in a place called Taranto to be interrogated by the British in a forbidding Section X. Why couldn't the British have asked their questions in Marseilles? Why had they hurried them on from Marseilles, bringing them all the way by sea to Taranto before interviewing them? He wished they were back with the Americans. The Americans hadn't known what to make of them, but had at least treated them with civility in Epinal. When they reached British HQ in Marseilles, Yaqub had reminded Hank of the letter he had written for him. The words had looked a bit erratic, as Hank had written them in the juddering lorry, while Arnie was driving. Hank had laughed, a bit unkindly, because Yaqub had been so hesitant about what to say, and in the end had offered to write in his own words. Yaqub did hope he'd been sensitive to the delicacy and proprieties of the situation, because Hank hadn't read it back to him.

But whatever it said, he was so glad he'd left the letter with the American, who'd promised to pass it on to Dwight to deliver to Léo's house. He could never have asked one of those British soldiers in Marseilles to write. They'd treated them like prisoners, pushing them around, and finally herding them onto the ship to Taranto. They didn't even bother to answer when he'd asked where Taranto was. But Barkat found out that it was in Italy, and had sunk into despair knowing that their separation from the battle grounds was final. 'Backwards all the time! The Germans brought us up through this Italy country after we were captured!'

For the first time since the forests of Alsace and the border crossing, Yaqub felt scared, as he was ushered into the windowless, grey room, with its table and two chairs. Why couldn't Barkat stay with him? He'd been shown into a different room. For interrogation they said. He wasn't sure what that word meant. He wasn't sure whether he should sit down or remain standing. 'Wait,' the armed Tommy had said.

Looking back, Yaqub yearned for the freedom of the French mountains. Even the endless, exhausted trudging now seemed exciting. At least they were at liberty then. It had been an exhilarating period of kindness, adventure and heroism. They'd lived as free men, patriots, warriors-to-be.

And here they were – or he was. Why had they been separated? Were the British testing them? Their own side? Making sure they told the same story? Were they being punished, rather than rewarded for their escape? Yaqub put his hand into his pocket. His fingers closed round the sock, caressing the thick wool to feel the curves of Eloise's feather-light egg. It had somehow survived the rough handling of the English soldiers. He didn't want to take it out of the safety of his pocket. He felt as if he was being spied on, even in this bare room. But he could remember its brightly painted colours, and he could remember her bright eyes and smiling mouth as he caressed it. It gave him courage to face the bewildering situation of being treated like an enemy of his own side.

He must have sat brooding for a couple of hours before an officer came in, with a bundle of papers and folders under his arm, which he spread out on the table. The top sheet of paper contained guidance notes on the assessment of Indian soldiers emerging from German captivity and on the three possible categories: black, grey and white. Black, dangerous to security. Grey, affected by enemy propaganda, but not a permanent danger. White, not affected and not dangerous.

Yaqub saluted as smartly as he could after years of lack of practice. He was instantly asked what salute he would give to a German. Puzzled, he demonstrated. Then he was allowed to sit down. Straight away the questions about Annaberg started. He wasn't sure at first why the officer wanted to know so much detail, but slowly realised that he was being in some way tested. He was asked about food, about conditions, then about Chandra Bose and then about how much food he got after Bose's visit. He was asked the exact date he was moved from Annaberg to another camp. But he didn't know that. He said it was a long time after Bose's visits. He told everything he could remember of Bose's speeches.

As the questioning continued, he felt the officer was trying to trap him with questions about what he was trained to do in later camps. He kept saying he had cut wood for the German officers' fires. But the questions kept hinting at military training. He was puzzled. Why would the Germans do that? Slowly it dawned on him that the officer must think he'd gone over to the Germans in those early days and been sent away for training. Surely he could tell that he wasn't that kind of man? He began to get upset, which seemed to interest his interrogator. As he was stumbling to explain his loyalty, his belief in everything he had been brought up to respect and everything he had learned in the Indian Army, his interrogator leaned forward and raised his voice, 'So why did the Germans let you escape?'

Yaqub tried to explain that it was Benoit, not the Germans, who had helped them to escape.

'But this Benoit was working for the Germans. There must be a reason why the Germans encouraged him to help you. Where did they want you to go after you escaped? Who did they want you to join and help?'

Yaqub hesitated as he recalled the fear of old Wilhelm, the kindness of Philippe and his wife, the bravery of the lorry driver despite his young children and the resourcefulness of 'bicycle-man.' He didn't want to get any of them into trouble. Perhaps he should not have mentioned Benoit. And as for Léo and his family ... He was aware how suspicious his hesitation must seem and stammered something disjointed and vague about not knowing real names.

'What were you told to do? What weapons did they give you?'

Defeated by the hostility of his interrogator, Yaqub risked sneaking his hand into his pocket again. The hump of the fragile egg shell gave him courage. He thought of Eloise, of how she had led the Americans, translated for them and risked her life. He felt angry at this man who was a superior and who should have a greater understanding. His hitherto submissive demeanour changed. He raised his head and looked the white man in the eyes, something he would never normally presume to do. He spoke loudly, almost roughly, demanding to know why these people would have risked their lives for him. He remembered the word 'Resistance'. He would be grateful all his life for everything they had risked to help him and his friend.

And he added that he had not held a weapon since the surrender at Mechili.

To his surprise, his disjointed vehement words, part English, part Hindustani, seemed to satisfy his interrogator for the time being. For he scribbled a few more notes, then gathered up his papers, saying 'Wait.' Yaqub was not sure if he heard a key turn in the door as he left. He didn't dare get up and try the door. He heard a nearby door open and shut. He wondered if it was Barkat's turn.

A private came in with a mug of water and a plate of army rations (English style). He realised that, as far as foreign food went, he much preferred the French food his hosts had shared. That was nourishing. But he should keep his strength up. Though for what?

The sky was getting darker behind the small window above his head when his interrogator returned. Yaqub wondered what had happened to all their Indian officers since their separation after capture. The viceroy's commissioned officers knew their men so much better. This man didn't seem to know how to look for honesty. He behaved as if he thought all Indian troops were dishonest.

'This Benoit, what was his job title?'

'What did he show you in the Maginot Line?'

'What were the Germans manufacturing there?'

'Where is the plan he gave you?'

'What did he want you to find out?'

Remembering Benoit's anxiety when he left them with Wilhelm, Yaqub tried to explain to his questioner that Benoit liked them, had been a friend to them and had been sorry for them. He was a man with a family and was terrified of the Germans taking revenge if he was discovered to have helped them. Did the Germans really send white people to death camps? He didn't want to say anything that would hurt Benoit. Would the English reward Benoit? He had had nothing to give him apart from some spices from the Red Cross.

The officer sighed. The two men were sticking to the same story as each other. They even gave the same minor details. They seemed simple rather than devious. 'Grey,' he summarised on Yaqub's file. 'In suspect camp during propaganda period. Fully aware of all subversion attempts at Annaberg. Knows many of the men who were subverted. But no evidence of treachery or of later presence in a legion camp or of desire to take up arms against the interests of the Crown. Escape probably genuine. To be offered help to write letters, in case they reveal more.'

After a toilet break, the private brought in some paper, a pen and some ink. 'D'ya want me to write?' he asked offhandedly.

It looked to Yaqub as if the young soldier found writing in English nearly as difficult as he did. He had screwed up his face, and put his arm in a defensive way around the paper, not like the clerks and scribes did. And he was pressing very hard and slowly with the pen. But between them they wrote a letter assuring his parents of his safety. He hoped someone would translate it for them.

Then they wrote to Eloise. At least, that's what he tried to do. But what could he say that would pass the censor now he was back with the military? What could he offer her if, as sounded likely, he was sent back to India? In the end, all he could say was that he had reached the British safely. They might send him home now. He would always remember her. Please write to him, and at the end of the war he would try to come back. He greeted her father, her mother and her sister too and thanked them all again for everything they had done. He wasn't sure if the soldier was still writing at this point, but he said he had written everything. And so Yaqub took the pen and drew her a picture of himself at the bottom, holding up his egg and waving. The soldier took it away, promising to send both letters after the censor had made his usual check.

In the censor's office, after a practised check, the duty censor wrote 'no incriminating details in letters' on Yaqub's file. 'I hope 'e's not threatening to blow us all up with that grenade in 'is drawing,' sniggered the private. 'Perhaps 'e really did join that Indian legion they're on about.'

'I'll be glad when they send us someone who can write neater,' retorted the censor, 'not to mention one of those VCOs who know the lingo. It will make my job a whole lot easier.' With that, he dropped the letter to Yaqub's parents into the sack for onward transmission, and tore up the one to Eloise, along with the other one that the American escort had dutifully handed over in Marseilles.

'He's not the only one to fancy a bit of French skirt! But there's regulations against mixing.'

16

Egg shells

Amina was startled to hear the doorbell. She had gone into the kitchen to put the kettle on, and now realised that she must have been just standing there, lost in thought. How long had it been? She'd just stood, looking at that message from Saira. 'We have found the house' was all it said. Why hadn't she said more?

She hadn't realised till now how much she had wanted Saira to reassure her. To tell her … But what did she really want to hear? Did she want Saira to tell her that there had never been another woman? That she had imagined it? That the Russian man in the forest had lived alone? She didn't think that would ring true after all these years. She trusted her instinct. All these years she had believed there was a reason for her husband's silence and withdrawal. And in the end she had decided that it was better to think there was someone than that he just hadn't wanted to come home to her.

A memory stabbed her sharply, and it was almost like a physical jarring, of the day she'd caught sight of him, three seemingly endless years after his return from the war. She had heard he was returning to help his family with the harvest, and there he was, setting out along the track with Yousaf scampering alongside. She felt she had brought disgrace on her family, but she didn't understand. All she knew was that Yaqub had now been back in his native land for three years, but she had hardly seen him and he had given no indication that their marriage would ever take place. She'd wept every night when he first returned from the war. He'd looked so thin and much older. But there had been another change too. He looked bitter. He no longer laughed or smiled. And he said nothing to her. People told her it was the war. But that was three years ago. He'd had time to recover. And he had stayed in the army, so it couldn't be the fighting that disgusted him. He had even transferred into their new Pakistan army when Independence came, and had coped with the terrible communal violence. Perhaps now he had seen the world, she displeased him. All she knew was that it felt as if her life was over.

Shaking herself, as if to physically rid herself of the painful memories, Amina filled the kettle and flicked the switch, before heading to look through the window by the front door to see who had rung the bell. She didn't want to open to an importunate salesman. Was there something that Saira didn't want to tell her till she got back? Had they found her? Was she still – seductive? French women were always so elegant, so poised. She'd heard that.

As they drove away from the cemetery (it was Will's turn at the wheel, and they knew the road now, so no problems with poor map-reading), Saira started wondering for the first time about the damage her grandfather had done. She thought she could now imagine how much her grandmother must have suffered from his silence after his return. But she hadn't really wanted to think about Eloise's reaction. Daniel's revelations the night before had been disturbing, with their implications that maybe Eloise had expected their PoW to return; maybe she too had had her hopes shattered.

Impulsively she suggested stopping briefly in Saint Loup to thank Eloise for her gift. Will tried to dissuade her, thinking they'd already stirred up too much in the old girl's shaky mind. A bit of Daniel's protectiveness must have rubbed off on him! But Saira had convinced herself.

'No more than ten minutes then, and I'll wait in the car.'

Again, there was no-one sitting conveniently outside on the bench. And it was a long time before Daniel opened the door, looking harassed. Behind him, yesterday's elegant hostess had dwindled into a cantankerous old lady in a faded red dressing gown, who was refusing to get washed or dressed, however late it was. But her face lit up when she saw Saira, and she beckoned her over to the bed.

'It's a bad day,' explained Daniel, unnecessarily.

To Saira's surprise, Eloise gave her a big hug (a greedy, possessive hug, quite different from yesterday's gentle embrace), sat her on the bed and started fussing round her, chattering away in French (where was her beautiful English?) with cooing words that sounded like some kind of baby endearments. She made Daniel bring over the basin and flannel she'd been spurning as Saira arrived, and started to dab at Saira's mouth, murmuring something about chocolate.

Daniel looked embarrassed, and tried to stay his wife's hand. But she shook her head crossly. My little one will get into trouble if she has dirty nails or face. I don't want teacher to punish her. She has to be a good girl. 'Bring her an apple!' she commanded. Daniel must have known it was easier not to reason with her when she was in this strange mood, for he went to get an apple, and Eloise polished it on her dressing gown and held it up for Saira. She's not wearing her hair ribbon? Where has it gone? 'Hair ribbon!' she commanded. Saira didn't know the word and looked towards Daniel who shrugged, and this time tried to explain something to Eloise – that they didn't have any of whatever it was.

Eloise began to argue, pointing towards the dressing table drawer, so Daniel opened it and showed her the contents. Eloise looked crossly at Saira, and for a moment it seemed as if she might smack her hand. But then her mind seemed to flip to another matter, and she asked Saira something directly, which involved a repeated word 'dictée.' 'I don't understand what has caused this,' Daniel said, 'but she's asking if you've learned your spellings properly, ready for the dictation test.' Eloise seemed unaware of the language shift and kept asking Saira till she nodded and said 'Oui' and Daniel added something reassuring, probably confirming that she knew her spellings.

This was like a nightmare distortion, Saira thought. Yesterday she'd decided that Eloise wasn't nearly as confused as she made out. But this was something else. She seemed, unaccountably, to have become Eloise's long-desired child. Was it possible that something yesterday had triggered some faulty link in Eloise's brain? Would Eloise keep nagging her till she responded dutifully with a 'Oui, Maman'? She desperately hoped something would break up this false scenario and divert Eloise. She looked, in appeal, towards Daniel, who took charge of the situation. 'I think it's best if you set out for school,' he said in English. 'I think that's all we can do at the moment.'

But despite the strangeness of the situation, Saira didn't want to leave without at least attempting to find out more about the little elephant. Perhaps producing it quickly would divert Eloise from this present charade. She took the little animal out of her bag. But to her disappointment, Eloise just got cross and told her (this bit she could understand) that she knew she couldn't take toys to school, and tried to take it away.

There was no way Saira was going to hand it over, so she stood up and pretended to give it to Daniel, whilst slipping it in her jacket pocket. She picked up the apple, before it became an issue, and headed towards the front door, catching a glimpse of the kitchen table littered with felt tip pens and decorated eggs. Eloise demanded to be kissed properly before she left. It was a heart-breaking moment as Saira embraced the bony old lady, who told her to be careful with her sums and make sure she got them all right. Saira thought for a moment that she had tears in her eyes, and wondered if Eloise knew, really, that all of this was make-believe and she'd never see her again.

Behind Eloise Daniel mouthed the word 'Sorry!' as he bent down to pick up the cat, and Saira gave him a discrete thumbs up sign, hoping that he wouldn't have to face a whole day of this irrational behaviour.

On the way to the car, Saira heard Eloise calling out in a cracked voice that she should be a good girl. And as she joined Will, Saira found it difficult to detach her mind from an alternative history, in which Yaqub, like Habib's father, had returned to his French girl after the war.

❧ ❧
❧ ❧

'Did you see a lot of dead bodies this time?'

Yaqub smiled wryly. This was the same question his youngest brother had asked him repeatedly when he'd first come back from the war in far-away Europe. Yousaf had only been eight then, and excited to have his big brother returning from captivity before most of the fighting troops. What a chance to boast to his friends!

Looking back, Yaqub was ashamed at how cold and off-hand he must have seemed to his little brother. He had been so wrapped up in his own hurt and bitterness on his return from the war. He must have sounded quite sharp when he replied that he'd only been in one big battle before they surrendered, and that most of the deaths in his brigade had been in their PoW camps from TB and malnutrition. That must have been such a disappointment for Yousaf. What could he tell the other boys? His father had later laughingly told him how envious Yousaf had been of his best friend Masud. For Masud had been able to boast, when his brother came back from fighting the Japanese, that he had killed three men in the jungle, close up!

The trouble was that Yaqub had found it impossible to talk to his family on his return. They'd been so overjoyed and had organised great family celebrations. But all he'd felt was confusion and numbness after his interrogation by Section X at Taranto, when the British had virtually accused him of treachery. He felt he had brought shame and dishonour on his family, by being suspected. But he felt unable to tell them about that.

When his home-leave was over Yaqub had resumed life in the Indian Army in a glazed and mechanical fashion. Then, with the end of the war in Europe and the return of the remaining PoWs, he learnt that all the captured Indian troops had undergone a similar interrogation. Apparently, there had been huge holding camps in England, where they were detained and questioned before being shipped back. He began to feel a bit better about his own experience and Barkat would goad him, 'It's time you stopped being so sensitive – you're as bad as a woman! Forget it. Get on with your life.' As the grim, hardened survivors of the jungles of Burma and the Japanese prison camps filtered back, he realised that his treatment by the Germans was positively kindly and humane in comparison with the Japanese. And even those prisoners had faced the same intense debriefing by the British. As they shared experiences, he began to realise how childish he'd been in the way he had reacted to Section X's distrust. He finally began to take an interest in what was happening around him. He would join in the off-duty huddles of men listening to the newspapers being read out and debating the political situation in India. He began to realise why the British had been so fearful at the end of the war about possible sedition within the Indian Army ranks. The last thing they needed was their own army turning against them back in India.

Now Yousaf skipped along beside Yaqub to the field, delighted to have him back for the harvest. 'Masud said they've been killing everyone who tries to cross the new border! Did you see killed people when you transferred from your barracks in India to your new quarters in our Pakistan?'

Yaqub's immediate thought was to deny the horrors of what he had seen. But then Yousaf would never understand the senselessness of war. He squatted down on the dusty track. 'Listen to me, Yousaf. What I have seen here, in our own land, is more terrible by far than the foreign war. Over there they had machines designed just for killing. Enormous guns, tanks, aircraft, land-mines, grenades. You could kill a man without ever seeing him. And all because you were following orders, in a war you knew nothing about.'

When Yousaf tried to interrupt, he silenced him, impatiently. 'But here, when we have almost won the struggle to be free of foreign rule, to be independent, to run our own countries, what do we do? We turn on our former countrymen. Our own neighbours. Madness overwhelms us. On the eve of Independence, we started killing those who used to be our friends and neighbours. It's not armed soldiers we are killing. It is mothers with their children, farmers with their animals, old men who can hardly walk. And it's not sophisticated weapons, its stones, sticks and our own bare hands we use.'

Finally, perhaps, Yousaf would understand how appalling it all was. 'Yes, I saw bodies, corpses pushed to the sides of the railway track and roads. They were killed close up, with knives and stones, by people with no reason to fear them. By people whose new land they were trying to leave. By ordinary people who had forgotten their humanity. That kind of killing is never glorious. It can never be the will of Allah.'

Yousaf looked at him solemnly. 'But you were safe. They respected you. You are a brave soldier. They didn't attack you on the train to Pakistan!'

Yaqub wondered how he could explain to his little brother about the tremendous bonds of loyalty that linked the regiment, so that they were prepared to defend each other to the death. He reached out and took Yousaf's hand. 'It wasn't because of my own bravery that I crossed the new border safely. It was because of the friendship and loyalty in the army. The British did their very best to ensure our safety. But it was our Hindu and Sikh brothers who were the brave ones.'

'Why were they braver than you?'

Yaqub patiently explained that those who had opted to remain in the Indian Army could simply have waved off those of them who had chosen to join the Army of the new Pakistan. But they had been colleagues and they had insisted on escorting them on the train. 'The bravest was the Sikh driver. He would have been the first to have been attacked by angry mobs. But he drove our train all the way to safety. And we saw terrible sights on the way.'

Yousaf's eyes were shining. 'Perhaps I'll be a train driver, instead of a soldier.' He pulled Yaqub up from the dust, and still holding him by the hand began to drag him towards the field, chuffing like a fast-moving steam train.

Then another thought struck his inquisitive mind. The chuffing stopped. 'Why don't you get married, like mother wants you to?'

Yaqub stared across the golden field in exasperation. His little brother, in his usual way, had gone straight to the point. Why indeed was he still hesitating? The sun shimmered in a heat haze. Even the birds seemed motionless and attentive. His mother's words scuttled and echoed in his head. 'Son, I want to see you married before I die.'

'I wasn't ready when I came back,' he said finally. 'The war had changed everything too much. I was confused, Yousaf, I was confused.'

It was still painful to remember the hope with which he'd waited for that first letter from France. While they were still in Taranto, waiting for a ship, he had written every day, with the help of that rather cocky soldier. Knowing how artistic she was, he'd taken great pains to embellish the margins of his letters with intricate drawings of cows and hens and a wounded soldier and Saint George with his dragon. And he had given her the address his parents used, so she could write back to him straight away, and had included messages for her parents and Marie.

But there was nothing when he got home. He had waited patiently for an answer to all fifteen letters. An answer that would shape his plans once the war was over. But that letter never came. And after a while, he did not feel he could write again, not even to Léo, until he heard from her.

How could he tell his little brother about that? That was the other part of his story that he had not discussed with anyone, along with the interrogation. And somehow the two things had festered together in his mind, making him increasingly bitter.

Even Barkat had been no help. He alone knew how devastated Yaqub had been. But all he'd say was that he was acting like a European. Love for them was like a fever, sudden, heated and delusional. How could you base a lifetime around your momentary loss of all reason? The only sensible way was to accept the wisdom of your parents, who knew you from birth. 'She was just flirting with you. It wasn't serious!' Yaqub felt that right from the start Barkat had made no attempt to understand. And after Barkat had happily married his first cousin, in accordance with expectations, he was not even willing to listen to what he called European nonsense. 'It was different over there. Their women are different. Their ways are different. Look at those German factory women. They all seem alluring at first. But that's no basis for marriage.' It had caused a rift between them that Yaqub regretted profoundly. It was as if he'd lost the friend with whom he'd shared so much. Sometimes he'd hear men bragging about their French or Italian 'girlfriends', but he didn't think they were sincere. He didn't have anything in common with them either. He stayed, wrapped in misery, becoming a loner.

'I'd changed too, Yousaf'

He sighed. He felt so far removed from the trustful young man who'd set out to war. He could see his mother worrying about his moodiness. And he knew his father had urged her to be patient. He, at least during his first leave, had accepted that his son needed time to adjust to life back home. 'Just give him time,' he had urged. He was wise beyond his limited horizons.

But Yaqub could tell that now that most of the returning

soldiers, even those who had been badly wounded, had settled down and married, his father felt he too should be ready. And perhaps he was hoping that marriage would help to settle him. Yaqub sighed. 'Come on, we need to get on with harvesting,' he said impatiently, trying to shrug off the black thoughts that threatened to return with Yousaf's pertinent questions.

But Yousaf was not easily deflected. 'Masud's mother keeps asking our mother what's wrong with you!' he chirped. 'She says why don't you want to give our mother grandchildren for her old age?'

Interfering old woman, thought Yaqub, beginning to swing and slash angrily at the millet with his blade. Then, as he settled into a rhythm, his thoughts began to take shape, as if they had been tossed up into the air like ears of millet, and had been floating disorganised for so long, but were eventually discarding all the chaff and falling into a more coherent pattern.

He began to realise how long the time since his return would have seemed to his mother. She would have watched the other soldiers returning at the end of the war, and settling down and producing children. No wonder, with women like Masud's mother goading her, that her sighs of, 'My one wish is to live long enough to see my grandchildren,' were becoming more frequent.

And perhaps the violence that he had witnessed within his own land had focussed him. This madness was not what he wanted for his country, for his people's future. They should not be tearing themselves apart as the Europeans had been doing. But how could the blood-lust be extinguished, once it had been roused? Perhaps it was up to men like himself to teach the next generation in his small village that violence achieved only pitiful results; to educate them about the world beyond, so that it could never manipulate and betray them as it had done his generation.

The next generation. Children. It was strange, but he had been so absorbed in his lonely misery that hadn't really thought about them for a long time. Barkat now had two children. Because of the rift he hadn't told Yaqub much about them, but Yaqub suspected that they anchored him.

'Don't you want children?' his brother persisted.

Yaqub straightened up, and looked across the fields. He had helped his family farm them since he was a child. He thought of how they struggled to produce a living from them. He always used to imagine his own children continuing with the same tasks. 'Perhaps,' he temporised. There were such high hopes at Independence. But would Kashmir be safe? Would it be a safe place for children? There were the rumours circulating in the Pakistan army. Fears that they could be used against their brothers in the Indian Army if the unsettled situation in Kashmir turned into a battleground. Would this area be torn apart still further?

He looked down at his brother. 'The world has changed so much.'

He thought of the rich plains of Alsace he'd seen, neglected, with their men away fighting or in captivity, and the women and children struggling to tend the land. His thoughts strayed to their journey across that distant mountain border. To the flames illuminating the sky, the lorry loads of looted goods, and the villagers he and Barkat had stayed with, who were turned out of their homes as the villages all round were destroyed. It was a long time since he'd thought of them and their cheerful endurance, and the fun he'd had with their children.

And then wayward images flashed before his eyes. A crimson coat, a red skirt, a stolen brushing of his lips on her neck, eyes promising the world. With an immense effort he pushed the images away. That was the past. It had obviously meant nothing to her. He forced himself to think of something else. He was now a free man, but a man with obligations to fulfil.

'Besides, I wouldn't want them to turn into little pests like you!' he teased.

Yousaf grinned happily. This was more like the brother he remembered. He pointed back down at the village. 'See that big new house on the far side? Masud's uncle is building that!'

His father had told Yaqub about the house that his little brother was pointing at. It was being built for Masud's uncle, a sea-man. Yaqub hadn't seen him for years. Even before the war he'd been away labouring on the big ships. Apparently he'd jumped ship after the end of the war and stayed on in England.

'He must be really rich over in England. He's sending back all this money to build a huge big house,' continued Yousaf. 'He must have a brilliant job there.'

Anything would seem good, Yaqub reflected, after the filthy, hot engine rooms of those big ships. He'd seen for himself the appalling conditions the lascars worked in. 'I could always go and get rich like Masud's uncle!' he teased. 'Then I could provide for any number of children!'

'Oh yes! And I could come with you! Take me with you! I could help you get rich!'

'You might not like it. It rains all the time in England and people are unfriendly.' Yaqub had noticed that the prisoners who'd been released in Germany at the end of the war and had been taken to England for questioning, all had different reactions. Some said it was friendly and welcoming, despite the climate. But most had found it hostile. They said it hadn't felt much freer than their prison camp, as they weren't encouraged to roam the streets. There had still been rationing and everyone seemed grey and tired.

'What shall we do there? Shall we have fields in England?'

'I'd be an electrician!'

That's what he'd said firmly and unexpectedly, without thinking, when first asked about post-war army training. Looking back, he wondered if this had been an unconscious tribute to Benoit, whose skill, knowledge and friendship had first helped them to escape. Perhaps a time would come when he'd actually do that training. They seemed to have been on a state of alert ever since, with no time for peace-time training. But that word was written down on his file, somewhere.

'I'll be one too! Shall we go by ship?'

'I'm teasing. I haven't done my electricians' training yet. We're not going anywhere just now. We've got this whole field to cut and we need to get on with it.'

Nevertheless, it felt as if things were clearer in his mind. He realised that, in all the horrors of what his own people were doing to each other, his old petulance about Taranto had finally slipped away unnoticed. 'Like an old sack with a hole, whose last-year's grain has seeped away! And that sack is now weightless.' He hadn't realised he'd spoken aloud. He laughed at Yousaf's astonished face.

'Don't worry. You've persuaded me, I'll speak to father tonight about Amina.'

Yaqub noticed that Yousaf was looking really pleased with himself, as he followed behind him, drawing the cut millet into piles. He realised that Yousaf was taking all the credit for finally persuading his big brother to see sense about his marriage, and smiled to himself as row after row of the blonde crop fell at his feet under his steady slashing. A time-honoured rhythm had been re-established.

Half way across the field a sudden thought struck him. He was amazed he hadn't thought about it before. He'd been too wrapped up in his own disillusionment. But how would Amina would be feeling? Here he was feeling that he had reached a tremendous decision, and thrown off the weight of the past. But all this time she had been waiting for him. Would the uncertainty have made her dejected and despised? Would she think that he had slighted her and her family?

He had known Amina all his life, but he had no idea of what she must have felt while he was away in the war. Of course, that would have been the same for all the girls. But what about after he came back? She didn't know about the humiliating interrogation, and she certainly didn't know about Eloise. But would she have speculated? Would she and the other girls have talked about him? Would they have guessed? That would have been shameful for her.

She was a fine girl. She didn't deserve his surliness and reluctance. He should be honest with her. Not by telling her of his strange madness, but by firmly putting it all behind him. By resolving never to think of it again. How many days of his life had it actually occupied? Seven? Eight? A mere fragment. How could he have placed so much hope and desire on so little time together? No wonder Barkat became exasperated with him. It was time for him to live out his appointed life in his own world and forget the brief dream completely.

He laughed out loud, and raised his arms to the sky, as if in thanksgiving, then punched his startled little brother affectionately in the chest. 'And how did you learn the women's work of marriage making?'

But one thing remained to be done. When he saw one of their sisters bringing their lunch to the field, he sent Yousaf over to meet her. Then he put his hand into an inner pocket and brought out the five fragments of painted egg shell, which he'd carried everywhere, even after it had broken during the riots. He crushed the pieces to fine flakes, threw them to the ground and watched them come to rest between the sharp stubble.

Now his father could speak to Amina's family.

Through the window Amina could see a small figure with a furry head. 'I thought you'd be looking out for me,' said the face below the fur hat, peering inquisitively from the other side of the raised net curtain. Amina's heart sank. Will's grandmother, – what was it she'd said to call her, – Betty! Amina had quite forgotten about her. But it had been mentioned at the end of the wedding. The two old ladies had politely said that they must keep in touch. And Betty had promised to come round on a particular afternoon. But Amina hadn't thought she really meant to come. Was it today?

At least she was neatly dressed. She pulled her wool wrap around her shoulders, willed a smile into position, and opened the door hospitably. 'Kettle is on! Come in!' How English she could sound now, she thought wonderingly, as her new relative-by-marriage stepped over the threshold, pulling off her hat and gloves and babbling something about the buses.

Amina was surprised how much they found to talk about. Not that she needed to say a lot. Betty did most of the talking. But it took a lot of concentration to follow what she was saying. Especially when she was munching biscuits (Amina was really glad she had some in the tin) at the same time. Did it all connect? Perhaps it wasn't just her own language deficiencies, Amina began to wonder. Of course they talked about Will, who seemed to be Betty's favourite grandchild and about Saira. And then Betty started to ask questions, personal ones.

'What made you come over here then? You must have found it really cold when you came! Did you always live in this house? How do you like it? It must all have been very strange at first.'

17

Mutation

It was wonderfully warm and steamy. The perfect place to ponder, until the water got too cold. Foxhill's public baths were Yaqub's one luxury of the week. Why did they call them slipper baths? Slippers were for wearing on the feet. His English was constantly enlarging, but this was unclear. But, whatever you called them, they were cheap and cleansing after a hard week, – and deeply relaxing. However much he valued the friendship of the men with whom he shared the crowded house, it was good to escape from it from time to time. Even from Yousaf. Some of them were old seamen, like Masud's uncle, who'd been in England much longer than the newcomers like himself, and they loved a good chat and could tell a tale or two. But sometimes a man needs silence.

He could hear the echoes of the turning and pummelling of the vast washing machines in the wash-house, the jokes of the men waiting on the wooden benches outside the cubicles, a man humming in the next bath, and occasional calls of 'More hot!' But they were all the background sounds of strangers. Nobody expected any response from him.

The big question really was: would it be fair? What would his wife make of this strange, cold, damp, hostile English town? She was used to being surrounded by her family and the support of the women of her village. Here there were only a few wives starting to come over and only a handful spoke her language, and they would not necessarily be living next door or even on the same street. If he loved her, how could he subject her to this life far from everything she knew? His children would adapt, he knew. Children always do. But what of his wife? Did he have any other choice?

It was ironic that he'd come here to debate with himself. After all, it was water that was the cause of his dilemma. Since he was last home in their village, the decision, of which there had only been vague rumours then, had been taken to build the huge dam. How could it have any benefit locally? Their village and all the surrounding ones flooded to make a big reservoir behind the dam. And where would the water go? To irrigate other people's land while their own vanished.

He could either send Amina and the children to start a new life in another village where she had no roots, or bring her here to join him. For one moment he allowed himself to dream of the blissful life they would have together again. Once he'd paid the fare he could stop sending as much money back (though there were still his parents to provide for in their new home) and he could build up just enough savings to start to buy a house here. Amina would make it a real home. Not a shared room with damp washing draped everywhere and one of the men cooking. She would shop properly at the big market. She would fill the house with wonderful cooking smells. And he would hear his children's laughter every day.

Not only laughter. The boys would learn proper English, far better than his, and get good jobs. But would she be able to adapt? Would she even like it? How could he hurt her, his beloved wife.

He had to admit he was tired of this life, scrimping and

saving to send money home and only going back occasionally to see everyone. He knew many men did this. But it was no way to be a family, especially with the boys getting older and needing more discipline. On the other hand, if daughters came along, would he find good marriages here for them?

Of course, more men were bringing their families now. He was sorry that Barkat had never come over, but had resisted the suggestion. He was settled back home, and his area was not under threat. But young Yousaf had been a loyal companion to him, and if he married soon, his wife would be a friend for Amina. He tried to think of the wives who had already come. Would they be supportive of his wife? He wasn't sure he thought they were all suitable. Two of the early comers were such loud-mouths. 'Brassy' he thought they called such women here. It was such a big decision. And he was worried about her happiness. It was so easy to be selfish and think of his own comfort.

His pay was steady now. She could be proud of him. He had status in the community now as an electrician at the depot. He was respected. And she was remarkably adaptable, given that she had seen so little of the world. He thought of her trusting smile, her faith in him. She would expect him to make the right decision. And she would make it work.

For she made everything work. He had never explained to her, when he got home, the confusion of feelings left by the interrogation. He knew he had been disturbed, untrusting, uncommunicative. He'd felt betrayed, but hadn't turned to the only people who hadn't let him down, his family. But somehow she seemed to understand something of his apartness, and had never pressed him to open up more. After their marriage she had got on steadfastly with her tasks and with making a secure home for him to return to each leave.

He could picture her now, her soft face glowing as she swept and scrubbed, with their third son, whom he hadn't seen yet, cradled in her shawl. Her face would light up when one of the pedlars brought fresh fruit or vegetables from the mountain foothills. She would turn them over, studiously selecting the best, savouring the tastes she would create for him from her store of spices.

She had listened attentively as he grew to trust her and spoke a little of his feelings. Of course she had no inkling of the other matter which had disturbed him. And these days he hardly thought about Eloise. That had been a boy's love, a whirlwind, intense but immature. He had put it resolutely behind him that day in the fields. The old ways were the soundest. The love that builds slowly is the love that lasts.

He leaned forward to pull out the plug. Yes, he would take the risk. He would bring his beloved wife and children over to share his life properly. And, although life over here was so different from what he had expected, he would protect them from the worst.

Amina got off the bus behind Betty. She could hardly believe that she was doing this. Saira would be amazed at her daring. But Betty was hard to resist. As soon as Amina had mentioned Minerva Street, where their first house had been, Betty had got excited, as her sister had lived on the next street with her young family until the day the bulldozers moved in. 'They didn't leave much behind in them days did they? Just cleared every one of the buildings in one section and then moved on to the next. Like locusts. Of course, they was terrible houses, time they came down.'

Amina was taken aback. She could still remember her

amazement when her husband brought her and their three children from the railway station to their new home in England. He must have worked so hard to buy such a big house. With its three floors there was plenty of room for all the family including Yousaf, who had his own room, and also for them to rent out two rooms to other young couples. She had thought it a fine house back then, and her Yaqub a shrewd businessman, and she had been devastated when the authorities decided to pull it down.

'Have you been back there recently? Did you know they was doing up them old Victorian baths? Practically the only thing they didn't knock down, along with the school. They have some big grant to do it all properly. They've uncovered all the lovely old tiles, and they're going to restore all the part with the big machines – did you do your bag wash there? Been shut up for years. Odd to have it as a museum! We ought to go and have a walk round.' Amina didn't follow all this, but somehow, Betty had organised her into her coat and steered her to the bus-stop. 'It will bring back, memories, you wait!'

As she stared at the rows of near-identical two storey pebble-dashed houses that now sidled up the hill where Betty insisted that Minerva Street had once stood, Amina remembered the effort of pushing the big second-hand pram up its steep pavement, especially in the snow. At first she had been surprised to see the women pushing their babies in prams rather than holding them close. But she discovered it was useful to put shopping in the pram despite the hard work pushing it back. And so many shops there had been, all gone now. She'd found it so confusing back then. How did people chose between all those strange shops? All the bread shops, fish and chips, tailors, tobacconists, grocers, hairdressers, off-licences, wool shops, dairies, hardware stores, bicycle repairs, coal merchants and green-grocers. And so many things like the lumpy vegetables hadn't been recognisable. It was easier to find the vegetables she wanted in the big market, though that was further to push the pram. It was better later on when one of the families they knew started a corner shop, which sold everything she wanted.

'There used to be a pub on each corner,' Betty was reminiscing, 'and one part way up the hill. Me and my sister would pop into the old King Billy.' Amina was horrified. She tried to explain how she hadn't liked going past the drinking shops when they were open. At first she hadn't understood the words the men shouted as they lolled outside, but she knew that they were not good words. Perhaps that was why Yaqub hadn't wanted her to learn English. As if he could have shielded her from the insults! Even the women would sometimes shout them, but usually it was children on the street. Suddenly she felt embarrassed. Surely Betty wouldn't have been among those women?

'Old school different,' she observed, changing the subject. Betty was instantly diverted onto the wedding and how lovely it had all been, whilst Amina recalled her terror at taking her boys to the school on the first day, finding her way there and back though the maze of little streets, and answering all the headmaster's questions. Yaqub had been unable to have time off work to take them, but he was so worried for her that he walked the route with them the previous evening, so she wouldn't get lost. The school was some distance from Minerva Street and seemed so large, with its echoing hall, long corridors and innumerable doors. And the headmaster was very frightening, though she could see he was trying to be patient. Yaqub had written the boys' details on a piece of paper. He was always so thoughtful. And the boys themselves spoke quite a bit of English by then, thanks to the tutor Yaqub had hired on their arrival, so they were able to explain some things. She had long been accustomed to daily life without Yaqub, and was surprised to discover how much he cared about her and the boys and how glad he was to have them with him at last. And he understood how hard it was for her. He had been a good husband and father, and she was so grateful that it had finally worked out for them.

'What did he do, your old man?' Amina looked puzzled, so Betty added, 'Did he work local?' Amina smiled and explained that he caught two buses. 'Very good job. Electrician. At depot.' She still felt proud of his job and the fact that two black-suited men had called round after his death with a signed card from many of his former colleagues.

They were nearly at the top of the hill now, two incongruous old ladies, puffing slightly and picturing the past. 'Remember the coal horses delivering? They struggled up here!' Reaching the top, Betty's thoughts flitted from the cart horses. 'Who'd have thought all them years ago?' She was pointing down at the gold-leaf dome below. 'If you'd told us there would be that great mosque down there, we'd have laughed!' Amina smiled as she remembered all the politicking of the men over the years. She'd never followed it all, the endless mosque committees, the rival candidates to be the first Muslim local councillor, the applications for grants here and favours there. She heard all the whispers among the wives. But that was not the way her Yaqub lived. He had never set himself up as a leader. And yet she knew, as time went on, how much his words were respected within their community. If he really felt strongly about something, and put it into words, others would fall silent.

'And there was that big building round the corner where the boys' brigade met. Our David and John and Peter, my sister's boys, loved it. All learnt the bugle. Did yours ... oh, I suppose not, they wouldn't have, would they!' Amina wasn't sure what that was about. 'Saturday school,' she said defensively. 'They went Saturday school. Very busy. And library. Learn good reading.' She was beginning to feel tired after the uphill walk.

It was rather a relief when her phone rang. She knew it would be her son. He seemed worried about her at the moment, and if he had rung home and there had been no answer, he'd want to know where she was. She almost laughed aloud at his horror when she told him where she was. Minerva Street! It wasn't there any more! She explained about Betty, and thought he sounded even more shocked. But when he offered to come over and give them a lift home, she accepted thankfully. Memories were tiring.

Back home, she insisted on making Betty another cup of tea. She felt rather proud of herself. Was she beginning to make a friend of her own with this new relative? Much to his surprise, Sid felt reassured. His mother seemed much brighter after this unexpected visitor. He courteously offered Betty a lift home on his way back to work. Will's grandmother was a bubbly old woman. But fancy them going back to the old places!

Perched in the back seat of his cab, Betty asked him what it had been like growing up in Minerva Street. 'We wasn't used to Pakis, pardon my language, but that's what we said back then. Not many of you around.' Sid corrected her gently, 'In fact there were quite a few of us Asian kids over here by then, and they were organising Saturday schools, Koran classes and mosques (Dad got involved with all that, I think), so we had plenty of places to meet up as well as on the streets and in the playground. There was always someone to take your side in a fight. And yes,' as Betty looked as if she was about to interrupt, 'there were plenty of fights. We never told my father. He had this philosophy of ignoring any insults and getting on as if he hadn't heard. He always told us the only way to survive was to show you were better than they were.' He smiled, and added, 'But we showed them with our fists.'

Betty cackled, and said unexpectedly 'You know, I think it would have been worst for your mother. She would have no way to stick up for herself.' Sid looked surprised, then said airily, 'Oh, no, we all looked after her. We protected her from all that. We never told her the half of what was going on at school. Just when we got good marks. And our teachers only told her the good things. One of us was always with her, translating, so she never had to speak for herself. She was sheltered from the worst!'

Betty shook her head, doubtfully, then changed the subject. 'She said you hadn't heard much from Will and Saira. Do you think they'll have found anything about your father in the war there?' Sid looked in the mirror, smiling at the abrupt change. 'Funny how the returning men never talked much about the war in them days, and now there's all these TV programmes. Didn't he tell you lads anything?'

'Not really.' Just once, when he and his brother were watching an old war film set in the desert, his dad had suddenly said that when his work mates were talking about Tobruk, he'd joined in, saying that his regiment had passed through there in '41. One of them had looked at him contemptuously, 'Your Indian lot was bloody useless! Caved in at the first shot. It was left to us to mop up.' Sid didn't want to tell Betty this; he had always assumed it was remarks like this that made his dad unwilling to talk about the war.

When he drew up in front of Betty's gate, he said impulsively, 'It's done my mother good to talk to you. She's seemed a bit depressed recently.' (Not that she'd have done much of the talking with Betty keeping up such a barrage of chat.)

'Glad you approve!' Betty said cheekily. 'Tell her I'll come again.'

Leaving Eloise for the third time was unbearably painful for Saira. Will felt helpless as she described the parallel universe the damaged old lady seemed to have entered and the shattered hopes she had revealed. He could only suggest that perhaps it was better to hold onto the gracious and dignified image from the second meeting. He stayed in the driving seat, and as Saira made no move to open the map, he just followed road signs, hoping to find some nice villages over the pass in Alsace. Saira stared out into the mist, and idly nibbled the apple Eloise had given her. She didn't take in very much of their surroundings, unable to refocus. She was startled when Will turned abruptly. He'd seen a sign to the Hohneck. 'Isn't that where Habib's father fought?'

Saira was surprised that he wanted to go up and take a look, and then realised that he was trying to divert her. It wasn't much of a distraction, though, stumbling up the hill, enveloped in cloud, and it was cold. She wondered if this was one of the threatened bits of hillside that you weren't meant to walk on. Below them they could hear the bells of grazing cattle. But, apart from the cattle they seemed to be the only other creatures on the slope. Saira shivered. 'It must have been terrible, up here in the snow and cold. And if the cloud was low like this, the enemy could just take you by surprise, emerging out of the whiteness.'

'Just imagine we're brave Tunisian skirmishers. We're stranded, with no radio contact, no medical supplies, eating our last rations as we wait for the enemy to strike! The snow is a metre deep all round and Himmler's men are holed up in a derelict hotel somewhere nearby.' Will must have been reading up on the background.

'Idiot!' But, as he continued to talk she could imagine the helmeted German soldiers emerging from the mist and snow, the gunfire, the flame-throwers and the explosions, then the bleeding bodies in the churned-up snow.

Suddenly the clouds parted, as if a curtain was being drawn back, and the sunshine lit up a patchwork of fields below them. Saira stopped, appalled to see how steeply the rocky face descended just a few metres in front of them. 'We could have stepped off into nothingness and plunged headlong!'

As Will turned away from the drop, he started to laugh. 'We could also have saved ourselves that scramble up!' He pointed to the car park and a large café! 'Hot chocolate!' Saira walked over to two large stones at the edge of the car park, and was pleased to see a plaque commemorating the Tunisians' bravery there in December 1944. And Will felt happy with the unexpected success of his diversion in lifting her sadness.

After that, the sun continued to shine as they drove downhill towards the wine villages. And even there, they didn't escape from traces of the war. They stopped in a pretty village for some of the Alsace tarte flambée, then chose one of the wine producers lining the old streets. Saira was apprehensive, following Will into the courtyard. What would she do while Will was trying out the wines? She'd heard that it was a really snobbish world, with all kinds of taboos. But when Will explained to the woman behind a sort of bar that he didn't know the first thing about wine ('I'm more of a beer man') and that he couldn't afford much but wanted to learn about Alsace wines, the woman couldn't have been more charming. She started to explain about the terrain and grape varieties, and Will had the glorious sensation of being taken-in-hand by a woman of experience – almost like those Frenchwomen he'd heard about who used to initiate young men into the joys of sex.

Meanwhile an old man came in, and, noticing that Saira wasn't tasting, tried to put her at her ease. His English was good, no doubt from years of selling his wines. She ended up telling him about her grandfather and their journey. As she talked, she noticed that Will was sipping his second glass. Wasn't he meant to spit it out, or something? The old man started to tell her about how the Germans often allocated prisoners to help them with the harvest, though they never sent any Indian PoWs. 'They were very fond of our wines, you know, the Germans. They were always very anxious to get the harvests in and the wines made. That last year of the war, with the Americans approaching …'

'Grandfather! You're not to go boring the customers!'

Saira looked across to the bar, and reassured the young woman that, because of her own grandfather, she was interested in any stories about the war. 'He'd hoped to join the Americans, liberating this area.' For the first time, she wondered why he hadn't been able to join the fighting. Was it just bureaucracy? It was odd that he'd just gone back to India without fighting again. She must ask her grandmother the reason. Meanwhile the old man was continuing with his story of how, with the Americans approaching, the Germans were trying to send the best wine off to Germany. 'Everyone had hidden away as many of the good bottles as possible. We had a false wall to one of our cellars. They used to tap all the walls, to try and find the hidden cellars!'

The woman smiled tolerantly at him, and uncorked another bottle, showing Will the label, before continuing his wine education. The old man was unstoppable now. Saira tried to imagine him as a small boy, in one of those silly smock things French boys wore in old photos. 'The harvest that year was almost impossible. The Germans had laid anti-tank mines everywhere to slow the Americans down. We'd watch carefully, but we never knew where they all were. So it was really dangerous up in the vineyards. One bad step, and pouf! And then, when the Americans got close, there was the shelling. Earth and grapes and sticks flying in all directions! We had to spend most of our time down in the cellars. Ours was one of the largest, so we were storing a lot of the statues from the church, to keep them safe. We would go down on our knees and pray to these saints for our neighbours and animals during the bombardments!'

Will was on to his fifth or sixth wine now, Saira noticed. She was losing count. He smiled at her and came over to listen to the old man. The woman slipped out. The old man eyed Will's glass. 'Now, that Gewürztraminer reminds me of when our water reservoirs were hit and our water supply ran out. We drank some of our Gewürz but, when our neighbour's cellar received a direct hit, we had to use some of the poorest wines with the lowest alcohol content to put out the fires. But it was still sad to see them wasted on the flames. What a smell, though! Now a good wine, like that Gewürztraminer, that would have produced an explosion!' He began to laugh.

So, of course Will couldn't resist adding a bottle of Gewürztraminer to his modest order. 'We'll have it with Luke at our farewell meal at Habib's tomorrow.'

They spent that night, their last night, in the shadow of a fortified church in another village. They were quite late looking for accommodation, as Saira wanted to linger among the otters and storks in the nearby sanctuary till closing time. So she was happy to go to the first guest house they came to. Will couldn't help laughing. 'I thought you said no more wine tasting! Do you realise that this guest-house belongs to a wine producer!' As they took their cases out of the boot, Saira saw that the basement of this modern house was indeed a big cellar, with dark outlines of men still busy inside.

Later, as she leaned out of the window to see if she could see any storks on their nests in the darkness, she said, with her back turned, 'It's going to be really odd getting home. This has all been a bit of a fairytale. I'm worried about reality.'

'You can smell the crushed grapes below!' said Will, coming and leaning alongside her, inhaling deeply. 'Your fairy tale is someone else's hard labour! I don't think I could live off the land, with all the uncertainty about crops, weather, pests, blight and harvests. I'm too used to city life, with the clubs, bars, cinemas …' and then he broke off, remembering that his life would be changed when they got back.

'That's what I'm afraid of,' Saira agreed. 'There's still so much to work out – and I don't just mean sorting out the flat and unpacking the wedding presents!'

Will put his arm round her. He wished he could explain how much more confident he felt than he had at the start of their honeymoon. How, when they'd been following Grandfather Yaqub's trail, it had felt intimate, as if the hints of that long-ago relationship illuminated their own. No, it wasn't just the hints. It was also seeing the time-worn constancy of Daniel and Eloise, whatever her wartime past. It was appreciating the turmoil that generation had gone through, the shake-up and levelling of the ranks, classes and races that made his and Saira's future possible. But he was no good with words.

He stroked the back of her neck, 'The storks are all asleep. Come to bed!'

On their way to Strasbourg next morning, Saira insisted on stopping in another pretty walled village to buy a few presents. They watched a couple of glass blowers at work and Saira was so taken with their skill that she bought an exquisite flower-like glass vase for her grandmother. She also, despite Will's groans, bought some furry storks for her younger brothers and sister. So, to retaliate, he bought two beer glasses with pictures of women in Alsace costumes revealing a great deal of leg and bottom, one of which he threatened to give to Asif. He smiled at her predictable reaction. Although he'd felt tongue-tied the previous night, after the tenderness their subsequent lingering love-making, it now felt easier to talk. In his old life, he'd thought that a good fuck proved your love and there was no need for words. How crude he'd been. He traced the design on the vase with his fingers. 'So delicate.' Then he said, unexpectedly, 'The old-fashioned vow to love and to cherish, – I think now I can stick to it, whatever the future throws at us!'

Saira was taken aback by his seriousness. She'd already shaken off last night's apprehension, so merely said lightly, 'Just as well. We'd better hurry now I've made us late.' Will felt snubbed. Women! Complex or what? You not only had to say the right things, but it had to be at just the right time. Why couldn't you just be yourself?

It seemed surprisingly familiar as they drove into Strasbourg, and it seemed much easier following signs to the underground car-park. They emerged into sunshine, dodging the skate-boarders, and walked along by the canals. Habib's street looked different in daytime, but they easily spotted the camel and palm sign. It felt as if they were walking into an old friend's as the door bell jangled, and Habib's warm greeting confirmed that impression. He waved towards a different table from last time, and brought them a dish of small savouries.

Luke breezed in a few minutes later, with a girl in tow. 'Sorry! Sorry! Deadlines!'

'Don't remind me!' groaned Will. 'I'm definitely not looking forward to starting work again.' Rather self-consciously, Luke introduced Mathilde, adding, in a warning tone, that they were the first friends he'd introduced her to. Saira eyed her curiously – younger than Luke, she guessed, student maybe, elegant in that very French way, but with a friendly laugh.

At Habib's suggestion they ordered the lunch-time menu-of-the-day, and he uncorked their wine bottle. Luke raised his glass, 'A good choice! You've been learning, I see. To your journey of discovery! I've told Mathilde all about your search for Saira's grandfather's escape route. And I gather you actually found a house he mentioned, right at the end? But start at the beginning!'

'How pretty!' Saira exclaimed as a beautifully garnished large oval platter was brought to their table. Then, between mouthfuls, she and Will tried to give a coherent account how exhilarating it had been to explore the Schoenenbourg underground fort, and how even the Struthof concentration camp had given them insights into the dangers surrounding his escape.

They were well into the main course, and Luke had been teasing Saira about border-crossing blisters, before they reached the point where they had found the Russian's house and then the surviving daughter, Eloise. At this point, Will had to explain why they were so interested in Eloise and her possible impact on Saira's grandfather. This was the bit that interested Luke the most. His journalist's nose scented a story. 'What is she like after all these years?'

'Confused!' said Will, succinctly.

Saira was annoyed. Despite that disquieting last encounter,

'confused' just didn't do the old lady justice. She tried to describe her – the soft cheeks, the wispy hair, the distracted look. The sense she gave of hearing far-off voices that they could not hear. The sense of her remembering everything and at the same time remembering nothing. 'I think she must have been very beautiful, once. She had this imperious air, as if she was used to people following her every whim, simply because she was so charming. It was touching how Daniel loved her and worried about her.'

As Habib brought them coffee and pastries and sat down with them, she stretched her hand to the jacket on the back of her chair and felt the little elephant. She didn't want to tell them about the last morning when Eloise had looked so slovenly and had acted as if she was her mother. So she explained about all Eloise's evasions as she talked about the farm, the animals, the pig-killing, but never about which men were actually there at the time. 'But then there was the song. I mean, none of you know this do you?' Through a mouthful of sticky honey-pastry, she hummed the childhood rhyme. They all shook their heads. 'There you are then! My grandfather used to sing that to me when I was little. She could only have heard it from him, I'm sure.'

Carefully wiping her fingers, she pulled out the elephant. 'And this was her parting gift!' She was touched to see how interested Mathilde was in how and when Yaqub would have made it, 'I am sure that was a very special present. It has significance for her.' Saira smiled gratefully at her. She was beginning to like Luke's new girl, and caught herself wondering whether Luke would finally get serious. Looking at the two of them, right at the start of a relationship, she felt like a mature married woman. She'd thought she and Will had been through so much together before they'd finally been allowed to marry.

But sitting here with these new friends she realised how much had also happened in this last week. Not just in terms of places visited and old events uncovered, but in the depth of intimacy between her and Will. She felt a bit remorseful for her flippancy earlier when he'd been serious.

Meanwhile Will was telling Habib about the Hawaiians and their memorial and how they'd gone in search of the Tunisians' battle near the Hohneck, 'and it was all misty and Saira got quite scared imagining them all firing out of the mist.' Habib was pleased that they'd seen the monument, and told them about how his father would take them every year to a big military cemetery above the vineyards of Sigolsheim. From the hundreds of Muslim graves, he would pick out the headstones of his comrades, introducing them and describing their quirks and exploits, saying, 'Never forget my friends!'

Habib's wife came out of the kitchen, wiping her hands on a towel, and Habib called her over to introduce Saira and Will, saying, laughingly, that she was the one who did all the hard work behind the scenes. She cuffed him round the ear, then said it was true really, women always did all the work while the men sat around talking. 'Your mother hardly ever came out of the kitchen. It was she who made the restaurant successful.'

Saira thought back to the wedding photo Habib had shown them of his mother and father, and she thought of her own grandparents. How did these soldiers who'd seen so much cope after the war with a settled life and in a new country, among strangers? Her journey with Will over the last week had thrown up new questions. She wondered why Habib's parents had left her village and come to Strasbourg.

Habib sighed and said that in the early days of their marriage his father had worked on the land and had helped with rebuilding the village. But, as some of the village's men returned exhausted and starving from Germany and the Russian prison camps and took over the work, there would have been little money to pay an incomer. So when his mother's family inherited an aunt's small shop in Strasbourg, they rented it to the newly-weds. Their five children were all born and grew up above the grocery store. 'My father gradually introduced some of the North African foodstuffs, as other families moved in, and later started to serve food at one end. But I don't think he ever imagined it becoming this gastronomic oasis in the city.'

It was good to think that Habib's father's story had a happy ending, Saira thought. But then Habib started to talk about the hardships, mistrust and disillusionment. Saira had heard of the Algerian war, but hadn't realised what an impact it had on life in France. Growing up in the shadow of its violence, with all the older boys going off to fight there, had coloured his childhood. He painted a picture of his father's isolation and depression, and his mother's struggles to hold her family together. He admitted that even he had turned away from his father, longing to be a typical French Catholic boy making his first communion and dreaming of leaving home to become an engineer; for it was only later, as his father got older, that he had returned with his wife to take over the running of restaurant.

'Imagine how it was for my father to see the wartime loyalty of the North Africa troops to France forgotten, the prejudice return with the violence in Algeria, and even his own son turn away from him.' He fell silent for a moment then continued, 'I ask myself, was it same for your grandfather in England?'

Saira realised that her grandfather had never said much about any hardships during his early days in England. It was her father rather than her grandfather who had talked about growing up in the shared-house with outside toilet before the slum clearances, and about going to a run-down school where all the Paki kids were mercilessly bullied. And she'd had her share of bigotry too. But all she said was, 'I don't think that many people in Britain now even know or remember that many immigrants like my grandfather fought for the British in the war. Especially not young people.'

'Ah the young. You know now, in our day, there is so much unemployment among the children of immigrants. And our President dares to call these malcontent young men of our suburbs … how to say?' 'Scum,' supplied Luke, grimly. 'Yes, scum.' Habib savoured the new word and said sadly again that he wished his father could have met Saira's grandfather. There was so much they would have talked about. Not just their military experiences, but whether they got a war pension, what it was like to settle afterwards in the country they'd fought for, and why they had so quickly became forgotten heroes.

It seemed a sad note on which to end their meal together. Luke and Habib had been there at the start of their journey of discovery, and understood the significance of what they had discovered. But Saira noticed Will looking at his watch, and knew it was time to leave for the airport. She stood up, full of emotion, hugging them and thanking them for everything they had done to set them on their journey and welcome them back.

'Come back soon to us,' Habib's wife urged.

Then Mathilde reduced them to thoughtful silence when she asked, 'How much of this story will you tell to your grandmother, about Eloise?'

18

Half truths

Yaqub, for he knew he was Yaqub, had been drifting in and out of a haze for a time that felt endless. There had been faces round his bed, people talking lovingly and touching his hands. From time to time different faces, English ones, often women's, had murmured 'this won't hurt', and the sharp jab had been followed by oblivion and then a surfacing to see the white sheets and anxious faces once more. Yousaf would come and go, and Amina was always there. How old and tired she was now, as she tried to persuade him to take some soup she had made specially. He made an effort, to please her; but he no longer felt the need for food.

He felt constantly drowsy, hardly able to focus on the faces. Instead there were faces from the past that loomed and faded, taking him back to times long past and forgotten.

Once there was water swamping, black, over his head, a German voice shouting, a tangle of weed and stinking mud, then a splashing and tugging. A girl's face was smiling lovingly, welcoming him – was it to his home? His journey was once more over. But this time he had lived a fulfilled life, with children and grandchildren. So sinking was peaceful.

Later, much later, he surfaced, still sensing a calm peace. He felt protected and wanted to tell Amina. He had taken comfort from talking seriously with her since he had been confined to bed. Her gentle smile had always reassured him. She leaned closer to hear what he was whispering. But now she was looking perplexed. He wanted her to understand that all was well. He repeated his words.

Still later, perhaps days later (he could no longer tell), he knew it was time to thank her for her steadfast love and to tell her that he too had loved her. He held her hand for a long time. Finally, he gathered his strength again to repeat the time-honoured words, 'I bear witness that there is no god but Allah.'

Amina was listening anxiously for the door-bell. She realised that she had been on edge and alert for the sound of it ever since Saira and Will's return, even that first night, despite the lateness of their home-coming. She kept telling herself that they would want to unpack, wash clothes, sort out wedding presents, finish decorating their new flat, catch up with their friends, – oh lots of things. All the time she made fresh excuses for them. Her son kept telling her that they were tired but very happy when they took round food to welcome them home that first night. But that wasn't enough. She so much wanted Saira to reassure her, to tell her … But what did she really want to hear?

A slight clanking as the latch on the wrought iron gate lifted, set her heart pounding. But the figure at the gate, she could see as she moved closer to the window, was not Saira. Oh dear. She so wanted it to be Saira, and it was Betty again. She didn't think she had the energy to cope with her today. And supposing Saira – and Will, of course – did come after all?

Like last time, it took a lot of concentration to follow Betty's flow of words. But she felt nastily pleased to hear that she too hadn't seen Saira and Will since their return. But however did they move from talking about their grandchildren to their husbands and how they'd died? She supposed it was through discussing why Saira and Will had gone to Alsace, and then the war and how their husbands had never talked much about it.

Betty's Bill, it seemed, had died in hospital and Betty thought that maybe it was the hospital ward, ever so old-fashioned still, with long rows of beds, not those modern alcove things for four or six, that had brought back his war experiences and set him talking as if the men in the other beds had limbs blown off by mines. And Amina found herself talking about how her husband had died at home, full of morphine to ward off the increased pain. She found enough words to tell Betty about the long months of suffering and also the welcome closeness they'd shared. About how all the family and the community had been there at the end. And also about that strangest time of all.

She had not spoken about it to anyone else, because she didn't know what it meant, and it had made her feel very uneasy at the time. But with Betty asking such blunt questions all the time, ('Do you say prayers when people are ill?' 'Do you confess everything when you're dying?' – she didn't really understand that bit, so just smiled, – 'Do you make wills or do you do it all different?') it was somehow easier. Abruptly she started to recount how she'd taken up a mug of soup one day (mugs being easier for him to manage than a bowl and spoon). It was a day when he'd been very restless all morning, not able to find a comfortable position in the bed, not wanting to talk, and seeming far away. But when she'd got upstairs with his soup she was surprised to see that he was leaning on one thin elbow, twisting his head and neck away from the pillows to stare at the wall behind the bed. He'd smiled at her. A very peaceful smile, she thought. And he told her that a holy warrior was looking down on him. Amina struggled to translate for Betty, as she'd never understood his words, 'George is giving me courage. He looks after soldiers.'

Well, she'd certainly taken Betty aback. Amina almost laughed at the surprised expression on her new friend's face. She felt a bit better about her own mystification, as Betty remarked that sometimes people say very strange things just before they die. 'Did he last much longer?'

At that point the door bell rang. Amina started. It must be Saira at last. But what unfortunate timing. She'd never be able to ask her all the things she wanted to, not with Betty there. 'Yes, two weeks more.' She got up stiffly. 'He died at tea-time,' she added, irrelevantly.

Saira swept into the room, her mind buzzing with all the things she wanted to tell her grandmother and all the things she'd decided to conceal. Will almost trod on her heels, as she stopped suddenly. He looked across her shoulder. 'Nan! How did you get here?' 'Bus,' said Betty, literally and complacently. She drew them both to sit down next to her on the sofa, and Amina felt a pang of exclusion. It was her they'd come to see, and here was Betty taking them over. Without bothering to ask about their trip, Betty plunged into what was uppermost in her mind. 'Have you got an Uncle George? I mean, he wasn't at the wedding. Not really a Paki name, is it?' As Will shot her a furious look, Betty remembered and added 'from Pakistan, like.' Saira shook her head in bafflement at this unexpected diversion.

Amina didn't feel happy about the direction the conversation was taking. She didn't want to dwell on Yaqub's death. Saira had been younger then, and they hadn't wanted to distress her too much. It would be far better to ask about their travels. Maybe their journey would shed light on some of the mysteries that had shrouded her husband's life, including this one.

'Then do you have a Saint George, like we do?' Betty continued relentlessly. 'He's the patron saint of England. We hang out his flag for football matches.' As Amina explained about Yaqub's puzzling words, Will looked at Saira, remembering that other confusing encounter. What was it Eloise had said? Something about a soldier with a bandaged head and Saint George. He didn't want to mention Eloise, and wasn't sure how to remind Saira. 'Crap!' he whispered, and after a few moments of incomprehension, Saira grinned conspiratorially, as Betty, her ears unexpectedly sharp, muttered a routine reproof that there was no need for that language.

Did this alter anything, this unexpected link between Eloise and Yaqub, even in their old age, Saira wondered. Was he thinking of the young French girl when he was dying? Of that distant attic room? She had spent the last two days telling herself that it was a long-ago romance. Over and forgotten. He'd made a new life. He loved them all. But supposing, at the end, he thought he was back there, did he think it was Eloise bending over him, not Amina? That was untenable. She couldn't let her grandmother even suspect that.

Yet again she wondered why her grandmother was so intent on knowing. Why had she asked Will? What would she do with any details? She had assumed that any confirmation of a love affair would make Amina unhappy. But perhaps she needed the 'resolution', as they called it now, of all those inexplicable things being finally answered. But not that last scene, her grandfather's death, it was separate in her grandmother's mind. It was better remaining so, though silence also felt like a falsehood. She realised that Betty was still prattling to Will and her grandmother was curled silently in her armchair, just waiting.

'And did you bring anything back with you from Alsace?' Betty demanded suddenly.

Saira smiled in relief. Of course, she would not show them the most precious thing, the little elephant, but the presents would be a diversion. She noticed Will looking guilty. He'd been impatient with the whole idea. You didn't do presents on your honeymoon! 'We weren't expecting you to be here, Nan,' he began. Saira gave him a small gesture of reassurance, and fetched the carrier bag from the hall. She gave Betty the pot of jam that Habib's wife had given them. 'Ooh! Blackberry! My favourite! Fancy it coming from a restaurant! It must be grand.' She'd probably have liked one of the saucy beer glasses even better, Will reflected.

Sitting down at her grandmother's feet, Saira handed her the fragile package and watched her grandmother's hands straying over the layers of tissue. 'It comes from a small town at the foot of the mountains that Grandfather had to cross to get to France. A lot of Muslim soldiers from the French colonies died near there, fighting to liberate the area.' But the story of Habib's father was for later. It was her grandfather's that mattered. 'We watched some of them being made.' Her grandmother reached the last layer. Her face lit up as she turned and twirled the delicate little vase in wonder. 'Aren't they clever! It is so pretty. I shall treasure it. To think of him being there! In the area where it was made!' And she continued to touch it wonderingly as Saira and Will started to describe their travels for the third time, having already told her parents and then Asif.

It was odd, Will thought, how the emphasis changed with each telling. Saira's father, who had never shown much interest in the scanty details of his father's escape, had seemed more interested in the parallel story of Habib's father and particularly Habib's own experiences of growing up in his father's shop and restaurant and of being a mixed race boy in a French school, 'There were only a few mixed race kids in our school at that time,' he'd said reflectively. 'Maybe it was even worse for them. At least we knew who we were.' Asif, on the other hand, had focussed on the escape and hiding, wanting to know how many tunnels there were, where the electricity came in and how the gun turrets worked. Like Will, he enjoyed the story of the Lost Battalion and their rescue by the out-numbered Hawaiians. But he too wasn't interested in their discovery of Léo's house. To him it was just the house at the end, nothing special, and as he didn't know anything about his grandmother's suspicions, Saira said nothing about visiting Eloise – he might not have accepted the implications.

Unlike her grandson, Grandmother Amina wasn't very interested in their attempt to discover her husband's prison camp or his hiding place in the Maginot Line. Perhaps she'd imagined his prison camp all too often during the years of his captivity. So Saira didn't show them her little candle-holder. It was very special to her, and she obviously hadn't conveyed the immediacy she'd felt down in that tunnel. And anyway, Betty was off on a tack of her own, asking if they'd tried to trace the man who'd helped her grandfather to escape. Saira felt rather sad that they hadn't paid more attention to that. Benoit's name had had no particular wartime significance to the customers in l'Aigle or the staff in the Schoenenbourg fort, and that had been the extent of their enquiries. It would have been nice, though, to have found some descendants to thank on her grandfather's behalf. 'No, no luck there. Too long ago.'

She also felt regretful that they hadn't found any clues about the route he would have taken over the mountains, and explained how the image of walking boots leaving a lasting imprint had affected her. 'It's the impression that he's left on our lives that's important, Saira dear,' her grandmother said gently. 'Even stones can get defaced by vandals. But what he's given you will live on in you. And in your children too.' How wise her grandmother sounded. Were they in danger of underestimating her sometimes?

Saira translated it and Will nodded, though Betty didn't take much notice. Having taken a ghoulish interest in their mention of the concentration camp, she was off again, 'I wonder if they caught all them men who helped your granddad escape and hung and cremated them all at that extermination camp? I wouldn't be surprised!'

Will didn't want to discuss the concentration camp which had jolted his long dormant beliefs, so instead told her that they'd met men who remembered other border crossings – and had lived to tell the tale. Betty looked quite disappointed that they hadn't all met a grisly end.

He noticed that Saira was hesitating. He knew they were fast approaching the part of their journey where they went in search of Léo's house. She had to say something. After all, she had texted her grandmother to say that they'd found it. And Amina seemed to sense that the moment had come. She was taking deep breaths, with an odd gulping sound. Saira focussed on the house itself. 'The house is still there and people still remember the old Russian who helped Grandfather and his friend. Of course it has been altered a lot,' she gabbled. Then she felt more courageous, and began to describe how she thought the house would have looked nearly seventy years ago. As she talked about the dusty attics, she realised her grandmother was stroking the little vase. 'So fragile!' she murmured. 'Like memories.'

'And eventually,' Saira continued, 'we found one of Léo's daughters. The one who helped the Resistance and the Americans.' Grandmother slowly straightened her back and stared straight ahead, as if waiting for a blow. She held tightly onto the little vase.

'His daughter was very old and confused. Not like you, Grandmother. And she didn't seem to remember Grandfather at all. She couldn't tell us anything about his days there. So he can't have made much impression on her – just one soldier among many who they rescued and passed on.' There, she hadn't really told her a lie.

Amina looked sharply at her favourite granddaughter. She was not being entirely open. She could tell. If only they wouldn't all protect her. The older she got, the more she saw through their attempts at kindness.

Saira saw the look. She wondered, guiltily, whether her family underestimated her grandmother's resilience as well as her understanding. Who would have thought, for example, that she would have made friends with Will's nanna and talked about such intimate things as her husband's death? How had she even found the words? She had always known that her grandmother was very understanding – she had, after all, been her main comforter during the year she had to spend apart from Will. She had always assumed that her grandmother understood the pain of separation so well because she still grieved the death of her husband. But had there been a much earlier pain when Grandfather had come back from the war, possibly – could it be – still in love with Eloise? Would her grandmother have sensed that? Or would she just have thought the war had changed him? But, imagine living with that question, that suspicion, for all these years. Didn't she owe her grandmother more than the half-truth she'd fobbed her off with? Only now did it occur to her that she might be assuming far too much responsibility, deciding what would or would not hurt her grandmother. It would have taken her grandmother a lot of courage to ask them to try and find out more for her. She had trusted them after all these years of silence.

Saira had never really thought about what her grandmother's earlier life would have been like. But there must have been big gaps for her, when Yaqub was away at war and then in his PoW camp and then when they were married and Yaqub had come over to England. Saira's dad and uncles, after all, had been born in Pakistan. She tried to imagine what it would be like if she had to face another long separation from Will. She knew how close they had become during their short time in Alsace, – was it really only ten days? It wasn't just the fact of being together at last, or of seeing new places, it was also sharing so many other peoples' lives and experiences. And then her grandmother had faced a completely new country, a big, dirty town after a small village. Would she have endured that as serenely as her grandmother?

And now her grandmother had asked for just one thing in return. Did she really want to know? Perhaps she did. Perhaps she needed to for some reason that Saira couldn't understand. But Saira didn't feel she could just pull out the elephant and say her beloved grandfather had made it for another woman. Suddenly she felt angry with him. How could he do that to her lovely, gentle grandmother? Of course, she and Will had discussed what she should say, and they'd both felt it was kinder to play down the significance of Eloise. But did she have that right? She had tried to imagine the impact of that wartime meeting on Eloise's life. But how much had her unconfirmed suspicions played a part in all Grandmother Amina's life alongside Grandfather and her growing family? Would it be a release for her or a new torture?

At this point they were all aware of the door handle rattling. Saira was initially pleased to be released from her thoughts, but then exasperated, on reaching the front door, to see that it was her brother letting himself in. Now she definitely wouldn't say anything. Not with Asif as well as Betty present. He was looking very pleased with himself as he greeted his grandmother. 'I knew they'd be here telling you all about their trip. And I've been doing a bit of research, so you can picture it better.' From his pocket he produced some photocopied sheets. 'Remember him referring to the gazogène he escaped in across the border? This is what it would have looked like!'

He pushed the papers into Amina's hands. Betty leaned over to look, exclaiming. 'I'm amazed it didn't finish him off, crouched up in a smelly old thing like that. He must have been pretty tough!'

A small smile played around Amina's lips. She agreed that it must have been dangerous, but, relapsing into her old habit of letting others translate for her, she told Asif that the time he nearly died was not then but, so another soldier had once told her, when his friend Barkat had rescued him from drowning. It was Saira and Will's turn to be surprised. Her grandfather had never said anything about a near-drowning. Where was that?

'Did they get medals for escaping?' Betty was clearly impressed. 'Especially his friend who saved him. Your army must have been pretty impressed by that!'

Amina looked surprised. She turned to Saira and said rapidly, 'It would be impossible for me to try and explain to her what it was like when he returned. There was something wrong, that I could not understand. I didn't get the impression that the British thought he had been brave in escaping. Anyway, I don't think the ordinary soldiers got medals from the British. But I don't think she knows anything about the British in India and the madness as they left. Do you want to try and tell her what was happening then?'

It was unlikely, Saira thought, that Betty would bother to take it in, so she just told Betty 'No they didn't. No medals for them.' She was remembering Daniel also alluding to the – did he also say 'madness' or was it 'confusion'? – after the end of the war. She tried to imagine Eloise, alone in a Paris freed from German occupation, making her hats and wondering what had happened to her Indian soldier, while her grandmother sat at home in their small village trying to understand how the war had changed her soldier-husband. Had she been disloyal to her grandmother when she promised to write to Daniel and Eloise? She had felt this immense sympathy when she promised. But she didn't want it to be a secretive, underhand correspondence which she hugged to herself (and Will, not that he'd do any actual writing).

She suddenly felt that it would be wrong to perpetuate the misunderstandings from the past. There was no way that anyone would ever know quite what had happened or how significant it had really been for Yaqub and Eloise at the time, but the elephant had been kept, as had some strange shared memory of St George. If her grandmother, towards the end of her life, needed to make more sense of that time, she had no right to withhold information.

She smiled across at her grandmother. This was not the time for further revelations, not with Asif and Betty there, but one day, soon, when they were alone, she would tell her grandmother more about Eloise and her fragmentary memories. And Amina, sensing her change of heart, smiled back, confident that the long wait for clarity would shortly be over. 'I make tea,' she announced in a very British way, graciously allowing Will to come and help. 'You learn traditional way!'

Once in the kitchen, she put her hand on Will's arm, which felt a very intimate, family gesture, and said quietly, 'Thank-you. You look.' That was all. She did not press him for more information, knowing now that Saira would tell her. And, that said, she made Will sit at the table and watch as she made tea. The unfamiliar kitchen setting and her quiet competence within it were a sharp contrast with his memory of Eloise's untidy kitchen and her helplessness.

For the first time he wondered how Grandfather Yaqub had decided between the two women and the very different lifestyles. He didn't think he would have been the kind of man to settle for tradition out of cowardice or lack of imagination. He had, after all, seen the world, and later, when his village faced change, he had the courage to make a life overseas. He had not turned his back on the west. But once he had made his decisions, he had stuck with them. Will couldn't help wondering whether he had ever been tempted to go back, years later, to try and find Eloise. He thought he might have wanted to do that. But then, from everything he'd been told about Yaqub's later life, he was a very upright and principled man. For him that would have been wrong. And yet, it seemed he hadn't forgotten. Perhaps it was even harder to live, honourably, with memories than to have them slip from you into a jumbled chaos like Eloise.

'She couldn't even make the tea now!' he found himself saying. 'It was so sad. Time has been unkind. Her husband does everything for her.' He was rather shocked to see a slyly gratified expression flit across Amina's face. 'Husband?' 'Yes, she married after the war, but they didn't have children.' A look of concern replaced the transitory triumph. Not to have children or grandchildren was clearly shameful. He could almost see Grandmother A. counting her blessings as she laid out the cups and saucers.

The burden that Amina had been carrying for so long began to shift. She had been right in her instincts about another woman, but now the threatening image had changed from one of youthful French sophistication to something sadder, older and more battered by life. She knew she would listen to Saira's account and explanations with an easier heart. 'Go!' She pressed two cups of sweet, fragrant tea into Will's hands. 'Tea good now'. Her Yaqub may have had a choice, but he had chosen her. He had been a good man. She could accept now that he was a soldier who had been hurt by the war but had grown to love her and had made it safely through to his appointed end.

As Will and her grandmother handed round the tea, Saira watched them both affectionately. She wondered if Will had said anything, for there was no doubt that her grandmother was looking brighter now. She slipped her hand in her pocket. The little elephant was safe there. That at least should remain a secret. But if she and Will had children, she hoped they would grow up knowing their resilient great-grandmother. And she could picture herself and Will, at some later date, showing their children the clumsy animal that their great-grandfather had made all those years ago. Would she let them play with it? She wasn't sure it had been made as a toy. It might get dirty or its crude stitching split and disgorge prickly straw stuffing. But she would tell them that it was a survivor and a symbol of all that wartime chaos.

Will eyed his nanna sternly. He could see her pulling a face as she took her first sip of the tea which was different from usual. She winked to show she was not cowed, but kept silent. There seemed to be a lot of undercurrents today that she didn't quite understand.

Acknowledgements

The inspiration for Footprints was the account given by former soldier Sahib Dad at a forum on the contribution of the Indian Army to World War Two, held during Nottinghamshire County Libraries' commemorations of the 50th anniversary of the end of the war.

This novel is not the story of Sahib Dad, but parts of the early chapters use information and events from his account. Yaqub in this fictional account bears no resemblance to Sahib Dad. Some further incidents are based on real events, but I have imagined the characters performing them, and they bear no relation to the originals. The story of Eloise is entirely fictitious, as is the journey over the mountains and the end of the story. All historical errors are entirely my own.

I am, however, very grateful for Sahib Dad's inspiration and the story of his escape and hiding in the Maginot Line until the arrival of the Americans.

*I dedicate this book to Sahib Dad's memory
and that of all the soldiers of the Indian Army
who fought in both World Wars.*

Many thanks also to all those who helped in the writing of Footprints, especially

Zahir and Nasreen Ahmed
Ellen Ainsworth
John Blackmore
Jean-Louis Burtscher
Alice and Marcel Colnat
Giselle Duhaut
Marie-Laure and Christian Eckler
Jean Jerome
Kamlesh Khetia
Mary Leake
Hubert Ledig
M. Yaqub Mirza
Denise Riotte
Jessica Smith
Charles Urlacher
Bernard Weigler
Astrid Wolffer

I hope they will enjoy seeing how their contributions have been used.

Made in the USA
Charleston, SC
23 March 2013